BILLY BUCKHORN

and the
WAR OF WORLDS

GARY ROBINSON

7th GENERATION
Summertown, Tennessee

Library of Congress Cataloging-in-Publication Data

Names: Robinson, Gary, 1950- author.
Title: Billy Buckhorn and the War of Worlds / Gary Robinson.
Description: Summertown, Tennessee : 7th Generation, 2024. | Series: The
   Thunder Child prophecy ; 3 | Includes bibliographical references. |
   Audience: Ages 12+ | Audience: Grades 7-9. | Summary: When an ancient
   evil alliance attempts to usher in a new age dominated by the
   Underworld, Billy and his friends must fight alongside their allies to
   prevent the apocalypse.
Identifiers: LCCN 2024020740 (print) | LCCN 2024020741 (ebook) | ISBN
   9781570674266 (trade paperback) | ISBN 9781570678219 (ebook)
Subjects: CYAC: Cherokee Indians—Fiction. | Indians of North
   America—Oklahoma—Fiction. | Supernatural—Fiction. | LCGFT: Paranormal
   fiction. | Novels.
Classification: LCC PZ7.R56577 Bj 2024 (print) | LCC PZ7.R56577 (ebook) |
   DDC [Fic]—dc23
LC record available at https://lccn.loc.gov/2024020740
LC ebook record available at https://lccn.loc.gov/2024020741

© 2024 by Gary Robinson

Front cover art by Chevron Lowery, chevronlowery.artstation.com
Cover and interior design: John Wincek, aerocraftart.com

7th Generation
Book Publishing Company
PO Box 99, Summertown, TN 38483
888-260-8458
bookpubco.com
nativevoicesbooks.com

Printed in the United States of America

ISBN: 978-1-57067-426-6
eBook ISBN: 978-1-57067-821-9

CONTENTS

Cosmic Twins

T he skies over Solstice City were bright and clear on that first day of summer in AD 1054. As the sun rose in the east that morning, the people were preparing for the largest annual summer solstice celebration the site had ever seen. Thousands would be attending the event to be held in this, the largest Native American city north of Mexico.

But no one was prepared for the spectacular cosmic events that would unfold that day, not even the Sun Chief's four sky watchers. These astronomers tracked the movements of the sun, moon, and star constellations and, in their dual roles as astrologers, interpreted the meaning of those movements for the chief and his people.

The watchers *were* the first to see it: a brilliant explosion in the heavens, visible in broad daylight, a sign from the Upperworld domain to the peoples of the Middleworld. As the four watchers rushed to inform their chief of this significant event, they argued over its meaning. *Is it the beginning of a new era? Or*

1

does it mark the beginning of the end of the world? No, it must be an indicator that something of great importance is coming.

As the four climbed up the stairs of the Sun Chief's royal mound, they continued to watch the skies for further signs. And they did not have long to wait, for just as they reached the summit, a fiery Sky Stone zoomed from the heavens toward the earth, no doubt hurled by one of the Upperworld beings. Leaving a trail of smoke and fire, the small object struck the center of the ceremonial plaza with such force that the ground beneath the astrologers' feet shook.

Screams of fear and uncertainty rose from the residents of the city. *Is the Sun, Creator's representative in the daytime sky, displeased with his children? Are the Upperworld beings trying to warn us of something? What are we to do?*

These were the questions on the minds of the dwellers of Solstice City as they gathered at the foot of the Sun Chief's mound. At that moment, as if choreographed by a cosmic designer, the Sun Chief emerged from his home atop the city's largest flat-top earthen pyramid. Wearing the feathered cape and carrying the staff that marked his divine status, he addressed his followers with a broad smile.

"Born unto us this day, in the presence of these signs, are twin sons!" he announced with great bravado. "Destined at this preordained time to become the twin Sun Chiefs who will rule with power and wisdom, directly chosen by Morningstar, lord of the Upperworld!"

A great roar arose from the people as they realized the signs from above were good omens, not signs of the end. This solstice day celebration would be like no other in recent memory. The Sun, the Thunders, and the Upperworld beings must indeed be pleased with them. All was right with the world!

In a grand naming ceremony, the Sun Chief gave the boys the names Shakuru, meaning "Sun" or "Of the Sky," and Monkata, meaning "He of the Earth." Expectations were high among members of the royal court that these two would embody the abilities and accomplishments of the Hero Twins. In mythic tales of the past, these powerful supernatural twins had rid the Middleworld of frightful flesh-eating monsters, banishing them to the depths of the Underworld.

As they grew, the twin sons of Solstice City's ruler were trained in the supernatural arts, including healing, spirit travel, communing with ancestors, and dispelling ghosts. The pair was also trained in the skills of the warrior.

By the time the twins reached their sixteenth birthday, however, Monkata had begun exhibiting darker, more negative traits. Not as agile, physically skillful, or smart as his brother, he grew to be jealous and self-absorbed, prone to taking actions that brought attention to himself and perpetuated rivalry between the two. His secret attraction to the darker arts also began having a negative effect on his physical form.

The fingers of his left hand began curling in on themselves, and his left foot turned inward, making it more difficult to walk. A slight curvature of the spine tilted him to one side. His whole demeanor made people think he was an elderly person rather than a young man.

On their twenty-first birthday, as their father lay dying, Shakuru was named sole Sun Chief, and Monkata was expelled from the community—forever. He vowed to return one day to take his rightful place on the chief's mound.

The exiled twin first traveled east to a village in Ohio he'd heard about. The people there were said to worship a powerful serpent figure who could heal you and grant you the power to overcome all obstacles in life. Although they'd created an earthen effigy of a snake, they had no real power, so Monkata moved on.

Returning to the Mississippi River, the twin followed the river south until he reached a place called Serpent City. It was here that an ancient Indigenous community had established a religious practice that rivaled that of the Sun Chief.

At the core of this community was the worship of both Horned and Winged Serpents, mysterious Underworld dwellers rumored to wield dangerous powers. Any mortal who could commune with those creatures and harness those powers must be powerful indeed! This group, commonly known as the Snake Cult, was led by a warrior sorcerer called the Head of the Snake, wrapped fully from head to foot in artful ink depicting a venomous rattlesnake.

The central figure of the cult's beliefs was the Great Winged Serpent, known as Quetzalcoatl to the Maya and KuKul-Kan to the Aztecs. He was the rightful lord of the three worlds: Upper, Middle, and Lower. He, and his court of subordinate Horned Serpents, had wrongfully been cast down to the Underworld by Upperworld beings or the Hero Twins—no one really knew for sure.

But what was the attraction to such a cult for mortal humans? Among other things, the Head of the Snake promised his followers that upon their death, they could reincarnate in a human life of their choosing, like a snake sheds its skin to be born anew.

Now *this* was a group Monkata could identify with! Upon reaching their compound of mounds located on a high point of land within a snaking curve of the Mississippi River, he immediately set about the task of using his considerable supernatural abilities and warrior skills to work his way up through the cult's ranks.

After becoming a close confidant to the Snake Cult's leader and learning the spells the man used to call on the powers of the Underworld, the evil twin beheaded the Head of the Snake and claimed the position for himself, naming himself the Snake Priest. He then convinced cult members that they must begin arming themselves for a revolution that would one day restore the Winged Serpent to his rightful place as lord of the three worlds.

Using mass hypnosis techniques learned from Snake Cult medicine makers, Monkata convinced his subjects to believe that his own physical deformities had been caused by the actions of his twin brother, who'd wrongfully seized sole control of Solstice City.

Years passed as the Snake Priest raised and trained his army and perfected his plan of attack. Finally, when he was sure the Sun Chief had relaxed his guard and Solstice City was busy preparing for another summer solstice celebration, the deformed twin launched his military campaign.

But the Sun Chief's spies had infiltrated the Snake Cult's inner circle and warned him of the plan. When the attack came, Shakuru's warriors easily repelled the offensive. During the battle, which was waged on the southern fringe of the city, Monkata was mortally wounded.

As the Snake Priest lay dying, his inner circle of warriors vowed to avenge his death, no matter how long it took. True to their vow, a small contingent of Snake warriors attacked when the Sun Chief was most vulnerable, during a sacred ceremony at the remote Spiral Mounds Ceremonial Complex on the Arkansas River in eastern Oklahoma.

After Shakuru and four men from his most dedicated protection unit were assassinated, the Snake Cult's strongest sorcerer cast the spell that tethered the Sun Chief's soul to his physical remains and simultaneously concealed his location.

That was until a Cherokee teen named Billy Buckhorn and his troop of supernatural and archaeological investigators stumbled on the spirit of the Sun Chief, along with the physical symbols of his office, the feathered cape and the staff, unseen by human eyes for almost a thousand years.

CHAPTER ONE

Countdown Begins

Billy awoke to the sound of thunder.

"Good morning, Fathers," the sixteen-year-old Cherokee said, acknowledging his role as Thunder Child, a position and responsibility he'd finally, but reluctantly, come to accept.

As he blinked and yawned and sat up in bed, he remembered the dream he'd been having off and on much of the night. His friend Chigger was trapped inside a very large bird's nest that rested on a dark mountaintop. In a fiery sky, an oversized fowl—maybe it was an owl or a raven, Billy wasn't sure—circled overhead. Coming up the side of the mountain was a one-eyed snake, its forked tongue flicking the air. But this serpent was more than just a snake. It was some kind of snake leader, it seemed.

Billy shook his head and put the dream out of his mind. Then, moving to the edge of the bed, he checked his cell phone sitting on the nightstand to confirm today's date: March 20, the end of winter and the beginning of spring.

"The final countdown begins," he said to his empty bedroom as awareness of his challenges and responsibilities settled once again into his waking mind.

But Billy wasn't just talking to himself these days. He'd been made conscious of a council of invisible allies who supported his mission here in the physical world. So, whether he spoke aloud or merely projected a thought in his mind, they heard him on some level.

There were the spirits of his deceased grandparents, Wesley and Awinita, who'd guided him many times on his journey along the medicine path. There was Morningstar, the revered Upperworld dweller from whom Billy had learned much since his initiation as Thunder Child. And he couldn't forget Little Wolf, one of the Cherokee Little People who'd been his companion off and on since childhood.

Of course, his dual cosmic fathers, the Thunders, resided somewhere between the natural and supernatural worlds. They'd chosen him last September, according to Grandpa Wesley, for a special purpose. That was when this incredible journey had begun. Their lightning strike had catapulted him into a new understanding of the closeness of the physical and spiritual worlds.

Finally, there was Creator, the source of it all, who resided throughout the universe and within each human heart. Respecting, acknowledging, and regularly communicating with Creator was one of the first lessons Grandpa Wesley had taught Billy as a young boy.

Billy rose from bed and performed the seven directions ceremony that he'd learned from Wesley long ago. As he finished the morning ritual, thunder rumbled again from above.

Lately Billy Buckhorn had become unexpectedly interested in—no, obsessed with—the weather. Of course, as an avid outdoorsman, he'd always been conscious of the weather, the weather as he directly experienced it while hunting, fishing, or collecting traditional herbs.

But now, he was obsessed with *weather reports and forecasts*, the kind found on the Weather.gov website or in bulletins from NOAA, the National Oceanic and Atmospheric Administration.

The obsession had begun a few weeks ago as he became familiar with the work of Native American weather makers from various tribes. First, there'd been a rare tornado that moved in an unusually straight line for several hundred miles. Billy and everyone else had assumed it was one of the results of climate change, but Grandpa Wesley and Cecil Lookout recognized it as the work of a tribal sorcerer, probably a Night Seer of the Owl Clan.

As Thunder Child, Billy had been instructed in supernatural weather making by Ojibwe tribal medicine man Andrew Blackbird. That was the teen's first direct training session with a member of the Intertribal Medicine Council. More sessions with the rest of the thirteen members soon followed as his bag of medicine spells and techniques grew.

Before Grandpa Wesley died, actually murdered by the witch of Buzzard Bend and her friends, he had warned of the possibility of freakish weather events due to the efforts of the Night Seers. According to the prophecy kept in Cecil's Osage family for a thousand years, these events would be part of the buildup to, and preparation for, the coming War of Worlds, when inhabitants of the Underworld would begin their campaign to retake control of the Middleworld.

The teen opened the laptop sitting on his desk, and a couple news headlines greeted him, as they often did. "Rare Earthquake Strikes Middle America" and "Oregon's Three Sisters."

"Very odd," the teen said.

Moving on, he navigated quickly to the radar feed visible on the National Weather Service website. The real-time image displayed moment-by-moment weather patterns in Canada, Mexico, and the US. Storms appeared in shades of blue, green, orange, or red, depending on the severity of the weather event. Other than a few scattered blue and green spots, the map was mostly quiet.

Billy knew that the first day of spring was also the vernal equinox, one of two days in the year when daylight and darkness were of equal length. In the northern hemisphere, this first day of spring was celebrated as a happy time when plants began sprouting again and animals came out of hibernation. He'd learned that many religions of ancient cultures—including those of the Middle East, Norway, and Central America—celebrated various forms of resurrected gods at this time.

The members of the Intertribal Medicine Council would be gathering later in the day to carry out their own ceremony to honor the change of seasons and hear a new message from the ancestor spirits.

But to Billy, the vernal equinox meant there were only ninety-two days until the summer solstice. By that day, the ancient Native American prophecy about the War of Worlds would be over and done with. Whatever was to happen would've happened by then.

An unexpected message popped into Billy's mind: "There will be adverse weather in diverse places soon—very soon."

Billy immediately knew this thought wasn't his own. Odd words and unusual phrases had dropped into his mind unexpectedly before, usually coming from a nonphysical source like Morningstar or his grandparents. One such message, "Strange changes are afoot," had come from Grandma Awinita during a stomp dance ceremony last September.

"You guys," Billy said out loud, looking up and around the room, "what are you up to?"

Then he remembered something related to that thought—a piece of paper he'd tucked away in a desk drawer. Opening the bottom drawer of the desk, he pulled out a very old, well-worn Bible with yellowed pages, one that had originally belonged to his grandmother.

A snippet of yellow paper peeked out of the pages at the back of the book. Billy opened it there—at the Book of Revelation, the last book of the New Testament—and read from the note Grandpa Wesley had placed there before his death.

"And ye shall hear of wars and rumors of wars: see that ye be not troubled, for all these things must come to pass, but the end is not yet. For nation shall rise against nation, and kingdom against kingdom: and there shall be famines, and pestilences, and earthquakes in diverse places."

Wesley said Grandma Awinita had read from that Bible every night before going to bed, so he'd continued the practice himself after she died ten years ago. Billy had thought about carrying on the tradition now that Wesley had passed, but he hadn't. The teen was all too painfully aware that generations of people claiming to follow biblical traditions had enslaved, betrayed, and murdered Native Americans while stealing lands and resources out from under them. So, for the time being, the old book remained merely a treasured souvenir of his grandparents' amazing lives.

As he returned his attention to the weather radar, his phone rang. The screen displayed a photo of his girlfriend, Lisa.

"Hey there," he answered in a weary voice. "Are you getting ready for our gathering today?"

"Of course," she replied. "But you sound tired. I thought you'd be catching up on your sleep after finishing all thirteen training sessions with the Medicine Council."

"My energy body is overflowing with the incredible knowledge I've learned from those powerful people," Billy said. "But my physical brain and body feel thrashed by it all. I'm exhausted when I thought I'd be energized. I don't know what the problem is."

"Stress," the Osage girl said. "Your problem is stress."

"You're probably—"

Before he could finish the sentence, the radar picture on his computer began changing unexpectedly. Out in the Pacific Ocean west of Northern California, a swirling blue-green mass of clouds was forming. Simultaneously, off the East Coast of the United States, in the Atlantic Ocean, a tropical storm also began a swirling pattern. Then, south of Texas in the Gulf of Mexico, a third rotating cloud pattern emerged.

Billy watched in silence.

"What is it, Billy?" Lisa asked. "What's going on?"

"Three synchronized hurricanes, in three different oceans, are forming on the radar map all at the same time," he replied. "I don't think that's supposed to happen, especially since hurricane season doesn't usually start for two months."

As he continued to watch, the three storms began creeping toward land and gathering strength. Then, within a few seconds, another anomaly developed, this time in the north over the Great Lakes region between Canada and the US. The mixture of churning blue-and-white clouds represented a snowstorm that started out small but rapidly blossomed, growing larger and larger. Now there were four different storms coming from the four directions.

"Adverse weather in diverse places," Billy muttered.

"What?" Lisa asked.

"Nothing," Billy replied. "You, your dad, and your grandfather should get over here as soon as you can. I believe the first step of the Night Seers' plan is beginning to unfold."

After ending the call, Billy ran to the kitchen to see if his parents, James and Rebecca, had left for work yet. Both were still at the breakfast table.

"Call in sick and fire up the big computer," he told them.

"What's up?" James asked.

"Adverse weather in diverse places," Billy replied.

"What does that mean?" Rebecca followed up.

"It means I think the Owls are beginning to roll out the first phase," her son replied. "And, here on the first day of spring, they've chosen weather to start things off."

"How do you know it's not just more climate change phenomena?" James said.

"You'll see," his son said. "I told Lisa to get her family over here pronto."

James dashed up the stairs to his office, where he had a desktop Mac computer with a large screen. After firing up the machine, he quickly pulled up the national weather radar.

"Holy guacamole!" he said when he saw the quickly developing weather patterns. "That's not normal."

Since Billy had last seen the radar screen in his room, a new line of thunderstorms had appeared as a wide, uneven wave of greenish clouds that began at the eastern edge of California and ran diagonally up to the southeastern corner of Montana. Within the moving green mass, areas of yellow, orange, and red indicated spots of intense weather.

Meanwhile, the original three hurricanes were beginning to make landfall.

"It's all happening so fast!" Rebecca said. "What are you going to do?"

"Time to consult a higher power," Billy said with a furrowed brow.

Billy ran back downstairs to his bedroom to lie down on his bed. After getting in a comfortable position, he began the sequence he'd often used to project his energy body out of his physical body. Within a couple of minutes, the familiar vibrational pattern surged through him, increasing in strength. The sound of ripping Velcro signaled his release from his flesh.

By picturing in his mind the nonphysical operations base above the belief zones, he was propelled through the energy layers to what he called his glass-domed "Home Among the Stars." Billy's Upperworld contact, Morningstar, arrived to meet him a few seconds later.

"I think it's beginning," Billy told the being, who stood much taller than any human. "Strange weather is afoot, and I could use some guidance. What should I do?"

"Volcanoes, earthquakes, and atmospheric phenomena probably aren't the main events," Morningstar replied. "You already know this at a deeper level, but you don't give yourself credit for having knowledge and resources directly available to you. You'll need to rely more on your innate intuition in the weeks ahead."

That wasn't the response Billy had hoped to get.

"I know that wasn't the answer you were looking for," the spirit man continued. "But you're going to face situations where you won't have the luxury of pausing the physical action while you spirit travel up here to the higher levels to seek guidance. You'll have to act swiftly and decisively."

Billy had already been stressed out, knowing the whole world was depending on him to make the right decisions and take the correct actions. Morningstar's advice wasn't really helping his peace of mind any.

"Look inward for the answer to your question about what to do," the Upperworld dweller said. "This morning when you performed the seven directions ceremony, did you really immerse yourself in it, or did you just go through the motions?"

Billy realized he'd been watching and waiting for signs outside himself in the world around him or from the Upperworld above him. He'd ignored his inner channels of communication. Now he knew he'd need all the elements of his multidimensional being functioning at the highest levels to face the coming challenges. He would, after all, be facing a possible end-of-the-world scenario.

His morning ritual *had been* less than productive, so, even though he wasn't in his body at the moment, he mimicked the action of letting out a breath of air as if to relieve tension. As soon as he did, he was back in his physical body.

He sat up in bed, blinked a couple of times, and quickly tried to gather his thoughts. Morningstar used the opportunity to impart one last message into Billy's mind.

"Remember when the Sun Chief transported you to a scene atop the chief's mound at Solstice City?" he asked.

"Yes," Billy replied. "Back when I was first learning about spirit travel."

"When you asked where this was, what did the Sun Chief say?"

"He said the more important question was *when*," Billy answered.

"You never really followed up on that idea, did you?"

Billy thought about all that had happened since that day in December. "I've been kind of busy, but yeah, you're right," he responded. "I never asked what he meant or how he did that."

"The time is coming very soon when you may wish you had that knowledge and could duplicate that process," Morningstar said and then ended the dialog.

"Great!" Billy said. "When will that happen?"

No answer came back.

"Hello?"

Still nothing.

Billy shook his head. "I hate it when you guys leave me hanging," he said out loud. "One of you shows up, imparts some piece of cosmic information, and then runs off back to the Upperworld, leaving me to sort it all out on my own. What a deal!"

He rose from his bed and thought about what he would do next. He remembered he was supposed to do the seven directions ceremony over again, so that's what he did. This time with real focus, feeling, and intention, he allowed energy from all seven directions to flow through him. That actually made a big difference.

Feeling more grounded and yet simultaneously more ethereal, he bounded back up the stairs to his dad's office. He was shocked at what he saw on the radar screen.

"It's only been a few minutes, but a lot has happened while you were gone," James said.

Billy gazed at the radar screen as rapidly swelling and swirling storms began to engulf the entire country.

"What did your higher power say?" his dad asked.

"That the weather isn't the main event, and I should rely more on my own intuition in times like these," the teen replied.

He paused to do just that.

"My inner source says this is all just a distraction so people won't notice when the main event begins. But, in the meantime, national resources will be tied up rescuing people from storms and floods and other catastrophes."

Outside, the winds began to blow as drops of rain fell on the roof of the Buckhorn's two-story log home.

"What we need to do first is prepare for long-term rainstorms and rising waters," Billy said. "Batten down the hatches, and all that."

A few miles northeast of the Buckhorn home, Billy's friend Chigger was feeling rather strange as he awoke—and the feeling was oddly familiar. The first time he'd felt anything like it was when he'd taken the purple gem from the crystal cave near Spiral Mounds, before whatever possessed him turned him into a raging maniac.

It was also the feeling he experienced when Carmelita Tuckaleechee had given him some of her strange tea or blown a handful of the purple powder into his face. He'd begun going to her cabin in January for so-called lessons in Cherokee traditional medicine. Except what was really happening, it turned out, was that the old *skili* was using the teen to gain information about, and access to, the Buckhorn and Lookout families.

When Billy, in his role as Thunder Child, had ended the witch's life, Chigger had been freed from her hypnotic spell. So why had that same sensation returned now?

His mother's voice rang out from the other end of the family's modest trailer home.

"You'd better get a move on," she shouted. "The weather's turning bad, and you don't want to be late for school."

"Yes, Mother," he replied less than enthusiastically.

He envied Billy for having gotten his parents to write him a medical excuse for skipping school on an extended basis. And then they'd signed him up to take the GED exam through the Cherokee Education Department, which his friend had passed with flying colors. Oh, to be like Billy!

But Chigger caught himself right there.

"Stop it right there, Charles Checotah Muskrat!" he said loudly, suddenly adopting Billy's habit of talking to himself. "Envy is one of the things that got you in trouble to begin with."

Chigger remembered that Billy had easily forgiven him for the mistaken path he'd taken with Carmelita Tuckaleechee. Keeping that friendship alive was most important now.

He grabbed his schoolbooks, along with the latest superhero comic book he'd received in the mail and the sketch pad he'd been doodling on. He headed out the door toward his truck.

"Come straight home from school," his mother called after him in a sharp tone. "Oh, and have a nice day."

That last bit came out overly light and sweet, and Chigger knew she was trying not to sound like his father. When the old man found out his son had been skipping school to learn Cherokee medicine from that witch, the crap had hit the fan. And the crap had continued to hit the fan every day since.

So Chigger had promised to show up for school every day, do his best to get good grades, and put out of his mind anything and everything having to do with Billy Buckhorn and all forms of Cherokee medicine, good or bad.

But how could he keep that last promise when elements of the supernatural were intruding into his life again, now possibly plaguing him with yet another mental disorder? It was Billy's grandpa, the medicine man, who'd freed the teen from the Horned Serpent's spell. The elder said Chigger might be influenced by the negative effects of that purple crystal for the rest of his life.

The teen was approaching the turn in the road that led to Billy's house, and the boy made a quick decision right then and there. He needed to talk to Billy more than ever. Now was the time. He made the turn, heading south toward Park Hill as scattered drops of rain fell.

He arrived at the Buckhorn home just ahead of the Lookout family, who pulled into the gravel drive behind Chigger's pickup. The boy made a beeline for the front door and knocked loudly as Lisa, Cecil, and Ethan Lookout got out of the van with the Indigenous Archaeology Alliance logo painted on the side.

"What are you doing here?" Lisa called angrily to Chigger just as Billy's mother opened the front door to the log house. Lisa still hadn't forgiven him for the trouble he'd caused when he was under Tuckaleechee's spells.

"I need to see Billy right away," the boy told Rebecca, loud enough so the Lookouts could hear.

"It's not a good time," Rebecca said. "Why don't you—"

"I gotta do it now," Chigger said. "It won't take long, and I can't be late for school."

Rebecca had known Chigger almost all his life, and she could tell he was distraught. "Okay. Wait out here on the porch."

Ignoring the boy, Lisa stepped quickly into the house, followed by her father and grandfather. Saying nothing, the two

Lookout men gave Chigger a look that seemed to say, "We don't blame you like Lisa does, but what can we do?" Billy's mother told them to go to her husband's upstairs study.

"I'll have Billy meet you in his bedroom," Rebecca whispered to Chigger as the Lookouts headed up the stairs.

As Chigger waited in Billy's room, a forgotten memory popped into his mind. The last time he'd been in Billy's bedroom, he was under the spell of *skili* Carmelita Tuckaleechee, who'd hypnotically commanded him to collect strands of his friend's hair so she could cast a spell against him.

"I thought you weren't supposed to associate with me," Billy said as he came into the room, a broad smile on his face. He hugged his oldest friend, noticing that Chigger's energy field once again emanated a faint purplish hue.

"I'm not, but I needed to tell you that those old feelings are coming back," Chigger said with concern in his voice. "You know, like when the purple crystal was just starting to take its hold on me."

"That's not good," Billy said.

"The same feeling I got whenever Tuckaleechee dosed me with her hypnosis medicine. Or really, anytime I was over there at her place, I could feel it a little."

"I didn't realize that. What do you think it means?"

"I think someone somewhere who's like Tuckaleechee is trying to access or activate the Horned Serpent's crystal. Or maybe there's another crystal like it somewhere else that's being activated."

"Either of those things are definitely not good," Billy said as his mind began to explore the possible meanings of this new information.

"I just needed to tell you that," Chigger said. "Now I gotta go."

"Hang in there, Chig," Billy said. "I'm glad you shared this with me. I'm still working on getting everyone to accept you back into the fold."

"I know you are. Thanks."

"If you need to talk and I'm not here, I'll probably be over at Grandpa's house taking care of patients," Billy said. "I'm slowly taking on his medicine practice, you know, healing the ailments of traditional Cherokees when I can."

After Chigger left, Billy opened the door to his closet and stooped down to pick up a hiking boot he kept on the floor in the back. Reaching inside the shoe, he fished around for something he kept hidden there: the key to his bottom desk drawer.

After unlocking and opening the drawer, he pulled out an ornately carved wooden box that he'd hidden under a pile of papers. It was the same box that Carmelita Tuckaleechee had kept in the fireproof safe in the back of her cabin.

"Now is the time, Buckhorn," Billy announced.

Carrying the box with him, he headed back up the stairs to rejoin the rest of the "Underworld Takeover Prevention Team," as he liked to think of them.

While he'd been downstairs, the storms coming from the four directions hadn't moved much. It seemed like they'd arrived at prearranged positions and would continue wreaking havoc in those four parts of the country. But the diagonal line of thunderstorms continued marching from west to east, ensuring that interior regions would also get battered by winds and receive a good soaking.

"What did Chigger want?" Lisa asked sharply. Having been captured, imprisoned, and drugged by Chigger's mentor, Lisa had remained the most critical and least forgiving of the boy.

"Not only did Chigger forgo his own safety by racing into that fire and rescuing Blacksnake's medicine book from Tuckaleechee's cabin, but he also went back into the burnt-out structure a few days later to retrieve this," Billy said.

He sat the wooden box on the computer desk and opened it. Members of his UTP Team moved in closer to get a better look as Billy removed a flat object wrapped in black cloth. Inside the cloth was a thin, highly polished slab of obsidian that was now slowly pulsating with a purplish glow.

"Whoa," Billy said. "It wasn't doing that before."

The group watched as the shiny black object emitted a low-energy glow, accompanied by a soft, synchronized hum every few seconds. It almost seemed like a cell phone in a slow vibrate mode.

"When I first saw it, I didn't know what it was," Billy explained. "But I remembered reading a passage in the back of Blacksnake's book that referred to some sort of supernatural viewer. It provided a spell and instructions on the viewer's use, if you knew how to read the unfamiliar language."

"It's an Aztec mirror, isn't it?" the elder Cecil ventured.

Billy was very surprised that the Osage medicine man could identify the strange object.

"A what?" James asked.

"An Aztec mirror," Cecil said. "Invented or created or discovered—whatever term you want to use—hundreds of years ago by Aztec sorcerers for contacting disembodied entities. These are legendary. There's even one in a British museum."

Wrinkled foreheads and questioning looks told Billy more information was needed. "Chigger gave this to me, hoping I'd know what to do with it," he said. "He had a faint memory of Tuckaleechee using it to contact other Night Seers or maybe even the ghost of someone she knew."

No one responded. It seemed the more they heard, the less they understood.

"That's not all," Billy continued. "Chigger came by today to warn me that he's begun picking up a supernatural signal like the one that came from the Horned Serpent's purple tail crystal, or similar energy coming from somewhere else."

The group's silence encouraged Billy to quickly come to the point he was leading up to.

"What it all means is this," he said with finality. "I think Chigger can be a valuable tool—no, a valuable weapon—against the darker forces in the coming conflict."

He paused to let that sink in.

"That's why I'll be inviting him to join our little group as soon as possible," he added. "My instincts tell me he'll be able to bring us intel from the other side we can use to effectively defeat whatever the Underworld is planning to do."

For the next thirty seconds or so, you could hear a pin drop in that room. To break the silence, Lisa's father, Ethan, made an announcement he knew everyone would be pleased to hear.

"We may have a guest joining us in the next day or two," he said. "She's a new investigator from the Department of the Interior, the DOI, and she'll give us an update on the leads she and the FBI have been following regarding the Sun Chief's remains and his stolen burial artifacts."

This obvious piece of good news seemed to fall flat. But it wasn't surprising. The group hadn't really made much progress during the past couple of months in their efforts to uncover details of the Owl Clan's apocalyptic plans for Middleworld retribution. Neither had they made much headway in their search for the skeletal remains of Shakuru, the Sun Priest; the artifacts from his burial that had been stolen; or the all-important missing piece of the Sky Stone.

Lisa's grandfather Cecil saw the need to shift the tense energy in the room. He'd already accepted Billy's action in forgiving Chigger's behavior while under the influence of the Cherokee witch, so that announcement didn't concern him.

"In spite of the weather, we still have a medicine lodge ceremony to prepare for, don't we, Spider Woman?" he said, looking at his granddaughter. "I believe that would be the best use of our time and energy now."

Lisa knew that her grandfather's use of her Indian name was meant to alter her attitude and force her to consider what was best in the long run. It frustrated her to no end that the tactic usually worked!

"I hear you loud and clear, Grandpa," she replied. "Let's go before I throw something at my boyfriend's head."

Out the door and to the van they went, driving through the slow, steady rain that was falling. The ceremony's location was the Cherokee Nation Cultural Grounds, the usual site of the tribe's annual powwow during the September Cherokee Holiday.

The Cherokee Nation had responded favorably to Billy's request for permission to temporarily set up the Intertribal Medicine Council's large community tipi on that spot. The young Buckhorn had become locally famous last fall, when he saved a busload of students from certain death, and even more famous when he helped police stop the actions of the malevolent teacher who was responsible.

The two Lookouts rode in silence on the short drive to the location. Lisa gazed out the window at the drizzling rain, hoping her medicine man grandfather wouldn't begin lecturing her about her attitude regarding Chigger, but Cecil was too immersed in worries about all the challenges the ITMC still faced to confront his granddaughter.

Fortunately, the twenty-four-foot-diameter lodge had already been erected, and all that was left to prepare were a few interior arrangements, beginning with the arrangement of buffalo skins that Thunder Child, Medicine Council members, and invited guests would be seated on. That was Lisa's job. A stack of dry firewood was also waiting inside the lodge to be used for the tipi's central fire, and Cecil worked on starting the fire they'd use for the ceremony.

The ITMC sometimes used a medicine lodge ceremony in place of a sweat lodge when they hoped to receive a message from the ancestor spirits. That was what could happen this evening as part of the group's spring equinox celebration.

ITMC member Eddie Abornazine, an Abenaki medicine man from Vermont, was next to arrive at the lodge. He would be leading the ceremony even though this medicine practice was one of the thirteen rituals Billy had learned as part of his Thunder Child training.

After greeting Lisa and Cecil, Eddie began his own preparations. Various other council members arrived during the afternoon, coming from all parts of the US and Canada. The main topic of conversation as they waited for the ceremony to begin was, of course, the weather. All were aware that this weather pattern was not the result of climate change.

Over at Tahlequah High School, Chigger was having trouble focusing on any classroom activities. The burn scars on his hands had now started to slowly pulsate with mild pain. The Horned Serpent's purple tail crystal had been the source of the burns when he had violently refused to release the gem from his grip.

During lunch, he tried to take his mind off the matter by reading his new superhero comic book, but he couldn't seem to focus. Then he opened his sketch pad to review his most recent drawings, which were all various kinds of weird monsters or hybrid creatures. Many of the images of these strange beasts had come to him at night in his dreams. Others had appeared in class when he'd lost interest in whatever the teacher was saying.

As Chigger sat in the school cafeteria, another creature popped into his mind. Quickly he sketched the horrific vision while it was still fresh. What emerged from the tip of his fast-working pencil was a furry nocturnal beast with giant antlers, that walked on two hind legs.

Windswept snow swirled around the ten- to twelve-foot-tall monster as he hunted for human flesh to fill his insatiable hunger. The howling wind in this vision seemed to whisper the word *Wendigo*, a word Chigger had never heard.

The mental image disappeared from the boy's mind as quickly as it came, and Chigger shook his head to make sure it completely cleared away. After the creative outpouring had finished, Chigger gazed at the sketch. As with the others, he hadn't been conscious while it was being drawn. And, like the other drawings, it had been signed *The Muskrat*.

He didn't remember drawing it, and he didn't remember signing it.

What the hell is going on here?

He couldn't answer that question or the others swirling around in his mind. But he knew he had to do something and do it soon.

CHAPTER TWO

Shaking Tent

Cheyenne medicine man Thomas Two Bears knew he had a problem that he needed to fix sooner rather than later. Billy Buckhorn had been the cause of the problem and would have to be dealt with eventually. But for now, as the head of the Night Seers of the Owl Clan, Two Bears needed to focus on three priorities.

One was finding a replacement for Night Wolf, or Carmelita Tuckaleechee, as she'd been calling herself. Another was locating the woman's Aztec mirror that went missing after fire swept through her cabin. If it fell into the wrong hands—Buckhorn hands, for instance—it could be a problem for the unfolding plan.

The third priority was retrieving Tuckaleechee's Owl Clan talisman, the inscribed pendant she'd sometimes worn. In fact, all thirteen members of the Owl Clan owned such an object. It was not only a symbol of membership but also a protector of power and a source of sorcery if you knew how to use it.

All the pendants contained the image of a thirteen-pointed star and were made of titanium, a mineral element immune to heat and fire. Thomas needed to find Tuckaleechee's talisman so he could pass it on to the new Night Seer member who would replace her.

The Cheyenne man had decided to drive his newly refurbished turquoise-colored 1958 Apache pickup truck for the journey. It had belonged to his medicine man grandfather back in the day but had been sitting abandoned in a barn for years.

The eighteen-hour drive from the Northern Cheyenne reservation to eastern Oklahoma was just what the old girl needed to break in the new engine he'd put in. The trip would take him through the Cherokee Nation, home to both Buckhorn and Tuckaleechee.

If the old Owl had just carried out her part of the plan and not gotten sidetracked by her feud with the Buckhorn family, I wouldn't be trying to clean up her mess now, Thomas thought. *I've got more important things to do.*

After passing through Tulsa, he had to take a back road, State Highway 82, that cut diagonally across the hilly, forested landscape. Then he followed an even smaller back road, a shortcut, that put him on Highway 10 just south of Buzzard Bend, the witch's rural homestead.

Turning onto Tuckaleechee's winding driveway reminded him of the time, maybe ten years ago, when the Night Seers met at her place for their annual gathering. The forest of dead trees covered with matted Spanish moss still emitted the sense of foreboding that Thomas had always liked so much.

At the end of the driveway, he parked the truck between the two burnt-out structures, the old Victorian house on the left and the even older log cabin on the right. Since Night Wolf had no children and no other family, the property had essentially been left untouched since the fire.

Somebody from the local community, maybe teens looking for a hidden place to party, must've visited the site. Broken beer bottles and beer cans with bullet holes lay scattered about. Graffiti painted in red on the only remaining wall of the house declared *High School Sucks* and *Tahlequah Tigers* and *You Reap What You Sow*.

Getting out of the truck, he made his way to what was left of the cabin and began picking through the charred debris. Near what was once the cabin's back wall, he found the object of his search: the witch's fireproof safe. Unfortunately, it was empty.

Using the toe of his shoe as a prod, he continued to sift through the cabin's sooty remnants, finding nothing of interest and no titanium pendant. He closed his eyes and, using a well-tested Night Seer technique, pictured in his mind the moment when the objects disappeared. A momentary flash gave him the clue he was looking for.

A Native boy, probably a teenager, stooped down and pulled an ornate wooden box out of the safe. Then, opening the box, the boy saw the black obsidian mirror and, beside it, the thirteen-sided pendant.

Was that Buckhorn? Two Bears thought. *Or was it that apprentice Night Wolf was using? What was his name?*

He couldn't think of it at the moment, but he'd have to remember to check with Jacki Birdsong and Geraldine Osceola, who'd stayed with Night Wolf for a while. They'd helped her end the life of the elder Buckhorn, Wesley, with their reversing spells.

Time to press on, he thought.

His next stop would be Wild Horse Mountain, Oklahoma, in search of a Cherokee medicine man named Raymond Bushyhead. Two Bears had heard good things about the man and hoped he was the right person for the job.

Keeping the membership number at thirteen was vital if the group was going to maintain its full supernatural powers.

Together, all the members were connected by a chain of energy that gave each of the Night Seers boosted abilities. The chain had temporarily been broken with the death of Tuckaleechee.

It was rumored that Bushyhead transformed himself, not into an owl but a different nocturnal bird called the black-crowned night heron. Night herons hunted for food at night or early morning at the edges of streams or lakes and hid in deep shadows during the day. Their piercing red eyes boosted their night vision considerably, and their black heads and backs made them harder to spot in daylight. Two Bears needed someone on his team who would be hard for the Buckhorns and Lookouts to see.

Wild Horse Mountain was just north of the crystal cave and across the Arkansas River from Spiral Mounds Archaeological Site. That might be a significant location in the very near future, according to what he'd heard from the head of the Serpent Society.

Once he neared the Wild Horse Mountain community, Two Bears looked for Bushyhead Road, so named because that family had lived there for generations. Signs pointed down a dirt road that led to the End of the Trail Trading Post, a general store owned and operated by the Bushyhead family.

The trading post was housed in a weathered wooden structure that appeared to lean a little to one side. It was obviously in need of serious maintenance. Two Bears parked out front, entered the building, and was greeted by an elderly Native woman who was stocking a shelf with canned corn.

Two Bears introduced himself and told her why he was there.

"The old fart is out back, whittling," she said, pointing toward an open door behind a counter. "You can go on out there."

Thomas found Bushyhead at a well-used workbench, carving some sort of mask out of a length of white pine with a hunting knife. The carver looked up from his work.

"I seen you last night in a dream," the man said. "I knew you was coming. Somethin' about number thirteen, which is good."

Two Bears introduced himself, described the Owl Clan, and asked Bushyhead if he'd heard of them.

"Yeah, I heard a ya. Who hasn't heard a ya? Night Seers been around since forever."

"Would you consider joining us?" Two Bears said. "We're doing something big and important, and we need a new number thirteen."

"I'll think on it," Bushyhead said and returned to his carving.

"I need an answer in a couple of days," the Cheyenne man said.

"How do I reach ya?"

Two Bears took a business card with a picture of an owl on it and handed it to Bushyhead. "My cell phone number is on the back," he said as he stood to leave. "What are you carving?"

The man held the wooden mask up, and that was when Thomas saw the coiled rattlesnake sitting on the mask's head. The reptile was poised and ready to strike.

"Whoa!" he said. "That's quite a piece!"

Two Bears knew it was no coincidence that his next stop would be with a man who claimed to be the Snake King.

"It's a traditional Cherokee warrior mask," the carver said. "Warriors dance with them at the stomp grounds to show they're not afraid to go to war."

Now Two Bears *knew* Bushyhead was the right man for the job.

As he walked back toward his truck, he thought about his next challenge. For months he'd been trying to renew the ancient alliance between the Owls and the Snakes. However, the head of the Snakes had played hard to get, and time was running out to make it happen.

Not only had the man played hard to get, but he played hard in general. The guy wanted to be the boss of both groups instead of being equals, so Two Bears knew he had to do a balancing act.

He needed to let the man think he was the boss without actually letting him take over. Tricky business.

Back in Tahlequah, Billy and Ethan arrived at the Intertribal Medicine Lodge in late afternoon, bringing with them Cherokee healer Wilma Wohali, the woman who'd helped free Chigger from the purple gem's unholy grip. She had agreed to take Wesley's place on the Intertribal Medicine Council and be the Keeper of the Southern Piece of the Sky Stone, if and when it was found.

Inside the lodge, Billy made the rounds and shook hands with each Medicine Council member, taking time to welcome them to his home territory.

As the sun set in the rainy western sky, all was ready for the unusual ceremony to begin. Originally an Algonkian ritual, it was usually conducted by a single medicine person who was located within a small lodge. All other participants would normally observe the process, also known as the shaking tent ceremony, from outside the lodge.

But everyone in attendance today was a medicine maker to some extent, so everyone would remain within the large tipi. As with the regular ITMC sweat lodge ceremonies, all were meant to hear today's spirit message from the ancestors.

After all were seated on the buffalo skins, Eddie Abornazine began the ceremony by smoking the sacred pipe, offering the prayer-infused smoke to the four directions. Other than the patter of raindrops on the tipi's canvas, the only sounds to be heard were Abornazine's soft ceremonial whispers between his inhalations and exhalations of the tobacco smoke.

Then, accompanied by Thunder Child, he started singing the songs that would call the ancestor spirits into the lodge. Others in the group who'd been to a previous shaking tent ceremony also joined in singing, which increased the power and intensity of the songs. After about a half hour of constant singing, the lodge began to quiver, only slightly at first.

But everyone continued singing more and more intently until the entire tipi, poles and all, began to shake violently. The ferocity of the vibration caused the ground beneath them to shake as well, until it felt as though the nomadic canvas structure would be shredded to pieces, the poles ripped apart and the dirt below them disintegrated.

And then suddenly the shaking stopped. All was quiet and still for a long few seconds.

Finally, the rushing sounds of whispering voices were heard, much like those experienced in the sweat lodge held near Cecil's house at the beginning of the year. But this time, instead of points of light flying into the lodge, all that could be perceived were the sounds of multiple entities passing through the canvas walls— whish, whish, whish—as the thirteen ancestor spirits arrived.

Using his own Abenaki language, Eddie asked the spirits to speak. "We are your humble servants, gathered to hear your message," he said. "What do you have for us today? What guidance can you offer to us who wish only to carry out your bidding?"

The lodge again quivered, then vibrated, then violently shook as the multiple voices began speaking as multiple discordant noises before coalescing into one. Then, sounding like wind personified, they spoke. The listeners could feel their words as much as they could hear them.

"The discord and disunity among you are obstructing your efforts," the multitude said. "Unless and until you are unified with Thunder Child, fully supporting his decisions and commands, your mission will fail, and all will be lost."

The voice seemed to take a breath, pulling energy and air up toward the smoke hole at the apex of the lodge. Then the message continued as the energy flowed back down.

"Only the solidarity of your unified energy will bring final victory. Only when your focus is fused as one can higher supernatural energies magnify your mortal efforts."

The voice seemed to pause to take another breath, but no further message was immediately forthcoming.

"Do you have more for us?" Eddie called out.

"Fear not what your enemies have in store for the Middle-world," the voices answered, "for fear is what empowers them. Fear is what emboldens them. Fear is their primary weapon."

Eddie felt that the spirits had finished their message. "We hear and understand you," he said. "We also ask for your patience as we attempt to follow your admonition."

"So be it," the whispering voice said.

The rushing sound of wind again permeated the lodge as the canvas shook and the poles rattled. Then all was quiet once more, except for the patter of raindrops. No one spoke. No one moved. Everyone turned inward as they absorbed the meaning of the message for themselves.

In Lisa's mind, there was no quiet or peace. She was painfully aware that she alone was the source of disunity and contention. She was sure the spirits' message was addressed to her, that probably every person in that lodge was waiting for her to own up to it. The perceived pressure was unbearable as she jumped up and ran out into the rain.

Ethan rose from his buffalo hide to follow her, but Billy stopped him in his tracks.

"I'll take care of this," he said, and Lisa's dad sat back down.

Following her out the lodge flap, Billy scanned the surroundings as the rain continued to fall. He spotted the girl heading for one of the small covered structures that stood at the edge of the circular dance arena. He made a beeline for the same spot.

Billy quickly caught up to her, and the two teens stepped out of the rain almost at the same time.

"How'd you get here so quick?" the startled girl asked with a gasp.

"One of the benefits of being Thunder Child," he answered with a smile.

She turned away from him, wiping both tears and rainwater from her cheeks. "Everyone knows the spirits were talking about me in there," Lisa said. "And I'm so sorry to have been the one to blame for our lack of progress."

"Don't be so—" Billy began.

Lisa reached up and touched Billy's lips with her forefinger. "I'll go back in there, take full responsibility, and apologize," she said, removing her finger and looking away.

"Not so fast," Billy replied.

The Osage girl looked back at him in surprise.

"You don't honestly think your attitude alone was the subject of the ancestors' message? You give yourself way too much credit for power over the situation," Billy said.

He was smiling as he said this, so Lisa was confused about how to react.

"I shook the hand of each council member today, and, except for two people, they had doubts and misgivings about me," Billy said. "You wouldn't believe how much they're all underestimating me and my capabilities. Really, only Wilma Wohali and your grandfather seem to maintain unwavering faith in my ability to rise to the challenge that I was chosen to face."

"I had no idea," Lisa said. "It's really that bad?"

"We're going to wait out here for a little while longer and then go back in there together." He paused as he made a decision. "And unless they admit their role in this failure . . . I may take a radical step and disband the Intertribal Medicine Council for obstructing the success of this prophetic operation."

Lisa was shocked.

"That's how big a deal it is," Billy said, looking out at the falling rain. "Morningstar said that I need to follow my own inner guidance and act swiftly, if need be, so that's what I'll be doing from now on." He turned back to Lisa and took her by the shoulders. "So you're either with me all the way or not," he said in all seriousness. "What's it going to be?"

She let out a breath of air and said, "With you all the way."

He pulled her to him and hugged her with more strength than she remembered feeling from him before. She sensed that he was different now, physically stronger, certainly larger, and surer of himself. It made her feel safer than she'd felt since her grandfather had announced last year that the time had come for fulfillment of the ancient prophecy.

Back inside the lodge, Lisa took her seat on the back buffalo skin as Billy retook his place at the head of the circle of seated medicine makers.

"I'm ready to hear your response to the message from the ancestor spirits," he said with a stern tone. "What do you have to say for yourselves?"

"I think—" Cecil began.

"I already know what you think, Cecil, and I appreciate it very much," Billy interrupted. "I need to hear from everyone else."

No one else spoke. They may have realized that Billy already knew what they thought too.

After a moment of silence, Billy spoke. "Except for the five Keepers of the Sky Stone, everyone else on the Medicine Council is excused. Please return to your home communities and prepare everyone you know for the coming calamities."

Billy heard a mixture of verbal reactions and saw a variety of confused expressions as a result of his declaration.

"Urge your fellow tribal members to pray in whatever way they do that," he continued. "Encourage them to intensify their practice of traditional ceremonies as much as possible. We don't have much time—maybe only a matter of weeks or days—before the convulsions begin."

Billy ignored the raised hands and raised voices that confronted him. "But most of all, what is necessary is faith—your faith in a positive outcome, your faith in the Thunders' choice, your faith in my ability to accomplish the mission I was chosen for."

The lodge fell silent again except for the sound of rain.

Cecil stood. "You heard Thunder Child," he said, breaking the silence in the lodge. "The Upperworld chose him to lead us during this dangerous time, so we must follow his guidance."

Members of the council realized there was nothing more to be said or done other than to gather their things and exit the lodge.

"Keepers of the Sky Stone, join me here in the center of the lodge," Cecil, Keeper of the Center, said.

Four elders—Eastern Cherokee Bucky Wachacha, Samala Chumash Doris Armenta, Ojibwe weather maker Andrew Blackbird, and newly appointed Oklahoma Cherokee Wilma Wohali—approached Cecil.

"Lisa, please wait for me at the house," Billy said as he, too, joined the Keepers.

After Lisa left, Thunder Child spoke.

"It's time to bring the pieces of the Sky Stone together," he told the five who'd gathered. "I'm well aware that the southern piece is still missing, but the remaining four pieces need to be put together, ready to go, when the fifth piece is found."

Cecil could tell that Wilma was not sure what was expected of her. "Remember what I told you about the purpose of the Sky Stone?" he asked her.

"When all five pieces of the Sky Stone are assembled," she said, "the Chosen One—that's Thunder Child—inserts the key, the Fire Crystal, in the center piece to unlock the . . . um, I'm not sure what."

"To unlock a portal between the Middleworld and the Upperworld," Cecil said, completing the thought, "allowing for the manifestation of spiritual forces to defeat denizens of the Underworld that will be attempting to regain control here."

"Got it," Wilma said. "This is all so new to me, but I believe every bit of it because of what I witnessed when I helped Billy and Wesley free Chigger from the grip of the Horned Serpent."

"For the rest of you Keepers, you have your piece with you now, right?" Billy said.

All four of them nodded.

"Good—take it out and hold it in your hand," Billy said.

Each one took their piece out of whatever it had been kept in.

"Cecil, I'll let you oversee the reconnection of the four pieces we now have," Billy said.

Cecil held his piece, the center, out toward the other Keepers. Andrew Blackbird, Keeper of the Northern Piece, held that piece out toward the top opening of the center. When the piece came within a few inches of the center, it was sucked out of Andrew's hand and into the center, as if the hub was magnetized and the piece was a chunk of metal.

That was when Cecil was reminded that all five pieces of the Sky Stone had once been parts of the meteorite that landed in Solstice City a thousand years ago.

Next, Bucky Wachacha's eastern piece fit itself into the right slot of the center.

"While I've got you here, Bucky, I need to ask you something," Billy said. "During my medicine training, you taught me how to find lost objects, for which I'm very grateful."

"Happy to do it," Bucky said.

"I assume you tried to find the southern piece of the Sky Stone using those supernatural techniques, so what was the result of that search?"

"We came up empty handed," Cecil replied before Bucky could get the words out. "We tried multiple times."

"Any ideas about why it didn't work?" Billy asked.

"As you learned with the search for Carmelita Tuckaleechee's place, there are ways to conceal objects, people, and even houses. It calls for the use of the right herbs and spells. Someone who knows how to do that must've taken the piece."

Billy nodded as he thought about the situation. "Okay, thanks for clearing that up for me," he said, turning to Chumash elder Doris Armenta. "Now we're ready for the western piece."

The western piece easily slipped into the opening on the left side. Each piece had reacted the same way as it came closer to the center. It was like they'd been away from each other too long and now they were at last together again and at home.

That left an opening at the bottom where the southern piece should go.

"Cecil, as the Keeper of the Center, you will hold on to the incomplete Sky Stone and guard it until we locate and retrieve the southern piece, which Wilma will personally fit into place."

Cecil and Wilma nodded their agreement.

"Cecil, when the stone is not with you, let's use my grandpa's house as a home base for now and keep it safe there."

Since Cecil, Ethan, and Lisa were already living there, that made sense.

"Wilma, you are welcome to stay here with us, if you want to," Billy said. "I'm sure they can find room at Grandpa's house. Or you can go home until we need you."

She nodded and said, "I'll let you know."

Turning to Andrew, Bucky, and Doris, Billy said, "Thank you for your long service to the Intertribal Medicine Council. Now, please return to your home communities and prepare for the apocalypse as I instructed the other council members. It's the most important thing you can do right now."

Billy could tell they were reluctant to leave, felt chastised for their lack of faith, but knew they needed to follow the Chosen One's directive. Without a word, each gathered their belongings and exited the lodge.

In the remaining silence, the sound of falling rain was the only constant.

CHAPTER THREE

Older than Cahokia

T he following morning, Ethan Lookout's cell phone rang, and when he looked at the screen, he saw that the caller was university archaeologist Augustus Stevens.

"Augustus, what's up?" Ethan answered in a friendly tone. "Good news, I hope."

"Sorry to say, no. I don't have any new information about your family's stolen artifacts," Stevens said. "But I do have something interesting to share that I hope to get your help with. Can we get together soon? I mean like today or tomorrow."

Ethan thought about what he needed to get done.

"And it would be ideal if Billy and Chigger could be there too," Stevens added.

Stevens, of course, had no way of knowing what Chigger had been through with the *skili* Tuckaleechee, but he had thought it odd that the boy wasn't present at Wesley Buckhorn's funeral. He had been part of what Chigger dubbed the Paranormal Patrol.

"Now I'm intrigued," Ethan said. "Let me check with Billy and get back to you."

When Ethan told Billy about Stevens's request, the teen paused a moment to check his internal receptors before answering.

"This could be important," Billy said, surprising Ethan with the decisive reply. "I'm glad that Chigger is invited. That means we'll have to meet after school is out. What about today at four?"

"I'll let Stevens know right away," Ethan said, "and find out where to meet up."

"Lisa should be there too," the teen added.

Billy had no trouble reaching Chigger or convincing him to meet with Stevens.

"Digger!" Chigger said enthusiastically on the phone. "I'd almost forgotten about him." He paused as he remembered the restrictions his parents had put on him. "I'll have to come up with a story to tell my parents," he said with concern. "Some new after-school club I'm joining . . . or . . . I don't know what."

That afternoon at four, the Indigenous Archaeology Alliance van pulled up in front of Stevens's house, which was located east of Tahlequah and stood on the west bank of the Illinois River. Ethan, Lisa, and Billy got out.

Billy carried a backpack with the ornate wooden box that held the Aztec mirror. He was anxious to ask his friend about the pulsating purple glow. A few minutes later, Chigger arrived, driving his own aging brown pickup. After greeting his guests, the archaeologist escorted them to his basement office.

"Chigger, I haven't seen you since our final expedition to the crystal cave," the college professor said. "What have you been up to lately?"

"Trying to stay out of trouble," the teen replied, hoping that Billy and Lisa knew his answer was meant for them as much as it was for Stevens. "For the last month or so, I've been playing around with comic book ideas and sketching unbelievable creatures that keep popping up in my mind."

This information surprised everyone.

"Oh yeah?" Stevens said. "What kind of creatures?"

"The kind that appear in nightmares or horror movies, chasing people and trying to eat them," Chigger said. "It's kind of a mystery to me where the ideas are coming from. I can show you the sketches sometime."

I'd like to see those for sure, Billy thought but didn't say anything.

"Anytime," Stevens said. "Anytime."

He turned his attention to papers and maps spread out on a worktable.

"Now to the reason I've asked you all to come," he said, moving a large map to the center. "I've taken a break from teaching classes this semester so I can focus on researching something that's recently caught my attention."

"Are those Native American mound sites you've identified?" Ethan asked, recognizing some of the locations marked on the map.

"Why, yes, that's exactly right," Stevens confirmed. "Spiral mounds, to be precise."

"You mean like the site where we found the Sun Priest's remains?" Billy said. "The site the Horned Serpent visited?"

"Yes and yes," Stevens said.

He pulled an old black-and-white photo from under the map. It showed several men with shovels, picks, and wheelbarrows busy digging up a large circular mound.

"The reason the archaeological site near the Oklahoma-Arkansas border was called Spiral Mounds in the first place is not readily evident now because these men destroyed much of the main burial mound in the 1930s," Stevens explained. "They were not archaeologists. They were treasure hunters, looking for loot they could sell to the highest bidder."

Stevens removed another, older picture from a file folder. "This photo of the site was taken earlier, a few years before the main mound was desecrated and destroyed by those profiteering pothunters," he said. "Look closely at the surface of the mound."

Everyone but Ethan looked closely at the picture.

"A spiraling ramp encircles the mound," Ethan said, already familiar with the archaeology of the site. "Starting at ground level, you could follow the path up and around the outer edge of the mound until you reached the top—a true spiral."

Guessing that Ethan probably knew the answer, Stevens asked him a question. "And what was depicted on the surface of the spiraling path all the way from the bottom to the top?"

"A serpent," Ethan replied. "But most mound archaeologists already know this. Do you have something new to share?"

"I do," Stevens said with a smile. He put the map back on top of the pile of papers and pictures, then pointed to the series of mound sites he'd circled. "Given Billy and Chigger's accidental discovery of the Horned Serpent in the cave on the Arkansas River, I began looking to see if there were any similar mound sites with caves situated nearby."

"Digger, please get to the point!" Chigger said loudly in exasperation. "The suspense is driving me crazy!"

Ethan immediately reacted to Chigger's use of the word *digger*. "Chigger, we archaeologists don't like to be called—" he began.

"It's all right, Ethan," Stevens interrupted. "Chigger, and only Chigger, has permission."

"Oh—excuse me," the other archaeologist said. "I didn't know."

"Every one of these spiraling mound sites along the Arkansas and Lower Mississippi Rivers features a cave within a mile or so," Stevens said. "There are at least a half dozen of them, maybe more."

Stevens waited to see if his listeners were getting the significance of what he was saying.

Ethan was the first to speak. "Since the Mound Builders believed that caves represented portals to the Underworld—"

Chigger interrupted Ethan with a burst of unexpected revelation. "There may be more Horned Serpents in those caves, and the nearby spiral mounds were created as places to worship them . . . or feed them or keep them from attacking people—like the people of Skull Island built a big place to sacrifice victims to keep King Kong from killing everyone in the village."

After a pause to mentally digest the logic of Chigger's outburst, Stevens simply said, "Absolutely. Good analogy."

Chigger smiled as Ethan took a closer look at the mound sites on Stevens's map.

There were nine locations, the most northern one being the Spiral Mounds Archaeological Site the team was already familiar with. There were three additional sites in Arkansas, also scattered along the Arkansas River.

The other five were located near the Lower Mississippi River, including one located near the place where the Arkansas River joined the Mississippi River. The southernmost mound site, called the Three Rivers Mounds, was in Louisiana.

"You're certain those mounds are all spiral mounds with a coiling snake path around the outer surface?" Ethan asked, not immediately accepting his colleague's conclusion.

"No, I'm not," Augustus answered. "It's a working hypothesis that I'm going to test out by visiting every one of those sites as soon as possible."

A thought immediately popped into Chigger's mind, but he kept it to himself for the moment.

"From the few archaeology reports on these mounds I've seen, they're thought to be older than Cahokia and may have been built by people who held competing religious beliefs," Stevens added.

Lisa, who'd been actively watching Chigger ever since he'd arrived and still didn't trust him, said, "Chigger, you look like you're about to explode. Out with it. What's going on in that little mind of yours?"

"I think it's a bad idea to go poking around in those caves," he said, relieved to be able to voice his concern. "More serpents might mean more purple crystals."

"The thought of more Uktenas never crossed my mind until now," Billy said as he processed the new information. Looking at Chigger, he added, "I think it's better to know if this is true as soon as possible and not wait to be unpleasantly surprised by it later."

Billy's mind quickly churned through possible scenarios as he consulted the calendar on his cell phone before coming to a conclusion.

"Spring break is in a few days," he said. "I think that would be a good time for us all to visit a few caves and nearby mounds, starting with the one Chig and I explored last Thanksgiving."

Chigger smiled and then frowned. "I can't go on a trip like that," he realized. "I'm not allowed to do anything with Billy or anything that has to do with tribal medicine."

Lisa's mind had also been churning with possible scenarios. "What about this?" she asked with an excited air. "A couple of years ago when I was going to school in St. Louis, Dad created an educational program to encourage Indigenous students to explore archaeology as a career."

"That's right," Ethan replied. "It was very successful."

"Dad, you could pretend to start a program here and select Chigger as your first recruit," Lisa explained. "Spring break would be the perfect time for the program's first expedition!"

"That's a great idea!" Chigger said enthusiastically. "How are we going to convince my parents to go along with it?"

"What if Dr. Ethan Lookout and Professor Augustus Stevens showed up at your home to announce that you'd been selected for this prestigious honor?" Stevens said.

"They'd think there'd been a serious mistake," Chigger responded with a frown. "The idea that their son had been chosen for such a lofty-sounding project would make them laugh."

But the frown slowly transformed into a near grin.

"But it's worth a try," he said. "They know all about me exploring the cave by the river and the discoveries we made at Spiral Mounds, so they might be fooled into believing it."

"I guess it *is* worth a try," Ethan said, looking at Billy, "since Billy wants both Chigger and Lisa involved." He mulled over the idea some more. "And we really wouldn't be 'fooling' your parents about anything, because you will be involved in a real archaeological exploration."

"Lisa, thanks for the idea," Chigger said humbly. "It means a lot."

"I did promise Billy that I'd give you a chance to redeem yourself, so here it is," Lisa said.

Everyone was quiet for a moment.

"Oh, I almost forgot," Billy said as he took the wooden box out of his backpack. After opening it, he removed the black felt covering to reveal the Aztec mirror with its pulsating purple glow.

"What the hell is that?" Stevens asked. "It's glowing purple, sort of like the dark crystal did."

Billy briefly explained that Chigger had apprenticed himself to a so-called traditional healer named Carmelita Tuckaleechee and then retrieved the object from her burnt-out cabin after her demise. It was a lot for Stevens to take in, but he *was* one of the few people in the world who'd seen the Horned Serpent!

"I'm hoping you have a clue about why it's pulsating," Billy said, looking at Chigger.

Chigger, in turn, looked at his burn-scarred hands. "The throbbing in my hands is synchronized with the purple pulsations in Tuckaleechee's viewer," he said. "Like I told you, Billy, my whole body has been feeling it. I think something has reactivated the purple gem in the bat cave, or some other stone like it."

"The bat cave?" Lisa said. "What's the bat cave?"

"You guys may call it the crystal cave, but it'll always be the bat cave to me," Chigger said. "The bats were what forced Billy to fall off the ledge to the ground below."

He looked at the black obsidian object before continuing. "Now I feel like this thing wants me to do something. Like it's calling me. It's creepy." He folded his arms and buried his hands under his armpits to protect them. "But I don't dare touch that thing. It might start controlling me like the crystal did."

"I'm going to get out Blacksnake's medicine book again and study the page that mentions this mirror," Billy said. "Maybe I can figure out how to translate the language written there."

He noticed that Chigger had started sweating and looked a little distressed. He put the device back in its box, and his friend was able to relax.

"I'll get everything prepared for our spring break archaeological expedition," Augustus said. I think it'll be a very productive trip!"

Meanwhile, about five hundred miles southeast of Tahlequah at the Three Rivers Mounds site, a handsome Native American man named Greyson Greenstone was also getting ready for spring break. It was, after all, one of the busiest times of the year for his Serpent World tourist stop.

Serpent World featured one of the largest exhibits of reptiles in North America, and families from neighboring states often visited the snake farm, as some people called it, with their kids who were off from school at that time. Admission was only twenty dollars for adults and ten bucks for kids.

CHAPTER THREE

This attraction sat on the same piece of land that the Three Rivers Mounds sat on, purchased many years ago by Greenstone, who was a member of the local Natchez tribe. The mound site was also open to tourists, and a separate admission fee of only ten dollars per person gave you access to a set of exterior stairs that took you to the apex of the Chief's Mound, a flat-top earthen pyramid.

In the site's interpretive center, on a three-panel display, you could read all about the Indigenous people who built the mounds, how they constructed the mounds, and their cultural beliefs. Many mound sites featured flat-top earthen pyramids, also known as platform mounds.

Greenstone was extremely proud of his Indigenous lineage, which generations of his family had recorded very well. Oral histories, aided by genealogical research, confirmed that on his father's side, he was a direct descendant of Moctezuma, chief of Mexico's Aztec Indians when the Spanish invaded and conquered them in 1521.

On his mother's side, he was a direct descendant of Monkata, the Snake Priest, also known by some as the Serpent King.

The saddest thing in Greenstone's life was the fact that he didn't have anyone to pass that lineage down to. The son he loved and treasured so dearly had died at age sixteen from an overdose of street drugs laced with fentanyl. The boy—whom his father had named Tesoro, or Treasure—had seemed to gravitate toward trouble and other troubled teens for most of his short life.

Greenstone's wife, Tesoro's mother, left soon after, another emotional blow to the man who remained stuck in the anger phase of grief. That anger became a motivating force bent on revenge that he carried out through a practice of the dark arts coming from both branches of his family tree.

Fast-forward to the present time, where Greyson Greenstone now headed up the Serpentine Foundation. Three Rivers

Indian Mounds Park and Serpent World were two-thirds of the successful nonprofit organization's operation. The third part was Serpentine Enterprises, a business program that used prison inmates of the nearby Louisiana State Penitentiary in Angola to produce jewelry crafted from the beautiful green-tinted serpentine stone.

This high-profile program was the pride of the prison's warden, because it was a part of the correctional facility's rehabilitation process, preparing inmates to return to a life without crime after prison. The jewelry was sold in the Serpent World gift shop and online, with a portion of the proceeds going to the inmates who produced the pieces.

"I want you all to be on your best behavior tomorrow," Greenstone told the members of his staff who'd gathered for an impromptu meeting. "We'll be hosting Thomas Two Bears, hopefully to finally seal a deal I've been counting on."

"But tomorrow is the monthly welcoming ceremony in the inner chamber," protested one employee. "Do you want him to witness that?"

"I do indeed," Greyson replied. "He needs to experience fully what we're all about, so he'll understand the power our organization wields."

"So, will Nahash Molok be present to perform the ritual?" another employee asked.

"He will," Greenstone replied. "So act accordingly. That will be all for today."

The following morning in the Cherokee Nation, Dr. Cecil Lookout and Professor Augustus Stevens arrived at the Muskrats' mobile home after Chigger had left for school. Hearing a couple of knocks at her front door, Chigger's mother opened it and was startled to see two nicely dressed men standing there.

"You guys must be lost," she said. "Or trying to sell me a vacuum cleaner."

"Is this the Muskrat family's residence?" Ethan asked. "Are you the mother of Charles Checotah Muskrat?"

"What's he gone and done now?" she replied, assuming the worst.

"What he's gone and done is get himself selected for a special educational program," Stevens said. "May we come in to discuss it?"

"I suppose—as long as you ain't serial killers or trying to sell me something."

She led the two into the kitchen, where she poured them each a cup of coffee. Then they proceeded to spool out the tale of the once-in-a-lifetime offer that would give her son the rare opportunity, during spring break, to explore the past through archaeological excavations while still a high school student.

"How much is this rare opportunity gonna cost me?" she asked. "We can't really afford any additional expenses, ya know."

"No cost involved," Ethan replied. "And we'll provide room and board while he's in the program."

"What's the catch?" she said. "There's gotta be a catch."

"No cost, no catch," Ethan replied. "Only opportunity. And Chigger has shown a real interest in this field. He could make a career out of it."

"I'll talk to his father about it tonight when he gets home from work," Mrs. Muskrat said. "Since there is no cost, I doubt he'll have any objections. It will be a good way to keep Chigger out of trouble while he's not in school."

After leaving the Muskrats' house trailer, Ethan and Augustus went their separate ways, each with preparations to make for the expedition and duties to attend to.

On his way back to Wesley's house, Ethan finally got the phone call from the Department of the Interior he'd been waiting for. He couldn't wait to get back to tell Billy, but he arrived at the house to find Lisa and Billy having a serious conversation on the porch. They broke it off as he approached.

"I've got some good news," he told the couple with a smile. Neither responded.

"Gee, Dad, what's the good news?" he said mockingly while looking at Lisa. When he still got no response from either of them, he forged ahead. "Remember me telling you about the Department of the Interior's new investigator?" he asked with obvious enthusiasm.

"No," Lisa said.

"Not really," Billy confirmed.

"I told you about it just the other day."

Neither teen replied.

"Okay, let's start over," Ethan said. "The DOI—that's the Department of the Interior—has appointed a new NAGPRA investigator to look into cases of stolen Native American remains and artifacts."

"That does sound like good news," Billy replied with mild enthusiasm. "And what does that mean exactly?"

"We'll find out exactly when the investigator, an Arapaho woman named Raelynn Little Shield, gets here tomorrow," Ethan replied. "I believe she has an update on the search for the Sun Chief's staff, cape, and skeletal remains."

"Well, that is pretty good news," Billy said with more enthusiasm. He stood and walked to the far edge of the porch. "But what we need are immediate leads that reveal the location of the stolen goods as soon as possible," he said, turning back to Ethan and Lisa.

"You'll get no argument from me," Ethan replied. "But let's keep things positive!"

"Yeah, keep it positive," Billy concluded. "I am hopeful that this Raelynn person is the right one for the job."

As a matter of fact, Raelynn Little Shield thought she was the perfect person for the job. She felt lucky and proud to be the first official NAGPRA investigator, a brand-new position within the US Department of the Interior. The thirty-year-old Arapaho woman from Crowheart, Wyoming, had gotten her double college degree in law enforcement and anthropology, hoping that someday she'd be able to do exactly what this job called for.

In the 1800s and much of the 1900s, anthropologists, archaeologists, and various other "collectors" dug up Native American burial sites wherever and whenever they felt like it. They carried their findings—including skeletal remains and cultural items buried with the deceased—back to whatever museum or university they worked for.

That began to change for the better in 1990 when Congress passed the Native American Graves Protection and Repatriation Act, commonly called NAGPRA. But the law really didn't have much in the way of "teeth," meaning there wasn't much done to enforce the law or investigate violations of that law. Until now.

The newly appointed secretary of the interior, a Native American woman, had made a lot of changes that provided for the inclusion of Native tribes and individuals in federal government operations they'd formerly been denied.

But the whole process was more than just a job to Raelynn. It had personal meaning to her, because a few of her own ancestors had been dug up and their skeletal remains carted off to a museum in Chicago for further study. She had witnessed first-hand how little respect earlier generations of white Americans had for anything to do with Native Americans.

So when Little Shield's first assignment was to take on the legal case brought by the Lookout family of the Osage Nation, it felt like she would finally be able to apply everything she'd learned and personally experienced to a significant, worthy cause.

Raelynn drove the rental car from the Tulsa airport to Grandpa Wesley's home, which only took a couple of hours. Using her phone's navigation system, she easily found the older white frame house located east of Tahlequah. The investigator collected her briefcase, designed to resemble a Plains Indian traveling bag, from the back seat and headed toward the front porch.

She was surprised to see a small collection of older Natives on that porch gathered around a young Native man who appeared to be doctoring one of them. It was a classic traditional Native setting, played out on reservations all across the country, except that this tribal doctor appeared to be about sixteen or seventeen years old.

An elder stepped out of the house and approached Little Shield, calling to her.

"You must be Ms. Little Shield," Cecil said with a broad smile. "Boy, are we happy to see you! Come on inside."

As the Arapaho woman crossed the porch, the young Indian doctor excused himself from his patients and followed the investigator into the house. He noticed the small deerskin medicine pouch she was wearing.

"You must be the Billy Buckhorn I've heard so much about," Raelynn said, extending her hand.

Billy shook it, saying with a smile, "Don't believe everything you hear."

He held on to her hand for a couple seconds, not immediately allowing her to withdraw it, to see if there were any images that appeared in his mind. His ability to "read" people when touching them had shown up shortly after being struck by lightning last September during the Labor Day weekend. Since then, the ability had appeared sporadically.

Now he briefly saw a short black-and-white mini-movie of an elderly Native American man smudging and praying over a small medicine pouch and then placing the pouch's strap around Little Shield's neck.

"Sorry," he said as he released her hand from his grip. "I have to make sure all the people we're working with now have good intentions. There are those who would do us harm or block our progress."

She smiled awkwardly as she turned to face Billy's entire Underworld Takeover Prevention Team, seated in the living room and eagerly anticipating the meeting and possible news. Raelynn made the rounds, greeting everyone in the room.

"I'll get right to it," Little Shield said, pulling some paperwork out of her briefcase. "The Reverend Dr. Samuel Miller of Limestone, Texas, was arrested by the FBI and is being held in the Texarkana prison awaiting trial. He's the one who bought the skeletal remains from Peter Langford, the director of the Spiral Mounds Archaeological Site. Langford is also there awaiting trial. Both are charged with the illegal sale of Native American human remains and other related charges."

That pleased everyone in the room.

"Miller admitted to being a broker for a buyer in another state, but, unfortunately, he hasn't revealed who that buyer is. He's not really motivated to talk, so we're at an impasse there for the time being."

That pleased no one in the room.

"As far as the cape and staff originally buried with those remains and stolen from the radiocarbon dating lab in Athens, Georgia, we do have one lead," Little Shield added.

From her briefcase, she pulled out multiple copies of a page containing two grainy photos and passed them out. A close-up of a muddy license plate was visible in one picture, and the side of a white van with a logo on the door could be seen in the other.

"These images were captured by a surveillance camera near the facility," she explained. "Both the license plate and the logo are partially obscured with mud. That seems to be intentional."

The Underworld Takeover Prevention Team peered intently at the photo's details as the investigator pointed them out.

"Fortunately, the FBI lab was able to reconstruct the portions that had been blotted out," she continued. "The plate and the logo belong to the state penitentiary in Angola, Louisiana."

"Huh?" was the collective response.

"That was my exact reaction," Raelynn said. "What does a prison in Louisiana have to do with Native American burial objects from eastern Oklahoma?"

While Little Shield had been talking, Billy had scanned her energy field to get even more of a read on the woman. Her energy seemed clean and her intentions true.

"Now that we've met you face-to-face and found that you don't have any hidden agendas, we can share a little more information with you," Billy said. He gave her a quick rundown of how the human remains and the burial items fit into the larger scheme of things, the ancient prophecy, the immediate timetable, and the consequences of not locating the stolen objects.

"That's all a little too far out there for me," she replied. "What proof can you offer to validate any of it?"

Billy searched the levels of internal and external spiritual guidance he had available to him. The apparition of an elderly Native American woman appeared just behind and to the side of Little Shield and presented Billy with a message.

"Your Arapaho great-grandmother just told me that she's proud of what you're doing now," Billy said. "Getting her remains out of that museum in Chicago and back to your tribe's homelands for reburial was very important to her."

The stunned look on Little Shield's face revealed the truth of Billy's message. She glanced back over her shoulder as if she might see the elder standing there.

"You saw her just now?" the investigator asked. "And she spoke to you?"

"Yeah, that happens sometimes," Billy replied.

Little Shield looked at the faces of the people seated around her to see if she could detect any hint of insincerity or falsehood. Neither were evident.

"You should tell someone in the federal government about this impending catastrophe so they can warn the American people," she said.

"Who would we warn, and what could we tell them?" Ethan replied. "They'd react the same way you reacted when Billy told you."

"Well, somebody's got to do something," she concluded as she began putting papers back into her briefcase.

"That somebody is you," Lisa said, getting up out of her seat. "And what you can do is fast-track this investigation! Those stolen items will play a big part in the prevention of national— maybe worldwide—disaster!"

"You know that's like trying to get the tail to wag the dog." Little Shield finished closing up her bag and threw the strap over her shoulder. "What I *can* do is make your case my top priority," she said with finality. "I'll rearrange my schedule and immediately head from here to question Samuel Miller one more time, and then I'll go straight to the prison down in Angola to talk to the warden."

Raelynn began heading toward the door.

"What if one of us goes with you?" Lisa asked. "Is that allowed?"

Raelynn stopped with one hand on the front doorknob. "I'm supposed to coordinate my fieldwork with the FBI and no one else," she said. "But, in general, my investigation has a low priority in law enforcement circles."

Opening the door, she turned to Lisa. "But I could use some company on the trip. How quickly can you be ready to go?"

"Is fifteen minutes soon enough?" Lisa said.

"Okay, we leave for Texarkana in fifteen minutes," Raelynn said as she stepped out onto the porch. "I hope I don't get fired for this. I love my new job."

Lisa gave Billy a quick kiss on the cheek.

"Let me know when you are in a room with Miller," Billy said. "I may want to eavesdrop."

"Sure thing," she said and literally skipped down the hallway to pack a suitcase.

Billy returned to his patients, who'd been patiently waiting on the front porch.

CHAPTER FOUR

Owls and Snakes Together Again

Greyson Greenstone wasn't always what he appeared to be. In fact, he was a rather unusual shape-shifter. Not only could he transform into an animal—a desert horned viper, to be exact—he could also shape-shift into a couple other human appearances.

Today, for the welcoming ceremony, he would be the charismatic orator Nahash Molok, the prophet who could handle snakes and reincarnate his followers into a new life of their choosing, or so he promised. Few people knew that the name Nahash Molok was Hebrew for "Snake King."

Now it was showtime for Molok. Or rather, time for his monthly ritual performance, held in his concealed underground ceremonial chamber constructed inside the center of the earthen platform mound at the Three Rivers Indian Mounds Park.

An audience of some two hundred souls had gathered this night, all eager to join the First Temple of the Reborn and one day hopefully be born again, as a snake is reborn by shedding its skin. That was what the recruiting messages promised. A banner above the stage included the image of a snake halfway through the skin-shedding process.

As he stood in the wings just offstage, the handsome, light-skinned, thirtyish Greenstone morphed into his stage persona: the gray-haired, darker-skinned, ethnically mysterious priest Nahash Molok. Then he grasped the greenish stone amulet that hung from his neck and took a deep breath.

"*Zôl-Coatl,*" he whispered in the ancient Nahuatl Aztec tongue, invoking the power of a very deadly snake.

He took a second breath, this time drawing in more than air. He drew in energy—dark energy from the lower supernatural regions, the source of his power.

"Serpent power," he whispered, "flow through me that I may spread it to the underlings of the Middleworld."

Now fully prepared, the orator stepped from behind the curtain and onto the stage. With great flourish, he fanned his serpentine-green cape in a wide gesture as if to share his power with the audience.

"In the Quran, the Prophet Muhammad says Allah told Moses to throw down his staff," the orator began. "And lo and behold, it became a writhing snake, demonstrating the prophet's divine power. And Allah said to Moses: 'Fear not, for you are my prophet.' Then Moses came before Pharaoh to free his people from slavery."

The man paused for effect as he gazed out on his audience. Faces of every shade looked back at him, eager to hear his every word and follow his every gesture. Multiple cameras recorded the spectacle for live streaming and later broadcast.

The orator continued with much bravado. "In the Gospel book of Mark, we find these words of Yeshua Messiah. 'And these signs shall follow them that believe: They shall take up serpents; and if they drink any deadly thing, it shall not hurt them.'"

Those few souls in the audience who'd attended the man's previous public events knew what was coming next. However, for most attendees, this was their introduction to his exotic teachings and their first time experiencing this man's legendary performance.

"Bring me the sacred cup of toloache, elixir of the soul and portal to the supernatural world!" Molok commanded.

Toloache was the Nahuatl Aztec word for the medicinal plant known as datura in North America, used for centuries by many tribes and cultures for spiritual vision quests. But if the plant was used unwisely, or ingested in too large a quantity, it brought sickness and death.

He raised his left arm, a gesture that allowed the sleeve of his robe to fall away and reveal a tattoo depicting the winding vine of a datura plant with its trumpet-shaped flowers wrapped around the arm. A similarly robed assistant rushed onstage carrying an ornate glass chalice. She handed the container to the orator, bowed to him, and exited as the man continued speaking.

"Then he took the cup, gave thanks, and passed it to his disciples, saying, 'Drink from it, all of you, for this is the gateway to the world of immortality.'" The orator swallowed the dark contents of the cup in one long gulp, then gasped for air, wiped his lips, and dashed the cup to the stage floor with a great deal of flourish. He turned to his audience. "When you join our ranks, you, too, will be able to partake of this mind-expanding potion at our monthly rebirthing ceremonies!"

Excited murmurs in hushed tones spread through the crowd, and the orator knew they were hooked. He then raised his right arm and signaled to someone stage right, again allowing the sleeve of his robe to fall away. The snake tattoo that spiraled along this arm from shoulder to wrist became fully visible then, further adding to the drama of the moment.

Two assistants quickly wheeled in a portable hundred-gallon terrarium and left it next to the pulpit. Inside that chamber, behind its glass walls, writhed a half dozen venomous snakes of various sizes and colors. Rattlesnakes, copperheads, cottonmouths, and cobras squirmed and twisted in a frenzied pile.

"Now I will demonstrate the combined power of trust, faith, and knowledge," the man proclaimed. "Today you will understand the truth of the command: fear not the serpent."

As if on cue, a rattlesnake in the terrarium hissed and struck at the glass wall that kept him imprisoned. The orator opened the container's lid, quickly reached in, and grabbed that very snake by the back of its head. The crowd gasped.

After pulling the reptile out of the enclosure, the man held the creature out toward the audience. It bared its fangs and hissed loudly, and audience members instinctively and collectively jumped back in their seats. As it writhed and wriggled, the man stepped forward to the stage's edge and marched back and forth so that everyone was able to appreciate the danger the snake presented.

What no one in the crowd knew was that this priest/performer/ entrepreneur/con man had for a long time been regularly dosing himself with rattlesnake venom—minuscule quantities at a time— to build up an immunity to its effects. And also, most of the poison had been drained from the snake.

Then he held the rattlesnake's open mouth about a foot away from his own face and uttered an incantation in a language unfamiliar to the people who watched. As he spoke, he moved his other hand in a smoothing, wavelike gesture in front of the reptile's eyes.

To everyone's amazement, the snake fell asleep and went limp in the orator's hand. He marched back and forth on the stage, displaying his impressive accomplishment. As the adulation continued, two beautiful dark-skinned female assistants came onstage. One took the unconscious reptile from the man and put it back in the terrarium. The other assistant, carrying a handheld microphone, spoke directly to the crowd.

"Everybody, let's make some noise for the incredible supernatural priest Brother Nahash Molok!" she shouted, and the room filled with applause as he left the stage. "Are you ready to believe?" she called out with a broad smile on her face.

"Yes!" came the resounding reply.

"Are you ready to come forth, join us, and start your journey toward immortality?" she continued. "All who do shall be reborn like a snake that sheds its skin, and begin a new life. Remember: judgment day is coming so very soon. Those who stole this land from its rightful owners will be removed from power! They shall be punished for their deeds, but the descendants of the colonizers who repent and denounce the actions of their ancestors shall be saved. Are you ready?"

A roar of approval and shouts of "We are ready!" came from various parts of the standing crowd.

"Well then, step to the back of the room, where you can pay your initiation fee, receive your welcome packet, and begin learning to merge mind, body, and spirit," she said, pointing to a row of tables with attendants. "Your packet also contains your first free portion of toloache, the gateway serum, and an amulet made of serpentine stone like the one Brother Molok wears."

That did it. People made a mad dash to the back of the room to be first in line. They'd heard the rumors, read the testimonials, and seen the online videos of these mysterious rituals. They longed to belong to something bigger than themselves and hoped there was more to life than the short, mundane physical existence here on earth. They *were* ready—that is to say, ripe for the picking!

Once he was offstage, Molok hurried to his dressing room, where he began changing clothes and identities once again. His true self, the one who held secret powers and controlled hidden forces, emerged. Or rather, it was uncovered and revealed, a sorcerer whose real name was known only to those in his inner circle but whose nickname was Snake-Eye. There was no obvious physical difference between Molok and Snake-Eye. The distinction was internal.

After adjusting the black patch that covered an empty right eye socket, the sorcerer pushed a button on his dressing room intercom.

"Has our guest arrived?" he asked an assistant as he brushed locks of gray hair back from his scarred, leathery brown face.

"Yes, sir," she said. "He's waiting in the meeting chamber below."

"Good, good, good," the man replied. "Let's get this alliance restarted."

Snake-Eye, followed by two assistants, stepped out of his dressing room, then walked across the backstage area and into a small elevator car. There were only three buttons on the control panel, and he pushed the middle one. That, he knew, would take him to another subterranean floor that contained his circular meeting chamber, along with a small conference room. That was where his guest would be waiting.

Snake-Eye had chosen this location for his rebirthing ceremonies on purpose. It was, after all, one of the oldest mound sites in North America. Some of his own ancestors had been involved in its construction and operation. They, too, had held ceremonies there for hundreds if not thousands of Indigenous people hoping for better lives now and after their deaths.

Stepping out of the elevator, the sorcerer signaled his assistants that they could return to the main floor. When the elevator doors closed, the man adjusted his eye patch one more time and walked into the conference room. There, he found his guest, Thomas Two Bears, the head of the Night Seers, seated at the conference table and sipping a glass of water. Molok greeted his guest and approached him with an extended hand.

"Thomas," he said in a friendly tone. "Welcome to my world headquarters, here on the second-largest Mississippian mound complex in North America. I've waited so long to meet you in person."

"I saw some of your—I don't know what to call it—performance," Two Bears responded in a less than friendly tone. "What kind of name is Nahash Molok, anyway?"

Snake-Eye relaxed his outstretched arm when he realized Two Bears wasn't going to shake his hand. "It's all part of my public persona to attract followers," the one-eyed man said. "It's from Hebrew, actually. *Nahash* is the word for snake, and *Molok* translates to 'king' or 'lord.' It means 'Snake King' or 'Lord of the Snakes.' The name is symbolic."

"What you preach is just a mishmash of things, isn't it?" Two Bears said in a criticizing tone. "A little of this and a little of that. But who and what are you really?"

The snake man pushed the shirtsleeve up on his right arm, making the spiraling snake tattoo visible. Then he clenched his right hand into a fist and held it tight as he replied. Mysteriously, Two Bears began feeling a constriction around his throat.

"The name on my birth certificate is, appropriately enough, Valerio Culebra," the man answered. "It means 'Powerful Snake' in Spanish. You see, my parents were very conscious of my lineage."

As Snake-Eye spoke, the Cheyenne medicine man began to feel like he was going to choke. The sorcerer continued talking.

"But ever since I lost this eye in an accident and began wearing the patch, some people call me Ojo Culebra, Spanish for 'Snake-Eye.'"

Two Bears continued to have trouble breathing. That was when he finally realized this Snake Cult leader was causing his discomfort. The Night Seer wasn't used to this predicament because he was usually the one using his supernatural powers to control someone else during these kinds of interactions.

"Here's a little genealogy lesson for you," Snake-Eye said. "According to oral histories, on my mother's side I am a direct descendant of Monkata, the Snake Priest. I believe you would be familiar with him. And on my father's side, I am a descendant of the great Moctezuma, ruler of the Aztec people when the colonizing Spaniards invaded Mexico. So, you see, I am Indigenous royalty all the way round."

Snake-Eye relaxed his fist, and Two Bears began to breathe more easily. He loosened his shirt collar, blew out a breath, and changed his tone.

"I apologize for my ignorant attitude earlier. It was uncalled for." He grabbed a cloth napkin from the conference table and wiped the sweat from his brow. "So where does your medicine come from?" he asked in a more friendly manner.

"From Maya and Aztec sorcerers in Mexico and Central America," Snake-Eye replied, also in a friendly tone. "My research revealed that much of the North American Mound Builders' culture seems to have come north from Mexico when maize—what you call corn—was brought this way."

"That's a concept I've never heard," Two Bears said. "Do you—"

"Look, Thomas," his host interrupted, clenching his fist again. "I didn't invite you here to get a third-degree interrogation! Have you forgotten the reason you're here—so we can once and for all seal the deal on a renewed alliance between the Owls and the Snakes?"

The one-eyed man began to pace the length of the conference room, getting angrier and slowly tightening his fist once again.

"Our organizations are after the same thing: to make the colonizers pay for what they did to our Indigenous peoples," he said in a gravelly whisper. "Tecumseh tried and failed to unite the North American tribes against the invaders, but now, more than any other time in our history, we have the power and ability to turn the tables and reset the balance."

Quickly, Snake-Eye returned to stand before Two Bears. He lifted his eye patch, revealing the hideous hole where an eyeball used to be. He stuck a finger in the hole and scratched a spot in the back of the empty eye socket that itched.

"So, what's it going to be?" he asked as he scratched. "Are we doing this or not?"

He replaced the patch and glared at the Cheyenne man with one cyclopean eye.

"Okay, okay. No need to get all riled up." The head of the Owl Clan took a swallow of water from the glass on the table and tried to compose himself. He realized he was no match for this sorcerer and that he'd probably lose if ever they were to go at each other at the supernatural level. "It's just that I've been in sole control of the Underworld retribution plans for so long. It's hard for me to trust anyone else enough to delegate any of the responsibility."

"The Snakes are only going to do what your Night Seers have already agreed to," Snake-Eye replied, losing patience again. "You began the campaign right on schedule with the well-placed storms, and we'll take the next step, also on schedule. I'm not going to rehash what our separate tasks are again. Been there, done that!"

"Right, right," Two Bears said, standing up. "We need each other for sure. Let's do this!"

He extended his hand, and the snake man shook it. Then, at the same time, each sorcerer pulled out a length of deer-skin they'd brought with them for the occasion. Each section of hide had a beaded image in the middle and one fringed end. They resembled the ancient traditional wampum belts that tribes in the Northeast created to represent intertribal agreements and treaties.

Each piece visually represented each man's organization. The beaded pattern on Two Bears's strip formed the image of an owl. The image on Snake-Eye's was the same image that appeared on the Serpentine Foundation's logo, a circular snake about to bite its own tail.

"Now we join our ancient orders back together once again," the snake man said.

The two men laid their leather strips side by side on the conference table, so the fringed areas were closest to one another. Then each placed one hand on top of his piece. In unison, the Owl and the Snake generated an internal electrical energy charge that passed through their bodies, into their arms, and down into the leather pieces.

The supernatural charges worked their magic on the separate lengths of leather, causing their fringed edges to intertwine and meld. Within a few seconds, the two hides became one—unified in purpose.

"The ancient alliance is renewed in the way the ancient treaties were ratified among our medicine peoples," Snake-Eye declared, holding up the newly created physical symbol of the joint agreement.

"The Owls and the Snakes in solidarity again," Two Bears confirmed.

"The Society of Serpents will be pleased to see this united emblem when we next convene in these council chambers to continue our work," the snake man commented.

"The first of May is our target date for the incarnation conjuring," Two Bears said. "The veil between physical and supernatural begins thinning then, as you know."

"So be it," the one-eyed man said with a nod of his head. He hit a button on the nearby wall-mounted intercom and spoke. "Layla, please come to the conference room and escort Mr. Two Bears on a tour of the compound. I want him to have a complete picture of our resources and capabilities."

"Yes, sir," a female voice replied. "Right away."

Snake-Eye turned to Two Bears. "I'd give you the tour myself," he said apologetically, "but I have much work to do in preparation for the upcoming arrival of the other eight Serpents."

"I'll pass on the guided tour," Two Bears replied. "I've got to keep moving if I'm going to have time to check on the progress being made by the other Night Seers."

"It must be hard to keep thirteen medicine makers in line," Snake-Eye said. "I'm glad there's only nine of us Serpents to contend with."

"Just before I got here, I was busy tracking down a possible new member of the Owl Clan to replace one that died," the Night Seer said.

"Oh, that's right. I forgot that you lost one. My condolences," the snake man offered. "What was her name again?"

"Most of her life she was known as Night Wolf, but more recently she used the alias Carmelita Tuckaleechee."

"I'm very familiar with the use of aliases," Snake-Eye said. "They have served me well. But you really underestimated the powers and abilities of that Buckhorn boy, didn't you?"

"Now the Owls and Snakes can deal with him and his so-called Medicine Council together," Two Bears said as Snake-Eye's assistant arrived at the conference room.

"Our guest is leaving," the snake man told her. "Would you see that Mr. Two Bears doesn't get lost on his way out?"

"Until next time," Two Bears said and followed the woman out.

Snake-Eye made sure the Night Seer was on the elevator before trotting over to an elaborately carved wooden desk that sat in the back corner of the conference room. He opened the desk's top drawer and pushed one of several buttons on a keyboard concealed there.

The button automatically connected him to eight cell phones belonging to the other members of his Society of Serpents. He typed a message that would be texted to the eight phones: *The alliance is renewed. Begin the second phase of the operation.*

He hit the Send button and waited to see that all eight of the other members of his secret society acknowledged his message. The next all-important personal step he'd take would be to contact Monkata, the ancient Snake Priest, down in Level Nine of the Underworld to let him know the deal between the Owls and Snakes had been completed.

The snake man knew it was unusual for the dark soul of a previous earth dweller to reside in the ninth level. Most ended up in the third level, the Shadow Zone. But, having served as the Snake Priest for the Winged One during his earthly existence, Monkata had proven himself worthy of residing in the land of the Underworld serpents.

Of course, all previous earth-dwelling Snake Priests before and after him had also earned the right to live in that world. Over the centuries, competition between them had become fierce, each striving to be the Winged One's favorite.

It was Monkata who had shown the current Snake Priest how to free the Horned Serpent from the crystal cave, and it was Monkata who had taught the Society of Serpents how to guide the creature down the Arkansas River and back to the original serpent cave.

And it would be Monkata who accompanied the Winged One when he materialized in the flesh during the Grand Thinning of the Veil. That would be a glorious day!

CHAPTER FIVE

Pieces of the Puzzle

Ethan and Cecil arrived early for a planned meeting with Augustus, who said he was finalizing their spring break expedition. Over the past few weeks and months, the Buckhorn and Lookout families had become very close, so knocking before entering the Buckhorn home was a formality no longer needed.

"Hello, is anyone home?" Ethan called after stepping into the front room.

"Up here," Billy answered from the upstairs office.

The Lookouts headed upstairs, where they found Billy observing weather patterns on one computer screen and watching a news report streaming live on another.

"You've got to see this," Billy said. "It's the wildest thing."

They all focused on an on-screen TV reporter.

"Reports are pouring in from all over the country," the young man said. He held a microphone in one hand and an umbrella in the other. A steady rain fell all around him. On-screen titles read

Live Report from Norfolk Tennessee. "Here's what a few local folks are saying about it."

The reporter held out his microphone as the camera panned over to reveal a middle-aged white woman, also holding an umbrella.

"It liked to scare us to death," she explained. "Every kind of snake you can imagine was gliding along the road just as pretty as you please."

As the reporter and the woman continued to talk, video footage showed several snakes moving along a rain-drenched paved road.

"They didn't pay no mind to any people nearby them," the woman continued. "They acted like they were glad to be out in the open."

The camera panned back to the reporter.

"Back to you in the studio," he said.

The view changed to a man and woman sitting behind a news desk with the KTUL-TV Tulsa logo in front. Behind the pair were several screens depicting snakes inching along roadways, racing across riverbanks, swimming in shallow lake waters, and coming out of caves.

"What would you call this?" the anchorwoman asked jokingly. "A serpent apocalypse?"

"Maybe snake-aggedon," the anchorman joked back.

As the pair chuckled to themselves, Billy turned down the volume.

"I can see how the continued rain, and now the flooding, would force all types of reptiles to flee to higher ground," Ethan said.

"I think it's more than that," Billy countered. "Snakes usually try to keep clear of people, hide out, and avoid interaction if at all possible."

"Yeah, that sounds about right."

"These snakes are on the attack," Billy said. "Charging at people out in the open. Pursuing and biting, showing no fear at all."

They continued to watch the news for a couple of minutes, and then Billy came to a conclusion.

"First the storms and now the snakes," he said with a worried look. "These aren't natural events. I didn't realize the Owls were powerful enough to create such large-scale troubles. I guess I was wrong."

A knock on the front door drew their attention away, and the three trotted downstairs to meet with Augustus. The archaeologist spread a new map out on the living room coffee table.

"I've mapped out our trip, starting at the Spiral Mounds site near the crystal cave," Augustus said. "Once we finish there, we get back up to Interstate 40 to head for Clarksville, Arkansas. Luckily, the mound site is not too far from the highway. Then we'll head through Little Rock to the next mound site, and our fourth stop will be at the mounds just outside of Pine Bluff, Arkansas. These mound structures all run parallel to the Arkansas River."

"How long will we need to be at each site?" Billy asked.

"I think we'll need a full day," Stevens said. "Plus travel time between sites."

"Chigger's spring break only lasts nine days start to finish," Billy said. "We won't make it to all nine sites in that time—especially when you add travel time. And we'll be rushing, so each stop won't allow for a thorough inspection."

Stevens thought about that for a moment. So did Billy.

"I have a feeling it might be important to check the Three Rivers site, the one that's farthest from us," Billy concluded. "And I'm not sure why, but Chigger should be there too."

"Well, it's not that far away," Cecil said, looking at the map. "We could go check out the Oklahoma site first, go see the Clarksville site next, and then head straight for the Louisiana site on the Mississippi River down south. We can work our way back, and since we'll have more than one vehicle, someone could drive Chigger back to Tahlequah when the time comes."

"Sounds like a plan," Augustus said with a smile as he stood to leave. "I'm excited," he added, sounding like a kid who was having a hard time waiting to open his birthday presents. "Now I've got to make some cheap hotel arrangements and check my departmental budget to make sure the university can afford this trip."

Meanwhile, Raelynn and Lisa had begun their drive from Tahlequah to the Texarkana federal prison, which would take about five hours according to Little Shield's calculations. With the Lookout teen as her traveling companion, the time passed quickly. They, it turned out, had a lot to talk about.

For Lisa, it was such a breath of fresh air to experience a little quality girl time. For weeks, she'd been surrounded by—no, absolutely drowning in—male energy. Her father, grandfather, Billy, Billy's father, and now Chigger and Augustus Stevens made the testosterone levels around her too much to handle.

For Raelynn, it was like talking to a younger version of herself. Ah, to hear the hopes and dreams of a Native girl about to step into the rest of her life. The two had similar interests in powwow dancing, tribal traditions, contemporary music, and the latest in high-tech gadgets.

Most importantly to both of them, the drive gave Raelynn the opportunity to hear the whole story of the ancient Native prophecy, the Lookout family's role in that prophecy, and the incredible journey that Billy as Thunder Child had been on. Finally, Lisa spelled out why it was crucially important right now to find the Sun Chief's remains, his cape and staff, and the missing piece of the Sky Stone.

"Dr. Hughes at the Osage Nation Historic Preservation Office has been so supportive in this," Lisa added.

"You're right," Raelynn said. "When it comes to NAGPRA issues, tribes usually want complete control over efforts to repatriate remains and burial artifacts."

"Hughes immediately gave us the green light as a family to participate in the investigation and take possession of the articles," Lisa said.

The pair finally arrived at the Budget Inn at the edge of Texarkana, and Raelynn apologized for the accommodations.

"Sorry for the two-star amenities," she said. "My department's travel budget only allows for low-budget travel, if you get what I'm saying."

"No problem," Lisa replied. "Whenever I travel with my dad, he always books the oldest, cheapest places he can find. He says it prepares you to step back in time for an archaeological dig, but we both know that's baloney. He's just cheap."

They chuckled and made light of the situation, and then Raelynn went over her plans to interrogate the Reverend Dr. Samuel Miller the following morning. Lisa spoke to Billy on the phone before turning in, and the couple apologized to each other for their earlier argument.

"I'm sorry for accusing you of pulling back from me," Lisa said. "I know you're under a lot of pressure and have the whole world on your shoulders. I'll give you some space for now."

"What a relief to hear you say that!" Billy replied, letting out a breath of air. "If and when this battle is behind us, I hope we can have normal lives and a normal relationship."

"Whatever that might be like," Lisa said. "I'm looking forward to it."

After that issue was out of the way, Lisa confirmed that they'd be talking to Miller around nine o'clock the next morning. Billy said he'd try to eavesdrop on the conversation via spirit travel.

"Let me know you're in the room if you can," Lisa said.

"I'll give you a kiss on the cheek," Billy replied.

Lisa remembered how Billy had signaled his presence the same way when he rescued her from the attack of the ghost wolves near Tahlequah several weeks before.

"Can't wait," she said before ending the call and turning out the light.

"It's highly unusual for a civilian to be involved in an investigation like this," Little Shield told Lisa the next morning on their way to the federal correctional facility. "But out of all the NAGPRA cases I've reviewed, yours is the most unusual, so I'm making an allowance. Plus, I really like you and your family."

At nine sharp, the two arrived at the prison and were admitted to a secure interview room that contained three chairs and a table bolted to the floor. They sat down at the table and waited.

At that same time back in Park Hill, Billy lay down in his bed and then rolled out of his body. It had become so easy for him to do now. He pictured Lisa in his mind and was immediately taken to the prison interview room where she sat. He floated down beside his girlfriend and gave her a light kiss on the cheek.

Feeling a sudden chill on one spot on her cheek, Lisa knew Billy was checking in with her. She smiled and touched that spot, trying not to alert Raelynn that anything unusual was happening.

In a few minutes, a guard escorted Miller, who was wearing an orange jumpsuit, into the room. The seventy-year-old white man did not look well at all, with sunken eyes and very pale skin. His thinning white hair was unkempt, and red sores dotted some areas of exposed skin.

As he entered the interview room, a loud noise was heard from outside, which caused Miller to cower and try to hide in a corner of the room. The guard grabbed the man and sat him down hard in a chair across from the two interviewers and handcuffed him to a metal loop in the middle of the table. Afterward, the guard took up a position near the door.

"I think this man is suffering from ghost sickness," Lisa whispered to Raelynn, recognizing the symptoms. "He was surrounded by the ghosts of Native American people whose skeletons had been dug up and hidden in his barn, along with hundreds of stolen burial artifacts. That's the way Billy found him just before my father called the FBI."

Raelynn had not heard this background information before, and it surprised her. She just nodded and then began the questioning.

"Should I address you as reverend or doctor or both?" she asked the man.

"I don't care what you call me. I've got nothing to—" Suddenly Miller jerked backward and looked up at the ceiling. "Go away and leave me alone!" he shouted up at an invisible threat.

Lisa realized that he might be aware of Billy's energy presence, but Raelynn tried to ignore the outburst.

"Mr. Miller, you illegally bought a set of ancient Native American human remains from Peter Langford, the director of the Spiral Mounds Archaeological Site," Raelynn said, drawing the man's attention back to her. "Who did you sell those bones to, and how much did you get for them?"

"I ain't answering no questions," he said. "I didn't have no bones. I didn't sell anything to anybody." He looked over at the guard who was standing near the door. "Get me out of here!" he shouted. "Take me back to my cell."

"But these nice people came all this way to see you," the guard said in a mocking tone.

"I don't care where they came from or why they're here," the prisoner protested. "I know my rights. Now take me back!"

Unexpectedly, Lisa shot up from her chair and pointed at Miller. *"Shonkay wahsahpay tatanka nikka wahko!"* she shouted. "An Osage curse be on you and your descendants from now and forever for disrespecting my ancestor's spirit and desecrating his buried remains!"

She turned and stormed out of the room, leaving Raelynn, Miller, and the guard in shock.

"Get me outta here now!" Miller yelled at the guard as he pulled on the handcuffs and stomped his feet. "That redskin witch cursed me!"

Raelynn followed Lisa out into the hall, and the guard shouted at the prisoner, "Calm down or I'll leave you handcuffed to that table!"

Miller continued to pull against the cuffs, but he calmed down somewhat. Meanwhile, the guard used the radio on his belt to call for assistance with the very agitated prisoner.

As the two investigators headed for the prison exit, Raelynn confronted her companion.

"Why did you do that?" she asked. "I could get in a lot of trouble."

"I'm sorry," Lisa responded. "I felt I had to do something to get the guy talking."

"What did you say to him?"

"All I said was *dog bear buffalo man woman* in the Osage language," Lisa said with a smile. "No curse. Just a list of random words."

"Let's get out of here before the warden comes looking for us," Raelynn said.

They headed for the rental car in the prison parking lot.

"I think Billy is going to come back here later today or tonight to pay a visit to that criminal," Lisa said as they reached the car. "To scare him into telling us who he sold my ancestor's bones to."

"Your boyfriend can do that?"

"If necessary," Lisa replied.

"Well, it's certainly an unusual interrogation technique," Raelynn said. "Let's hope it works. Next stop: the warden's office at the Louisiana State Penitentiary in Angola."

Across the country to the east, in the Great Smoky Mountains National Park, Cherokee park ranger Joseph Saunooke had noticed that the number of visitors to the park had drastically dropped in the last few weeks. And he knew why. It was the Tlanuwa, a creature straight from the legends of the Cherokee people, brought back to life through some unknown supernatural process.

Rumors of an enormous predatory bird snatching up pets in the park spread like wildfire throughout the hiking, camping, and outdoorsy communities. And, of course, the ongoing torrential rains hadn't helped either.

National Park Service officials tried to dismiss the rumors as merely the fearful fantasies of urbanites unaccustomed to the wildlife in the region. A wide range of predators, officials said, were responsible for the plague of pet disappearances.

"Mountain lions, wolves, bears, and coyotes are all prone to nabbing small dogs and scampering back into the forest," the director of park communications told a TV reporter. "The best solution to the problem is for visitors to stop bringing their pets with them to the wilderness."

Joseph Saunooke and his uncle Bucky Wachacha had tried on four separate occasions to perform medicine rituals meant to drive the Tlanuwa from the area. But those efforts failed, because the medicine man who'd conjured the oversized bird kept performing daily rituals designed to maintain the creature's peak performance.

"We need to find that medicine man, Yonaguska," Joseph told Bucky. "Billy Buckhorn heard that name directly from the mind of the creature, and even though we thought the man was long dead, he must still be living around here somewhere."

"What do you suggest we do?" Bucky asked. "Drive up and down every road on the rez until we locate him or someone who knows him?"

"Can't you use your 'Finding Lost Objects' formula to locate a missing person?"

"I ain't Google," the elder replied. "It don't work that way."

Amos Yonaguska, the medicine man they were discussing, came from a long line of old-school medicine people. Like Carmelita Tuckaleechee, whom Amos had known for decades as Night Wolf, he was over one hundred years old. Most people on the Eastern Cherokee reservation thought he'd died years ago, and he liked it that way.

"Out of sight—out of mind," he often said.

Some of his ancestors had been founders of the original Owl Clan, and he'd been among those who restarted the modern incarnation of the group. He'd never questioned the legitimacy of the ancient faction, nor had he wavered in his participation in the reformed organization.

However, his commitment began to waver with the murder of Wesley Buckhorn, one of the best-loved healers to ever walk Turtle Island. As far as Amos was concerned, it was a step too far. He was on the fence now about what to do. Should he voice his disapproval of the Night Seers' actions? Resign? Or should he just ride it out to the end, which was approaching quickly?

If Yonaguska protested the Owls' recent actions, Two Bears would respond by doing something very unpleasant to him. That was a fact. So this was a hard decision to make, and he was running out of time.

Raelynn, who was still using the economy car she'd rented at the Tulsa airport, now drove with Lisa toward the Angola prison on Interstate 49. The trip would take about five hours.

The two young women joked about that number—forty-nine—both having grown up in the powwow tradition and familiar with the Native American cultural meaning of it.

They knew the after-hours event known as a "forty-nine" was a dance sometimes held informally in a secluded location after a powwow that allowed for flirting between males and females participating in the event. Song lyrics often included English lines, such as the most famous "When the dance is over, sweetheart, I will take you home in my one-eyed Ford."

As the two continued driving and singing Indian songs, Lisa's boyfriend did indeed pay a visit to Miller in his prison cell. Billy had first seen this "bone collector" via spirit travel back in the man's barn in Limestone, Texas. At the time, Miller was haunted by dozens of ghosts of the Native Americans whose skeletal remains he had collected. The reverend doctor had become aware and afraid of spirits due to that experience.

When Billy appeared to Miller in his prison cell, the man acknowledged his presence.

"You don't scare me none," the man said, gazing in Billy's direction. "I seen plenty of ghosts. What can you do to me?"

Billy hadn't expected this kind of response and decided he needed to produce some kind of physical action to get to the man. Thinking back to events during his amazing Thunder Child initiation ceremony, Billy got an idea. He'd use a supernatural technique he'd learned from one of the members of the Intertribal Medicine Council.

He looked around the cell and spotted a small object sitting on a shelf in one corner. It was the man's aluminum drinking cup. Using all the focused energy he could muster, Billy forced the cup to fly across the cell and slam into the wall right next to Miller's head.

The man jumped away and yelled, "What the hell?" He backed into a corner. "What kind of spook are you? You keep away from me, you hear?"

Billy did just the opposite. He quickly positioned himself above the man and then slowly dropped down on top of him. Cold shivers passed through the man's body. He jumped onto his cot and pulled the blanket over himself.

"Guard! Guard!" Miller yelled as loud as he could. "You gotta get me outta here. I'm being attacked by a ghost!"

Hovering above the man, Billy whispered in his ear, "I'll be coming back over and over again until you tell them who you sold those bones to."

"Guard! Guard!" Miller called again. "Help me! Help me, please!"

All the nearest guard did was report Miller's further mental breakdown to the prison psychiatrist.

While Billy was dealing with Miller, Raelynn and Lisa arrived in the area of Angola, Louisiana, late in the afternoon to look for accommodations. Using her phone, Lisa located a cheap motel in St. Francisville, the nearest town with a motel that fit the federal travel budget. They'd surprise the warden with a visit first thing in the morning.

In the meantime, they decided to take a drive up to the Three Rivers Indian Mounds Park, which they'd seen signs for earlier in the day. Lisa remembered it being one of the mound sites on Augustus Stevens's map that would be visited during their spring break expedition. Lisa told Raelynn about the upcoming archaeological journey planned by her father and Professor Stevens.

A narrow two-lane paved road took them to the Three Rivers area, a large piece of land bounded by waterways on all four sides. An entrance sign made it clear that this was property owned and operated by the Serpentine Foundation and its executive director, Greyson Greenstone. Lisa snapped photos of everything on her phone while Raelynn drove.

As they got closer to the actual mounds, they passed a large, tacky-looking tourist stop called Serpent World, "home to more reptiles than any other place in North America." The Serpent World sign featured a drawing of a circular snake that was about to bite its own tail.

The most visible landmark within the collection of mounds was a flat-top earthen platform mound that had obviously been reconstructed. On top, in the center, sat a replica of the chief's house that once overlooked the entire site.

"This seems like a small version of Cahokia," Lisa commented. "But that's a state park, and this is private property. I wonder how many mound sites are still on private property."

A gate blocked the road leading into the mound park, but there was a marker explaining the history of the site on the side of the road. The two women got out to read the plaque, which said there were originally about a dozen mounds there and pointed out that the round mound closest to the Mississippi River had been reconstructed to include the spiral ramp that originally led from ground level up to the top.

"I'll have to tell Billy about this place and send him these pics," Lisa said. "This site is on their list of spiral mounds to visit."

The next morning the pair presented themselves at the entrance to the Angola penitentiary. Raelynn flashed her Department of the Interior investigator ID to the guard and asked to see the warden.

"Mr. Broussard only sees people with appointments," the chubby, gray-uniformed man said without looking at the ID. "His calendar is booked with back-to-back meetings and duties all day."

"That's okay," Raelynn said. "If he can't see me for a few minutes now, I'll be back later today with a couple of FBI agents and a search warrant for his office. I'm sure that won't inconvenience him more than a couple of days."

That got the guard's attention.

"Uh, wait just a moment, please," the man said as he picked up the phone on his desk. "I'll tell him you're here."

While they waited, Lisa looked around the reception area and found a stack of brochures that boasted of the prison's Greenstone Rehabilitation Program, which paid a select few prisoners to fashion jewelry from pieces of the greenish serpentine stone. She put a brochure in her back pocket.

After a quick chat with his boss, the guard said, "He's right down that hallway," and pointed toward the back of the room.

The pair of investigators walked briskly down the hall and into the warden's office. After they explained the nature of their visit and showed Broussard the surveillance photos Little Shield had brought with her, the warden began to look worried. He examined the two pictures closely, noting that the van's side-door panel displayed the Louisiana Department of Corrections seal, as did the license plate.

"I assure you no one from my staff drove all the way to Athens, Georgia, to steal Native artifacts!" Broussard said. "That's six hundred miles, and we have no authority to drive any farther than nearby New Orleans or Baton Rouge!"

"Those photos were taken by surveillance cameras across the street from the lab's loading dock, Mr. Broussard," Raelynn said. "Someone on your staff obviously took the van without your knowledge."

Raelynn caught a hint of recognition in Broussard's eyes and on his face when he heard that notion. But he quickly deflected to cover.

"I tell you right now, Ms. Little Shield, I'm going to do a thorough internal investigation into this matter," he said. "I'm determined to get to the bottom of this."

"I'm glad to see that you're motivated in the right direction, warden, but we'll let the FBI take it from here."

His face went from bright, hopeful, and determined to sunken and defeated in an instant.

"I'll leave these copies of the photos to help you with your thorough internal investigation," she said. "Good day."

After leaving the prison office, Raelynn and Lisa decided to visit Mr. Greyson Greenstone, executive director of the Serpentine Foundation, before heading back to Tahlequah.

They returned to Serpent World and parked in the asphalt parking lot, which was riddled with potholes and long, meandering cracks. A very large, faded sign, visible for possibly half a mile in either direction, stood on the roof above the attraction's front glass doors. It announced such features as *The Largest Collection of Reptiles in North America* and *World Famous* and *Fangs Galore*. Drawings and photos of lizards, alligators, snakes, and various other reptiles adorned the outer walls on either side of the entrance.

A young female cashier sat on a tall stool behind a glassed-in box office just inside the door. A name tag on her Serpent World T-shirt identified her as Ruthann, and she was busy reading something on her phone.

"We're here to talk to Executive Director Greenstone," Raelynn said.

"How many tickets will that be?" she asked, oblivious to what Raelynn had just said.

"As I said, we're hoping to talk to Mr. Greenstone," Raelynn repeated more loudly, this time flashing her ID. "We're NAGPRA investigators with the Department of the Interior."

"Mr. Greenstone was called away this morning," the cashier said. "I'm not sure when he'll be back. But you could leave your name and phone number so he can call you."

"Well, Ruthann, we won't be in the area that long," Little Shield said. "Do you know where he went?"

"There was some kind of problem over at the prison," Ruthann said. "He had to go see the warden."

That struck both Lisa and Raelynn as more than a coincidence. Ruthann caught the questioning looks on the investigators' faces.

"You don't know about Mr. Greenstone's prison rehabilitation program?" she asked. "I thought everybody around here knew about that."

"We just didn't know that your Greenstone and the prison's Greenstone were the same, and, if you'd really looked at Ms. Little Shield's ID, you'd *know* we're not from around here," Lisa said with a touch of sarcasm.

"Oh, sorry," Ruthann responded. "Why don't you leave a business card so Mr. Greenstone can give you a call?"

Raelynn pulled a card out from her briefcase and handed it to the girl.

"I'll give this to him the next time I see him," the cashier said. "In the meantime, why don't you two tour the reptile exhibit free of charge?"

"Thanks, but no," Lisa said. "We're more interested in touring the mounds. My dad's an archaeologist who specializes in Indigenous mound sites."

The cashier reached under the counter and produced two certificates that had *Three Rivers Indian Mounds Park* printed on them.

"These will get you into the mound park for free," she said. "I'm sure Mr. Greenstone would want you to see the mounds at no charge."

Lisa thanked the cashier for the passes and stuffed them into the back pocket of her jeans as she and Raelynn left the building. Neither of them spoke until they reached the car.

"You know serpentine is a green stone, right?" Raelynn said as she unlocked the car.

"No, I didn't," Lisa said. "I'm not familiar with it at all."

Then she caught on to what her companion was getting at.

"The name Greenstone must be an alias," Raelynn concluded. "The Greenstone Rehabilitation Program makes jewelry out of green stones."

"The director of the Serpentine Foundation is named Greenstone," Lisa added. "But what does that have to do with anything?"

"Don't know yet," Little Shield replied. "A deeper dive into all things serpentine might reveal a lot."

They got into Raelynn's rental car and drove away.

Meanwhile, Greyson Greenstone was having a rather heated conversation in the warden's office.

"How could your guys be so careless?" he screamed at Broussard. "It should've been a pretty simple job for a couple of convicts who are doing time for armed robbery to break into a college archaeology lab!"

"I don't know how that happened, Mr. Greenstone," the warden replied. "I told them to hide anything that would tie the van to the prison. When they left here, they'd completely covered the prison logo and the license plate with mud."

Greenstone grew angrier by the minute, and his face began turning red. He clenched both fists tightly and glared harshly at Broussard. The warden began feeling like he couldn't breathe, and panic set in.

"Please, Mr. Greenstone, we didn't do it on purpose," he pleaded as he choked. "I'll do whatever it takes to make it right."

"You bet your ass you will!"

Greenstone focused so much energy on choking Broussard that the spell he used to maintain the Greenstone identity began to fade. His one-eyed-man persona with the eye patch and serpent tattoos was bleeding through.

Just then, the guard from the front desk came into the room. "Mr. Broussard, are you all right?" he asked. "I heard shouting down the—"

He stopped short when he caught a glimpse of Greenstone's partial transformation. As the sorcerer split his focus between Broussard and the guard, more of the Snake-Eye persona became visible.

"What in hell's name is happening?" the guard yelled as he began to choke. He reached down and grabbed the radio mic that hung from his belt and yelled into it as best he could. "Code 10-5. Warden's—"

Both Broussard and the guard felt sudden sharp invisible blows to their necks that collapsed their windpipes and cut off all oxygen to their lungs and brains. The two men simultaneously fell to the floor.

The effort Greenstone had put into the double choking had caused his Snake-Eye persona to appear full blown. He looked down at his body to see if the transformation had completed itself. Slim legs and arms had become stout, muscular limbs. His smooth, well-manicured hands had also become stubbier and rougher. And the tattoos on his arms peeked out from below his now ill-fitting shirtsleeves.

Snake-Eye looked at the two dead men lying on the floor of the warden's office. This wasn't the first time he'd ended someone's life. And he knew from experience that the cause of death would be listed as "mysterious" because there had been no physical contact and therefore no physical evidence.

Time to eliminate evidence, he thought and casually walked back to the front desk.

Locating the surveillance system, he placed his hand on top of the electronic recording unit. He gave it a quick zap of electromagnetic current, just enough to blur any details that displayed who entered and exited the building that morning.

He confidently walked out of the building, got in his car, and drove back to his headquarters located deep inside the Chief's Mound.

CHAPTER SIX

Spring Break

Members of the project officially known as the Interstate Spiral Mounds Archaeological Expedition left Wesley's house on Monday morning of Chigger's spring break. The group would have a week to check out as many spiral mound sites on Professor Stevens's map as they could before Chigger would have to be back home.

The continuously rainy weather was causing Cecil's arthritis to act up, and he wasn't feeling much like crawling in and out of caves or climbing up mounds, so he didn't participate. Billy's parents, James and Rebecca, were, of course, busy at their jobs and couldn't take off a week for the expedition.

"I'm so pumped!" Chigger exclaimed when the Indigenous Archaeology Alliance van picked him up from home. "It's almost like getting the Paranormal Patrol back together!"

"Chigger, please don't call us that," Billy said. "That name was a joke."

"The Paranormal Patrol?" Lisa responded. "Is that what you called yourselves?"

"Like I said, it was a joke," Billy said. "A funny nickname."

"So that's where you got the idea of using a nickname," Lisa said, knowing that Chigger wasn't aware of the name Billy had given their little group.

"It's time for a new nickname, I guess," Chigger said, furrowing his brow and appearing to be in pain as he brainstormed.

"We already have a—"

"How about Mound Diggers Extraordinaire?" Chigger said, interrupting Billy. "Or . . . Supernatural Sleuthing Services, Incorporated. Ooh! I know. Something to do with preventing the Underworld from taking over!"

"Wow, that sounds really familiar, doesn't it, Billy?" Lisa said. "Amazing!"

"Okay, okay," Billy said with an air of defeat. "I guess we—"

"What exactly have you been calling us?" Lisa asked her boyfriend, interrupting him. "The Underworld Takeover Prevention Team, I think it is."

"Really? You already came up with a nickname and didn't tell me?" Chigger exclaimed. "Underworld Takeover Prevention Team, huh? Has a nice ring to it. That's UTPT, for short."

"Okay, I admit it," Billy said. "I got the idea of having a nickname from you, Chigger."

"And it's an effective nickname because it reminds us of what we're trying to do here, right?" Lisa commented.

"When you're right, you're right," Billy said. He was glad to see Lisa connecting with Chigger. He wanted that trend to continue.

There were three vehicles in the caravan: Ethan's archaeology van; the university van, which was towing a boat; and a third van that carried additional gear they'd need for the expedition, driven by a graduate archaeology student named Brad.

Ethan, Lisa, Billy, and Chigger rode in Ethan's van while Professor Stevens drove the university van. Brad, driving alone in the third van, would be helping to load and unload gear as well as assist Stevens with any actual excavation or recordkeeping to be done.

As her father drove, Lisa described the experiences she'd had with Raelynn after leaving the Texarkana prison and what they'd learned about the Three Rivers Indian Mounds Park and the nearby Angola prison.

"Raelynn promised to ask the FBI to fast-track their investigation," she said, wrapping up her report.

Ethan remembered he wanted to get more details about Billy and Chigger's original adventures on the Arkansas River. "Tell me more about your experiences in this first cave we're headed for," he asked. "I think you called it the crystal cave."

"I like to call it the bat cave," Chigger said. "And I think our story says why."

Billy and Chigger, who sat in second-row seats, took turns recounting those events, which had occurred last November and December. That seemed like such a long time ago to the two friends. Ethan and Lisa were so astonished by it all they could scarcely believe what they heard.

"Talking about all that really makes me miss Grandpa Wesley," Billy said with a sad tone in his voice. That was when he remembered something very important he'd brought. He fished around behind his seat and came up with a canvas tote bag. "I found these in a back closet at my grandpa's house," he said as he handed one of the objects to Lisa.

It was one of the round medallions Wesley had made for their expedition to recapture the Horned Serpent. It featured two snakes that had been tied together, forming a loop around a center hand with an eye in the palm. The medallion hung from a metal chain so you could wear it around your neck.

"That is an impressive piece of work," Lisa said, showing it to her father.

"All five of us wore these on that trip because, surprisingly, they repelled the beast," Billy said. "I suggest we wear them again, but there aren't enough to go around."

Chigger grabbed one from Billy's bag. "I for one wouldn't set foot in that cave again without it," he said as he slipped the chain over his head.

Billy went on to explain how Professor Stevens had discovered the image's power to repel the creature when it attacked him in his basement office. That detail added even more to the amazement Lisa and Ethan already felt about the boys' experience.

The drive to a boat ramp near the Spiral Mounds Archaeological Site took less than two hours. Stevens had arranged for a canopy-covered motorboat large enough to take all of them and much of their equipment upstream to the cave site. As everyone began transferring equipment from the vans to the boat, Augustus saw that the crew from Ethan's van was wearing the eye-in-hand medallion.

"I'll take one of those," he said.

Billy gave him the last one, and Augustus put it on.

"We're one short," Augustus said. "When we get to the cave, I guess someone will have to stay with the boat."

When all the people and gear were loaded into the boat, they headed out. During the short boat ride, Billy said, "Now I can show you the place where I died."

No one quite knew what to say to that. But Chigger always seemed to have a way to lighten any situation, whether he meant to or not.

"And I can show you the place I helped save Billy's life by calling the Cherokee Nation marshal on our satellite phone," he bragged, a smile beaming from his face.

After a brief silence, Lisa was the first to break the tension with a laugh. "Chigger, you crack me up!" she joked. "And you don't even know how you do it."

They soon rounded a curve in the river and came to the flat landing space at the bottom of the cliff. Billy tilted his head upward, and everyone looked up to see the mouth of the cave.

"This is it," Billy said.

"The bat cave," Chigger added.

Billy looked at Chigger and asked, "Are you picking up any negativity here? Any purple-type energy?"

"Not really—maybe a tiny bit. But now that we're here, I don't know why I let you talk me into coming along," Chigger said. "I'm not going in there. I'm staying in the boat."

"That's good," Augustus said. "You can give your medallion to Brad."

"Gladly," Chigger said, handing the object to the grad student.

Wearing raincoats, everyone but Chigger clambered out of the boat and onto the shore. Billy led the way up the slippery wet footholds that had long ago been etched into the cliff face. Lisa was up the steps next, and she stood beside Billy, who was taking in the rainy westward view.

Billy grasped the small medicine pouch containing the Uktena scale that hung from his neck. It was a gift from Grandpa, who said it was powerful warrior medicine, and the teen needed some of that now. He, too, was feeling reluctant to reenter the world of the Horned Serpent. However, since the team looked to him as their guide and leader, he turned on his flashlight and marched into the darkness.

Ignoring the upward path to the left that led to the crystal part of the cave, they followed the ramp to the right downward toward the serpent's prison. As they reached the pedestal where they'd left the purple crystal months before, Billy was in for a shock. The crystal was gone, and the stone door was open.

"That's certainly not the way we left things," Billy said, peeking in through the open doorway. The Horned Serpent was nowhere to be found. "Crap!" he said loudly. "Chigger's not going to like this one bit!"

Then he remembered the horde of bats that had been hanging from the ceiling. Shining his flashlight upward, he scanned the cavern's roof. A single, seemingly harmless bat fluttered around near the apex, apparently not in a hurry to get anywhere.

"Double crap!" he shouted. "There should be about a hundred bats hanging from the ceiling. Where could they be now? Let's get back to the boat."

Once everyone was back in the boat, Billy broke the news to Chigger.

"Crap, crap, and triple crap!" the teen exclaimed. He scanned the river in both directions. "That thing could be anywhere!"

As the motorboat carried the crew back downstream, the one lonely bat departed the cave and flew south across the river to a small ghost town known as Skullyville. Three frame houses, a general store, and a cemetery were now the only remnants of a once thriving community that included a Butterfield stagecoach station.

The bat dropped down to a spot in the backyard of the house closest to the cemetery and began its transformation into Norman Redcorn, a Caddo Indian medicine man and member of the Society of Serpents.

Time to report to the Head of the Snake, Redcorn thought and stepped into the old house. *He'll definitely want to hear about this.*

Back at the boat ramp, Stevens and his assistant snapped the waterproof cover tightly over the boat and hooked it up to their van. They'd need it to access at least one other cave during the expedition. The caravan headed east for Clarkesville, Arkansas, the next stop on the Underworld Takeover Prevention Team's tour.

Within a couple hours, the caravan reached the Mountain Shadow Motel southeast of town, where they'd spend the night. After stashing their stuff in three neighboring rooms, the gang of six had some dinner at Fat Daddy's BBQ.

That was when Chigger pulled out his sketchbook to show off the recent batch of comic book sketches he'd been working on.

"I don't know where these ideas are coming from," he admitted. "Sometimes they show up in dreams, and other times they'll just pop into my head while I'm wide awake."

He let Augustus see them first since Chigger had first offered him a look. Then the drawings got passed on to Ethan. The Osage man, familiar with a variety of tribal stories and beliefs, reacted immediately.

"These aren't just any random monsters and creatures you're drawing here," Ethan said. "These all look very much like mythological beasts from the legends of Indigenous people all across the country. And some of them resemble the composite Underworld beings depicted in Mississippian Mound Builder societies," Ethan said.

"Let me see those," Billy said, and Ethan passed the sketchbook to him.

He scanned the pages, seeing all manner of two-legged and four-legged creatures, some with human features, some with horror-movie-creature features. But one in particular caught his attention, because Billy had seen the beast with his own eyes: the metallic-winged Tlanuwa. And Chigger had not been with him when he'd visited the North Carolina national forest location where the creature spoke to him in January.

"You're absolutely right," Billy told Lisa's father. "Grandpa Wesley and I saw this one when we visited our Eastern Cherokee cousins." He pointed to Chigger's drawing of the large bird as he passed the sketchbook back. "Chigger's exposure to the purple crystal and his time under the influence of Carmelita

Tuckaleechee must have put him directly in touch with supernatural Night Seer energies."

Chigger folded his arms and looked down, feeling ashamed of himself. Billy saw this.

"No, no, no, Chigger," he said. "I'm not blaming you for anything. I'm just confirming the same conclusion I came to before. You're a valuable asset we should use. You can possibly help us discover what the dark side is up to or maybe even where our missing Sun Chief is."

Chigger looked up with a much happier expression on his face as the food they'd ordered arrived at the table. Everyone ate in silence as they mulled over the possible meanings of this new revelation.

"But why are your drawings signed *The Muskrat*?" Lisa asked pointedly.

"Good question," Chigger replied. "Like I said before, the drawings and the signature seem to happen while I'm in a fog or unaware of what I'm doing."

Everyone waited for more explanation.

"I sort of think it's a hidden part of me that wants to come out, that wants to be seen," he said finally. "I looked up muskrats online, and they're creatures that mostly operate at night, building nests and finding food. Since my last name is Muskrat, I believe my inner self wants to be less afraid to do things that force me to be braver."

No one had anything to say to that since no one expected such insightful comments from the boy.

Ethan broke the silence and changed the subject. "Ever since we entered the crystal cave and saw the setup where the Horned Serpent had been captured, a thought has been nagging at me," he said. "Mound Builders believed in Horned Serpents and other such creatures as Underworld spirits, not physical beings. Someone had to actively conjure that Uktena to bring it into physical existence."

"Yeah, Grandpa said Cherokees considered them to be water spirits," Billy added. "Only very rarely did anyone actually ever see one."

Ethan continued to point out what that might mean. "So, a thousand years ago when the Sun Priest imprisoned the Uktena in the bottom of that cave, a conjurer first had to use an incarnation spell or a manifestation formula to bring the creature into the Middleworld."

"That's so obvious now," Billy replied. "Why didn't any of us think of it?"

"So, follow my logic here," Ethan said. "A thousand years ago, followers of the Snake Cult assassinated the Sun Chief after the beast had been locked in the cave. Therefore, someone from that cult must've manifested the beast in the first place. If you remember the history, the Sun Chief's twin brother had run off to join the Snake Cult when he was expelled from Solstice City."

"Oh my gosh," Chigger blurted out. "That means the Snake Cult is active again. They're the ones who must've taken the purple crystal and freed the Uktena."

Everyone stared at Chigger in disbelief for a moment. Actually, they were in a confused state, in disbelief that Chigger was thinking surprisingly deeply today, but in full belief that, unfortunately, he was probably right!

Or was it just really good barbecue that was doing the talking?

The following morning, as rain continued to fall, the crew headed for the next mound site, which sat within a state park called Morrison Bluff Park. The park was on the south side of the Arkansas River and contained a handful of man-made mounds.

A small gravel parking lot gave the group a place to park their three vehicles. A gravel path led from the lot to the unrestored central circular mound, which had been eroded by wind and weather. This site was not as well developed to accommodate visitors as other Native mound sites, and no interpretive signs were available.

Using a pop-up canopy as cover, Augustus spread out a site map on a small folding table he'd brought. Along with it, he had a brief report on the site written by an archaeologist who'd surveyed the Clarksville mound area many years ago.

"According to the report, the central circular mound is a burial mound and originally included a spiral path that led from ground level to the top," Stevens said. "But that has all eroded away now."

Ethan studied the documents to verify the facts for himself. "No excavations have been conducted here, have they?" he asked Augustus.

"That's right, but what's most interesting is what's visible along the steep slope due north across the river. I think we should climb up the mound and use binoculars to take a look."

Brad unzipped an equipment bag and began pulling out several pairs of binoculars. He handed them out to everyone. Chigger, the most eager of the bunch, grabbed the first pair and scrambled up the hill. Quickly focusing the lenses, he found something.

"Yep, there's a cave over there all right!" he shouted excitedly.

Tilting the binoculars upward, he also spied something he hadn't expected to find. Above the cave's entrance was the image of some kind of creature. But because it was very old, parts of it had faded and other parts had broken off, making it hard to tell exactly what it was supposed to be.

"Good thing we brought the boat along, because there doesn't seem to be any other way to get to the mouth of the cave," Stevens said.

"What are we waiting for?" Chigger asked excitedly. "Let's go!"

He scrambled back down the slope and headed for the vans.

"Wait a minute," Lisa said as she and Billy strolled casually down the hill. "Wasn't he the one who didn't think it was a good idea to go poking around in these caves?"

"That's Chig for ya," Billy said. "He runs hot and cold. Gotta love him."

A quick boat ride took the crew to the north side of the river. A dead tree trunk onshore provided an anchor point that Brad tied the boat to. Everyone took turns standing on the wet bow of the boat and leaping to the nearest spot of land.

"I don't think all of us should try to climb up this slope," Stevens said. "The rain has made it slippery. Brad, Ethan, and I can go."

"Record what you see on your phones," Lisa suggested. "Send us pics, please."

The three teens remained on the shore near the boat.

"Are you picking up any bad vibes around here?" Billy asked Chigger as they waited.

"Only a tiny bit," Chigger said. "About the same as at the crystal cave."

As he reached a flat area—or sort of shelf—in front of the cave, Ethan was first to draw the group's attention to the partial image above the cave opening. He snapped a couple of phone pics.

"It's the Winged Serpent," he said loud enough for everyone to hear. "Believed by early Mound Builders to be the lord of the Underworld."

He texted the photos down to Billy's phone.

Billy and Chigger studied the crude image, noticing that it looked a lot like the Horned Serpent but with smaller horns and the addition of back feet and a pair of wings.

"You mean there could be giant creepy horned snakes that fly?" Chigger said in astonishment. "Boy, the situation just seems to get worser and worser."

The three archaeologists began exploring the mouth of the cave, snapping photos on their phones, and making notes in their field notebooks. Ethan continued texting the images down to the three near the boat.

At first there was nothing out of the ordinary. But as the explorers moved deeper into the cavern, they turned on their headlamps and came across unexpected sights. First, there was clear evidence that a wall once blocked the entrance to a passageway that branched off the main room. Piles of crumbled stones lay scattered about.

"Remind you of anywhere else we've been?" Chigger asked Billy when he saw the first photos.

Billy just nodded.

Stepping through the wall opening, the team moved through a narrow passage and deeper into the cave. Another cavernous room opened up, where broken pottery shards lay in clusters. Wearing latex gloves, Ethan stooped down to pick up and examine several of them. He placed several pieces together, like putting a jigsaw puzzle together, and a fractured image emerged.

"It's another Winged Serpent," Billy said when the photo was transmitted. "It looks like the people from the mound village across the river may have left offerings to this Underworld god here."

The archaeological team moved on through the darkness, and more photos arrived on Billy's phone. Billy was shocked when he saw a smooth wall panel with writing on it—writing that looked almost identical to the markings on the serpent's door in the crystal cave. Billy explained to Lisa how the Sun Chief had given him the ability to speak the language of the markings but hadn't given him the key to decoding the writing.

"My mouth needed to be able to easily form the words so the Sun Chief's spirit could speak the words using my body," he said. "For a short time, he inhabited my body."

"Now I get it," Lisa said. "You told us about that when my family first came to meet you, but I didn't really understand it fully."

The three teens waited for more photos to show up on Billy's phone, but nothing came for a while.

What's going on? Billy texted.

Hang on, came the reply.

The phone went dark and silent for a while longer.

Hello!? Did we lose the signal? Billy sent.

We haven't decided whether or not to send you these pics. They're too disturbing.

You'd better send the photos right now or we're coming up!

Okay, but don't say I didn't warn you.

"Never mind," Chigger said. "I don't think I want to see whatever it is."

"Too late," Billy replied. "Here they are."

What the teens saw next was shocking. Human bones lay on the cave floor near a large slab of stone. Several skulls were stacked one on top of the other in a crevice not far away. One full human skeleton lay on the slab, complete with the necklaces and bracelets that the person was wearing when they were placed there.

"What the—?" Billy said.

"How gruesome!" Lisa said.

"Gross!" Chigger yelled and quickly moved away from his friends to throw up.

Chigger was exactly right, Ethan texted. *People from the mound city probably were being sacrificed to the Winged Serpent god by serpent priests to appease the creature.*

After seeing the images of skeletons, the three teens climbed back into the boat to wait as the cave explorers quietly finished making notes in their archaeology notebooks. No one spoke after the crew returned and the boat headed back to the south side of the river. The team spent another night at the Mountain

Shadow Motel outside Clarksville. At dinner, Stevens was ready to discuss the expedition's next move.

"We do have time to visit one more mound site and nearby cave before heading down to the Three Rivers Mounds," he said. "I recommend we explore as many sites as we can."

He waited for comments from the team, but everyone was still in a state of shock or disbelief about what had been found.

Chigger was first to speak. "Since you guys arranged this trip so I could come along, I vote to do whatever Digger says we should do," the teen said. "What we saw at the last cave was bad, but maybe the next one won't be."

After a little more discussion, the team agreed to follow through with the plans.

"All right," Stevens said. "We'll stop at the Natchez Mounds next. This one's been excavated and documented by archaeologists. It's now a well-developed park that a lot of people travel to see. It sits on a high point overlooking the Mississippi River."

"What about a cave?" Chigger asked. "Is there one close by?"

"There is," Stevens replied. "About a mile from the mounds. But it's been closed off to the public for decades. A locked gate prevents anyone from entering."

"Good," said Billy. "The last time I visited a cave with a locked gate, something inside the cave broke out. It looked like a creature from Chigger's sketchbook."

"You didn't let me finish," Stevens said. "The locked gate prevents anyone from entering who doesn't have a key. But the woman with the key is meeting us there tomorrow morning at ten. I got permission to go in just in case we decided to visit."

"The gate is there to protect the priceless ancient cave drawings from vandalism," Brad said. "Back in the 1920s, people added their own graffiti and defaced the drawings closest to the cave entrance, so it had to be closed off."

Augustus pulled a file folder out of the satchel he carried and placed it on the table. "Here are a few photos of those rock art images," he said. "The first pages of pictures come from near the cave entrance. Later pages come from deeper in the cave."

He passed around the loose-leaf pages from the folder. Billy was amazed at the beauty and variety of the images. The first couple of pages displayed drawings recognizable as outlines of people and animals. Later pages contained more abstract drawings, possibly depicting spirits, space aliens, suns, stars, strange-looking insects, and combination creatures. The final page was filled with various versions of Winged Serpents.

"I've seen plenty of dragons in movies and comic books," Chigger said. "But these flying reptiles don't look like any of those."

"I guess you could think of these as Indigenous American dragons, but they don't breathe fire," Ethan said. "Some tribes called the creature the Sky Snake and believed in its power for both good and evil."

Discussions continued for a while longer, but after dinner, everyone was emotionally drained. An early bedtime was had by all.

Billy took advantage of the extra time by spending it with Lisa. Standing under an awning and out of the continuing rain, he knocked on her motel door. She was surprised to see him standing there.

"Can we talk?" he said.

"Sure," she replied, opening the door wider and sitting in a chair near the window.

"I want to apologize again for not being a very attentive boy-friend lately," he said, taking a seat on the edge of the bed. "There's so much to do, and I'm overwhelmed with just . . . everything all at once!" He anxiously pulled at the ends of his longish dark hair.

"My head understands perfectly," she said. "But my heart's not too happy about it." She pulled the curtain back and looked out at the rain.

"Would you mind doing something with me?" he asked.

She looked at the bed Billy sat on with a raised eyebrow. "I hope you're not thinking—"

"Oh, gosh, no!" he said hurriedly when he realized what she meant. "I thought we could do some spirit traveling together," he said after turning a bright shade of red.

"Okay, what did you have in mind?"

"I thought we could gang up on Miller in his prison cell and convince him to tell who he sold the Sun Priest's bones to."

"Ooh, how romantic!" Lisa said with a chuckle.

Billy looked deflated but recovered when she said, "I'd love to!"

The couple lay down in bed on their backs, side by side. Billy began humming the melody he used to create the physical vibrations that allowed for the release of their energy bodies. In a few moments, the pair floated above the bed near the ceiling.

Billy reached out, took Lisa's hand, and pictured the imprisoned Miller in his mind. Off they rushed to the Texarkana prison cell where the thief lay asleep. Once inside the man's cell, Billy sent a mental message to his companion.

"You go over and put a hand on his chest while I begin hurling objects at him," Billy communicated. "The coldness will wake him up."

This was all still a fairly new experience for Lisa, but she carried out her boyfriend's instructions. As soon as she placed her nonphysical hand on the sleeping man's chest, he woke up with a start. He pulled his blanket up to his chin, but it didn't help.

Then Billy, seeing a bookshelf above Miller's cot, moved quickly to knock books down on the man's head. Miller jumped up and ran to the door of his cell. He was faintly aware that some ghostly presence was with him.

"Help!" he yelled out into the hall. "Help me! Something's in here with me!"

No one came to his aid, so Miller cringed in the far corner of his cell. Billy and Lisa drifted over and took up positions on either side of the man. Each one leaned in to whisper in Miller's ear.

"Who did you sell the Sun Chief's bones to?" they asked simultaneously and then thrust their spirit hands into the man's head.

The stereo audio input, accentuated by the cold sensation in the center of his brain, penetrated Miller's mind. He ran back to his cot.

"Leave me alone, do you hear me?" he shouted. "I'll tell you what you want to know!" He calmed himself down and looked up, not sure where in the cell his visitors were. "The man's name was Coyote or Coat-ell or something like that. He's some kind of Mexican Indian. He said he was buying 'for his boss down in Louisiana.'"

"Who is the boss?" Billy and Lisa asked.

"I don't know," Miller replied. "I swear I don't know."

The pair of energy bodies floated up toward the ceiling of the cell. "Do you think he's telling the truth?" Billy asked Lisa.

"I think he's too scared not to."

Satisfied they'd gotten what they needed, the couple returned to their physical bodies.

Sitting up on the edge of the bed, Billy said, "You want to give Raelynn a call in the morning to let her know what we found out?"

"How do I say we got this information?"

"Maybe from a confidential informant?" Billy said. "Will that work?"

"I did tell her about spirit travel," Lisa said.

"You mean our unique reconnaissance capabilities?"

"I don't think a jury would believe us, but then again, they wouldn't believe any of this!"

After a chuckle and a quick kiss goodnight, the two retired to their separate motel rooms.

The following morning, Lisa called Raelynn to report what Miller told them, and the team moved on toward Natchez Mounds park.

But when they got closer to the park, Chigger began feeling sick.

"Something's not right here," he said. "The burn scars on my hands are tingling, and it feels like witchy energy is around."

"Maybe you should stay in the van while we go in the cave," Billy suggested.

"Good idea," Chigger readily agreed.

Following signs in the park, the three vans arrived at the cave and parked in the nearby lot. A middle-aged Native woman who said her name was Jonna Boudreaux met them at the cave entrance with the key. A bandanna with a Native design held back her long gray hair, and she wore a pendant containing greenish-colored stone that Lisa recognized as the serpentine she'd seen during her visit to Serpent World.

Billy tried scanning her energy field but found it sort of camouflaged by a shield of dirty brownish emanation. Boudreaux stood beside a sign that announced, *Entrance to the closed cave is only permitted for recognized archaeologists, tribal members with approval, and tribal ceremonial leaders.*

"It's a good thing you called ahead to make arrangements and get permission to go inside," she said, pointing to the sign.

"Yeah, good thing," Ethan replied, a little annoyed.

"Are you that Native archaeologist I've heard about?" she asked Ethan.

He nodded.

"You must feel like a traitor to your Native people," she said in an accusatory tone. "I know I would."

"You have a right to your opinion, but—"

"Save it," she interrupted. "I don't want to hear it." She unlocked the gate and pulled it open. "Be sure not to touch anything in the cave, and I mean anything. I know how you archaeologists are. If it was up to me, I wouldn't let you in, but my boss says I gotta."

She left them and walked away from the cave toward the parking lot.

"She's wearing a serpentine stone pendant," Lisa said quietly after the woman was out of earshot. "I recognize it from the prison's inmate rehabilitation brochure and the stones for sale at the tourist shop."

Chigger had been watching what was happening at the cave entrance and saw the woman approaching. As she got closer, his pain increased, so he hid under a tarp that covered some of their gear.

The woman passed right by the van where Chigger was hiding. When she was next to the vehicle, she stopped to peek in the back window. Seeing nothing of interest, the woman moved on. A couple minutes later, Chig peered out the van's back window in time to see her get into her car. The farther away she got, the less his hands hurt.

That woman is some kind of witch, he thought. *Better warn the team.*

While he waited for the rest of the team in the van, Chigger got out his sketchbook and began sketching a few new animal images. These had appeared to him in the last couple of days.

First, he drew a bat that had a sort of human face with green eyes, then a badger with a different human face wearing a bracelet containing a green stone, and finally a white bird with long slender legs that was wearing a pendant featuring a green stone. This one had a woman's face that surprisingly resembled the woman he'd just seen. Chigger wasn't sure at all what those three drawings had to do with anything, and he wasn't even sure he'd keep them.

Finally, the team returned to the van with more photos on their phones. He'd already seen most of the images from the pages in Digger's file folder. But he hadn't seen the images captured by the team at the deepest part of the cave, what Ethan called the Dark Zone.

There were the most beautiful and mesmerizing photos of crystal clusters literally growing out of the cave walls. There was a whole room filled with them that reminded him of the crystal cave, but with a big difference.

In the crystal cave, the stones were white and clear quartz, amazing looking in their own way. The stones in this cave were a mix of differing shades of purple and green.

"I don't know if the purple and green crystals have to do with anything, but we're trying to document everything we can on this trip," Augustus said. "It may be useful later."

Then Chigger told the team about his reaction to the woman with the key to the gate.

"She's some kind of *skili* for sure," he said. "And she must be a pretty strong one too."

"What do you mean?" Billy asked.

Chigger pulled out his sketch of the white bird wearing a green pendant. "There's this," he said, displaying the drawing.

The resemblance to the woman they'd just met was unmistakable, as was the medallion she was wearing.

"And I never felt as strong a vibe from Tuckaleechee as I felt when this woman passed by the van," he said. "Never."

CHAPTER SEVEN

Looks Can Be Deceiving

T he three expedition vans left the Natchez Mounds area, first heading west across the Mississippi River and then taking the small two-lane State Highway 15 headed south. The road ran alongside the Mississippi River and would take them directly to the Three Rivers Mounds and Serpent World. Even taking their time, the drive only lasted a couple of hours.

Augustus thought it would be good to just drive through the area first to get oriented to the landscape. From the main road, the group could see the collection of mounds within the park, but the closer they got to the mound site, the worse Chigger felt.

"I got a bad feeling about this place. My *skili* senses are going through the roof!" Chigger began rubbing his hands up and down his sides and legs like his whole body itched or tingled or something. "Keep driving!" he said anxiously. "Please keep driving and don't stop until we're on the other side of this place."

The three vans proceeded to a place called Red River Ferry Landing. There were no bridges across the Mississippi for miles in either direction. You had to take a ferry boat, large enough to carry cars, to cross the river. Once they'd taken the boat ride across to the east side of the river, the three vans followed a winding road up into an area called Tunica Falls, named after another tribe that used to live in the region.

Finally, they arrived at the five-bedroom house Brad, the grad student, had rented for the team. It was a place where they might stay a couple days. The house sat on top of a bluff on the east side of the river and provided a clear westward view of the Three Rivers Indian Mounds Park on the west side of the river.

After unloading the vans and getting settled in the house, the team gathered around the dining table just off the house's large kitchen.

"I believe Chigger isn't just sensing witch energy or some purple crystal energy," Billy said to start the team's discussion. "Intuition tells me he's sensing something I could only call Underworld energy. And a big dose of it is coming from this area."

"Raelynn and I felt that something was off when we came here before," Lisa chimed in. "And possibly Greyson Greenstone is involved, but I'm not sure how."

Brad found a local newspaper folded up on the front porch when he unlocked the front door. As the group discussion continued, he opened it and scanned the front page.

"Could this be related?" he asked, interrupting the conversation.

He spread out the front page in the center of the table. "FBI Called in to Investigate Prison Murders," the headline announced. A smaller headline read, "Search Continues for Mystery Man."

Lisa grabbed the paper and quickly read the main paragraph. "The warden and a guard were murdered. We just talked to them a few days ago." She read some more. "The men were strangled to death, but somehow no markings were found on their necks. No hand impressions, fingerprints, or signs of wire or rope."

"Bizarre," Augustus said.

"Speaking of bizarre," Billy said, "could we possibly be near the serpent-worshipping center that Monkata the Snake Priest was involved with a thousand years ago?"

No one had an answer to the question, and no one wanted to believe Billy was probably onto something.

"Meanwhile, we haven't been able to locate a cave around here," Augustus said to bring the team's attention back to the expedition. "All eight of the other spiral mound sites have a cave nearby."

"I think there is one here somewhere," Brad said. "It's just that no archaeologists have found it or mapped it."

"I think it's time I did some more out-of-body reconnaissance," Billy said. "I'll make a flyover tonight so we'll be more prepared for tomorrow morning's meeting. Do you want to come with me again, Lisa?"

She nodded.

"Set an alarm for midnight, and I'll give you a hand if you need help lifting off."

That night around midnight, Billy rolled out of his physical self and floated up through the bedroom ceiling where he slept. He drifted into the upstairs room where Lisa was sleeping to find her awake and sitting up in bed. He floated to her and gave her a little spirit kiss on the cheek as he'd done before. She, of course, felt the touch as an intense cold sensation.

"Ah, Billy, you're here," she said, knowing that he could hear her. "For some reason I'm too anxious to get relaxed tonight. You go on without me."

He gave her another cold kiss on the cheek and drifted up through the rental house roof. Before moving on, he took in the view from high above the landscape. To the north of him he noticed a break in the topography where an inlet from the river had cut a ravine into the hilly terrain. Water from the river filled the narrow inlet for several hundred feet. He made a mental note to investigate that later.

To the west, the wide and winding Mississippi River spread out below him, forming a sort of double S curve. On the west side of the waterway sat the Three Rivers collection of mounds, nestled within the lower part of the S.

The mound nearest him was indeed a spiral mound that had either been restored or may have never been damaged, because the spiral path with the snakelike pattern was fully visible. To the west of that mound was the Chief's Mound, a flat-top pyramid, complete with a fully restored residence that looked identical to the one at Cahokia. Several other smaller round mounds dotted the land surrounding the central Chief's Mound.

Billy moved across the river to get a closer look. One of the things he watched for was anything that emitted a glow only visible to him while in spirit-travel mode. That was how he'd spotted the four medicine pouches buried by Carmelita Tuckaleechee in the four directions around Lisa's dormitory in January. Using an old Cherokee spell, the *skili* had wanted to bring conflict and confusion into Lisa's life, and that had succeeded for a short while.

The Chief's Mound had a set of steps up one side to allow tourists to climb to the top and look inside the chief's residence. But Billy was surprised to find a doorway at ground level on the back side of that mound. The spiral mound was too perfectly round and the spiral pathway to the top too smooth to be the originals, so he concluded that they, too, had been restored. Again, on what could be considered the back side, there was a doorway at ground level.

Time to move inside, he thought.

He slowly penetrated the outer layer of the flat-top pyramid, expecting to experience layers of dirt. Instead, he discovered that the visible outer layer was made of some sort of synthetic material that looked like dirt and grass. The next layer was a network of steel beams and pillars. The mound was, in reality, a three-story building disguised as an earthen pyramid!

The central ground-floor space was a theater containing about two hundred seats with a stage in front. A banner hanging above the stage read *First Temple of the Reborn.* Other levels of the space mostly contained offices and meeting rooms. A small elevator connected the levels, and there was an additional set of stairs that seemed to lead to another underground chamber.

Things are definitely not what they appear to be, Billy thought and moved out of the building.

He headed for the spiral mound, not knowing what to expect there. He passed through that structure's outer layers to again discover a hollow interior space. But this area was far different from the one inside the Chief's Mound.

The large circular chamber seemed to be divided into two halves. The half he was in contained a central round table with nine ornate chairs positioned evenly apart. On the table in front of each chair sat a black viewing screen. Each one emitted a dim purple glow.

A meeting chamber of some kind, Billy thought.

Then he was shocked to see a huge stone carving of a Winged Serpent hanging on the back wall. It was similar to the images he'd seen in the caves near the spiral mounds the expedition had just visited. Only this image contained more details than those crude, ancient cave drawings. The purple-and-green body on this wall hanging looked like a muscular rattlesnake, but the head was oversized and had horns like the Uktena. Also, the creature had two clawed back feet and a pair of batlike wings.

An American dragon, Billy thought, echoing Ethan's description.

Billy floated down closer to the table so he could take a better look at the setup. The screens were exactly what he thought they were: Aztec mirrors. But these were larger than the one Chigger had discovered. Additionally, these were perfectly round and set in a round frame that depicted a snake about to bite its own tail.

Next, he propelled himself through the partition that separated the two halves of the mound. As he hovered in the center of the vaulted space and saw what was below, a chill passed through him. If he had been in his body, he'd say he was chilled to the bone.

On the ground level near the back of the area sat a large rectangular stone slab like the one he'd seen in the Arkansas cave. Intricately carved patterns in the slab created the outline of a human body. Chutes carved into the corners of the slab looked like they were made as drainage channels to drain liquid away from the top of the slab.

On the wall behind the slab hung a large round sun stone like the one on display in a museum in Mexico City that Billy had seen pictures of. Billy realized what he was looking at.

This looks like a human sacrificial chamber like the ancient Aztecs used to collect the heart and blood of human victims as offerings to the gods.

The shock of it jolted him right back into his physical body lying in bed across the river. He immediately sat up, his mind racing, his thoughts grasping for meaning.

I can't wait—I've got to tell the team about this.

He jumped out of bed and raced through the house, turning on lights and making lots of noise.

"Everybody, wake up!" he yelled. "I've got something you need to hear!"

As he described scenes from his exploration, each member of the team experienced their own sense of horror.

"You expect us all to go on a nice little tour tomorrow and pretend we don't know what we know?" Chigger said.

"Yes, I do," Billy said. "And, Chigger, I need you to have your *skili*-detection senses turned on and in high-alert mode."

"But you know it's gotten really hard for me to be near any-one or anything that puts off that vibe," Chigger said in a kind of whiney voice. "I . . . I—"

"Dammit, Chig!" Billy said angrily. "I've always protected you and made allowances for you because of our friendship! But these are the most serious and dangerous times we've ever faced, so you need to man up and do your part. We've still got to find the Sky Stone and the Sun Chief's staff. I've got a feel-ing they're here somewhere. And possibly Shakuru himself!"

No one said a thing. No one moved. No one looked at Chigger.

He knew Billy was right. Tears began forming in the corner of each of Chigger's eyes. He jumped up from his seat and ran from the room and out of the house before anyone could see him tear up.

Out on the front porch, he pounded a fist against the wooden porch railing. "Why are you such a frigging wimp, Muskrat?" he said out loud. "Billy's right. It's time to man up! You owe him a lot!"

He continued to stand on the porch and gaze out at the dark, hilly landscape beyond the house. Maybe the courage he needed lay out there somewhere, because he didn't quite know where else to find it.

Unexpectedly, Lisa joined him on the porch a few min-utes later.

"What do you want, Lisa?" he said sharply as he wiped his eyes. "Did you come out here to criticize me? I know you never liked me."

"I'm here because I love Billy, and Billy loves you like a brother," she said in a calming voice. "You are without question his dearest friend, so I'm trying to be your friend too."

She paused to give that time to sink in.

"At first I doubted that you had anything to contribute to our efforts," she admitted. "But I've seen firsthand your abilities, your sensitivity to supernatural forces. It's kind of like your superpower, and we need that superpower now."

Chig looked at her for the first time, seeing that she was being sincere. She smiled.

"Superpower, huh?" he said.

"So suck it up, put on your big boy pants, and get your butt back in there," she concluded, still smiling.

Chig smiled too and nodded. He followed her back inside the house and to the group meeting. Billy was surprised to see them both.

"Sorry, everyone," Chig said, looking at Billy. "I'm here to do whatever the team needs me to do. I'll figure out some way to overcome or block out the negative energy."

Standing next to Billy, Lisa bent down and whispered in his ear, "Sometimes it takes a woman's touch."

"Sure," Billy replied, only half paying attention to what Lisa said, because when Chigger mentioned blocking out negative energy, a light went on in Billy's head. "Why didn't I think of it before? I learned a technique from a Medicine Council member that protects you from physical or supernatural attacks!"

"Gee, Chigger, that sounds useful," Chigger said with a sarcastic tone. "Maybe Billy will show you how to do that."

"Of course I will," Billy said. "I'll teach it to you before we go back to bed tonight so you can practice it some. I have a feeling you might need it tomorrow."

The following morning, the team carried a sense of dread with them as they drove back across the river. They had an appointment with the director of the Three Rivers Indian Mounds Park. The closer they got to the mound site, the more distressed Chigger became.

But he'd promised to grin and bear it for the good of the team. So he began performing the steps Billy taught him the night before. He started repeating the phrases Billy had taught him, and also visualized a specific sequence of images.

The three vans parked side by side near the park's interpretive center. The team saw a dark-skinned man wearing a straw hat with an oversize brim and a dark-green raincoat, standing near the center's front door. The front of the hat bore an image of a round Aztec sun stone calendar just like the one Billy had seen the night before.

"The design on his hat matches the sun stone in the secret chamber," Billy said quietly so only those inside the van could hear. "And his aura is a muddy brown like the woman at the Natchez Mounds. I'm thinking they may be able to prevent others from seeing their true energy fields."

"This place puts out a terrible vibe," Chigger said in a shaky voice. "The energy is strong, and that guy is definitely on the dark side of things. But the protection formula seems to be working."

"You guys should let me and Augustus do the talking," Ethan said. "We do anthropology-speak quite well."

Wearing rain ponchos, the seven members of the expedition approached the man. Something prompted Chigger to pull the hood of his poncho tightly around his face, making it hard for the man to see him clearly.

"Welcome to our archaeological center," the man said with a smile and a slight Spanish accent. "I must apologize on behalf of Mr. Greenstone. He was called away. I am Miguel Coyotl, a member of the Serpentine Foundation's board of directors."

Billy and Lisa gave each other a quick glance, recognizing a version of the name Miller had given them.

"And in case you're curious," Coyotl continued, "I am a Nahua Indian, what you might call Aztec."

"Oh, that's cool," Lisa said. "I didn't know you guys were still around!"

"Why, yes, there are thousands of us alive and well all over Mexico," Coyotl said. "And hundreds more scattered across the Southwestern United States."

Augustus introduced the team by their first names, and then Miguel led them into the interpretive center. The center of the main room was occupied by a large model of the mound complex as it might've looked more than a thousand years ago. Walking from exhibit to exhibit, he described the significance of all the items on display.

It was all Chigger could do to keep focused on creating the protective spell. In addition to the *skili* energy coming from their tour guide, he also sensed a similar vibe coming from the direction of the round spiral mound and a weaker signal from somewhere near the river.

Their guide noticed that Chigger was acting a little strange, and said, "Young man, are you all right? You don't look well."

"Oh, man," the teen answered, "I don't feel well, and I don't know what it is. Maybe I'm coming down with something."

"Possibly you should go lie down," the guide said.

"No, I can't miss any of this," Chigger said. "I've got to write a report on everything I learn on this trip to turn in to my school. I'll just hang back a little and listen at a distance."

"Suit yourself," Coyotl said and completed the tour of the interpretive center.

After they'd seen everything inside, the man led them to a large viewing window at the back of the building. The angular Chief's Mound and the round spiral mound were both visible from that vantage point.

"I'm sorry to say that it won't be possible to tour the rest of the site," the man said. "The rain makes it too slippery to climb the stairs up to the chief's house."

"Our main interest is in investigating the spiral mounds along the Arkansas and Mississippi Rivers," Augustus said.

"So we're really looking forward to visiting your spiral mound and reviewing any reports you may have on the archaeology of it."

"That mound is off limits to visitors," Coyotl said sharply. "Uh, the structure is too unstable and prone to disintegration. We have engineers trying to fix the problem."

Billy stepped over to the edge of the window to see if he could get a glimpse of the back side of the Chief's Mound. "I thought I saw a door on the back side of the Chief's Mound at ground level," he said. "Where does that go? Is the mound hollow?"

"When did you see that?" Miguel asked.

"When we drove into the area yesterday, we came from the north," Billy replied. "I saw it from that angle."

"It's just a storage area where we keep maintenance equipment and supplies," the Aztec answered.

"This is really disappointing," Ethan said.

"I am sorry," Coyotl said, and began walking back toward the entrance of the interpretive center.

No one followed the man.

"We'd also like to find out if there's a cave nearby associated with these mounds," Ethan said. "Our archaeology maps don't show anything like that, but all the other spiral mounds have one nearby."

"There was an old cave across the river, but it collapsed long ago," the guide said. "Totally inaccessible now."

Miguel continued walking toward the entrance. There was nothing else for the team to do but follow him. At the door, he bid them farewell and rushed them out. Back at the vans, the team huddled together.

"This place is fishy as hell," Chigger said. "And so's that guy, Coyote or Coyotl or whatever his name is."

"This has to be the guy Miller sold Shakuru's remains to," Lisa said.

"We need the FBI down here to investigate this place," Ethan suggested.

"They're coming to investigate the prison murders, so maybe Raelynn can get them to spend some time here," Lisa said. "I already told her about Miller's prison confession."

"Meanwhile, we've got to get Chigger back home," Billy said. "His spring break is almost over."

"Who's going to drive him back?" Augustus asked.

"You don't need me or Lisa here," Billy said. "We can get him home while you archaeology types finish the expedition."

No one objected.

During the time Billy and the team were touring the Three Rivers interpretive center, Greyson Greenstone, Snake-Eye, was busy preparing for the next meeting of what he called "the Nine." These members of the highly secretive Society of Serpents had been handpicked and trained for these very prophetic days. Now that the old alliance of Owls and Snakes had been renewed, it was time to act.

The site of the meeting would be the very cave once used by serpent worshippers, beginning more than two thousand years ago. The cave, in fact, had not collapsed as Coyotl said, but had been the very portal used by the original Snake Cult when they first called forth the serpent beasts from the Underworld. Now, upgraded and outfitted by Snake-Eye, the cave would once again serve as the portal.

A secret history, known only to Snake-Eye and a few others, validated the notion that Monkata did indeed find his way south from Solstice City to this spot, then called Serpent City. It was a place for outcasts and misfits, those who didn't have a place with other dwellers of the Middleworld. All the knowledge Monkata had learned and the skills he'd mastered as a son of the original Sun Chief served him well as he climbed through the ranks of the leadership in this community.

Using sorcery, spells, and words learned from Maya and Aztec sources, the Snake Cult had achieved unprecedented results. The reptilian creatures they called forth and sent out into the world were the stuff of legends—literally.

From his detailed studies, Snake-Eye knew these water monsters had many names in the legends of several tribes, names like Sinti Lapitta among the Choctaw, Awanyu among New Mexico's Pueblo Indians, Mazacoatl among the Aztec, Unktehila among the Sioux, and Uktena among the Cherokee. And there were plenty of others.

Modern anthropologists had dismissed these legends as fanciful myths, created by so-called unsophisticated Natives. But Snake-Eye and his followers knew the truth. And the truth would soon be revealed again when the Winged Serpent physically took to the skies! A power shift unlike anything the Middleworld had seen in centuries was about to take place, orchestrated by the Snake Priest of the modern age.

But what the snake man didn't know was that three unassuming Native teens, with the assistance of residents of both the Middleworld and Upperworld, were orchestrating a counteroffensive meant to halt that power shift in its tracks.

For Billy, Lisa, and Chig, the ten-hour drive from Three Rivers back to Tahlequah gave the three teens time to sort out their conflicts and differences while strengthening the bond between them. Lisa happily volunteered to sit in the back seat so Billy and Chig could have some quality "bro time," as she called it.

"I'm really impressed with your drawings of monsters," Billy told Chigger during the trip. "And I'm doubly impressed since finding out from Ethan that most of those creatures come from traditional tribal cultures."

"Yeah, I'm kind of impressed with me too," Chigger said. "Like I said, they just pop into my mind from time to time."

"I'd like to let Cecil take a long look at them," Billy said. "Can I borrow your sketchbook to make copies?"

The suspicion and jealousy that hid within Chigger's mind immediately flared. The influence of Underworld energies immediately got a grip and took control. He almost reacted to Billy's question without thinking.

But at the last minute, his rational mind intervened and stopped him from expressing the fear and defensiveness he felt. That all happened within two seconds.

"Of course," he said in a calm tone. "Why would I object to such a logical request?"

"Umm . . ." Billy replied. "Why would you?"

"I wouldn't," Chigger said. "I don't. I'm not."

He blew out a breath of stress, releasing it from his mind and body.

"You don't know the whirlwind of chaos that just went through my mind before I answered you," Chigger admitted. "It was like slogging through lava to get to the other side."

"Okay," Billy responded, not sure what to do with this information.

"Whirlwind of chaos," Chig repeated thoughtfully. "That would be a great title for a graphic novel!"

He wrote that down in the margin of one of his drawings.

Before they reached Chigger's mobile home, they switched drivers, and Lisa took the steering wheel while Billy hid in the back of the van. They still didn't want Chigger's parents to know Billy had anything to do with the archaeology expedition.

The following day, Billy returned to Wesley's house to resume his medicine practice. As soon as a Cherokee neighbor or nearby patient saw that the white frame house's front door was open, news of Billy's return spread rapidly. Within a couple of hours there were dozens of Natives lined up in front of the house to see him.

Unfortunately for Billy, the first person in line that morning was not there to receive treatment. The elderly Native woman was there to accuse the teen of devil worship and the summoning of demons! She launched her attack before he had a chance to speak.

"Do you know what the Bible says about communicating with the dead?" she asked as she sprang up from her seat and pointed her hand-carved cane at him.

"Please tell me, *Agataanhi Agayuhli*," Billy said calmly, referring to the woman as a wise elder.

"Do not turn to mediums or necromancers. Do not seek them out, and so make yourselves unclean by them," she quoted. "That's from Leviticus 19:31."

"Beloved, do not believe every spirit, but test the spirits to see whether they are from God, for many false prophets have gone out into the world," Billy replied. "That's from my grandpa Wesley and the book of John, chapter four, verse one."

The woman was undeterred and proceeded to get to her main point. "My daughter, Mattie Acorn, came to you for comfort in her time of grief a few weeks ago, and you told her to her face her son killed himself! You, son, are a liar, because my grandson would never do such a thing!"

Billy remained silent as he focused on a translucent scene that was unfolding behind the grandmother. A Native teen named Aaron that Billy recognized as the boy who'd hanged himself in his mother's attic in February was replaying an encounter between himself and his Cherokee father. The boy was in the process of revealing he was a two-spirit person—a Native way of saying he was gay. Then, in the vision, the boy tried to explain that this used to be an accepted trait within the tribe.

That was when the dad removed his belt and commenced to brutally beat his son. The injured boy ran to his mother for protection, but she ignored his plight, fearing her husband's violent reaction. That night, after everyone had gone to bed, the boy quietly climbed up the stairs to the attic and hanged himself.

This scene played itself out for Billy's benefit within a matter of seconds.

"Your grandson, Aaron, just showed me the reason he ended his own life," Billy said, shocking the elder. "Your family failed to love this boy unconditionally, and he couldn't bear the thought of living his life that way. So he ended it."

The woman was silent.

"I think you're supposed to love them, not judge them," he added.

Still the woman remained silent.

"Now, I didn't try to talk to Aaron," Billy said. "He reached out to me from the Afterworld because he needed you to know."

Billy waited one more time for a response but got none.

"Now, if you'll excuse me, I have patients who need me," he said, turning to the next person in line.

The woman left, still too shocked to respond.

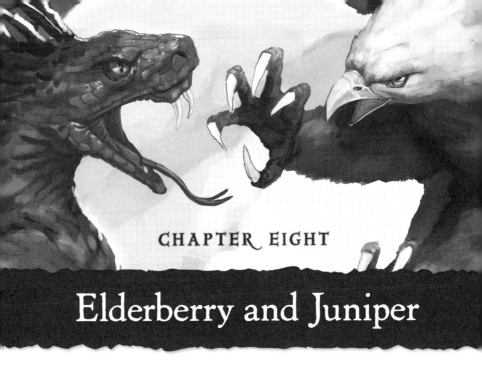

CHAPTER EIGHT

Elderberry and Juniper

Willy James of the Mississippi Choctaws had been a member of the Owl Clan for longer than Thomas Two Bears had been the group's leader. Neither man ever particularly liked the other, but recently their conflict had escalated.

Of course, Willy knew the importance of the upcoming Thinning of the Veil between the physical world and the supernatural world, a prophecy handed down through generations of Native sorcerers and conjurers. But he believed he had the right to exploit the phenomenon any which way he pleased and not have to follow the Night Seers, group plan devised by Two Bears.

That was why he'd conjured the beast from the depths of Manitou Cave in Alabama and hadn't waited for the Owl Clan's approved timetable to do it. The beast was now safely contained in a special cage at the back of James's property. Try as it might, the beast had been unable to break out of its prison.

But now, James decided, it was time to make use of the southern piece of the Sky Stone he'd stolen from Elmore Proctor. Billy Buckhorn and the Intertribal Medicine Council were helpless to stop the Underworld takeover without it, and they'd probably been desperately searching for the missing piece ever since Elmore Proctor died.

What to do? What to do?

James unlocked the door to the spare bedroom at the back of his house. The air in the room was musty, and a layer of dust covered what little furniture occupied the space. Stepping over to the closet, the old man knelt down and began prying up three of the floorboards. Once those were out of the way, he lifted the fireproof safe out of a hidden compartment—a safe identical to the one Carmelita Tuckaleechee had owned.

Every member of the Owl Clan owned such a safe in order to protect and store their Aztec mirrors and their thirteen-sided membership pendants. Additionally, Willy James also kept the stolen Sky Stone piece there, inside a pouch filled with the invisibility herb known as hellebore. When combined with the concealment spell, the herb and its purple flowers prevented other medicine men from locating any object.

James removed the piece from the pouch and returned the safe to its hiding place. The pie-shaped wedge of the Sky Stone piece felt a little different in his hand than it had felt the last time he held it. The change was slight but noticeable. The object seemed to exert a sort of tugging sensation, like it was gently being pulled in a westward direction.

Odd, he thought. *What would cause that?*

He needed to think, so he walked out to the back screened-in porch of his aging frame house. Standing near the porch door, he held up the object to examine it in a ray of sunlight that shone through a break in the canopy of trees.

All the Night Seers knew he had this rare thousand-year-old item, so he could offer it up to the organization—for a price. Or he could offer it to the head of the Snake Cult for possibly a larger price, and not necessarily a financial one. The one-eyed snake man was most likely going to end up being king of the Middleworld after the upheavals. He was clever, ruthless, devious, and much stronger than Two Bears could ever hope to be.

That's it!

James could offer the Sky Stone piece to Snake-Eye in exchange for a lofty position within the ruling elite after the Underworld takeover. He smiled widely at the delicious thought of outsmarting Thomas Two Bears and becoming a man of substance in the approaching new world order.

Suddenly a loud roar and a thunderous crash came from the back corner of Willy James's property.

"Oh, crap, I forgot to feed the beast!" he said out loud.

The Choctaw quickly headed out the back door of the porch to see what was happening. Three steps were all he was able to take before the Underwater Panther did what the legends said it would do. The creature jumped on James, knocked him to the ground, bit off his left hand, and carried it away with him. The beast disappeared into the woods beyond Owl Creek.

Writhing on the ground in extreme pain, the Choctaw medicine man screamed. That was when he remembered the nearest neighbor was a quarter of a mile away and couldn't hear him. He'd purposefully moved to this house so no one would come snooping around and accidentally discover what mischief he was up to.

He tried to figure out what to do, but the agony prevented him from collecting his thoughts or even stringing together a sentence in his mind.

The phone! I should call the Indian hospital on the phone!

James tried to stand up, but the loss of blood made him dizzy, and he passed out. He lost control of his right hand, and the Sky Stone piece slipped from his grip. His lifeblood continued to trickle from his body.

About 450 miles to the northeast, on the Eastern Cherokee reservation, medicine man Bucky Wachacha felt something change. It was only a small supernatural nudge, and if he hadn't been sitting quietly drinking coffee, he might've missed it. But it was definitely *something.*

Ever since Thunder Child had dismissed the Intertribal Medicine Council, Bucky had felt bad about letting the boy down. He felt particularly bad about not having found the missing Sky Stone piece. After all, finding lost objects and people was his strongest medicine power.

It had been Bucky who, in 1992, found a Cherokee boy who had gone missing. The use of the Cherokee-language formula and prescribed herbs had revealed the boy's location at the bottom of a dry well, safe and mostly unharmed except for a badly sprained ankle.

It had also been Bucky, in 2001, who located a gold ring that had been stolen from an elderly Cherokee woman. Bucky's spell located the ring at a nearby pawn shop, and the shop's surveillance camera showed the woman's own teenage granddaughter selling the ring.

Long ago, Bucky had learned a key secret about finding lost objects. That key was the understanding that all things had a spirit or an energy. In other words, all things were alive. This secret was part of what the medicine man had shared with Thunder Child. In a way, the object itself would reveal its location when you knew how to connect to it as one living being to another.

Now Wachacha's mind was urging him to try finding the Sky Stone piece one more time. Maybe that was what the subtle nudge was about. The supernatural search for it had failed before, which could mean that a concealment spell had been at work. That was the only thing Bucky could think of that would keep his own formula for finding lost items from working.

So now he would try again. What did he have to lose? Nothing. The process involved several steps. First, Wachacha went to the back room of his house and opened a leather case he kept in the back of a closet. The only thing in the case was the old lined journal where he'd written his formulas in the Cherokee syllabary. He laid the writing tablet out on a folding table in the corner and sat in the chair next to it. This was his spell-casting spot.

Flipping through the yellowed pages, he found the formula he needed, which also spelled out the herbs to be used. Returning to the closet, he opened a cabinet drawer that held little bottles of dried herbs.

"Elderberry and juniper," he said to himself as he searched through the bottles. "Ah, there you are," he remarked when he found them.

Back at the table, he took a pinch of each herb and placed them in a stone ashtray. Next, he removed a hand-rolled tobacco cigarette from a plastic bag and lit it. He'd "doctored" several of the cigarettes a few weeks ago so they'd be ready when he needed them. Finally, he put a flame to the herbs, and they began smoking.

Between puffs on the cigarette, and as the herbs burned, he repeated the formula for finding lost items. The spell, in essence, asked for assistance from his spirit helper, Little Fox, who lived among the Little People.

"Take a stand, little man, and set your feet firmly on the ground" was the essential meaning of the words in English. "Point the way to the missing piece for which I search."

The next step called for Bucky to close his eyes and open his spirit to receive whatever answer was to come, be it a location on a map, a picture of a place, or a name whispered in his ear.

Now all Bucky had to do was wait. An answer would come. It might take a day or two. It might come in a dream at night. He didn't know when or how, but it would come.

With a feeling of satisfaction, the Cherokee elder returned the medicine journal to its place in the back closet and then went to the kitchen to reheat his cup of coffee. As the black brew warmed, a sad realization settled into his mind.

Our medicine ways are probably coming to an end, he thought. *Billy Buckhorn is our best hope for carrying traditional healing into the future . . . if we are to have a future.*

At about this same time, Thomas Two Bears, from his ranch-style house in Montana, decided it was time to review his version of the future. As the head of the Night Seers, he'd just returned home from recruiting Raymond Bushyhead to replace Carmelita Tuckaleechee in the Owl Clan and felt confident the organization was back to full power.

He was also confident that the conjured weather patterns had achieved their purpose of distracting governmental agencies and closing down certain national parks. One park in particular, the location of the largest known cave in North America, had been closed to the public. It was destined to play a pivotal role in the master plan.

Two Bears sat in the centermost room of his house, a locked, windowless space he used for Night Seer business. Herbs, potions, formulas, and, of course, his Aztec mirror were kept out of sight in this secure location.

Today his goal was to connect with the spirit of Benjamin Blacksnake down in the Shadow Zone to check on preparations being made in the lower regions. First, Two Bears began reciting the spirit vision incantation while applying oil he kept in a near-by jar made from bilberry leaves and rattlesnake venom.

He'd memorized the verbal sounds of the spell, which came from the ancient Aztec language, although he didn't know exactly what they meant. As long as he used the right oil and pronounced the words correctly, the spell always worked, because an Aztec medicine maker had long ago officially given the spell to the Night Seers for their use.

Within a few minutes of chanting and polishing, the black obsidian surface began to glow with a faint purple light.

Next, Two Bears visualized Benjamin Blacksnake in his mind, based on an old photograph of the man. The purple glow intensified, and Two Bears imagined himself being projected through the black spirit viewer.

Having used the viewer many times, he was quickly propelled through the Land of Gray Fog, through the Forest of Dread, and across the River of Fear. He found Blacksnake waiting on the opposite shore at the edge of the Shadow Zone. Benjamin seemed agitated.

"I haven't been able to get anything done ever since Night Wolf arrived," he complained. "She's constantly pestering me to perform the soul-sealing ceremony so we'll be eternally joined together no matter where we are."

"Not something you're interested in, huh?"

"Not in the slightest! I've got more important tasks to accomplish now that the Owls and Snakes are aligned again."

"That's why I'm contacting you now," Two Bears said. "Have you made any progress?"

"You'll be happy to know that I've secured the cooperation of all domains down to and including Level Six, the Pit of Bitter Wind. There's only one more level to clear, the Nightmare Mountains overlooking the Lake of Fire."

"Dammit, Benjamin, we're running out of time!" the medicine man said. "We've got to have an unrestricted connection to Level Eight, the Lair of Banished Beasts, in order for the mass creature conjuring to work!"

"I'll get it done," the shadow spirit replied. "You just make sure that me and my Shadow Zone army are warned before those beasts come tearing through here on their way to the Middle-world. I don't want to get trampled."

Two Bears broke off the connection without answering. At least he had some good news to tell the Owl Clan for his next Aztec mirror report to them.

"Not interested in the soul-sealing ceremony, huh?" a female voice behind Blacksnake said.

He turned to find Carmelita "Night Wolf" Tuckaleechee standing behind him. "No, not really," he admitted to her for the first time. "I have a lot to do before the Grand Thinning, so I don't have time for any of that nonsense."

"Nonsense, is it?" Her dark, shadowy figure began emitting a deep red glow as her anger grew. "You want to talk about non-sense?" the *skili's* ghost asked as her voice took on a raspy edge. "I'll show you some serious nonsense."

While in the Middleworld, the witch had often transformed into a large owl, but here in the Shadow Zone, her alter ego was, and had always been, the Night Wolf. With no physical resistance, the unimpeded transformation took place quickly, and within seconds, a growling she-beast lunged for Blacksnake.

Just as quickly, though, the sorcerer became the Raven Stalker, adopting his own true self. Able to avoid the fangs of the attack-ing four-legged creature, the raven latched on to the wolf's back with formidable claws that sank into her hackles.

The two struggled viciously, ripping and tearing at each other's shadowy ghost bodies. No matter how much damage one animal did to the other, neither one surrendered, neither one weakened. Without bodies of flesh and blood, no one suffered serious injury, and no one would die as a result of their savage struggle. They were already dead.

First to acknowledge this truth, the raven withdrew from the conflict and hovered above the wolf, out of reach.

"Enough, Kituwah!" Blacksnake yelled, using the medicine name the witch had first used as a young Cherokee woman. He quickly morphed back into his human shadow form. "I could send you straight to the Lake of Fire or the Pit of Bitter Wind with a simple command and wave of my hand! Let's just stop this."

"You led me to believe we'd reincarnate as immortals when Thinning Time came!" the *skili* said as she, too, reverted to human form.

"I needed you to keep believing that so I'd have a reliable contact in the Middleworld," he admitted. "Nothing more."

"You son of a scorpion!" she shouted angrily and charged at him once again.

He quickly raised his hand, thrust the palm toward her, and uttered a single word in the Nahuatl language, the tongue of the Underworld. "*Themo*—descend!"

The ground beneath her feet undulated, became unstable, and gave way. She was swallowed up as if she'd stood on quicksand and, within a few seconds, was gone.

"I don't think the Shadow Zone is big enough for both of us anymore," Blacksnake said and returned his attention to his Underworld takeover preparations.

CHAPTER NINE

A Myth Visits Chigger

B ack in Tahlequah, Chigger was back in school and staying focused on schoolwork. But at night he was plagued by nightmares. One in particular came night after night.

At the beginning of the dream, a man with an eye patch was caressing a very large snake. This was taking place in a cave. Then the man noticed he was being watched and became enraged. He turned toward Chigger and began chasing him. Luckily, that was when Chig woke up.

"What do you think this dream means?" he asked Billy by phone one day during lunch.

"It could just be a delayed reaction to the horrible photos we saw in Arkansas," Billy offered. "Or the one-eyed man might represent your own fears that you need to face. But you need to go inside yourself to find out what it means to you."

Chigger thanked his wise friend and vowed to do just that. "The Muskrat out!" he said, ending the call.

Meanwhile, Billy's dad had a surprise waiting for his son when he got home from the expedition. He told Billy he had set up a remote meeting with a language expert over the Internet.

The day of the meeting, Billy and his dad sat in front of the computer in James's office. When Mr. Buckhorn launched the meeting, a window opened to reveal an older Latina woman with glasses and graying hair sitting in front of a bookshelf.

"Billy, I want you to meet Dr. Catalina Esperanza of the Indigenous Language Academy in Albuquerque, New Mexico," James said.

"*Piyali*," the woman said. "*Quen-amici-tzintli*. Hello. How are you?"

"Uh . . . I'm fine," Billy replied, curious about what was going on. "What language are you speaking?"

"I greeted you in the Nahuatl language, also known as Mexica," the woman answered. "It's the language of the Aztecs."

Billy looked at his father, who was seated beside him.

"I sent Dr. Esperanza the photo of the writing on the Horned Serpent's stone door from the crystal cave," James said. "I heard about her work in Indigenous languages and thought she might be able to help us figure out where this language came from."

"The writing on the door is Nahuatl," Catalina confirmed. "It is one of many known magic spells used in ancient times by Aztec sorcerers. There are still thousands of Indians in Mexico who speak that language in addition to Spanish."

"The Sun Chief from Solstice City—that's Cahokia—told me it was an old sacred language," Billy said, thinking about the implications as he spoke. "That means that some of the old knowledge passed down in Native North American communities might have originally come from Mexico?"

"And other parts of Central America," the scholar added. "The language and religion of the Maya people is even older and contains earlier versions of some of the same beliefs."

Billy thought about the images and writing dedicated to serpent deities they'd seen recently in caves along the Arkansas and Mississippi Rivers.

"Do those beliefs include a winged serpent, or a sky snake of some kind?" he asked.

"Yes, both belief systems speak of the sky serpent," Catalina explained. "The Maya worshipped this serpent as a creator god whose presence was marked in the night sky by a prominent constellation."

Thinking out loud, Billy said, "The man who led our tour of the Three Rivers Mounds said he was an Aztec Indian. His last name was Coyotl, I think he said."

"The origin of the word *coyote*, which you may know from many tribal cultures as—"

"The Trickster," Billy interrupted. "No wonder Chigger had such a strong reaction to the guy."

"And other words like *chocolate* and *tomato* are derived from original Nahuatl words," the linguist added.

"You learn something new every day," Billy said.

"Well, I have to get back to my teaching duties now," Dr. Esperanza said. "I'll email you a link that'll take you to an English-Nahuatl translation website and some background on the Aztec-Maya cultures."

"Thanks for your time, Dr. Esperanza," James said. "We really appreciate it."

He ended the call and closed the meeting software.

A light went on in Billy's head as he realized something. "This is incredible! I may be able to read some of the strange passages in Blacksnake's medicine book, maybe even figure out how to use the Aztec mirror!" He hugged his father. "Thanks, Pops. This could be a real game changer."

That night Chigger dreamed that dream again, and it proved to be a mental tipping point. Waking to a pounding heart and heavy breathing, he sat up in bed waiting for his body to calm. After turning on the light sitting on the nightstand beside his bed, he looked around the darkened room.

The faces of superheroes and sports figures stared back at him from posters on the wall. A handful of participation trophies he'd won for archery and blowgun competitions at Cherokee Holiday competitions seemed to scream "Unremarkable!" at him.

What caught his eye was the pair of satellite phones, plugged into their charging stations, that sat almost forgotten on a corner bookshelf. Each had a tiny green blinking light that indicated they were fully charged and ready for action.

Originally, he and Billy had received a single sat phone from the Cherokee Marshals Service as a reward for their work in stopping Ravenwood, the fake high school gym teacher, from harming any students after he'd imprisoned and impersonated the real gym teacher.

The Marshals Service gave the second phone to Billy as part of the search-and-rescue campaign to find Lisa after Tuckaleechee had kidnapped the girl. Billy, in turn, had entrusted the pair of unique communication devices to his friend as a sign of their continuing friendship.

Now the two little green lights blinked at Chigger like a signal that said, "Go! Go! Go! Go face your fears like Billy said! Go do something important with your life! Go back to Three Rivers and find the Fire Crystal and the Sun Chief!"

Whoa there, Chigger! he told himself. *Settle down and think about what you're saying. This isn't like you at all. A move like that could be dangerous!*

Another part of Chigger replied, *Billy said you were an asset that could be helpful in preventing the Underworld from taking over, so this is your chance. This is your opportunity to prove him right!*

　　　　　　　　　　　CHAPTER NINE

Chigger pictured in his mind these two little versions of himself sitting on the bookshelf near the sat phones, arguing back and forth.

"What will you tell your parents or the school?" Chigger number one said.

"I won't tell them anything," Chigger number two replied. "I'll just go—take my hidden stash of cash, put gas in my truck, and go."

Then Chigger heard a third voice, one not coming from inside his head but possibly from under his bed: "So, you're just going to run off without telling anyone what you're doing?"

Chigger was so startled by the new voice he jumped out of bed, pulled out the hunting knife he kept in the nightstand drawer, and whispered loudly, "Who said that? Who's in here with me? Don't try anything. I've got a knife!"

A small Native American man peeked out from under the bed and said, "Put that knife away before you hurt yourself."

"What the—?" Chigger blurted out. "Who—? How—?"

"I'm not coming out until you put the knife away," the little man said.

A light went on in the back of Chigger's mind as a glimmer of recognition began to grow. He put the knife back in the drawer, and the little man crawled out from under the bed. He had one braid of long black hair and wore a pair of deerskin leggings.

"Do you know who I am yet?" he asked.

"Yeah, you're a myth," Chigger said with a smirk. "One of those little fairy-tale people the elders are always carrying on about."

"I beg your pardon," the short guy replied smugly. "I have been, and continue to be, the friend and medicine helper to none other than two of the most powerful Cherokee medicine men who ever lived: Wesley and Billy Buckhorn."

Finally, total recognition and understanding settled into Chigger's brain.

"You're Little Wolf, aren't you?" the teen said as he began to accept the situation. "Billy told me about you long ago, but I thought he was just pulling my leg." Chig sat down on the edge of his bed. "How come I never saw you before?"

"Your mind wasn't open to the possibility," Little Wolf replied. "You've only recently opened up to deeper parts of yourself to allow other dimensions in."

"Other dimensions?" Chigger's mind became a whirlwind of chaos. "Why are you here now?"

"To help you face your fears and find the Fire Crystal," the little man said. "You're going to need all the help you can get."

Chigger kept quiet as he came closer to making a decision.

"What are you, a boy or a muskrat?" Little Wolf said.

"Not just any muskrat," the teen answered with finality. "*The* Muskrat!"

And that was that!

That night Billy got an unexpected mental invitation from Morningstar, who asked the teen to meet him in the fourth Upperworld level at a place Billy had named his Home Among the Stars. Billy was really curious to find out what this meeting was about.

"You've already received your medicine training from all the members of the Medicine Council," Morningstar said. "I want to add one more tool, or maybe you'd call it a technique, to your arsenal of supernatural abilities."

"Always happy to learn something new," Billy replied. "What do you have in mind?"

"Out-of-body time travel."

"Not an answer I was expecting to hear," Billy said. "Not even close to anything I could ever imagine."

"It's something that might be useful someday somewhere somehow," the spirit man said. "And you sort of experienced a sample of it during a dream you had back when you were first learning about spirit travel."

Billy thought about what Morningstar was telling him, and then a flash of memory reminded him that during that dream, he'd traveled back in time to Solstice City in the era when Shakuru was the Sun Chief.

"I asked Shakuru where that scene took place, and he told me to ask not only where it was but also when it was!"

"Bingo!" Morningstar said. "Okay, ready for the lesson?"

"As I'll ever be," the teen answered.

"First I'll take you to a pivotal point in your past and allow you to interact with that moment, and then I'll show you how we got there."

Morningstar whisked them away in spirit-travel mode, but Billy recognized that it was somehow different from just moving from one place to another. There was an additional element to their movement that he couldn't quite identify.

Within a few seconds, the two of them hovered above a river next to a cliff, right at the level of a ledge outside the entrance to a cave.

"It's the bat cave!" Billy said when he recognized the location. "Well, that's what Chigger calls it."

"You're right," Billy's tour guide replied.

"Can we go in?"

"No, we cannot," Morningstar said. "It's one of the restrictions of time travel. Your future self and your past self can't be too near each other. Just wait and watch."

In another moment, loud screams came from within the cave, accompanied by the beating and fluttering of dozens and dozens of bat wings. The out-of-body Billy watched as the physical Billy came running and screaming out of the cave, unable to see where he was, as a barrage of berserk bats scratched, nipped, and battered the boy.

In the next instant, the physical Billy, wounded and bleeding, plummeted off the ledge, crashing onto a small jetty of land thirty feet below. The last of the bats came out of the cave, followed by Chigger, who was yelling, "Billy, Billy, are you all right?"

No signs of Billy were visible on the ledge other than drops of his blood, so Chigger peered down at the ground below, and there his friend lay in a bloody heap, not moving. Screaming "Billy! Billy!" at the top of his lungs, the teen scrambled down to his wounded buddy.

Unable to revive his pal, Chigger asked a crucial question in his mind, a thought that Morningstar and out-of-body Billy could hear as if it were spoken.

What would Billy do?

"That's your cue," Morningstar told out-of-body Billy.

"Oh, crap!" Billy responded. "Really?"

Out-of-body Billy swooped down and whispered in his friend's ear, "Use the sat phone to call the Cherokee marshals office."

To Billy's surprise, Chigger immediately jumped up, ran to the canoe parked close by, and pulled the sat phone out of a backpack. The rest, as they say, is history, as the emergency call brought a medical helicopter to the scene, which got Billy to the ER in time to save his life.

Morningstar and out-of-body Billy floated up and away from the scene.

"What would've happened if we hadn't gone back to this place at this exact time?" Billy asked.

"You would've died, and that would be the end of your story in the Middleworld," the spirit man replied, matter-of-factly.

Billy was dumbfounded by that answer. He couldn't wrap his mind around it at all.

"But that was never a possible outcome," Morningstar added, "because you were predestined to become Thunder Child and carry out your life's purpose."

Billy continued to float quietly above the river scene, still trying to grasp it all.

"If you think about it too much, you'll drive yourself crazy," Morningstar said. "It just goes to show you that time isn't what you think it is."

Billy decided to follow the spirit man's advice. He stopped trying to figure it out and chuckled. "This is the big moment that Chigger likes to brag about," he commented. "How he helped save me from dying and all."

"If I were you, I wouldn't burst your friend's bubble. Let him have his moment of glory."

"You're right," the teen said. "Now show me how this works."

Morningstar took Billy back to his present time and current location to begin the lesson, a lesson the teen was destined to use once more during his lifetime.

CHAPTER TEN

Brave or Crazy

A round four o'clock the next morning, Chigger tiptoed quietly from his bedroom to the front door of his family's mobile home. The previous afternoon, while his mother prepared dinner in the kitchen, he'd packed a bag and stowed it along with a bedroll in the back of his truck. And earlier, on his way home from school, he'd filled the pickup's tank with gas.

Now, as he stepped out on the porch and ever so gently closed the door, he made sure the envelope addressed to his mom and dad got pinched between it and the doorframe. He hoped the note he'd written his parents told them enough about why he was doing what he was doing without giving away where he'd be doing it.

I am doing something important that will help humanity, a line of the note said.

As he sprinted to his truck in the dark of night, a roar of thoughts cascaded through his mind. Thoughts like *This is a really bad idea* and *This is the craziest thing you've ever done, Muskrat* and *I hope you packed enough snacks to carry out this bad idea.*

Thankfully, the truck engine started right up, allowing him to slip away without much noise. And he was off! Heading south toward what he knew to be a dangerous situation in order to help his best friend in the world prevent dark forces from taking over that world.

The first stop on Chig's journey was Billy's house, where he quietly left one of the two sat phones and a charger leaning against the front door, along with another note.

Next stop—possibly hell on earth, Chigger thought as he put his truck in gear and continued heading south.

As the sun rose later that morning, Billy decided to conduct the seven directions ceremony on his front porch. When he opened the front door and peered out at the sky, he heard a clunk on the floor. Looking down, he saw the phone, charger, and note lying at his feet. He recognized the paper as a page from Chigger's sketchbook.

If I find the Sun Chief or his staff, I'll give you a call, the note read. *I realized I did need to man up, face my fears, and do my part. I'm going to use my superpower. Meanwhile, wish me luck and keep the phone nearby. PS: No one but you knows where I'll be. Don't tell my parents.*

The note was signed: *The Muskrat.*

Billy looked up from the note and gazed southward, as if he might catch a glimpse of his friend in the distance.

"Chigger, you silly, silly boy," he whispered. "As if I didn't already have enough to worry about."

The idea of Chigger out there on his own, possibly stepping into a situation more dangerous than he could possibly imagine, short-circuited Billy's morning ceremonial plan. He called Lisa.

"What exactly did you say to Chigger when you gave him that little pep talk on the front porch of the rental house down at Three Rivers?" he asked.

"I told him his sensitivity to negative supernatural forces was his superpower."

Billy didn't say anything.

"Billy, are you still there?" Lisa asked. "Is something wrong?"

"I couldn't imagine what would motivate Chig to do something rash like this."

"Like what?"

Billy read the note to her.

"Congratulations," he said angrily. "You found the *one thing* that might prompt Chig to take action. Dangerous action, at that."

"Billy, you gotta know I never dreamed he would try to do something like this on his own," she replied. "What's he going to do—sneak into the Three Rivers Mounds and do a search?"

"Something like that—or worse."

"What are we going to do?" Lisa asked, genuinely concerned.

"I don't know about you, but I'm going to get busy studying the Nahuatl language so I can decipher some of the spells in Blacksnake's medicine book."

He ended the call and tried to calm himself. After sitting quietly for a couple of minutes, he took Blacksnake's book off the shelf next to the bed and opened the bottom drawer of his desk. Grabbing the box that held the Aztec mirror, he bounded up the stairs to his father's office with the book and the box.

But before checking his email for the language link Dr. Esperanza had promised to send, Billy clicked on a weather update video waiting for him on his dad's computer. The video began to play.

"Multiple streams, rivers, and lakes across North America are now overflowing their shorelines as the stationary weather patterns continue to dump copious amounts of water on the already drenched ground," a voice-over announcer said as images of rising waters filled the screen. "The National Weather

Service has issued evacuation warnings in communities that border those waterways. Fire departments, search-and-rescue teams, and the Red Cross are standing by in case unprecedented flooding reaches predicted levels. Updates will follow in the days ahead."

"Focus, Buckhorn," Billy said aloud as he closed the video. "The weather is merely a distraction and not the main event."

He searched for the email about the Nahuatl language and found it. He clicked on the underlined blue link within that email and was taken to a page called Nahuatl Portal that contained several more links. The links had names like Nahuatl Translator, Nahuatl Word List, and Symbols of the Nahuatl Written Language.

"Aha," he said when he saw the "Symbols of the Nahuatl Written Language" title.

He clicked on that link and, within a couple of seconds, found himself staring at a screen filled with the same type of writing he'd seen on the stone door at the bottom of the bat cave. The characters were nothing like either English letters or the symbols of the Cherokee syllabary.

Quickly flipping to the back of Blacksnake's medicine book, Billy found what he knew was there: a few pages filled with the same writing! The last page of the medicine book included a crude drawing of what appeared to be the Aztec mirror along with a few lines of text.

But he quickly realized that he was not equipped to translate the text in Blacksnake's book to English—or Cherokee, for that matter. When he first encountered the writing on the stone door, it had been the Sun Priest's spirit that had made it possible for Billy to speak the words needed to recapture the Horned Serpent. And Shakuru wasn't around right now to help him with such things.

"Dr. Esperanza!" Billy said as the idea burst into his mind. "She could do it!"

He took out his phone and photographed the pages containing the Nahuatl writing. Then he texted the images to his father with a message asking him to see if the linguist could do the translation, maybe offering to pay her for the service.

He ended the message to his father with *Chigger's life may depend on it.*

As Chigger drove south toward Three Rivers, he was determined not to let his own fear stop him from doing what needed to be done. Before leaving home, he'd purposefully turned off his cell phone to avoid receiving the calls and texts he knew his mother would be sending.

But he was sure to keep the sat phone handy and charged in case Billy tried to reach him. It was about halfway through the drive—near Pine Bluff, Arkansas—when his phone rang. Chigger answered, hoping Billy wasn't going to start a fight with him.

"Is there any chance I can change your mind about this?" Billy said.

"Not a chance," Chig said firmly.

"You know this is crazy, right?"

"Of course it is," Chig said. "But I have a superpower."

"Lisa told me," Billy replied. "Use it wisely."

"Have you forgotten who saved your ass from the Raven Stalker?" Chigger said.

"And helped save me when I died at the bat cave," Billy confirmed. "No, I haven't forgotten. You won't let me. Friends till the end, you and me."

"Friends till the end," Chig replied.

After ending the call, Chigger took a very deep breath and reached inside the collar of his shirt. Locating the fine chain, he pulled the Night Seer talisman up and away from his chest. Holding the titanium pendant in one hand, he briefly examined the thirteen-pointed star engraved on its surface.

His plan for getting himself admitted into the inner circle of people who probably had the Sun Chief and the Fire Crystal hadn't been totally worked out. But he hoped Tuckaleechee's pendant might get him admitted to the group. It would support his story of being the *skili*'s faithful apprentice. He practiced his act.

"As she lay dying, she took the talisman off and gave it to me," Chigger said, looking at his emotion-filled face in the rearview mirror. "She charged me with carrying on with her work to restore the Underworld to its rightful control of the Middleworld."

Satisfied with the performance, he returned the pendant to its place underneath his shirt. *That high school drama class is finally going to pay off,* he thought.

"Time to fly by the seat of your pants, Muskrat," Chigger said aloud as he passed a highway sign telling him he still had about 250 miles to go. "The first thing you need is a place to stay during this, um . . . adventure."

He turned on his cell phone, which immediately blew up with a dozen text messages and missed call notifications from his parents. Ignoring those, he used the phone's assistant app to find a cheap motel near his target area. The app responded by showing him a photo of the two-star Sportsman Inn located thirteen miles west of the Three Rivers Mounds—room rate $120 per week.

"Perfect!" Chigger said enthusiastically and then told the cell phone assistant, "Directions to the Sportsman Inn on Highway 1."

Back at Billy's house, Lisa had been busy behind the scenes doing whatever she could to help with the search for the Sun Chief's remains and ceremonial staff. One thing she'd done was secretly take a photo of Coyotl when they visited Three Rivers.

She then sent the photo to Raelynn with the message: *We're pretty sure this is the guy Reverend Miller sold the Sun Chief's remains to. His name is Miguel Coyotl, an Aztec who works with Greyson Greenstone at Three Rivers.*

Soon afterward, Raelynn was put in touch with the FBI agent who'd been assigned to investigate the murders at the Angola prison. The agent was also assigned the additional duty of finding the stolen burial artifacts and human remains belonging to the Lookout family, and he wasn't very happy about it.

Agent Jeremiah Swimmer, originally from Oklahoma, was one-quarter Cherokee and the nephew of Chief Swimmer of the Tahlequah Police Department, so he seemed perfect for the job. He was stationed in the FBI's field office in New Orleans, geographically close to the Angola prison and Three Rivers mound complex and not too far from the federal prison in Texarkana.

As Swimmer drove from his office in New Orleans toward the Texarkana prison to meet Raelynn Little Shield, he thought about how he'd gotten this assignment. It was the day before in his supervisor's office.

"I'm already in charge of searching for one or more mysterious murderers," Agent Swimmer had complained to his FBI supervisor. "I won't have time to go looking for some bones and artifacts that went missing! Give the case to someone else!"

"The Lookout family and the NAGPRA investigator both requested the case be assigned to an agent with at least a little Native blood," the supervisor countered. "They figured someone like you would be especially interested."

"Well, they figured wrong," he said angrily. "I'm only interested in working on real criminal cases with national implications for significant career advancement!"

"This is a nationally significant, groundbreaking case," the supervisor responded, rising from his office chair and moving toward the seated Swimmer. "News outlets all over the country will be watching to see how well the Department of the Interior and the FBI work together."

The supervisor, a robust white man in his fifties, leaned back against the front of his desk and spoke directly to Swimmer in a low, controlled voice. "The president has even taken an interest, because he made campaign promises to Indigenous leaders that his administration would take Native American issues seriously. So you see, the director of the FBI reached out to this field office with high expectations. That means my ass is on the line. Which means your ass is on the line." He poked Swimmer in the chest with a stiff index finger as he said "your ass." "Which also means there will be no significant career advancement without this case, because you will no longer have a career to advance."

The supervisor stood up. "Do I make myself clear?"

Swimmer, who now understood his situation perfectly, also stood up. "Yes, sir, special agent in charge, sir!" He saluted his supervisor.

"There is no saluting in the FBI, Swimmer," the supervisor replied. "You know that."

"I forgot, sir. Sorry, sir."

"You're dismissed, agent Swimmer," the supervisor said as he sat back down behind his desk. "Go do your job."

Swimmer pulled into the Texarkana prison parking lot, slipped on a raincoat, and jogged toward the prison's visitor entrance. Little Shield was waiting for him just inside. When he saw the beautiful Native American NAGPRA investigator for the first time, his opinion of this assignment immediately changed.

"I'm FBI Agent Jeremiah Swimmer," he said with a broad smile. "Call me Jerry. You don't know how much I've been looking forward to working with you on this groundbreaking case."

As they shook hands, the DOI investigator felt a warm glow all over. She got a good feeling from this man. The pair quickly took care of the business they came to conduct, which was to show Reverend Miller the photo of Coyotl and confirm he was the one who picked up the skeletal remains of Shakuru, the Sun Chief.

Before Swimmer and Little Shield left the prison interview room, Miller made an observation.

"Me and people like me have been collecting Indian bones and grave goods for a couple hundred years, and nobody raised a stink about it," he said. "Why all the fuss now?"

The man's insensitivity got to Raelynn. "You and people like you have been desecrating Indigenous burials and disrespecting Indigenous peoples' cultures and beliefs far too long," she said angrily. "Because we had no voice in the federal government or the legal system, you and your buddies got away with it."

She stood from her seat and walked around the table where the three of them sat. Miller, who was handcuffed to a metal loop anchored in the middle of the table, tried to retreat from her but couldn't.

She bent down and whispered in his ear. "I will personally see to it that you suffer for what you've done for the rest of your miserable life," she said. "Whether or not you're found guilty in a courtroom, I have connections to powerful medicine people who have more ways to torment you than you can ever imagine."

"Okay, okay, I get it," he replied in a whispered, fear-filled voice. "They already visited me in my cell and made their point. I'll fully cooperate." He paused for a moment, then spoke loud enough for both investigators to hear clearly. "I hope that Peter Langford fella from Spiral Mounds and that Coyotl guy are getting the same treatment I am! They're just as guilty."

"Oh, they're on our list," Raelynn said, surprising Agent Swimmer. "We've neglected to follow up with Langford much, and now I've got plenty of questions to ask him."

A prison guard came into the room and took Miller back to his cell.

"Langford is here too, isn't he?" Swimmer asked Little Shield.

"He sure is," she replied. "And I've got new information I need to ask him about."

"Okay, let's do it," Swimmer said.

Then the FBI agent and the DOI investigator headed to the warden's office to request an interview with Langford. The warden was happy to oblige.

A guard ushered Langford into the interview room and handcuffed him to the table. The man, who'd mostly been ignored since arriving at the prison, was actually pleased to have visitors.

"To what do I owe the pleasure of your company?" he asked the pair. "I don't get many visitors here."

After introducing herself and Swimmer, Raelynn opened her briefcase, took out a file folder, and opened it. "I've been studying the visitor logs from the interpretive center where you worked," she said, flipping over a couple of the pages. "I noticed a few repeat names I need to ask you about."

"Okay, shoot," Langford said. "I'm an open book."

"The ones I'm interested in are all Indigenous," she said. "Their individual separate visits were spread out over a year, but, in your logbook, they all wrote that they came from other spiral mound archaeological sites along the Arkansas and Mississippi Rivers. Did you find that odd? No one lives at those locations."

"Not really. A lot of Native Americans visited my spiral mound site, but I didn't really pay that much attention to what people wrote in the visitor log."

She read from the list. "Jonna Boudreaux, Houma tribal woman, Emerald Mounds. Travis Garfish, Coushatta tribe, Redbone Mounds. Joseph Saracen, Quapaw, Pine Bluff Mounds. Dominic Yazza, a Tunica Indian woman from the Poverty Point Mounds. Jimmy Cypress, Chitimacha tribe, Toltec Mounds. Lavinia Tahsequah, Comanche, Clarksville Mounds. And Norman Redcorn, a Caddo man from a town near your Spiral Mounds site in Oklahoma. And finally, Miguel Coyotl, Aztec, Winterville Mounds in western Mississippi."

"So, what's your point?" Langford asked. "I'm not getting it."

"Two things jump out at me," Raelynn said. "First—Miguel Coyotl is the man that Samuel Miller delivered the human burial remains to, the remains that came from the mound site you were in charge of."

"If you say so," Langford replied.

"Second, all eight of those people listed TRMBOD as the organization they represented."

"What do those letters mean?" the prisoner asked.

"I was hoping you could tell me," Raelynn said.

"TRMBOD—that doesn't ring a bell."

"I think it means Three Rivers Mounds Board of Directors," the DOI investigator said.

"Again, if you say so. I don't have a clue."

"Mr. Langford, do you really expect us to believe you didn't know why they were visiting your site?"

"I don't have to sit here and listen to this. Yeah, I'm guilty of trying to make a buck selling old Indian artifacts, but I didn't think anybody really cared about old dead Indians."

Raelynn reacted much as she'd done with Miller, but this time Agent Swimmer stepped in to calm her down.

"Guard, we're done here," he called out. "You can take the prisoner back to his cell."

This upset Raelynn even more, but she held her tongue for the time being. Once Langford and the guard were out of range, Swimmer spoke to her.

"Think about it, Raelynn," he said calmly. "Your words and actions here could jeopardize the cases against these two men. You don't want that."

He waited for her to get control of herself.

"I understand why you're upset," he continued. "But we must maintain a professional attitude during this investigation. Are you with me?"

She blew out a frustrated breath of air and nodded. "Yeah, I'm with you," she said. "Thanks for talking me down."

Once their business at the Texarkana prison was taken care of, the two investigators drove to the Angola prison to follow up on the murders. On their way, they dropped Raelynn's car at the nearest car rental location. As the drive progressed, they easily dropped the usual law enforcement formalities in exchange for calling one another by their first names.

"I believe the murders and the missing artifacts are tied together," Raelynn told Jerry.

"I hadn't thought of that," Jerry replied. "Then I'm doubly glad we're working together."

Raelynn filled him in on everything she and Lisa had discovered earlier at the Angola prison and at Serpent World.

While Raelynn and Jerry were on their way to the Angola prison, Chigger was recovering from a nightmare he'd had after checking into the Sportsman Inn. It was a repeat of the nightmare with the man wearing an eye patch, petting a very large snake. Only this time there were more details, frightening details, that caused him to toss and turn all night.

In this dream the man took off the eye patch, revealing the sunken eye socket underneath. In one hand he held a large ornate knife made of some kind of glassy black stone. The man ran his thumb across the blade of the knife, making sure it was sharp.

Soon the dream's view widened, showing that the man stood before a stone table. Lying on the table was a man in an orange jumpsuit who was tied up and gagged. As the one-eyed man raised the knife over his head, the eyes of the man on the slab widened with fear. The knife thrust downward toward the captive man's chest, and that was when Chigger woke up with a jolt.

"What are you getting yourself into, Muskrat?" he said loudly as he sat up in bed, his heart racing.

Then he remembered a couple of nightmarish dreams Billy had described since beginning his medicine journey. Billy had said the dreams were warnings, so he'd be alert in the next few days.

"If Billy can do it, so can I," he affirmed.

The following morning, he drove to the Serpent World tourist attraction to see what he could learn. He was looking for any information that could lead him to Serpent Foundation meetings or other gatherings related to the Three Rivers Mounds.

As he entered the building, he was greeted by Ruthann, the same young lady whom Lisa and Raelynn spoke to. Surprisingly, she offered him a free ticket to see the snake exhibits and even threw in a guided tour.

"It's time for my morning break, so I could personally show you around, if you like," she suggested.

Chigger, who wouldn't recognize when a girl was flirting with him even if she hit him over the head, accepted the offer. As the two strolled among the reptile cages and glassed-in habitats, Chigger didn't sense any negative vibrations from the girl, and he concluded that she wasn't involved in any of the secret ceremonies in the area.

The boy didn't realize the girl had a superpower of her own.

"Are you from around here?" the girl asked. "I don't think I've seen you before."

"I'm just sort of traveling around," Chigger said. "You know, seeing what the world has to offer. I'll probably be in the area for a few days."

Ruthann smiled, encouraging the boy to open up.

"I heard about a group around here called the Church of the Reborn, or something like that," Chigger said, surprising himself with his own courage. "Do you know how I'd find out more about that? It sounds like something I might like to check out."

Ruthann led him over to a bulletin board filled with business cards and announcements. She pointed to a flyer inviting people to attend an introductory service of the First Temple of the Reborn. There, in a photo on the flyer, stood the one-eyed man from Chigger's nightmares, holding a large venomous snake!

He gasped at the sight of the image, then had to quickly cover by pretending to cough.

"Who's that guy?" he asked between fake coughs.

"His name is Nahash Molok," Ruthann said. "He's a priest or preacher—I'm not sure what you call him—but he demonstrates how you can handle deadly snakes without being hurt. I've heard it's pretty impressive, but I've never seen him perform."

"What kind of name is Nahash Molok?"

"I think it's Hebrew. Something to do with—what else—snakes, but I'm not sure."

Chigger took a closer look at the flyer. The caption below the photo read: *Come join us for a rebirthing ceremony to shed your old skin to be reborn into a new life! Learn how to overcome all obstacles that stand in your way!*

"How do I meet up with this snake preacher?" Chigger asked.

"They have a welcoming ceremony every Saturday night in the Chief's Mound," the girl replied. "There's a little auditorium in there they call the 'inner chamber.' It's for people to sign up to get saved, or reborn, or whatever."

So Billy was right. The mound is hollow.

"Where do I sign up for this welcoming thing?" Chig asked.

"I could talk to Mr. Greenstone's assistant about it," Ruthann answered. "Greenstone is in charge of everything around here. But only if you promise to do one thing."

"What's that?"

"Ask me out on a date," the girl said with a shy smile.

The boy blushed. He'd never been asked out or picked up by a girl. "Sure," he replied hesitantly. "Let's figure out a time we can get together."

Secrets of the Underworld

C higger had arrived in the Three Rivers area at about the same time Agent Swimmer and Raelynn had arrived at the prison to conduct their joint FBI-DOI investigation. Crime scene techs had already finished their work in the warden's office gathering physical evidence, and a part of that effort had been an attempt to recover usable images from the blurred surveillance video footage.

After checking in to their rooms at the budget hotel in St. Francisville, Jerry and Raelynn began reviewing the crime scene files that had been emailed to the FBI agent. The cause of death for the warden and the guard was listed as strangulation. However, neither victim displayed any outer markings on their throats that would've normally been visible in such cases.

"That's definitely odd," Swimmer said. "How can you die from strangulation without having your throat squeezed, which would produce some kind of markings?"

"That's definitely outside my area of expertise," Raelynn said. "But look at these still frames from the surveillance camera."

She laid out the two blurry photos on the table. Even though the FBI crime lab had been able to improve the sharpness of the images a little, the identities of the men visible in the pics couldn't be determined. The image on the left depicted a slender, well-dressed man entering the prison office building. The picture on the right, shot from the same camera, showed a larger, stockier man leaving the building a few minutes later.

"What am I looking at here?" Jerry asked.

"There is no recorded image of the slender man ever leaving the warden's office, and there is no recorded image of the stocky man ever entering. How's that possible?"

"It's not," Jerry said.

"Unless—" Raelynn began and then paused to complete the idea forming in her mind.

"Unless both images show the same man, a man that somehow has the ability to morph from one identity to another," she said.

Jerry laughed too loudly and too long before realizing Raelynn was serious. "Oh, you're not joking. What would ever give you such a wacky idea?"

"Well, if you think that's wacky, hold on to your seat," she replied. "You'll want to give me the World's Wackiest Award after I tell you what the Lookout family believes is going on."

Raelynn spent the next fifteen minutes detailing the whole story that Lisa had shared—the thousand-year-old prophecy, the Intertribal Medicine Council, the discovery of the Horned Serpent last fall, the abilities of Billy Buckhorn, and the murder of Wesley Buckhorn.

She also shared, for the first time, the reason why the Lookouts were in a hurry to locate the stolen human remains and burial items belonging to their ancestor, which included the expected coming catastrophes being caused by Underworld forces.

"You do win the World's Wackiest Award," Swimmer said when she'd finished. "Nothing you just said is believable or even remotely possible."

"You just wait," Little Shield replied. "You'll change your tune before this is all over. I guarantee it!"

In the meantime, James Buckhorn had followed through on his son's request to contact Aztec-language specialist Catalina Esperanza and ask her to translate the Nahuatl language passages he'd sent her. She agreed to do the translations and record herself reading the passages out loud just out of a sheer fascination with the old magic spells.

Now, as Billy sat down at his bedroom desk to look at the resulting translations and listen to the recordings, he was nervous. He didn't want to accidentally unlock some old formulas that might have unintended consequences—bad unintended consequences—for him, his family, or his friends.

"I hope I don't regret this," he said out loud as he opened the ornate box that held the Aztec mirror, which continued to emit a pulsating glow.

Dr. Esperanza had emailed several audio files that contained her voice speaking the words. But before playing the first one, Billy read the English translation that had been typed out. It was a step-by-step guide to activating and using the mirror.

Step one was to place the mirror on the little metal easel that came with it. Step two was to polish the black glassy surface with a few drops of the concoction made of rattlesnake venom and bilberry leaves that had been stored in the box. Step three was to repeat the spirit vision formula in the Nahuatl language four times.

Step four was to stare deeply into the mirror's black surface and visualize who or what you wanted to see through the viewing device. Billy really didn't have a goal in mind. He just wanted to see if the thing worked, how it worked, and what it did if it was activated.

As soon as Catalina's recorded voice finished repeating the vision spell, the pulsating stopped as the surface of the mirror transformed into a transparent window of some kind, a window into a dark world.

Billy realized he could probably see into that dark world more easily if he turned off the lights in his own room. After hitting the switch, he sat back down, moved the mirror closer to him, and concentrated.

As his eyes adjusted and his mind became more focused, his view of the scene beyond the mirror became clearer, but all he saw was roiling gray fog.

Where have I seen this before?

Then he remembered! It was a layer he discovered once when he was out-of-body and then again when Mattie Acorn wanted him to give her information about her deceased son. The boy's confused spirit was drifting in a space filled with fog.

As Billy continued to watch the image in the mirror, the fog began to dissipate. In its place, a dense, dark forest became visible. Along with the image, there also came a dense sense of foreboding that Billy could feel.

He immediately looked away from the black glass and brought his attention back to his present physical location. He stood up, ran a hand through his hair, and let out a tense breath of air. As he did, the image in the mirror faded away, to be replaced again with the purple pulsating glow.

What dark force must've created this thing and why? What did Chigger say when he gave me this thing? Billy racked his brain, looking for the memory. *Oh yeah. He said Tuckaleechee used it to contact other Night Seers and possibly the ghost of someone she knew. That means she could visit the Shadow Zone!*

Then another thought appeared in his mind. *Maybe there's a map of the Underworld somewhere!*

CHAPTER ELEVEN

Excitedly, he sat down and looked through the printed translations Dr. Esperanza had sent. What he found wasn't that helpful, but it was better than nothing. A passage in Blacksnake's book, written in the Nahuatl language, said that Aztec and Maya priests often visited the nine levels of the Underworld and left records of those regions.

As his mind searched for sources of information on the subject, his thoughts turned to his nonphysical home away from home up on the fourth level.

Morningstar should be able to give me some answers, he thought.

The teen climbed into bed and easily ran through the sequence of steps that allowed him to disengage from his physical body. Once that was done, he quickly moved upward until he reached his glass-domed base of operations among the stars.

He waited for Morningstar to appear as the Upperworld being usually did when Billy came seeking answers or guidance. Billy continued to wait, but nothing happened. Morningstar never showed. The teen returned to the physical realm and his body lying in bed.

Disappointed, he sat up in bed and considered his options.

"Time to do an Internet search!" he said to no one as he moved back to his desk and opened a favorite browser that didn't track searches or store personal digital information.

When he entered "Levels of the Underworld" in the search field, he was surprised—no, overwhelmed—when he got results that included websites on Hades, the Underworld region of ancient Greece; a Wikipedia entry on Sheol, the land of the dead in the Old Testament; a book called *Inferno* about the nine rings of Christian Hell; Buddhist beliefs about lower afterlife levels; the Chinese teachings on the ten lords of the Underworld realm; and on and on and on. He counted no less than forty-five entries from cultures and religions all over the world, including both the Maya and the Aztec!

Just goes to show you how familiar we humans are with the negative side of life and death.

Billy clicked on a link labeled "The Aztec Underworld" and began reading. Generic descriptions of the top few Underworld levels sounded very familiar, like something maybe he'd already experienced. But for the levels below that, the explanations were vague and sketchy.

"You're not going to find what you're looking for this way, Buckhorn," he said aloud.

Then a light went on in his mind.

"Oh my god!" he blurted out. "Where were you when they were passing out brains?"

He realized that Lisa's grandfather knew all about these levels. He was the one who'd explained where the House of Bones was located and taught his granddaughter how to rescue someone from there. Billy picked up his cell phone and pushed a button on the side.

"Call Cecil Lookout," he said, and the elder's number began ringing.

Within moments, the elder, who was on the front porch of Wesley's house, answered. "Thunder Child, how can I help you?"

"I'm trying to figure out how the Aztec mirror is connected to the Underworld," Billy said. "Something tells me I might need to know how to navigate those regions in the near future."

Silence was the only response he got.

Billy thought he'd lost the connection. "Hello, hello? Can you hear me?"

"I heard you plenty good," Cecil replied. "But that's considered forbidden knowledge. The holy ones who shared it with me said the temptation to abuse it was too strong to trust just anyone with it."

Billy didn't understand why this elder, head of the Medicine Council that chose him to be Thunder Child, would hesitate in responding to this request. "Am I just anyone?"

"No, you're not, but you're not the first one to ask me for this knowledge," Cecil said and paused before continuing.

Billy waited.

"Things ended badly the only other time I ever shared this knowledge," the elder finally said. "But I realized later it was my own damn fault for choosing the wrong person to trust."

Cecil paused again as his own inner guidance told him, *If not Billy Buckhorn, who then will you pass this sacred knowledge to before you die?*

"I'll be right over," the elder told Billy. "Be sure to have the Aztec mirror, Blacksnake's medicine book, and the Nahuatl language translations handy. We may need them."

Cecil ended the call and rushed to the closet in the back room of the old house. There he reached up to a top shelf above the clothes rack and pulled down a folded-up length of buffalo hide. Inside it was a rolled-up piece of deerskin—a scroll of sorts—that he'd placed there the day he and Ethan had moved into Wesley's former home.

He didn't bother to unroll the scroll, because he knew exactly what was inside: the oldest known sample of symbolic markings used by anyone in the Osage tribe. Oral history, passed down through at least ten generations, said the animal-skin scroll was created as a record of a rare meeting of tribal medicine men from the four directions who all had the same nightmarish dream on the same winter solstice night.

As he drove his old pickup truck to Billy's house, Cecil became more confident that this was the time and place to share this secret knowledge. Once inside the house, the elder climbed the stairs to the second-floor office that Billy's Underworld Takeover Prevention Team now called the War Room.

Billy's father, James, had gladly donated what had been his home office to the effort to stop the Underworld takeover, even relinquishing use of his desktop Apple computer. Billy had also set up a big flat-screen TV connected to their satellite dish, along with a large map of North America and a bulletin board for posting any information relevant to Underworld takeover prevention.

After Cecil arrived at the Buckhorn house, he began telling Billy the story of the scroll.

"In that shared dream of long ago, all four medicine men, from four different tribes, descended into the nine realms of the Underworld," he said. "Each was led by a supernatural guide who wanted the men to know what lurked below, continually threatening the inhabitants of the Middleworld. The four guides identified themselves as the Four Shadows."

"The Four Shadows?" Billy interrupted. "I've never heard of them."

"What I learned is that every person, and also every being, operating in the Middleworld has a shadow self," Cecil said. "The Four Shadows are the undersides of the Four Winds. But right now, let's focus on the story of the scroll."

Billy reluctantly agreed, and the elder continued. He said that, using a system of agreed-upon markings, the four men, who became known as the Trustees, recorded a condensed version of their shared experience on the first scroll. They made three copies of the scroll and swore to each other to pass the story of their experience, along with their copy of the scroll, down only to the most trusted younger member of their tribe.

That next generation Trustee, in turn, swore the same oath so the story and the scroll would continue to educate succeeding generations.

"And so, it came to me, as a young Osage medicine man, to not only become Keeper of the Center and Protector of the Prophecy," Cecil told Billy, "but also to be one of the four Trustees of the Scroll for my generation."

"You're just full of surprises," Billy said as Cecil carefully unrolled the scroll on the conference table. The nine sets of clustered symbols laid out in neat rows on the deerskin reminded Billy of some of the characters of the Cherokee syllabary. "What language is this?" he asked. "I don't recognize it at all."

"It's not an official language," the elder said. "Four medicine men who spoke different languages created it specifically to record this information. I'll explain more when we have time."

"Okay," Billy replied. "What's it say?"

"What I'm about to tell you is a combination of what the markings say and what I was asked to memorize some sixty-five years ago," Cecil explained. "When I finish, you will become one of four Trustees of the Scroll for your generation. That's the way it works."

"Whoa," Billy remarked as the feeling of a little more added weight rested on his shoulders. "As if the Thunder Child responsibility wasn't enough."

"Exactly," Cecil said. "For unto whomsoever much is given, of him shall much be required. Do you know who said that?"

"Spider-Man's uncle Ben?"

"No, Jesus—recorded in the Parable of the Faithful Servant." That took Billy by surprise.

"We'll come back to that another time," Cecil said. Pointing to the first line of the writing, the elder pressed on. "Okay, let's focus. Underworld Level One is the Land of Gray Fog, which I believe you've already experienced."

"Yes, I've seen another person trapped and confused there, and I visited that level myself," Billy replied. "I saw it again through the Aztec mirror. What's the purpose of that, anyway?"

"According to the tradition I learned, it's a buffer layer to prevent humans from accidentally finding the path to the Underworld."

"Oh, that makes sense," Billy said.

"The second level is called the Forest of Dread, guarded by a pack of ghost wolves that sorcerers can summon to the Middleworld."

"Seen that too," Billy said. "Those wolves almost got to Lisa a few months back. Nasty bunch."

"Next on the path is the River of Fear," Cecil continued. "It's not a level, but another barrier to keep non-dead humans out. The river is filled with ferocious, soul-shredding ghoul fish and can only be crossed with the help of the Pullman."

"The Pullman? What's that?"

"In Native canoe cultures, paddling a canoe is called pulling," Cecil replied. "A Native warrior spirit paddles, or pulls, his canoe back and forth across this river. But he'll only take you across to the other side if you can give him one of the accepted passwords."

"Which is?"

"I can't tell you yet," the elder said. "But I will when the time is right."

Billy didn't like this delay, but he knew better than to try to force anything with Cecil. "Okay, what's next?" he asked.

"On the other side of the river is the Shadow Zone, where human souls may be trapped due to their own negative deeds, character defects, or even addictions while on earth."

"I think I saw that during my Thunder Child initiation ceremony," Billy said.

"Probably. It's the dwelling place of ghosts, who unfortunately can be reincarnated in the flesh using certain spells and formulas."

"Benjamin Blacksnake and the Raven Stalker come to mind," Billy interjected.

"Right you are," the elder replied. "And that's where the Four Shadows live."

"Sounds like the name of a famous singing group," Billy said.

"Enough with the jokes, please."

"Sorry. This is so horrific sounding I have to do something to keep from crying."

"Okay," Cecil said as he pointed to the fourth line of markings on the scroll. "Below that level is the Negative Afterworld Belief Zone."

"The House of Bones location," Billy said.

"Yes, in the Valley of Stalking Skeletons, which you saw," Cecil said.

"Up close and personal like." A shiver ran up Billy's spine as he remembered the experience.

"Now things get really interesting, because each of the remaining five levels has its own lord or guardian," the elder said. "The fifth level is the Territories of Torment, ruled by the Scorpion Queen. Armies of ants, tarantulas, and scorpions stand ready to carry out her every whim."

"Level by level, this just gets worse the further you go," Billy commented. "What's number six on the billboard chart?"

"Level Six is called the Pit of Bitter Wind, where you'll find the twin lodges of the brother and sister spirits Disease and Despair."

"Not the deadly double D's!" Billy said with a chuckle. "Reminds me of my high school math grades!"

Cecil realized Billy couldn't help himself and gave up his joke protests. "Let's see if you can keep that sense of humor all the way to the bottom," he replied. "In Level Seven there are the Nightmare Mountains overlooking the Lake of Fire. This is where the idea of Hell came from."

"A hot time in the old town tonight."

Cecil just glared at Billy.

"One too many?" the teen said.

Cecil nodded. "The Lair of Banished Beasts is on the eighth lower level," he explained. "Physical caves and caverns, along with bodies of water, provide direct access to this level, as you've seen. Conjurers access the beasts through dark underground or watery portals."

Billy thought about that revelation, realizing what the caves his team had recently visited were all about.

"Actually, let me revise that," the elder said. "A really powerful sorcerer who knows the proper spells can conjure any dark soul or beast from any of these levels and bring them into the Middleworld."

Billy shivered at the thought.

"Finally, we reach the bottom, the Valley of Death at Level Nine," Cecil continued. "This is where the Winged Serpent—supposed lord of the Underworld—is said to live. Snake worshippers down through the ages believe he was once lord of all three worlds."

Before rolling up the scroll, Cecil had one more item to share. "I don't have any actual proof of this, but I believe there are actually several Horned Serpents, what your tribe calls Uktenas, who serve under the Winged Serpent. They may be like a royal court or something similar."

"Now that's a cheerful thought," Billy said.

As Cecil rolled up the scroll, he looked at Billy. "So why are you seeking these secrets of the Underworld?" he asked. "I thought you already had enough on your plate."

"I haven't been able to reach Grandpa Wesley, Awinita, or even Morningstar in a very long time," Billy said in a worried tone. "It feels like I'm on my own now, and it's kind of disturbing. But I still need answers."

"You've got us," the elder said.

"And you don't know how much I appreciate that."

"But?"

"But I need to know the full picture of what I—what we—are possibly up against so I—so we—won't be blindsided by unknown forces when the Underworld erupts into our world."

CHAPTER TWELVE

The Muskrat Makes His Move

As Bucky Wachacha sat in his modest living room watching an old black-and-white episode of *Gunsmoke*, he got the message he'd been waiting for. The spirits were ready to reveal the location of the lost Sky Stone piece to him.

"About time!" he declared to whoever might be listening.

He could now perform the second part of the formula to find lost objects. The spell consisted of two main steps. First you filled a small white porcelain bowl with fresh water from a flowing source. Then you took a common sewing needle and floated it in the center of the bowl. Then, while visualizing the lost object, you repeated the Cherokee words that made up the formula.

After getting the bowl, the water, and the needle, Bucky began the process.

"My name is Buchanan Wachacha, and my people are the Tsalagi," he said aloud in the Cherokee language. "Now I come to you, the Provider of everything that is right. I know that you, Foreseer, will certainly answer my inquiry. You, Ancient One, will tell me what I need to know."

He repeated the words four times and continued to picture the missing Sky Stone piece in his mind. To his pleasant surprise, this time something started to happen.

Slowly but steadily, the floating needle shifted its position within the bowl until the point of the needle aimed itself in a southwest direction. He positioned himself behind the bowl and then aligned himself with the direction the needle pointed.

Continuing to picture the object he was searching for, Bucky said, again in Cherokee, "Now show me the way. Take me to its location. Take me on a journey."

With his eyes closed, his spirit began to travel. It rapidly hurtled across the landscape just above the treetops, then over a mountain ridge, and then back down nearer the vegetation. Within a few seconds, Bucky found himself looking down on a gruesome scene. Some unknown fearsome creature was making a meal of a human corpse.

The sight almost caused Bucky to eject from the spell, but he forced himself to remain fast. Remembering his objective, he visualized the missing Sky Stone piece once again and was immediately moved to a position not far from the grisly feast and barely above the ground.

There, lying half-buried in the dirt, was the section of the stone he'd sought for so many years. After the revelation, he zoomed back across the miles and into his own body.

"What the hell was that?" Bucky asked himself.

He searched his mind for an answer.

It was definitely in Mississippi Choctaw territory. But where exactly? Could that possibly be a Choctaw medicine man lying dead on the ground? And what kind of strange creature was that?

"Time to call Cecil Lookout," Bucky said.

When Saturday night came at Three Rivers, Chigger was nervously ready to attend the snake man's inner chamber ceremony. His plan was to get noticed by Molok so he could gain entrance to the snake man's organization. How exactly that would happen Chigger wasn't sure. What could go wrong with that plan?

In whatever way that was to play out, he hoped it happened before he had to go on a date with Ruthann, because he was more intimidated by that prospect than the thought of infiltrating the Serpent King's inner sanctum. Lisa's suggestion that Chigger had a superpower had given him a surprising and continuing sense of calm confidence about his ability.

Chigger parked his pickup truck in the Three Rivers parking lot as other cars also pulled in. Singles, pairs, and small groups of people of varying ages, all wearing raincoats, headed for the side door of the central mound, the door that supposedly led only to a storage area.

As the teen approached the mound, the purple energy levels increased. Before entering, he closed his eyes, repeated the protection formula, and visualized an invisible shield going up around him.

Just inside the door, a table had been set up where a couple of people sat with sign-in sheets in front of them. Chigger took off his rain poncho and made sure the thirteen-pointed star pendant was visible. When it came his turn in line, he wrote his name as Nathan Nighthawk, a fictional Native American superhero he'd created for a comic book he hoped to write someday.

The character even had an email account, so he entered that as the primary way to contact him. He was handed a stick-on name tag with *Nathan* printed on it, so he stuck that to the front of his shirt.

Time to get into character, he thought.

Chigger stepped into the auditorium and studied the space for a moment.

Just like Billy described it.

An usher stepped up and showed him a place to sit near the back.

"Can I sit nearer the front?" Chigger asked. "I really want to experience this up close."

The usher took him to the only open seat in the front row, which was the last seat on the left side.

"What a unique pendant," the girl in the next seat said as she reached out to touch it.

Chigger blocked her hand. "Better not touch," he said. "It's a talisman given to me by a Cherokee medicine woman."

The girl pulled her hand away and made a gesture as if to say, "Sorry."

Just then, the lights in the little theater dimmed, and a hush came over the audience. As he'd done so many times before, the one-eyed man mesmerized his audience with his apparent supernatural powers, his handling of serpents, and his promise of providing a renewed life—all for a price.

As he watched Nahash Molok's performance—and an impressive and sometimes frightening performance it was—Chigger noticed the man regularly looking at him. Was it the talisman he wore, or was it something else that attracted the man's attention? Whatever it was, the teen hoped it produced the desired result.

At the end of the spectacle, after audience members had been invited to sign up in the back of the room to join the First Temple of the Reborn, one of Molok's female assistants approached.

"Brother Molok has requested to see you backstage," the assistant said. "He's never done that before. It's quite an honor."

Chigger couldn't move because his muscles would not cooperate. The confidence he'd maintained up until this moment quickly dissolved. Now that he'd achieved the hoped-for result, he was terrified.

"Uh, oh . . . okay," he muttered.

The assistant waited.

"Oh, you mean right now," he said.

Finally, he was able to muster the courage to rise from his seat and follow the woman up a set of stairs on the side of the stage. She disappeared behind a curtain, and Chigger reluctantly followed. He was ushered into a nearby offstage dressing room, and then the assistant left.

Molok sat in a director's chair in front of a large mirror surrounded by glowing globes of white light. He was focused on his own face as he wiped makeup off with a towel. The eye patch and strap lay on the counter, along with several partially filled makeup bottles.

Chigger flinched noticeably when the man used the towel to wipe inside the empty, sunken eye socket.

"What are you doing here, boy?" the man asked without diverting his eye from the mirror. "Nathan, is it?"

"I just wanted to see what it was all about," Chigger answered nervously. "My mentor told me about you before she died."

"Yeah? Who was that?"

"Carmelita Tuckaleechee over in the Cherokee Nation."

"Is that where you got that Owl Clan pendant?" Molok said, turning his seat in Chigger's direction. "She gave it to you?"

"Yes, sir."

The man put his eye patch back on and studied Chigger with a singularly piercing stare. The boy had never felt so prodded and probed, and yet the man never touched him.

"Why do you think she did that?" Molok asked.

Chigger swallowed hard before answering. "Because I spied on certain people for her and got her access to a Cherokee family she was having a feud with."

"Hmm. Now you've come to be my apprentice, is that it, Nathan?"

"Maybe not a full-blown apprentice," Chigger replied. "Just someone willing to learn and help out. I know I'm not the smartest person you'll ever meet, but I'm loyal."

"I can tell by your energy field that you have an affinity for things of a supernatural nature," the one-eyed man said. "You see, a person can't hide his true self from me. I picked up on your vibe out in the audience right away."

Molok considered his next steps before speaking again.

"I may have a job for you," he said finally. "Meet me here tomorrow at noon, and we'll see if you're cut out to be involved with the Society of Serpents."

"That's great," the teen replied with a nervous smile. "Looking forward to it."

Back home, Chigger's parents were angry, upset, and worried when they discovered their son had run away from home. Any parent would feel that same mix of emotions. But the couple had more reason than most to be concerned. Their son had already experienced—and caused them to experience—the worst nightmare imaginable, his descent into madness due to the strange purple crystal he'd brought home.

And, as far as they were concerned, it was all Billy Buckhorn's fault.

Also, they'd never believed any of the explanations Billy and his grandpa Wesley gave about some giant ancient horned reptile that had come to life. That was proof enough the whole Buckhorn family was prone to flights of fancy and not to be trusted.

Sure, Billy and his grandfather were among those who'd rescued the teen from the spell he'd been under, but their ongoing practice of tribal voodoo was probably the very reason Chigger had gotten mixed up with that Cherokee witch in the first place. What was the Cherokee word Chigger used? *Skili*?

Now their son had run away, and all he had left them was a note that included the line *I'm doing something important that is helping humanity.* Probably some kooky idea planted in Chigger's brain by that attention-seeking boy who thought he was some kind of powerful medicine man.

Chigger's parents decided they needed to call both Chief Swimmer of the Tahlequah Police Department and Deputy Marshal Travis Youngblood of the Cherokee Nation Marshals Service to report the disappearance of their son, Charles Checotah Muskrat, under mysterious circumstances.

Chief Swimmer and Marshal Youngblood knew each other well because their jurisdictions overlapped somewhat, and previous cases had called for them to work cooperatively several times. Both had been involved in the Raven Stalker incident and the search for Lisa Lookout when she was kidnapped by Carmelita Tuckaleechee.

Chigger's mother made two copies of the boy's note so each agency would have a copy, and she personally delivered them to their separate headquarters. The complete note read: *I'm leaving home, maybe for good. Don't try to find me or ask the cops to go looking for me. And don't bother Billy about it. I'm doing this on my own. I am doing something important that is helping humanity.*

"Running away from home isn't a crime," Chief Swimmer told Mrs. Muskrat on the phone. "It is our duty to return a sixteen-year-old to his home if we find him, but we don't have the manpower to mount a search for a voluntary runaway."

"Billy Buckhorn confirmed that Chigger has his satellite phone with him," Deputy Marshal Youngblood told her. "But we've tried calling your son, and the calls never go through. That's unusual for a sat phone. He must be inside a structure that blocks the signal."

In a last-ditch attempt to get help from law enforcement, Chigger's father went to the Cherokee County Sheriff's Office, because Billy Buckhorn's house was located outside the city of Tahlequah but inside the Cherokee County boundaries.

"That Billy Buckhorn knows where my son is, but he won't talk," Sam Muskrat said. "I want you to go arrest him and make him talk!"

"I can't go around arresting people based solely on your hunch," the sheriff replied. "My hands are tied unless you have some evidence that the Buckhorn boy is harboring the runaway or has in some way actively caused, aided, abetted, or encouraged the runaway to leave home."

With no other options available, the Muskrats resorted to doing what they usually did. Chigger's mother argued incessantly with her husband, blaming him for anything and everything that had to do with their current situation. Chigger's father, in turn, retreated into a bottle of whatever alcohol he had on hand and, when that ran out, restocked his supply repeatedly.

Chigger had left any mention of those typical behaviors out of his note, but they were topmost in his mind when he'd fled his home.

FBI agent Jerry Swimmer continued his investigation of the murders at the Angola prison, which included detailed research into the Greenstone Rehabilitation Program. Prisoners that participated in that program did everything from mining the raw serpentine ore from the nearby hills to creating finished pieces of jewelry for sale in the Serpent World store and on the Serpent World website.

And the project had been praised for its innovation and effectiveness by legislators and prison administrators all the way up to Washington, DC. However, during interviews with a few prisoners and prison guards, Swimmer learned that some participants were expected to do "extra" jobs for Mr. Greenstone, whether they liked it or not.

The men who performed these additional chores were expected to do so without asking questions. Otherwise—and this had happened more than once—those men might disappear and never be heard from again.

The men who worked the rehabilitation program got paid for their efforts, but the prison held the funds for them until the day they finished their prison sentence. And they were grateful to have that money to help them start life again after they got out.

But the deaths of Warden Broussard and the front desk guard had spooked everyone at the prison and everyone associated with the prison rehab program. So when Swimmer first began trying to get answers to his questions, no one agreed to speak to him. But after he offered to keep all interviews anonymous, and created a foolproof way of doing that, men began coming forward to talk.

That was when certain rumors came to light—rumors of a secret cave where secret ceremonies were held by some kind of cult. No one seemed to know more than that. No one knew where the cave was located, no one knew what the cult was called, and no one knew who was in the cult.

After these interviews had gone on for several days, and after Swimmer had reviewed all the interview transcripts, the agent decided it was time to interview Mr. Greyson Greenstone himself. The only problem: no one had seen the man since the warden's death.

His administrative assistant had put papers that required Greenstone's signature on the man's desk every afternoon. The following morning, she'd enter his office and find the papers in a neat stack already signed. But when had he come into the office? Sometime in the middle of the night, the assistant assumed. But why? Greyson had always been somewhat mysterious, but now more than ever before.

After reviewing the evidence at hand and reading all the interview transcripts, Swimmer came to a conclusion.

Maybe Raelynn's idea isn't so wacky after all! But how am I going to verify this possibility without sounding wacky myself?

Back in the Cherokee Nation, when Billy learned of Bucky Wachacha's discovery of the dead medicine man and the missing Sky Stone piece, he was thrilled and immediately wanted to check it out for himself. Later in the day, the teen went out-of-body and used his own version of the formula for finding lost objects he'd learned from Bucky.

He was able to access the exact location by focusing his vision on the lost Sky Stone piece, but he was appalled when he arrived at the scene. The Underwater Panther had returned to the medicine man's body to continue its ongoing meal. It was all Billy could do to keep himself from being propelled back to his physical body as he watched the creature gnaw on a leg bone.

It's the very creature that escaped from the Manitou Cave in Alabama!

Looking away from the grisly scene, Billy saw the southern piece of the Sky Stone lying in the dirt only a couple of feet from the body. At last!

We've got to get over there to get that piece before another Night Seer gets ahold of it, but with the creature so close, it will be impossible to grab it.

The following morning, Billy, Lisa, Cecil, and Ethan set out on the five-hundred-mile, nine-hour drive in the archaeology van. Billy brought the sat phone along in case Chigger tried to call.

"My memory ain't what it used to be," Cecil said. "But I think Elmore Proctor's widow said he had a Choctaw apprentice years ago named Willy something—Willy James, I think it was. I wonder if this is that guy."

"That's a good place to start," Ethan said. "When we get to the Mississippi Choctaw reservation, we'll ask for him. Someone's bound to know where he lives—er, lived."

As they drove, Billy's mind kept wandering back to Louisiana and the Three Rivers Mounds, where Chigger was very foolishly trying to investigate the whereabouts of the Sun Priest and his staff and cape.

Chigger showed up at the Chief's Mound to meet Molok at the appointed hour, not knowing what to expect and nervous about what the snake man might want him to do. Before entering the mound, the teen performed the self-protection spell. Then he entered through the side door, as he'd done the night before, and walked into the auditorium, which was dimly lit.

"Ah, right on time, my boy." Molok's voice echoed through the space. "Come on up onstage and take the stairs you'll find at the back."

Chigger followed those directions, finding a set of stairs leading down a couple of levels. Molok was waiting at the bottom. The man stared at him briefly and said, "I can't believe how much you look like him."

"Look like who?"

"Never mind," the man replied as he opened a door that led into a round room. "Follow me."

After taking only two steps into the space, Chigger froze in place. At first, he wasn't sure what he was seeing. The floor seemed to be moving or squirming or writhing. Then he realized why. The floor was covered in snakes!

And they weren't just any snakes. They were all venomous—rattlesnakes, copperheads, and such. Chigger knew this because he'd taken summer wildlife classes given by his tribe. The heads of venomous snakes are triangular-shaped, and all the triangular-shaped heads in the room now looked at him.

Molok walked slowly through the area just as casually as you please. But Chigger continued to stand stock still. Maybe the reptiles would lose interest and look away. Or maybe they would think he wasn't there anymore if he didn't move. He really didn't know what to expect.

To his horror, they began moving toward him! Their little forked tongues flicked as they moved in his direction. Now he was petrified and couldn't make his legs move no matter how hard he tried. But, surprisingly, none of them coiled to strike, or rattled their rattles, or made any threatening moves.

Instead, they seemed to be attracted to him, to perceive him as a friend, slithering gently around his lower legs and rubbing up against his hands like they wanted to be petted.

"That's impressive, boy," Molok said. "They like you, and they don't like most people. They must feel your vibe and approve of your presence. I am surprised."

"No one is more surprised than me," Chigger said, still not moving. "Actually, I'm shocked."

"Well, you've passed the first test," Molok said. "Welcome to my domain! We have a few private dorm rooms in this building if you'd like to stay here."

"Uh, that sounds okay," Chigger replied, though he wasn't sure it sounded okay at all. But he realized that was what needed to happen if he was ever going to locate the Fire Crystal and the concealed Sun Chief. "I've just got a few of my things to move in with me. I can go collect those and come right back."

He opened the door and left the snake room as quickly as possible. Molok followed him out into the hallway.

"Good," the one-eyed man said. "You've come at the right time, because we have a lot of things going on. Plans to make, preparations to complete, and prophecies to fulfill. And you'll be here for the next meeting of the Nine."

"The Nine?" Chigger said. "What's that?"

"Oh, I'll tell you all about it after you get settled in," Molok replied. "Glad you're here, son."

The man abruptly looked away, as if he'd just made a mistake he didn't want to acknowledge. He quickly moved down the hallway.

"See you back here later," he called back as he strode off.

What was that all about? Chigger wondered.

As he drove back to the Sportsman Inn to collect his few belongings, he knew the first thing he needed to do was call Billy on the sat phone. Billy, who was in Mississippi searching for Willy James's house, answered the call on the third ring.

"I'm really glad to hear from you," Billy said.

"I've been inside the Chief's Mound at Three Rivers," Chigger told his friend. "It's hollow, just like you said, and they have a few dorm rooms there. I'm moving into one."

Billy was immediately even more worried for his friend's well-being than he was before. "That sounds very risky," he said. "How'd that happen?"

"I'll fill you in later. I've got to pack and move in."

Billy gave Chigger an update on the search for the Sky Stone piece.

"I met the one-eyed man I dreamed about," Chigger said before ending the call. "He's really into snakes, and his snakes seem to be into me."

"Just be careful and keep in touch," said Billy before the call ended.

After the call, Billy gave his traveling companions an update on Chigger's progress as their van came to the end of a dirt road in the Bogue Chitto neighborhood of the Mississippi Choctaw rez. When he'd seen the Sky Stone piece while out-of-body, Billy had failed to do some additional exploration of the area that might have given him a road name or local landmark. Consequently, it took the group longer to locate the medicine man's house.

"This seems like the right place," Billy said when the van came to a stop. "But before we get out, I want to see if I can sense the location of the Underwater Panther and possibly get into its mind. It worked on the Tlanuwa."

With eyes closed, he mentally probed the surrounding area. The fact that he'd already visited the property while out-of-body helped the process considerably. Try as he might, there was no mental indication that the beast was still around.

What Billy discovered was what seemed like the lingering memory of a recent event. It resembled the experience he'd had when he encountered the ghost of a long-dead Cherokee man along the Trail of Tears.

But instead of the thoughts of a well-spoken historical Native man, this was more of a bundle of bedlam or a whirlwind of chaos, to borrow Chigger's phrase. The mental sphere didn't have a focused core. It was a loose collection of raw cravings, random impressions, and disorganized memories. The Tlanuwa's mind had been far less jumbled and easier to access.

This might be a remnant of the creature's consciousness, Billy thought. *But the beast may have eventually disappeared sometime after the conjurer died.*

"I believe the beast no longer exists," Billy reported. "I think it's safe to go into the backyard now."

"No need to take any chances," Ethan said as he accessed a cabinet in the back of the van. Stored on a secure rack inside the cabinet was a twelve-gauge shotgun. He pulled the gun down from the rack and reached into a box of shells to grab a few. "You never know when you might have to protect yourself on an archaeology dig in the backwoods," he said by way of explanation for why he carried such a weapon.

"Lead the way," Billy told Ethan as the rest of the crew fell in behind the man with the gun.

Around back they found what was left of the medicine man's decaying, mangled body. Lisa suddenly felt sick and turned away from the group. She vomited in the bushes and then backed away from the revolting scene.

In a back corner of the yard, Billy saw a metal cage where the Night Seer had apparently been keeping the beast. Bars on the cage's door had been bent and ripped much like the ones Billy had seen at Manitou Cave. On the ground nearby and inside the cage, various cattle bones were scattered around.

"I guess the thing got hungry and escaped," Billy noted. "The feeding schedule must've been intense."

Circling widely around the corpse on the ground, he headed for the spot he'd seen the Sky Stone piece. He let out the biggest sigh of relief in his life when he found the object still there, half-buried in the soil. He picked it up and scraped the dirt off it.

Billy turned to Cecil. "Where's the rest of the Sky Stone?" he asked. "You didn't bring it with you, did you?"

"No," the elder said. "I didn't want to risk anything happening to it. As a matter of fact, I was worried about it being unprotected at Wesley's house, so I rented a deposit box at the First National Bank in Tahlequah. It's safely tucked away there."

"Sounds perfect," Billy replied as the four of them headed back to the van.

"What do we do about the beast thingy?" Lisa asked. "He might still be out there and could kill someone else."

"In my experience," Cecil replied, "once a conjurer dies from unnatural causes—suicide, murder, or disease—the things he conjured simply cease to exist."

"And what about this man's grotesquely mauled body?" she said. "Don't we have to notify somebody?"

"Of course we do," Billy said, stopping in his tracks.

"Maybe we should find a phone booth and call the Choctaw tribal police," Ethan said as he unloaded the shells from the shotgun. "That way they won't have a cell phone number to link to any of us. We can notify them of the man's death anonymously."

"Good thinking," Cecil said as the team climbed back into the van.

"Spoken like a man who's faced this situation before, Dad," Lisa replied. "Hmm?"

"No comment," Ethan responded.

CHAPTER THIRTEEN

Inner Sanctum

Back at Three Rivers, Chigger had moved into a dorm room inside the Chief's Mound. His Nathan Nighthawk undercover persona seemed to be working just fine. More than just fine, really. It seemed that Molok had accepted the teen into the fold too easily. What was that about? Chig hoped to find out soon.

At ten the following morning, a woman that Chigger had seen before came to his room.

"My name is Layla," she said. "I'm Brother Molok's primary assistant."

"Nice to meet you, Layla," the teen replied. "My name is Chi—Nathan."

He hoped she hadn't noticed his slip of the tongue.

"Nathan, he'd like you to come to the spiral mound in about fifteen minutes," she said. "He wants to introduce you to the Serpentine Foundation's board of directors."

"Uh, okay. That sort of seems like a big deal for someone who just got here."

"It *is* a big deal, so you should wear something nice," Layla said.

"I don't really have anything nice with me," he replied.

"Okay, come with me. I know where there's a closet of clothes just going to waste."

Chigger followed Layla to a higher floor within the mound complex. She entered another dorm room a little larger than the one Chigger was staying in. The walls were decorated with photos and artwork of stone pyramids that he wasn't familiar with.

"Where are these pyramids from?" he asked.

"Those are Aztec and Maya temples, built hundreds and hundreds of years ago in Central America," she replied as she opened the door to a closet in the back of the room. "Brother Molok says those peoples were the original builders of pyramids and mounds."

Inside the closet, Chigger saw a variety of shirts, pants, and jackets hanging on a rack.

"I think you're about the same size, so this stuff should fit you," Layla said. "Pick out something and try it on."

Chigger felt funny about trying on the clothes. "Whose stuff is this?" he asked. "Whose room is this?"

"This room belonged to Molok's son, Tesoro," she replied. "He died suddenly a couple years ago, and Nahash has never gotten over it."

That explains a lot, Chigger thought, but kept it to himself.

"I don't think I should be wearing any of his clothes or even be in his room," Chigger said. "Brother Molok probably wouldn't like it."

"It's all right, Nathan. He's the one who suggested it."

Uh-oh. What have I gotten myself into? Chigger thought. But he said, "Okay, if you say so."

He picked out a bright multicolored shirt that featured a fanciful tree in the center with deep roots. It included several Indigenous designs.

"Good choice," Layla said. "Put it on, and we'll head for the meeting chamber."

As they walked toward the spiral mound, Chigger silently went through the steps to initiate the self-protection shield Billy taught him. He followed the assistant through the ground-level door into the round structure and had to allow his eyes to adjust to the dimly lit space.

As his pupils dilated in the dark, he could feel a palpable pulsating pressure against his whole being. It was the strongest he'd ever experienced and momentarily caused him to falter in his tracks. He quickly regained control of himself and increased the strength of his protective shield.

In a few moments he was able to see the large round table in the center of the room with fancy chairs spaced evenly around it, one of them empty. The men and women seated in the chairs all looked to be Native and wore medallions with some sort of winged creature on them. In front of each place at the table sat what Chigger knew to be an Aztec mirror pulsating with a dim purple glow.

Nine of those dang glowing viewers. How am I ever going to survive this?

"Nathan, come and meet everyone," Molok's voice rang out as he stood up from his seat at the table. When he saw what Chigger was wearing, he said, "Ah, you're wearing my son Tesoro's favorite shirt. That settles it."

Not sure what that comment meant, Chigger tried to smile and seem enthusiastic as he shuffled toward Molok's seat. "Thanks for inviting me here," he said. "I hope I'm not interrupting anything important."

"One of the Nine is running late, so we really haven't started our proceedings yet," the one-eyed man said.

Molok introduced the teen to each person in the circle. They were all Natives from various tribes, and they all had a purple energy vibe. One of the women seemed familiar, but Chigger wasn't sure where he'd seen her before.

"Miguel Coyotl is just returning from Mexico, and we can't start until he shows up," Molok said. "You can meet him later."

Chigger immediately recognized that name from the tour of the Three Rivers Mounds compound a few days before.

I hope that guy doesn't recognize me when he shows up.

"What do you guys talk about in here?" Chigger asked, trying to sound naive and innocent. "It must be something interesting and important." After a pause, he added, "Is it about the take-over? I know it's coming soon."

The statement surprised everyone in the circle.

"Dammit, Molok!" one of the men said. "What have you been telling the boy? No one outside this circle is supposed to hear about our business!"

"The boy was apprenticed to one of Thomas Two Bears's Night Seers," the snake leader said in an authoritative tone. "He's supernaturally tuned in, and he's here as my guest! So watch your mouth."

After Molok calmed down, he looked at Chigger. "Nathan, why don't you go next door to see if you can help with the set-up for tonight's rebirthing ceremony? I'll check in on you later."

Molok pointed to a door on the room's back wall, and Chigger headed for it. Then, suddenly, he hesitated as he remembered Billy's description of that space with its Winged Serpent wall hanging and the ornate slab resembling an Aztec sacrificial altar.

Aware that he was being watched by members of Molok's inner circle, the teen walked briskly through the door. On the other side he found a small team of workers busy preparing for the ceremony. The workers were all men wearing orange jump-suits with the words *Angola State Pen* stenciled on their backs.

The large wall hanging of the Winged Serpent dominated the space, just as Billy had described it. The image presented a frightening specter with its reptilian body, two clawed back feet, and bat-type wings spread wide across the wall.

Those cave drawings we saw are nothing compared to this thing!

Below the wall hanging sat the carved stone sacrificial table, also just as Billy had described it. Chigger thought of the flyer he'd seen on the Serpent World bulletin board about the rebirthing event: *Shed your old skin to be reborn into a new life!* the flyer promised. *Learn how to overcome all obstacles that stand in your way!* That didn't sound like anything that involved human sacrifice. Did it? Not unless the process included skinning someone alive!

Scattered around the room were several large candles, both black and white ones, sitting on fancy candlestick holders, all waiting to be lit. Brass bowls sat on pedestals surrounding the sacrificial table, and inside those bowls was some kind of dried herb. Clusters of purple and green gemstones also decorated the area immediately around the table.

A worker entered from a door in the back wall. He wheeled in a large silver urn and parked it behind the table. Removing the urn's lid, he revealed its contents: some sort of thick red liquid. Was it blood? A second worker wheeled in a glassed-in terrarium filled with writhing snakes, the same container Molok used during his welcoming ceremony.

Again, I ask myself, what have I gotten myself into?

"Can I help you?" a nearby orange-clad worker asked, startling Chigger. The tattoo-covered worker was placing printed programs on nearby chairs.

"Uh . . . Brother Molok sent me to help with the setup," Chigger replied.

"We're pretty much done," the man said. "The show begins at eight tonight. You should come back then. You wouldn't want to miss that."

"What exactly goes on in the rebirthing ceremony?" Chigger asked.

The worker realized that the setup looked rather misleading to an outsider. "People who've been to the welcoming ceremony and signed up to join the temple will *symbolically* die to their old selves and be reborn through ritual and by being washed in the blood," he said.

"Washed in the blood of what?"

"Well, serpents, of course," the man replied, as if it was the most obvious thing. "Snakes that have already shed their skins at least once. It's the final step in the ceremony."

"Oh, I see," Chigger said with both relief and disgust. "But why snakes? Aren't they considered evil—symbolically?"

The worker stopped what he was doing and looked at Chigger. "Man, you've got it all wrong," he said. "Haven't you ever noticed that the most common symbol for doctors and medical personnel is a staff with one or two snakes coiled around it? People used to believe in the healing power of serpents all over the world before they were demonized."

Chigger thought about it for a moment and realized it was true. Ambulances sometimes had blue stars with one or two white snakes wrapped around a pole in the middle. The helicopter that took Billy to the hospital from the bat cave had that symbol painted on the side and bottom.

"Got it," Chigger replied. He turned to leave and called back, "Thanks," to the worker.

Out of the corner of his eye, he saw yet another worker wheeling in a portable wardrobe rack containing several articles of clothing. To the teen's astonishment, hanging on the front of the rack was a feathered cape just like the one he'd seen last fall at the Spiral Mounds Archaeological Site in Oklahoma. Also on the rack, attached to it with some kind of clamp, was a staff fitted with a pinkish-orange crystal on top.

The Sun Chief's missing cape and staff! I have to call Billy!

When he got back to his room inside the Chief's Mound, he tried to call his friend on the sat phone, but the call wouldn't go through.

This building has something in the walls that blocks the signal, he thought.

He considered his options. He wanted to get this information to Billy as soon as possible but didn't want to risk being seen with the sat phone during the day. He decided to wait until after dark to make the call.

About half an hour after Chigger left the rebirthing chamber, Miguel Coyotl returned from his trip to Mexico, where he had acquired a fragile and precious ancient document. It was an Aztec book of spells and formulas written in the Nahuatl language. Sections of the magical work had been passed down orally for generations among the Aztec people.

But Molok needed the full manuscript, because it contained a long-forgotten spell that would be needed when the Thinning of the Veil arrived.

"It is a wonder to behold," Molok said after Coyotl unwrapped the leather-bound volume and laid it on the conference room table. He turned a few of the book's sheepskin pages, careful not to tear the brittle yellowed material. "What about the Spanish-language index?"

Coyotl removed a second volume from his briefcase and laid it next to the first. "This index is what's going to allow us to quickly find the passages of text we need for the incarnation ceremony," the Aztec said. "Otherwise, we might never find the right page in time."

Molok picked up the index and flipped through a few pages. It was a much newer book, published only about a hundred years ago, so he didn't have to be as careful with it. He found what he was looking for.

"Reembody the souls of the dead," the man said, translating the Spanish entry. "This is it! We'll finally be able to incarnate dwellers of the Shadow Zone in the flesh! They'll walk again amongst the living here in the Middleworld!" Molok grabbed Coyotl by the shoulders and shook him in delight. "Good work, my friend," he said with a broad smile as his mind filled with glorious possibilities.

He knew Benjamin Blacksnake and others like him were among the ghosts who lived in a part of the Shadow Zone. And he also knew Benjamin had been preparing to lead an army of them during the Thinning of the Veil that was to come. And it was coming very soon now!

"I hate to burst your bubble right now, Molok," Coyotl said in a serious tone. "But members of the Nine have expressed concern about your new so-called apprentice."

Molok was not pleased by Miguel's change in tone. "Oh yeah? What have those jealous busybodies been saying?"

"That you've let your grief in losing your son get in the way of the business at hand," the Aztec replied. "That you could be jeopardizing our whole operation!"

"That's nonsense!" the snake man replied. "Just drop it, Miguel!"

As the sun was setting over the Three Rivers compound, Chigger put on a hoodie and stuffed the sat phone into one pocket. Outside the Chief's Mound, he walked around as if he were taking a casual stroll. Once he was sure no one was watching, he pulled out the phone and hit the speed dial number for Billy's phone. His friend answered after two rings.

"They're here," Chigger said excitedly in a loud whisper. "The Sun Chief's staff and cape. I just saw them in the spiral mound."

"What? That's incredible!"

"They're being used tonight in some sort of ceremony," Chigger said. "It's what they call a rebirthing ceremony, where a person symbolically dies and is reborn."

"Good work, buddy," Billy replied. "I didn't know you had it in you. Maybe now the FBI will raid the complex to retrieve the artifacts."

"I've got to go," Chigger said. "I don't want anyone seeing me using this phone."

He ended the call and headed toward the door at the back of the Chief's Mound.

"Hold on there," a man's voice said from behind him.

Chigger turned back in time to see Miguel Coyotl coming around the corner of the pyramid mound.

"What are you doing out here?" the Aztec man asked.

"Just taking a walk. I'm headed back to my room in the mound where Brother Molok invited me to stay."

As Coyotl got closer, he showed some recognition on his face. Chigger, on the other hand, had immediately recognized the guide who'd led them on a tour of the site a few days earlier.

"Hey, wait a minute," Coyotl said. "You look a little familiar. Do I know you from somewhere?"

"Don't think so," the teen offered. "I just have one of those familiar-looking faces." He began walking briskly back toward the mound entrance.

"Now I remember!" the man said. "You were the kid who was kind of sick with the archaeologists group. That's it."

"No, you must have me confused with someone else," Chigger said and turned to go.

Coyotl grabbed the boy by the arm and pulled him back. When he did, the sat phone, which was larger and heavier than a cell phone, fell out of the boy's hoodie pocket.

"What's this?" Coyotl asked as he picked up the device. Recognizing what it was, he said, "Who have you been talking to on this thing?"

"Nobody important. Just my buddy back home."

"On a satellite phone? Not likely. You don't come across one of these every day."

The muscular man brusquely escorted the easily controlled scrawny teen toward the spiral mound. As he was whisked along, Chigger got glimpses of ornate Aztec tattoos that adorned Coyotl's neck and forearms. On one arm, a warriorlike face glared menacingly at him with tongue extended. On the other arm, the artful image of a jagged dagger appeared to have one eye. On the side of the man's neck, an intricately designed sun with an intimidating human face stared back.

Once inside the round mound, Coyotl locked the boy in a supply room and headed to Molok, who was preparing for the ceremony in a dressing room behind the rebirthing chamber.

Meanwhile, back in the Cherokee Nation, Billy had quickly called Lisa to report Chigger's discovery, who in turn called Raelynn. That got the investigator's blood pumping, and she texted the breakthrough news to Agent Swimmer.

"You've got somebody on the inside of the Three Rivers property?" Swimmer said when he called the investigator back. "How'd that happen?"

"I just found out about it myself," Raelynn said. "A friend of the Buckhorn and Lookout families took it on himself to infiltrate the organization."

"That was either extremely brave or extremely foolish," Swimmer replied.

"No doubt" was all Little Shield said.

"Well, I may not be able to get a search warrant until tomorrow afternoon, so I hope the boy is all right until then."

"Me too," Raelynn echoed. "In the meantime, we have to get back down there so we're ready when the warrant comes through."

As the two investigators got off the call, each felt like this was the breakthrough their case needed. And it had come thanks to the reckless actions of a naive teenager who now needed to be rescued. Could they get there in time to save him?

Chigger sat in that dark closet for quite a long while as he waited for Coyotl or Molok to come fetch him. And then who knew what would happen next? Probably nothing good.

After leaving the boy in the closet, Coyotl had marched back to the Chief's Mound and located Chigger's room. He turned the place upside down until he found the boy's Oklahoma driver's license. *Charles Checotah Muskrat,* the plastic ID read.

"Greenstone, you fool!" Coyotl barked loudly as if Snake-Eye, who was in the spiral mound, could hear him.

The Aztec immediately headed to confront the snake leader.

"Here's proof you've been duped!" the Aztec blurted out as he burst into the man's dressing room.

"That's just not possible!" Molok replied as he glared at the intruder. "The boy's energy field is definitely aligned with the Underworld."

Snake-Eye's eye patch lay on the dressing table, leaving his empty eye socket exposed.

Coyotl thrust Chigger's ID toward Molok, who took it and examined the license closely, noting the boy's real name.

"He was part of that archaeology team I showed around not long ago," Coyotl explained. "I remembered him because he was acting kind of funny that day—like he was sick or something."

Molok was stunned. How could he have been so foolish?

"You let your longing for your dead son cloud your judgment!" Coyotl said. "No telling who the boy told about what goes on behind closed doors here."

Molok thought for a moment, recalling his interactions with Chigger. "I don't think he actually saw anything that was incriminating," he replied with relief. "He doesn't know anything about the secret cave or details of our future plans."

The one-eyed man thought about how he'd misjudged the situation and grew angry.

"He took advantage of my grief," he said, throwing the blame on the boy. "And you're right. We don't know what he told outsiders."

Molok made a quick decision.

"Cancel tonight's public ceremony and bring the boy to the rebirthing chamber," the sorcerer said. "Tie him down to the rebirthing table good and tight!"

Five hundred miles to the northwest, Billy was having a conversation with Lisa on the living room couch about the circumstances at Three Rivers when he felt a sudden *ping* in the middle of his being.

"Chigger's in trouble!" he said as he sat up straight and searched inwardly for more details.

"What kind of trouble?" Lisa asked.

"The kind of trouble we can't wait for the FBI to investigate— the kind of trouble we always knew he might have when he ran off to infiltrate Serpent World!"

"What can we do?" she asked.

"The fastest thing is to spirit travel to check on him. After that we can figure out next steps."

Lisa stood up and grabbed her boyfriend's hand. "Let's go," she said. "Right now!"

The couple ran to Billy's bedroom and jumped into bed— not to do what most teenagers might think of, but to leave their physical bodies behind.

The pair easily rolled out and then up through the rooftop. Linking their energy fields together, Billy led the way farther upward and then southward across the landscape. With Chigger's image firmly planted in his mind, they were whisked directly into Molok's ceremonial rebirthing chamber.

Not wanting to alert the snake man to their presence, Billy and Lisa hovered near the ceiling of the half dome. Chigger was tied down on a table and seemed to be unconscious. No one else was visible within the space.

Billy communicated to Lisa that she should stay put while he moved closer to investigate. She did as he asked, though she wasn't happy about it. Billy zoomed down close enough to touch his friend on the face, hoping the cold sensation would wake him. It didn't. Then he spoke into Chigger's ear, but that, too, failed to produce a response.

Finally, he tried thrusting his spirit hand into Chigger's brain. Nothing.

Two male voices could be heard coming from behind the stage area, so Billy immediately returned to his position up near Lisa. From there, the pair could hear the men's conversation quite well as they approached Chigger.

"Thomas Two Bears confirmed everything I've been telling you," one man said.

Billy and Lisa recognized the speaker as Miguel Coyotl, the one who gave them the tour of the Three Rivers Mounds and the one Reverend Miller sold the Sun Chief's remains to.

"He probably stole the Night Seer pendant from Tuckaleechee, along with her Aztec mirror," Coyotl continued. "And, according to Two Bears, he's best friends with that Thunder Child kid we've heard about."

"I don't know how I could be so gullible," the man with the eye patch replied, shaking his head. "I really let my guard down. But he looks and sounds so much like Tesoro."

The two approached Chigger lying on the slab as Molok thought about what to do. Then an idea suddenly came to him.

"I think I know a way to kill two birds with one stone," he said with a sly smile. "And you, my friend, have just supplied me with the means of pulling it off with that new sorcerer's manuscript you brought."

He grabbed a fistful of Chigger's hair, raised his head off the slab, and spoke to the boy as if he could hear him. "Let's see if the souls of you and your buddy can survive the mountains of Xibalba!"

Molok released his grip on Chigger's hair, and his head hit the slab with a thud.

The snake man turned to his Aztec comrade. "When that Thunder Child character discovers his friend's soul has been cast down, he'll no doubt rush to the rescue."

"No one escapes the grasp of the dark abyss without the help of an Underworld dweller, so both of these troublemakers are doomed!" Coyotl declared.

Then the two men quickly left the chamber.

Billy signaled Lisa it was time to leave, but the girl was not ready to go.

We should try to revive Chigger," she told Billy. "We've got to get him out of here."

"The eye-patch guy must've cast some kind of sleep spell on him," Billy replied. "Nothing's going to wake him up."

"What did he mean about surviving Xibalba?"

"That's what the Maya Indians call the nine levels of the Underworld," Billy said. "I'll explain later. For now, we've got to get back home."

Without further delay, Billy enveloped Lisa in an energy bubble and dragged her with him back home. Back in his body, Billy jumped out of bed. Once Lisa was reconnected to her physical self, he took hold of her shoulders and looked into her eyes.

"I'm sorry," he said heatedly, "But I've got to figure out how to rescue Chigger's soul, and I've got to do it now. Let your dad know what's going on. You and he may be able to motivate Rae-lynn and the FBI to act sooner rather than later."

Mentally, Lisa released her objections and agreed to follow Billy's wishes. She knew he was now acting as Thunder Child. He needed to do what he needed to do, and she needed to do what he asked of her.

"May Waconda go with you," she said, kissed him on the cheek, and headed out the door.

Billy made a quick call to Cecil, who answered after the first ring.

"I need that password now," the teen said.

"What's happened?" the elder asked.

"A group worse than the Night Seers has Chigger, and they're about to cast his soul down to one of the Underworld's lowest levels," Billy said, aware that this statement sounded totally insane. "If they haven't already."

That news shocked Cecil to the core. "The password is *Thatiyay Dopa*," he said. "It's a phrase, really, that the Trustees of the Scroll were told to use to get across the River of Fear."

"*Thatiyay Dopa*," Billy repeated. "Do you know what it means or where it comes from?"

"It's in the Lakota language, which is similar to Osage, and means Four Winds." He paused before continuing. "You're going, aren't you? Down to rescue him?"

"Yeah."

"Someone—Lisa or I—should monitor your body while you're gone in case you're the one who needs rescuing."

"Probably wouldn't hurt," Billy said. "Whoever it is should get over here as soon as possible, because I'm going now."

"How will you begin the journey?"

"Hopefully through the Aztec mirror. Blacksnake's medicine book hints that the mirror is not only a viewer but also a portal. I've been successful in activating its mirror mode, so now I'll try to activate it as a portal."

"Remember to travel as Thunder Child, representative of the Upperworld, not as Billy the Cherokee teen. And use the powers the Medicine Council taught you," Cecil said. "They could be useful down there."

"I'll try to remember that," Billy said and then added, "See you later—I hope," before he ended the call.

CHAPTER FOURTEEN

Deep Dive

Sitting down at the desk in his bedroom, Billy followed the steps he'd used before to activate the Aztec mirror. Within a few seconds, the mirror's black surface had morphed into the viewing mode, and the gray fog became visible. Then he executed the extra step suggested in the medicine book for converting the mirror from viewer to portal.

"*Mee-keetz Kah-lah-co-hu-ah-yan,*" he said aloud, speaking the Nahuatl words for "doorway to death," which were hand-written on the page about the black mirror.

The mirror's hard obsidian surface quickly transformed into some sort of thick black liquid. Even though the mirror stood on its stand at about a forty-five-degree angle, the liquid remained within the mirror's edges and didn't spill out onto the desk.

Completely unsure about the wisdom of proceeding, the teen lay down on his bed and tried to relax.

"Dammit, Chigger!" he said aloud. "Look what you're making me do!"

The urgency and uncertainty of the situation interfered with the process a little, but he eventually rolled out of his physical body. In his spirit body, he propelled himself to the obsidian mirror but realized he was too large to squeeze through the twelve-inch portal.

Concentrating intensely for a moment, he shrank himself down to about one-fourth of his normal size.

Thanks for that lesson, Lisa.

Cautiously propelling himself forward, Billy moved into and through the liquid, which proved to be only a thin, undulating membrane. Once through, he was surrounded by the gray fog he'd experienced before. Remaining still, he patiently waited for the fog to dissipate, and as he did, he caught a glimpse of his own spirit hand. It glowed! Then he looked at his other hand. It glowed as well! He looked down and saw that his whole energy body glowed. He felt like a glow-in-the-dark stick at Halloween!

But the fog finally disappeared, and a dense, dark forest came into view, which Billy knew was the Forest of Dread. It wasn't all that different from the woods surrounding Carmelita Tuckaleechee's place.

He remembered the pack of ghost wolves that guarded the forest, and prepared himself for a possible attack. He kept still and quiet, listening for the threatening patter of paws to come his way. He hoped they wouldn't notice him, forgetting that he glowed from head to foot.

He really didn't have time to think about it though, because he soon heard them approaching from three different directions, emerging from behind moss-covered trees. There were five of them, growling as they crept toward him.

That was when he remembered he was glowing.

No wonder they found me so fast!

The beasts fanned out, forming a semicircle that gradually closed in on him. His first thought was to simply perform a stretch-zoom, as he'd done many times when traveling out-of-body. He was sadly disappointed when this maneuver failed to work. He'd also forgotten about the denseness of the lower regions. It almost felt like he was in his physical body again.

Like moving through molasses!

Then a solution popped into his mind: the spell for temporarily blinding an enemy he'd learned from Lillian, the Alaskan medicine woman. He quickly spoke the spell in the Tlingit language four times while concentrating on the result he wanted. Then, thrusting his hands forward and spreading them out across the faces of the wolves, he cast the spell on all five of the snarling beasts.

Each of the animals stopped right where it stood and tried to blink away the blindness, growling and yipping as if a blanket had been thrown over its face. In the confusion, Billy was able to slip past the pack and into the gloomy forest behind them.

He realized his glow was going to be a continuing problem, and stopped to see if he could turn the brightness level down. The first time he'd met Morningstar, the being was too bright and had dimmed his own brightness.

Now Thunder Child focused on feeling his own spirit body and imagined he had a dimmer control knob in his mind. Mentally he turned the knob in a counterclockwise direction. As he did, he sensed that his own brightness level was diminishing.

It worked!

As he slogged farther into the forest, he became aware of the sound of rushing water in the distance.

The River of Fear!

He kept moving in that direction and, with much effort, reached the river's edge. The dark, choppy waters splashed and crashed violently against the shoreline. Peering through the purplish mist that hung over the water, Billy searched for the Pullman that Cecil had described.

A burning torch first came into view, and soon afterward, the bow of a canoe. A red skeleton wearing a Plains Indian feathered headdress paddled the craft toward Billy.

There's the Pullman, right on cue.

"Who is it that wants to cross the River of Fear?" the skeleton asked in a threatening tone.

"Billy Buckhorn of the Cherokee Nation," the teen replied. "I have to—"

"Be gone with you, mortal child," the Pullman replied authoritatively. "You have no place in these regions."

The skeleton began pushing his canoe away from shore. But when he had spoken the word *child*, Billy remembered who he really was and what the passphrase was.

He gathered his strength and spoke in a more commanding tone. *"Thatiyay Dopa!"*

The Pullman stopped moving away from shore and slapped the water with his paddle. "By what right do you utter that name at this river's edge!" he demanded.

"I am Thunder Child, spirit warrior of the Upperworld! I instruct you to carry me across the river!"

Before taking any action, the Pullman looked back across the water toward the opposite shore. Thunder Child followed his gaze to the other side, where four tall, dark figures were just emerging from the murky purple darkness. They soon arrived on the far riverbank and stood shoulder to shoulder. Their hooded black robes fluttered and flapped as though perpetual winds surrounded them. Their appearance, apparently, told the skeleton all he needed to know.

"I am at your service, Thunder Child," he said in a more cooperative tone of voice. "It has been so very long since someone of your stature has asked me to pull for them."

The skeleton quickly carried his passenger across the choppy waters, directly toward the four dark shapes waiting on the other side, and deposited him at the edge of the Shadow Zone. Then, sounding much like wind blowing through trees, the voices of the Four Shadows spoke in unison, as the voices of the ancestors had done during the shaking tent ceremony.

"This is unexpected, Thunder Child," they whispered. "What dire circumstances have brought you to such dangerous regions?"

He told them of his quest to rescue the soul of his best friend from somewhere in the lower levels. Upon hearing that explanation, the four proceeded to heatedly discuss the situation in what sounded mostly like blasts of air. When all opinions had been expressed, debated, and exhausted, the foursome turned to Thunder Child.

"There is only one who can safely escort you in these regions," their unified voice said. "We have called him, and even now he approaches."

A figure about the same size as Thunder Child approached from the same direction the Four Shadows had come.

"Who is it?"

"Your shadow self," the voices replied.

"Huh?" Billy said.

Just then the silhouette of a person came into view. It was the very likeness of Billy Buckhorn, but somehow reversed. Not like looking in a mirror, but a mirror image just the same. But this version *felt* different.

"The shadow self is made up of parts of you that you don't necessarily like or acknowledge," the voices said. "The negative things you pretend don't exist but are really just hidden away."

Thunder Child did not get the concept at all.

"Just as your physical body casts a visible shadow, your spirit body casts an almost invisible nonphysical shadow."

Thunder Child walked around to get a view of his shadow self from a different angle. But the figure didn't seem to really have another side.

"If you've ever had a nightmare where someone is chasing you, but you don't know who it is, that's your shadow self."

"Why does he chase me?"

"Usually to give you a message, but like most people in their dreams, you never stop to find out what your shadow wants to tell you, because you don't want to hear what he has to say."

"My friend's soul is trapped somewhere down here in the mountains, so I don't have time to try to understand this," Billy said impatiently.

"Your shadow self knows his way around here and moves fast, so you'll have to try and keep up," the voices said as they began to recede into the murkiness.

"We need to steer clear of Blacksnake and Tuckaleechee," the shadow self said in a voice that sounded older and gruffer than Billy's regular voice. "Both of them hate your guts."

"I get that," Thunder Child replied. "How do we avoid them?"

"First you've got to adapt yourself," the shadow said. "Don't try to control the glow with a dimmer. Turn it off or reverse it. It'll be easier for you to move around down here, and make you harder to see."

Thunder Child experimented with that idea until he could feel the actual change.

"Good for a beginner," the shadow said. "Now stay close to me, but never touch. That would be like matter and antimatter colliding. We'd both implode."

"I still don't get this," Thunder Child replied as the shadow turned away to begin their journey.

The Shadow Zone was not like Thunder Child had pictured it. Instead of the clusters of trees that occupied the Forest of Dread, this level seemed to be made up mostly of dilapidated old buildings. Some resembled Greek and Roman ruins. Others seemed Egyptian or Middle Eastern. Still other areas reflected a variety of diverse regions of the Middleworld, including Native American.

But it was all black and white and shades of gray. No color.

"The Shadow Zone is divided into sublevels," the Buckhorn shadow said as they began to move. "The topmost level is filled with shadow selves like me. Another area is inhabited by souls who allowed their weaknesses, cravings, and bad habits to rule their lives on earth. Selfishness, greed, envy, gluttony, rage, and the like all have their own little subzones."

"Wait. That sounds like the sins that preachers talk about," Thunder Child said. "Did those people get judged and condemned to spend eternity there?"

"No, they put themselves there—it's a cause-and-effect sort of thing."

"That makes sense. What about the other parts of the Shadow Zone?"

"Predatory souls—the ones that exploited and preyed on others—end up clustered together. Coming from different earth cultures, they're drawn to each other in little communities. Unfortunately, one of the Native American areas is close to the tunnel we need to take to get to the next level down."

"Why is that unfortunate?" Thunder Child asked.

"Because that's where Blacksnake and Tuckaleechee hang out, so we have to move quickly and calmly." Pointing with his lips, the shadow self indicated the direction they needed to go. "The tunnel down to the next level is this way," he said and moved out quickly.

Thunder Child was pleased to find he could now move more easily since he'd altered his outgoing energy level. His shadow self zoomed away from the old buildings toward a region filled with grassy, rolling hills. Thunder Child had to move fast to keep up.

They reached the tunnel with little difficulty, and the shadow self immediately entered the opening, which resembled a mine entrance with a downward tilt. After a couple of minutes, the pair emerged from the shaft into another, totally different environment.

"This must be the Negative Afterworld Belief Zone," Thunder Child said as he surveyed the vast desert spread out before him, "where the House of Bones and Valley of Stalking Skeletons are." What he hadn't noticed when he was trapped in the skeleton prison was that the whole region was infused with a purplish color.

"The deeper we go, the more purple things get," his shadow said, acknowledging Thunder Child's thoughts. "Again, we gotta move quickly so we don't attract attention."

But as soon as they stepped out of the tunnel, the sound of rattling bones came from somewhere near them. The unexpected but familiar sound startled Thunder Child, and his energy field momentarily glowed. It was immediately noticed by a dozen or so skeleton people.

Moving like a horde of hungry zombies, the skeletons marched toward the pair. Rather than run, the shadow surprisingly charged straight at them. Thunder Child watched in shock as the dark version of himself transformed into a large black ball. Within seconds, the ball rolled into the tightly packed cluster of walking bones, breaking them into harmless scattered piles.

"That racket is bound to attract more," the shadow self said.

Thunder Child readjusted his energy field, and the pair moved on. Keeping to the fringes of the desert landscape, they remained close to the cliff walls that enclosed the valley space. Soon they came to a cave that looked every bit like the lower part of the bat cave, as Chigger had dubbed it.

"Stay low to the ground so the bats won't notice us," Thunder Child's Underworld guide instructed. "If they find you, they could trap you down here."

"I have so many questions about this," Thunder Child said.

"No time now."

The shadow shrank himself to half his size, and Thunder Child did the same. Rather than race through the cave, the pair had to move slowly through a cavernous space that was filled with hundreds of the black aerial mammals hanging from the ceiling. Just before reaching the far side, the Buckhorn shadow stopped and transformed back to his original size.

"To get past the Scorpion Queen in the Territories of Torment, we have to fly," he said.

"Why is that?"

"Scorpions, fire ants, and venomous tarantulas cover every square inch of the ground and walls."

"That's not creepy at all."

When the two reached the lower cave opening, they found the ground just beyond it teeming with active crawling insects.

"Time to fly," the Buckhorn shadow said.

Thunder Child activated his stretch-zoom move, not sure how well it would work with him in his modified energy mode. When it proved successful, and he was airborne, he followed his shadow self as closely as possible.

The Scorpion Queen was too busy eating a tarantula leg by leg to notice the two humanlike figures passing overhead. Each of her scorpion underlings stationed nearby held a human soul between their front pincers as they repeatedly stung their captive with their venomous tails.

Horrible, horrible, horrible! Thunder Child thought, forgetting that thinking thoughts was the same as talking out loud in nonphysical realms.

This drew the immediate attention of the queen. She dropped her meal and scurried after the two intruders, moving almost as fast as they flew. Flying close behind his shadow self, Thunder Child looked ahead for an opening in what appeared to be a solid rock wall. Was there an exit? He couldn't see one.

"You have to make your own exit," the shadow said. "Think *Hole in the wall*, and one will appear. Then dive into it."

A few seconds later, the shadow appeared to dive straight into the solid rock as a small opening quickly appeared and just as quickly disappeared.

"Here goes nothing," Thunder Child said as he pictured a hole just a little larger than himself.

Surprised and grateful, he jumped through the opening that appeared and then closed behind him. He found his shadow self waiting on the other side, standing at the edge of a slippery slope made of glassy black obsidian.

"Onward and downward," he said.

The slope landed them in the Pit of Bitter Wind, home to the brother and sister spirits known as Disease and Despair. Their twin lodges were piled high with the mangled spirit bodies of people. These, again, were the souls of those who believed it was their Underworld destiny to arrive here and remain here forever.

"The fear of death is such a powerful force," the shadow said. "That vibrational energy brings you directly here."

"The opposite of the love of life," Thunder Child responded.

Those words, expressing the positive energy he felt to his core, repelled him from the setting and catapulted Thunder Child and his shadow self beyond the sixth level. They arrived at the base of a mountain range.

"Good," the shadow said. "We've finally reached the Nightmare Mountains. In your mind's eye, can you see your friend here?"

Thunder Child pictured Chigger in his mind. Suddenly, the memory of the dream he'd had the morning of March 20 sprang into view. There was Chigger, trapped in a nest on top of a mountain.

"He's on a mountaintop," he said. "I saw this in a dream!"

"Let's go!" the shadow said.

As the pair soared upward, Thunder Child could feel intense heat coming from somewhere not too far away. Then he remembered the Nightmare Mountains *overlooked* the Lake of

Fire. It was sad to think there were countless souls burning in there due to their own beliefs!

Nothing he could do about that now. He had a mission to complete!

He and his shadow self reached the mountain peak and found Chigger's energy body lying unconscious in a small round crater—and it had a distinct purplish glow, which immediately alarmed Thunder Child.

Then he noticed something else. The indentation in the rock where Chigger lay kind of looked like a bird's nest, but it wasn't. And there was no bird circling above or snakes climbing from below.

In my dream, those must've represented the Owl Clan and the Serpent Society.

"No time for philosophy now," the shadow self said. "Things worse than owls or snakes are probably looking for us as we speak."

"Do we have to go back up through the levels to get to Chigger's physical body?" Thunder Child asked.

"Not at all," his shadow replied. "Lift him up out of the crater and picture his physical body in your mind. Then do your stretch-zoom thing, and you'll be there in no time."

Before doing anything, Thunder Child had to ask a question that had been haunting him since he and his shadow first met. "So, when the Underworld takeover launches, will you and I be fighting against one another?"

"I was wondering if you'd ever ask that question. If you psychologically accept me and incorporate me into your total self, you and I will be fighting as one, against a common enemy."

Suddenly a very loud roar coming from some unknown beast echoed through the smoky atmosphere.

"That would be coming from the Lair of Banished Beasts in Level Eight below us," the Shadow said. "That's your cue to get going."

Thunder Child stepped into the crater and picked up Chigger. He looked at his shadow self one last time, nodded a farewell, and then took off.

Seconds later, he and Chigger were floating above the Muskrat's physical body where it lay tied to the ceremonial slab in the inner chamber of the Three Rivers spiral mound.

Still there, my friend, Thunder Child thought. *Hope you're still alive.*

He drifted down to the physical body and deposited the spirit body into it. Thankfully, when the two merged, the physical body began to stir and awaken. Thunder Child was thoroughly relieved. But the boy's human form now emitted a powerful purple aura as well.

Weakly, Chigger tried to sit up, but quickly realized he was tied down. Fumbling with the knots, he eventually freed himself. However, when the teen first tried standing, his legs collapsed beneath him.

Whoa, steady as she goes, Thunder Child thought. *Wait till you get your land legs back.*

"Who said that?" Chigger asked as he looked around the empty room. "Who's there?"

You heard that?

"Of course I did," the teen replied. "As plain as day."

Chigger, it's me—Thunder Child. You know: Billy. I just brought you back from Level Seven of the Underworld.

Chigger was understandably confused. He sat back down on the slab.

"You did what to who from where? What exactly is happening?"

We'll talk later. Right now, you need to get out of here. You might still be in danger.

Then, just as Chigger was remembering what had happened before he blacked out, the door to the chamber burst open, and a half dozen men and women holding guns and wearing FBI

CHAPTER FOURTEEN

jackets flooded in. They fanned out and began searching every square inch of the space.

Behind them came a Native man, accompanied by a Native woman. Both were professionally dressed in business attire. As the pair walked toward Chigger, the woman held up a photo they both looked at.

"That's him," she said to the man. "What a relief!"

"Are you Charles Checotah Muskrat?" the man asked when they reached Chigger.

"Yeah, who wants to know?" the teen answered as he tried to stand again.

"I'm FBI agent Jerry Swimmer, and this is Investigator Raelynn Little Shield." Swimmer grabbed Chigger's arm to help hold him up. "Did you realize you were infiltrating an organization run by our primary prison murder suspect?"

Chigger gulped. "No," he said sheepishly.

"Do you have any idea where everyone is?" Raelynn asked.

"What do you mean?" Chigger replied, looking around the room.

"The whole Three Rivers compound seems to have been abandoned," Swimmer said. "There's no one in any of the buildings. The Serpent World tourist trap is closed, and all the exhibit animals are gone."

"You called and told Billy you saw the Sun Chief's cape and staff," Raelynn reminded the teen.

"Oh yeah," he replied. Chigger searched his memory bank for more useful bits and pieces. "Just before the one-eyed snake guy put me out, I remember hearing him say something. What was it?" He rubbed his forehead and took a deep breath.

"Maybe we should have you see a doctor to make sure you're all right," Raelynn said.

"Yeah, yeah, yeah—we'll take care of that in a minute," Swimmer said impatiently. "Who is this one-eyed snake guy?"

"Brother Nahash Molok," Chigger said, trying to shake off lingering grogginess. "Oh, you don't know, do you?"

"Know what?"

"Nahash Molok and Greyson Greenstone are the same person."

Swimmer was speechless as Little Shield began to gloat a little.

"I was right!" she said, looking at Swimmer with a smile. "Not so wacky after all."

"I don't—"

"Retreat to the cave!" Chigger blurted out. "That's it. Retreat to the cave. That's what Molok told Coyotl."

Thunder Child watched as the FBI arrived on the scene, and he floated up and out of the spiral mound. His own quick aerial survey of the mound complex told him the place really had been abandoned, so he rejoined his physical body back in Park Hill. After opening his physical eyes, he saw that Lisa was asleep in the bed next to him. He nudged her, and she woke up.

"Strange changes are afoot," he said as she opened her eyes and looked at him.

"I can't put my finger on it, but something about you is different," she said. "You were a sixteen-year-old when I lay down beside you. Now you seem much older. Not how you look, but how you . . . feel."

"What are you talking about?" her boyfriend asked.

He jumped up and looked at himself in a mirror. Nothing seemed different—at first. But when he looked more closely, he did see something. Was it his eyes? They seemed deeper, older.

"It's an optical illusion," Billy said, dismissing the whole thing. "Come on, we have work to do."

The couple headed upstairs to the War Room.

Back at Three Rivers, Chigger was released by the FBI after explaining in detail what he'd seen, heard, and experienced there over the past few days. Then he gathered all his belongings from the dorm room, climbed into his pickup, and headed for home.

During the drive, he took stock of himself and what he'd been through over the past few months. He came to several conclusions, one of which was that he needed to get better at thinking things through before jumping into situations. The second was that he indeed could take care of himself if he had to, and the third was confirmation that he'd never abandon Billy Buckhorn no matter what.

By the time he arrived home, he knew exactly what he'd say to his parents in his own defense when they began scolding, punishing, and grounding him for running off. Much to his surprise, he didn't have to say or do anything when he reached his front door, because the Buckhorn and Lookout families had already paid a visit to Sam and Molly Muskrat.

Billy, who somehow seemed different, had spun a tale that began with a lightning strike last September during the Labor Day weekend. The other two Buckhorns had filled in certain gaps and validated some of the more unbelievable details of the story.

Then all three Lookouts had shared their perspectives, which included the thousand-year-old prophecy and Billy's part in that cosmic story. Finally, they'd explained how their son, Chigger, had played such a vital role in the latest chapter of the unfolding saga.

CHAPTER FIFTEEN

End Times

E arth Day falls on April 22 every year, and that was the date Billy chose to hold a gathering that would bring together all the players, and potential players, in the campaign to prevent the Underworld takeover of the Middleworld.

After his visit with the Muskrat family, a flash of insight—from what source he wasn't sure—told him it was time for more revelations. Time for what was hidden to be seen by more people. Time for what was concealed to be divulged to the world at large.

So, with the help of his parents and the Lookout family, he planned a gathering and invited everyone who'd witnessed and could validate previous supernatural events in his life, along with other people who would probably be impacted by the up-coming ones.

The place he chose to hold the gathering was the abandoned Tsa-La-Gi Amphitheater located on the grounds of the Chero-kee Heritage Center less than a mile from his own house. The outdoor theater had been the site of hundreds of sold-out performances of the *Trail of Tears* dramatic play that reenacted portions of Cherokee history.

After permission had been obtained from the Cherokee Nation administration, preparations for the gathering included a cleanup of the seating area and the cutting down of trees and shrubs that had taken over the stage area. The tribe also donated the services of its maintenance and landscaping staff to help with the preparations.

From concept to implementation, the whole thing came together in an incredibly short time. Invited guests began arriving an hour before the event's twelve noon start time. That was good, because Billy wanted to have time to greet and interact with people, some of whom weren't sure why they were even there.

At a few minutes past noon, Cherokee medicine woman Wilma Wohali stepped onto center stage and looked up at the one hundred or so people scattered among the seats of the semicircular amphitheater. She saw the Buckhorn, Lookout, and Muskrat families, members of the Tahlequah Police Department, the high school principal, and a school bus driver.

Medical doctors and nurses, US marshals, a Cherokee preacher, a college archaeology professor, a night watchman, a DOI investigator, and an FBI agent were also there. A handful of reporters from area newspapers and broadcast media were also present.

"*Osiyo,*" Wohali said and proceeded to welcome everyone in both English and Cherokee. Then she offered a traditional prayer in the Cherokee language before returning to her seat in the front row, a row that included the twelve other members of the Intertribal Medicine Council, who'd been invited to attend.

Next, Lisa and her father, Ethan, stepped onto the stage area carrying a large banner that had been rolled up on a spool. Lisa attached the free end of the banner to a flagpole that stood on the left side of the stage. Ethan then unfurled the banner and stretched it across the width of the stage, attaching the other end to a second flagpole.

Displayed along the length of the banner was a timeline that started with last September's Labor Day weekend on the left and ended on the near future date of June 21, summer solstice, on the right. People in the audience studied the image, but most didn't understand what it meant.

Billy took the stage and began his explanations.

"We're here today to share secrets and issue warnings," he said. "Most of you know me as Billy Buckhorn, grandson of Awinita and Wesley Buckhorn and son of James and Rebecca Buckhorn. But a very ancient and for the most part unknown organization called the Intertribal Medicine Council declared that I was the one chosen to fulfill a thousand-year-old tribal prophecy, giving me the warrior name Thunder Child."

That bit of news set off a round of murmurs from the crowd.

"Many of you in the audience are here because you witnessed recent events in my life," he continued. "I ask you to simply share with everyone else what you saw and heard, even though at the time we decided not to. We'll start with Dr. Jackson, who was my medical doctor back in September."

Then, one by one, members of the audience came forward to share what they'd personally seen. Dr. Jackson explained how a lightning strike on the lake had created the weblike scars on Billy's neck and hand. Mr. Sixkiller, the Tahlequah High School principal, testified to the dangerous actions of a fake gym teacher who was really a shape-changing Raven Stalker attacking students.

Police Chief Swimmer revealed what he and several of his officers had seen with their own eyes as they shot a giant raven that was about to kill a female student, and then the creature morphed into an old man before dissolving into a pile of ashes.

Deputy US Marshal Travis Youngblood told of the panicked satellite phone call he'd received from Charles Checotah Muskrat, who reported the mortal bat attack on his friend after they entered the crystal cave on the Arkansas River.

Next, nurse Rebecca Buckhorn tearfully shared how she'd felt when ER doctors pronounced her son dead after the Life Flight helicopter brought him to the hospital. The relief she'd experienced next was evident in her voice as she then recounted his surprising and miraculous recovery.

Chigger's mother, Molly Muskrat, revealed the horrendous sequence of events their family had experienced as a result of their son's attachment to the strange purple crystal he'd brought home from that cave near the river.

Archaeology professor Augustus Stevens began the next chapter of the story, relaying that at first he couldn't believe what he saw. But after the mythological Cherokee creature known as the Uktena, the Horned Serpent, physically attacked him, he had to admit it was real.

His testimony was followed by that of the night watchman at Spiral Mounds State Park who was temporarily blinded by a large creature with reptilian eyes. The creature had damaged portions of the mound that held the bones and burial items belonging to a historical figure known as the Sun Chief, a distant ancestor of the Lookout family.

Then, for the first time, elder Cecil Lookout repeated publicly a portion of the tribal prophecy that foretold the events that were now unfolding, and how the ITMC had arrived at the conclusion that Billy Buckhorn was indeed the Chosen One.

Lisa Lookout described how she was attacked by a pack of wolves in the wildlife refuge south of Tahlequah and was then rescued by Billy, who was traveling out-of-body at the time. She went on to reveal details of the actions of Carmelita Tuckaleechee, who drugged and kidnapped her.

James Buckhorn told how the same Cherokee witch, a member of the Night Seers of the Owl Clan, had orchestrated the murder of his father by means of evil medicine.

Near the end of the presentation, Chigger nervously stood onstage to recount the things he'd witnessed as Billy's oldest friend, along with his recent successful efforts to sneak inside the headquarters of the Serpent Society.

Finally, FBI agent Jerry Swimmer and Investigator Raelynn Little Shield reported on their joint investigation, which included the murder of the Angola prison officials. That investigation was tied to their attempts to locate and recover human remains and burial artifacts belonging to the Lookout family.

As the full incredible story neared a conclusion, Rebecca's preacher brother, John, came to the stage. Most of what was being shared this day was news to him, and he was shocked by it all, to say the least.

"I am astonished and humbled by what I've heard so far here today," the preacher said. "I spent many years criticizing and condemning the beliefs and practices of the Buckhorn family, but that is no more."

He paused as he looked into the faces of those listening to him.

"In the past I wouldn't have hesitated to take advantage of this opportunity to preach hellfire and brimstone at you all," he said. "But, thanks to my nephew, I'm a changed man. So instead, I'm here today to bear witness to the truth of the words spoken by all these people. I'm here today to implore you to heed their words and follow their warnings. I truly believe we're in the Latter Days spoken of in the Bible. We are verily facing the End Times!"

No one spoke or even moved as the preacher returned to his seat. Before taking the stage again, Billy walked over to his uncle, shook his hand, and thanked him for his words.

"I want to thank my uncle John for his comments," the teen said as he returned to the stage. "Now, to the reason I wanted you to hear about events of the recent past. The point was to prepare you for the next part of today's presentation."

Many whispering voices in the audience began speculating about what was coming next.

"For maybe the first time in my life, I agree with my uncle the preacher," he said. "The time has come to issue the warnings I spoke of earlier—warnings you need to take seriously."

That quieted all the whispers.

"Between now and the summer solstice, the combined efforts of the Owl Clan and the Serpent Society will bring forth the worst the Underworld has to offer," he continued. "Beasts thought to be only figments of the imagination of Native American peoples will roam the earth in search of human flesh. Ghostly denizens of the Shadow Zone will walk among us in physical form, wreaking whatever havoc they please."

Gasps of fear echoed through the amphitheater as the audience heard these ghastly forecasts.

"Worst of all, the Winged Serpent—rumored lord of the Underworld and believed by some to have once been lord of all three worlds—will rise up like some ancient dragon to reclaim his place over us all. It is said that he rules other serpents—the legendary Uktenas known from Cherokee traditional stories—who will do his bidding and unleash their extraordinary powers against us."

That did it. A hundred people began talking at once, expressing belief or disbelief, dread or denial, and every other form of reaction one could imagine. As the din reached a crescendo, Billy stepped offstage for a brief moment and then returned with his Lightning Lance.

Holding it aloft, he spoke the spell that would call forth the lightning, as he'd done once before. Roiling dark clouds quickly formed overhead. A bolt of atmospheric electricity shot down from above, striking the tip of the lance, followed by an immediate crack of thunder.

That, of course, silenced the crowd as a sweet but pungent aroma spread through the amphitheater, a typical smell following a lightning strike. Holding their collective breath, the audience waited for the Chosen One's next words.

"All of you here now are witnesses who I call on to spread the word of the impending disasters," he said in the voice of authority. "It's up to all of us to prepare the Middleworld for what will happen within the next few weeks. Whatever religious or spiritual tradition you follow, now is the time to practice it with all your might."

No one budged as these words echoed throughout the amphitheater. Every person there remained momentarily frozen in place.

Finally, Lisa and Ethan rose from their seats and began to roll up the timeline banner. Likewise, Cecil rose from his seat and began urging his fellow members of the Medicine Council to follow him to an area behind the stage. James and Rebecca Buckhorn approached Chigger and the Muskrat family to ask them to stay a little longer.

After most of the news media and the audience had dispersed, Lisa asked Chigger to join her backstage. There he found his best friend about to address the thirteen members of the Medicine Council. He and Lisa stood by to watch the proceedings.

But first, the Chosen One had something to say to his oldest friend.

"Chigger, the Lookouts and Buckhorns voted to officially include you in our inner circle as part of the Underworld Takeover Prevention Team. Your contributions to our efforts have been noticed and appreciated, and from now on you'll be welcome at any and all of our meetings and decisions."

"This means a lot to me," Chigger replied, trying to hold back a tear. "But from now on, please call me the Muskrat. That's the new warrior identity I've adopted."

Billy and Lisa didn't know how to take this announcement. Did he really want them to call him that? If so, how could they call him that and keep a straight face?

"Gotchya!" Chigger said at last, wearing a broad smile. "Had you going there for a minute, didn't I?"

"Ha ha, very funny," Billy said with a slight smile. "Always the joker." He quickly dropped the smile and gave his friend a serious look. "Now, please get into your most serious frame of mind and observe what's going on."

Lisa escorted the Muskrat back a couple of steps as Billy moved closer to the circle of thirteen elders.

"As of this minute I'm reactivating the Intertribal Medicine Council," he told them. "We have retrieved the missing piece of the Sky Stone, and our first order of business, with Wilma's help, is to join that final piece to the stone."

He unwrapped a swatch of deerskin, revealing the southern piece within it. Handing the piece to Cecil, who then passed it to Wilma, Billy invited her to slip it into place. As the other pieces had done, this one seemed to fly out of her hand and into its place as if a powerful magnetic force animated it.

At last, all four directional sections were rejoined to the center piece. Cecil handed the complete Sky Stone to Billy, who hoisted it over his head.

"I implore you, my Thunder fathers, Morningstar, Thunderbird, the Hero Twins, and all the dwellers of the Upperworld, to guide the Fire Crystal to us and to its rightful place in the center of this reconnected stone from the sky."

A rumble of thunder came as an immediate response.

Then Cecil spoke on behalf of the assembled council of medicine makers. "We seek forgiveness for underestimating your powers and abilities to carry out the duties for which you were chosen," he said. "We stand united in our pledge to support all decisions you make and actions you take. Also, we offer our guidance when asked."

"Thank you," Billy replied. "What would be best now, if possible, is for all of you to remain here in the Cherokee Nation until the summer solstice. Gather once a day every day to pray for guidance and deliverance until this ordeal is over."

Once he'd obtained their commitment, Billy returned to the seating area, where Agent Swimmer and Raelynn Little Shield had waited. "I ask Creator to especially empower the two of you," he said to them, "and those who work with you, to guide you in your search for the Sun Chief, his ceremonial cape, his staff, and the Fire Crystal. Positive results are of utmost importance, sooner rather than later."

The last conversation the teen had that day was with a member of the medical profession: Dr. Abramson, the psychiatrist who'd visited Billy after his near-death experience.

"Why am I here, son?" the doctor asked. "You've proven the mythologies to be true. Now I see the Upper, Middle, and Underworlds are more than just beliefs, more than mere representations of the layers of the human mind."

"I met my shadow self while on my Underworld journey," the teen replied. "I need him to become a permanent part of my total being before the Underworld rises up."

"Astonishing!" Abramson exclaimed with wide open eyes. "That means Carl Jung's theories are true! What was it like?"

"I'm afraid there's no time for a discussion of the psyche now," Billy answered.

"Right you are," the man said. Taking a small calendar book out of his jacket pocket, he checked his schedule. "Come to my office tomorrow at noon. I have time then, and we'll get started."

The two shook hands, and the psychiatrist departed.

Later that day, the print journalists wrote and filed their news reports, while TV reporters edited their broadcast news segments.

The afternoon papers and evening news shows carried details of the day's highly unusual gathering, and as expected, viewer and reader reactions covered the full range of possibilities.

Some preachers railed against the "heathens." Others told their congregations to prepare for the Second Coming. New Agers proclaimed Billy Buckhorn the Red Messiah. Scientists, atheists, and materialists denounced the whole affair as pure fantasy.

But the reactions didn't matter to Billy. The truth was out there now, and people were free to make up their own minds about what to do with it.

That night, before going to bed, he thought about his upcoming meeting with Abramson and wondered what exactly the doctor might do to help him accept his shadow self. That thought brought up a memory of his journey to rescue Chigger from the Underworld.

"I should write a book about these experiences," the teen told himself before turning out the lights. "But no one would ever believe it."

It was about three in the morning when the dream began. Billy found himself floating alone in a canoe on a gently flowing stream. When the craft beached itself on a sandy shore, he stepped out and moved toward a line of trees at the edge of a forest. Looking into the woods more deeply, he saw a small group of people warming themselves at a campfire.

Moving closer, he was delighted to see that two of the people were his grandparents, Awinita and Wesley. Happily, he began running toward them before discovering a third person sitting across from them on the other side of the fire.

This other person was more like a shadow than a person. He seemed dark and featureless and yet familiar. The shadow man rose from his seat and moved toward the teen, who, for some reason, felt threatened by the move.

Billy turned to run as the setting transformed from forest to desert, with flat sand stretching as far as the eye could see. It immediately reminded him of the Valley of Stalking Skeletons and the House of Bones.

"You know you're only running from yourself," a voice from behind said.

That made Billy stop dead in his tracks. He turned to face his pursuer and recognized his shadow self, who was approaching slowly now.

"The longer you delay it, the harder it gets," the shadowy figure added.

"But I thought everything from the Underworld was bad," the teen replied, sounding very unsure and vulnerable. "This is so confusing."

"The Underworld is a place of fear, doubt, and negativity. It exists partly because of humanity's view of things. Everything in the Middleworld is understood by comparing opposites—you know, duality."

"Someone else told me that," Thunder Child remembered.

"Just think of me as your wilder side," his shadow said.

"Okay," the teen said as his resistance dissolved. "What do I need to do?"

"Accept that I am part of you, a part you often judge harshly and would prefer to keep hidden from other people—a part that displays qualities you don't want to admit you have. By accepting me, you become more whole."

Billy blew out a big breath of air. "Okay," he replied. "Let's get this over with."

The shadow now stood within reach. "Close your eyes and say the words," he said.

"I accept that you are part of me," the teen said. "A part whose existence I've always tried to hide—a part I no longer reject."

At that moment, with eyes still closed, Billy's dream self felt a heavier energy merge with his own. It didn't feel bad necessarily, just different. Surprisingly, he did somehow feel more complete, more like he was worthy of the Thunder Child title.

He awoke from the dream and looked around his bedroom. Nothing had changed, but everything seemed different. Something prompted him to look at himself in the mirror. Rolling out of bed, he walked to the mirror hanging on the back of his closet door and received the shock of his life.

"Whoa," he exclaimed as he took in the unexpected image.

Looking back at him was a slightly taller and more muscular version of himself. Long locks of black hair now flowed down his back, with a single stark white streak that started in front at the hairline.

Because of his journey to the Underworld and his acceptance of his wilder shadow self, Billy had finally transformed from being Cherokee teen Billy Buckhorn from Park Hill, Oklahoma. He had become, at least for now, the spirit warrior known as Thunder Child.

"You really are Thunder Child now," he said to his mirror image. "Billy Buckhorn is no more."

I've got to tell Abramson about this.

Suddenly, exhaustion overtook him. The dream and the integration process had worn him out, and he easily fell back asleep.

CHAPTER SIXTEEN

Latter Days

Ever since the FBI raided the Three Rivers compound, teams of searchers had been combing the countryside in search of the cave Molok and his followers had possibly retreated to. Maps, old and new, of every kind were consulted: county, state, federal, topographical, archaeological, aerial, and so on.

A battalion of FBI agents hunted for the cave on foot, climbing up and down the mountainous landscape on the east side of the Mississippi River. Other agents in boats ferried up and down the Mississippi River looking along its shoreline.

Nothing was found.

The closest anyone may have come to locating it was when a motorized boat operated by the Louisiana Department of Wildlife entered a river inlet just south of Fort Adams, Mississippi. They followed the inlet, which formed a narrow canyon between two ridges, for about a half mile until it dead-ended.

They abandoned the search when they realized the area was just across the state line in Mississippi and not Louisiana. It was outside their jurisdiction, and they didn't think to call a Mississippi state agency to follow up.

On the day after Thunder Child's gathering at the amphitheater, Swimmer and Little Shield gave the full Underworld Takeover Prevention Team—or UTPT for short—a report on their failed search efforts.

"Your search may have failed because your crew doesn't include someone with the necessary sensitivities," Thunder Child said.

"What you might call a specialized superpower," Lisa chimed in.

"All right," Swimmer replied. "Who and what are you talking about?"

"We're talking about this young man right here," Cecil answered, indicating Chigger. "His superpower is basically an acute ability to perceive the presence of Underworld energies."

"No offense, but I doubt anyone has that ability," Jerry replied.

Swimmer's own investigative partner disagreed. "I don't know about you, but I've personally witnessed enough proof from these people to believe anything and everything they tell me," Raelynn said angrily. "So let's hear what they have to say now."

Having been effectively chastised, Swimmer's tone mellowed. "Okay, what are you suggesting?" he asked the team.

"We're suggesting you take Chigger—"

"I now prefer to be called the Muskrat," Chigger said in a serious tone.

"I thought you said you were kidding," Lisa said.

"I guess I really wasn't."

Thunder Child revised what he'd planned to say. "I'm suggesting you go back to the Three Rivers area and take the Muskrat with you. And follow his lead. He'll eventually find that cave because of the negative Underworld forces concentrated there."

"That's a brilliant idea," Raelynn said, daring her partner to disagree.

Swimmer looked at the Muskrat. "Will your parents even allow you to go back down there? After what happened before?"

"They've completely changed their minds about me being involved with Billy and the whole Underworld takeover prevention stuff," Chigger said. "They've seen the light."

The FBI agent carefully considered what he'd say next before speaking.

"Well, I can't just snap my fingers and make a new search happen," Swimmer said finally. "I have to get new approvals from higher-ups in the FBI, and they have to get approvals to expend more resources. You know, the whole red tape thing."

"Whatever," Raelynn and Lisa said simultaneously and smiled at each other.

"Just get it done," Raelynn said, looking at Jerry as she rose from her seat. "I hope we have better news to share the next time we see you," she told the team in a pleasant tone of voice as she headed for the Buckhorn's front door.

"Me too," Jerry said and excused himself to follow his partner.

During the next few days, Thunder Child continued to feel overwhelmed as he faced the impending calamities without the support he'd expected. He needed spirit warriors by his side in the coming conflicts, but how would he get them? Where was the outpouring of miraculous supernatural help that was supposed to come? Why had his grandparents and Morningstar abandoned him in this approaching hour of great need?

Those were the questions and doubts that plagued the sixteen-year-old. He drove out to Lake Tenkiller just before sunset for some time alone to think. Then he remembered he wasn't completely alone.

"Just me and my shadow strolling down the avenue," he said aloud as he paced along the shore, remembering a very old song his grandpa Wesley used to sing from time to time.

The rains that had been falling since the first day of spring had ended, and the lake's water level was noticeably higher. The overly soaked ground nearby was like mud soup, and so he stayed on the pavement as he strolled.

He stopped momentarily to gaze at the cement boat ramp he'd used many times over the years to launch fishing expeditions with Grandpa, or Chigger, or both. Orange rays of sunlight streaked across the Oklahoma sky before withdrawing and fading with the disappearing sun in the west.

In the growing darkness, Thunder Child decided to take a few steps onto the angled boat ramp. During the past couple of days, the sun had returned to the sky, and sunsets were a welcome change after more than a month of cloudiness.

He reached down and touched the concrete surface of the ramp. It was still warm to the touch, having basked in the day's sunlight for several hours. Thinking the warmth would feel good on his back, he lay down on the upper part of the ramp. It was dry, and he knew no one would be launching a boat at that hour. Cradling his head in the crook of his arm, he gazed upward as the stars began their nightly display.

The Path of Souls—better known to most as the Milky Way— became brighter and brighter with each passing minute. His mind drifted back to a night at the end of last summer when he and Chigger had done a little night fishing.

Life was so simple then, before the lightning strike changed everything.

As the last remnant of western light disappeared and the field of stars began to brightly shine, the teen reached up and touched the side of his neck where electricity from the stormy sky had left its weblike scar.

"What was it your grandpa Wesley used to call the stars?" a voice in the darkness asked.

"Campfires of the ancestors," Thunder Child replied without thinking.

His mind suddenly snapped to attention.

"Wait. Who said that?"

Thunder Child looked around. No one was in sight. But then a shimmering apparition began forming out over the water. As the vision developed, Thunder Child saw a circle of seven traditionally dressed Native men and women facing him.

The man closest to him spoke. "We're here to offer you at least some guidance," he said.

Thunder Child wasn't sure who these spirits were, only that they weren't the ancestor spirits who spoke to the Intertribal Medicine Council. This group of elders only numbered seven, while the ancestors that interacted with the council numbered thirteen.

"This is the Circle of Prophets," the spokesman said. "Though from different tribes and different eras of history, we tried to save our people from the onslaught of foreigners who destroyed our way of life. We continue to guide our people as needed when possible."

Having seen old photos of some of those historical Native prophets, Thunder Child surveyed the circle. He recognized Wovoka, the Paiute holy man who'd introduced the ghost dance, and Black Elk, the Lakota holy man whose visions had been shared with the world. The others weren't familiar.

"I am known as Tenskwatawa, the Shawnee Prophet," the spokesman said.

"Very nice to meet you," said Thunder Child. "I used to be Billy Buckhorn, but now I'm known as—"

"We know who you are," the prophet said. "That's why we've come bearing a message."

"A message? I could use a good message about now."

"Morningstar has been very busy, as have your grandparents," the prophet said. "Don't judge them too harshly, and don't sit around waiting for them to answer your every question. When in doubt, rely on yourself."

"I guess I have been whining and complaining a little."

"Also, I want to introduce you to one of the ancestors whose campfires you see up there in the sky every night."

That piqued Thunder Child's interest. "Who is it?" he wanted to know. "Is it someone who'll help us defeat the Underworld?"

"Possibly. If anyone from the past could help, it would be him. He knows all the spirit warriors, the Native American warriors from the past. But I need to warn you. He still needs some convincing, and that'll be part of your job when you meet him."

The floating image of the prophet circle flickered and dimmed a little.

"If you know Native American history, you'll be familiar with my brother, Tecumseh, the Shawnee warrior who tried to unite the tribes against a common American military foe."

"In the end, he failed, didn't he?" Thunder Child said. "Or am I missing something?"

"Yes, his earthly life concluded before his dream was realized," the prophet replied. "But lately his deep sense of disappointment over that failure has returned."

"I think I could work with that, use it as a discussion starter."

"Good," the apparition said, continuing to fade. "He might agree to meet you up at your out-of-body dome."

"Okay, thanks."

"If you forget everything else I've said, remember who I told you to rely on."

"When in doubt, rely on myself," Thunder Child said.

"That means *all* the multiple dimensions of yourself that exist in multiple time frames."

The apparition disappeared, leaving the teen to wonder just what the Shawnee Prophet was getting at. He looked up at the velvet black sky filled with distant twinkling lights and mentally expressed his gratitude to the Circle of Prophets, hoping to see them again in the future.

As Thunder Child continued to prepare for the imminent Underworld uprising, two secretive allied groups had been at work busily preparing to execute that uprising. The entire endeavor depended on a large and unusual energy shift known as the Thinning of the Veil, or simply the Grand Thinning.

The veil could be described in many ways: the space between the natural and the supernatural worlds, the space between the seen and the unseen, the barrier between the living and the dead.

In normal times, a minor thinning of the veil took place each year during the overnight transition from October 31 to November 1, the time of Halloween, or All Hallows' Eve, as it was originally known. In Mexico and Central America, it was thought of as the Day of the Dead.

But the upcoming Thinning of the Veil was very special, occurring only once in every Long Count of 5,125 years, according to the way the Maya tracked time. Therefore, only communities that had maintained and passed down their ancient traditions even knew of this phenomenon or when it would come around again. That was one of the things the Maya calendar did very well—if you knew how to read it.

So, behind the scenes and mostly out of sight, the Owl Clan and the Society of Serpents had been honing their magical skills, practicing their dark arts, and restocking their inventories of herbs and potions. Cosmic clocks, ancient manuscripts, and signs in the night sky all pointed to the first of May as the start date for this uncommon phenomenon.

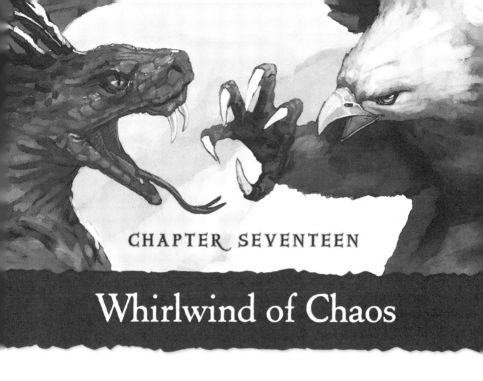

CHAPTER SEVENTEEN

Whirlwind of Chaos

I n many cultures for a time, May Day, the first day of the month of May, was a date to celebrate the coming of summer. Festivals, flowers, dances, and multicolored streamers marked the day as the final defeat of winter.

But among many European practitioners of darker traditions, May Day was known as the "witches' sabbath," a time for worshipping the Devil and his demons. The cosmic timetables of the Owl Clan and the Snake Cult agreed, and now the long-awaited supernatural window had arrived.

On May 1, at precisely 12:01 a.m., the incantations began. Having gathered in one secret underground location, the Indigenous sorcerers and conjurers were ready to carry out their coordinated plans.

"Owl Clan, activate your mirrors," Thomas Two Bears commanded.

Eleven of the thirteen Night Seers, seated in a circle inside the entrance to Mammoth Cave, initiated the spells that brought their individual Aztec mirrors to life. They executed their duties by the dim light provided by small battery-powered LED lamps.

Just as Two Bears had predicted, flooding from the massive rainstorms had closed Kentucky's Mammoth Cave for months. It was the perfect location, chosen months ago for this precise day and time. This, the largest network of caves in North America, was the perfect location for conjuring the banished beasts from their abode in Level Eight of the Underworld.

"Let the conjuring begin!" Two Bears announced, and each Night Seer commenced with the specific spell he or she had learned and practiced. Casting their spells through Aztec mirrors amplified their effectiveness and increased the speed of the results.

Two of the thirteen Night Seers, however, were not present. Eastern Cherokee Amos Yonaguska had failed to answer any of Two Bears's calls in the last few days. And the news of Willy James's death had only recently reached the Owl Clan leader.

Their absence was troublesome to Thomas because it meant the group's powers would be diminished. Despite this setback, Two Bears felt a sense of pride at what he was now accomplishing. It brought to mind an argument about the "Thinning Time" he'd had decades ago with former Owl Clan leader Benjamin Blacksnake when that Cherokee sorcerer was still alive.

"That's the most ridiculous idea I've ever heard," the elderly Blacksnake had ranted. "Mammoth Cave is one of the busiest tourist spots in the nation, and you'll never be able to get the park shut down long enough to hold the conjuring!"

"That's where you're wrong, Benjamin," Two Bears countered. "When we execute our massive changes to weather patterns, that will no longer be a problem. The ongoing rain will flood out the cave and force park personnel to close it. There'll be no visitors for weeks."

"No Night Seer has ever been able to control the weather at such a large scale," the famous Raven Stalker replied. "It can't be done."

"But the unified effort of all thirteen Night Seers can do it," the younger conjurer proposed. "I believe we can achieve it if we synchronize our spells, just as I believe we can conjure all the beasts ever known in tribal cultures when the Thinning Time arrives."

"That idea is no good either," Blacksnake snarled. "It's hard enough to conjure one beast from one tribal region at a time. Forget trying to conjure all the banished beasts known to all the tribes. The spells aren't strong enough to cover the whole country!"

Debates like those raged between the two Night Seers for years—that is, until Two Bears's powers eclipsed those of Blacksnake's. That was when the Cheyenne medicine man cast an old tribal destruction spell on the Cherokee man, sending him down to the Shadow Zone. Blacksnake had always erroneously blamed fellow Cherokees for his demise.

"It seems to be working!" the Coast Salish Night Seer exclaimed, bringing Two Bears back from his memories of the past. "I can feel the old Bakwas creature emerging from the Northwest area where my people are from."

"*Ehpayva!*" Two Bears shouted in his Cheyenne tongue. "It is good! It has begun!"

The secret order of Native dark magicians known as the Owl Clan had for decades collected and stored the legends and tales from tribes across the nation. Among those could be found multiple versions of accounts of a variety of dangerous creatures that had threatened Native communities since ancient times.

Accompanying these stories were a variety of tales that told of the times when the beasts were destroyed or banished by the Upperworld's Hero Twins to make the Middleworld safe for human habitation.

So now, during the Grand Thinning, not only would the creatures pictured by Mound Builders long ago come forth, but so would all the horrifying beasts ever known by any of North

America's tribes. This time the creatures would appear in the Middleworld to strike terror in the hearts of everyone.

And that thought pleased Thomas Two Bears immensely.

"When the conjuring is complete, we'll all head to Cahokia for a grand rendezvous with our allies, the Society of Serpents," he said. "Be sure to wear your Night Seer pendants so they can recognize you."

The Owls continued their work, satisfied that their magical efforts were successful.

Six hundred miles southwest of Mammoth, the nine members of the Serpent Society had initiated their complementary set of serpentine conjurations and concoctions. These dark magic crafters were concentrated in one highly secret underground location, the hidden and forgotten old cavern complex across the river from the Three Rivers compound.

Informed by the traditions and manuscripts of tribal magicians south of the border, their efforts were producing distinctly different results. Eight of the nine Serpents focused on calling forth the eight Horned Serpents—the Uktenas—while Snake-Eye worked on summoning the legendary and feared Winged One himself from the lowest level.

Additionally, Coyotl, the second-in-command, monitored Blacksnake's work to manifest certain residents of the Shadow Zone. The Aztec hoped the newly rediscovered reembodiment spell—which the Cherokee sorcerer would activate from his Underworld location—would do the trick.

Coyotl's recent studies had taught him a lot about this ancient spell. The reentry point into the land of the living didn't require the use of caves as portals. Instead, the souls of the dead would reenter the Middleworld using their own physical remains wherever they lay buried. In other words, cemeteries. The bones would become interdimensional stepping stones, allowing souls to burst forth from denser regions.

As they worked in the hidden Louisiana cave, Serpent Society members began posing questions they'd wanted to ask their leader for quite a while. And for the first time, Snake-Eye seemed to offer concrete answers.

"There are a couple things I have to warn you about, even though you may have figured these out on your own," he said to the group. "If you are killed or die from disease, your spells are automatically canceled. That means the Uktena you've conjured will cease to exist."

"I hadn't thought of that," Raymond Bushyhead, the newest member, replied.

"I'm happy to say that won't happen if I die," Snake-Eye continued, "because I'm supernaturally linked to Monkata, and his Underworld power protects the Winged One from that fate."

That brought on more questions about the emergence of the Winged One.

"Has the Winged Serpent actually ever been conjured before?" Norman Redcorn asked.

"Most definitely," Snake-Eye said. "Rumor has it that my own ancestor, Snake Priest Monkata, successfully brought the creature up from Level Nine a thousand years ago."

"Ancient cultures around the world once worshipped the Winged One as the Great Serpent," Coyotl added. "Even the early Hebrews did so while they were captives in Babylonia."

"It will be the beginning of a new glorious age when Monkata and I together control the Middleworld," the snake leader said. "And you'll all be there as our most trusted advisers."

"I know we're supposed to gather at Cahokia immediately after the Winged One manifests in the flesh," Raymond Bushyhead said. "But how will you ever restore that site to its former grand status as Solstice City? That'll take a lot of work over a long period of time."

"Not really," Coyotl replied. "Imagine the mighty Winged Serpent rising into the sky and destroying all life below. The Mundanes will be shocked and shaking in their boots in fear of death from the sky and will do whatever we want them to."

"Destroyed how? Will it breathe fire like a dragon?" Bushyhead asked.

"Oh no, this is no European-style dragon," Coyotl corrected. "Its very breath is death, according to the ancient texts. How it kills you exactly, I'm not sure."

"Molok has repeatedly told us the Underworld takeover will be directed toward the descendants of the colonizers," Jonna Boudreaux commented. "You know, as punishment for their betrayals of Indigenous people."

"How can you be sure who will suffer and who will be saved?" Travis Garfish asked before Coyotl could answer.

"The only thing we can be sure of is chaos," the Aztec admitted. "Unleashing the Underworld means unleashing chaos in the Middleworld—on really everybody."

That answer doused all interest in asking any more questions about what was coming.

East of Tahlequah, at 12:01 a.m., Chigger sat bolt upright in his bed as a wave of negative purple energy coursed through him, bringing on an overwhelming sense of chaos and doom.

The whirlwind of chaos is here, he thought.

Looking at the digital clock-calendar on his nightstand, he saw the date and time: one minute past midnight on the first of May. Then images of grotesque creatures, like the ones he'd been drawing for weeks, began popping into his mind. One after another they came like a blizzard of bleakness. Traumatic memories of his destructive ordeal with the Horned Serpent's tail crystal last fall flooded his brain, immediately leading to a paralyzing panic attack.

Oh no, what's happening?

Remembering an old black-and-white war movie he'd seen on TV, he impulsively called out, "Mayday! Mayday!"

Then he looked down at the burn scars on his hands, which were painfully pulsating with a purplish glow. He was extremely glad to see that he wasn't irrationally clutching the dark crystal as he'd done for several days last December.

He remembered to use the protection technique that allowed him to decrease the impact of the negative energy and regain control of his feelings. Once that was in place, he slowly breathed in, held the air for a count of four, and then exhaled. He repeated that pattern four times, allowing his mind to clear out the sense of panic.

That was something he'd learned from Lisa. Another thing he'd learned from Lisa was that Billy was no longer Billy. He was now truly and completely Thunder Child.

"You need to call him Thunder Child from now on," she'd said. "We've all begun calling him that because it strengthens him and reinforces our trust in him."

Now, a few minutes into the month of May, Chigger was able to clear his mind enough to realize that major shifts were taking place, that the Underworld takeover had begun!

"It's happening now?" Thunder Child exclaimed when he answered Chigger's sat phone call. "Are you sure? I thought we had more time!"

"I'm sure. The whirlwind of chaos has arrived."

Thunder Child knew the first thing he needed to do after hearing Chigger's revelation was notify the rest of the Underworld Takeover Prevention Team. But at that time of night, they'd probably all be asleep and hard to reach. Lisa had created a group text for just such emergencies as this, so Thunder Child sent the text anyway.

I need the UTPT over here now! Chigger felt a strong purple energy surge just after midnight. It might be the beginning of the UT.

It turned out that Cecil already knew something was up and was also awake. The supernaturally sensitive elder had felt the hint of a wave of disturbance the same time Chigger had. He texted a message back.

I'm awake. I'm getting Ethan and Lisa up now. We'll be over ASAP.

Thunder Child woke James and Rebecca and put on a pot of coffee in the kitchen. Within about fifteen minutes, the whole team, including Chigger, had gathered in the upstairs War Room.

"I'm not ready—we're not ready for this," Thunder Child said as his mother brought in the coffee pot along with enough cups for everyone. He tried to keep a sense of panic out of his voice.

"We're all very aware of what still needs to be done," Cecil said. "Let's try to stay calm and think this through."

"Staying calm is a tall order right now," Chigger said. "The purple energy is so strong I want to crawl out of my own skin!"

"What are you, a muskrat or a mouse?" Lisa said in a firm voice. "Remember your training. Use your breathing exercise."

That had an immediate calming effect on the teen.

"Thanks, Lisa," he said. "That helps."

"I'll assemble all the members of the Medicine Council in the lodge as soon as possible," Cecil confirmed. "Our energy, as a group, can be focused on countering the negative energy with positive energy."

"When we're finished here, I'll head up to Level Four and try to connect with Tecumseh," Thunder Child said. "I'll need everyone's positive, supportive energy for that meeting as well."

Nodding heads confirmed their support.

"My next call is to Raelynn," Lisa said. "She's number four in the list of favorites on my phone. We've got to get Muskrat down there so he can use his superpower to scan for the Snake Cult's hideout—with or without the FBI's help."

"Lisa, I appreciate the effort," Chigger said. "But it's *the* Muskrat."

Everyone paused and stared at the teen.

"Are you being serious right now?" Lisa asked. "*The* Muskrat?"

"Very," the Muskrat replied.

Lisa just rolled her eyes.

"Well, Digger has a boat," the Muskrat said, breaking the silence. "I bet he'd let us use it, or he might even drive it up and down the river once he finds out we're still looking for the hidden cave."

"Good idea," Ethan said, looking a little surprised at the smart suggestion.

"Don't look so surprised," the Muskrat said.

"You know, continuing this search is probably pretty dangerous," Ethan said.

"Danger is my middle name," the Muskrat offered.

"I thought Checotah was your middle name," Lisa said and smiled.

"Ha ha. Very funny." The Muskrat chuckled.

"Okay, everybody, this is serious," Thunder Child said. "Let's get on with it."

"We can talk about correcting the Muskrat thing another time, maybe," the Muskrat added.

"I'll start phoning Augustus right away," Ethan said, ignoring the last remark. "If he doesn't answer, I'll just go over to his house and pound on the front door."

"I'll go with you," the Muskrat said. "He and I have a special bond." Then he remembered an important point. "Everyone, be sure to wear your eye-in-hand medallions at all times!"

"Got it," came the simultaneous reply.

Thunder Child went back to his bedroom to begin the process of spirit travel up to Level Four. Once he was out of his physical body, he could sense a generalized heaviness in the atmosphere, which was new. It felt like he was perceiving the energy field not of an individual person but of the Middleworld as a whole.

Before attempting his rise to Level Four, he paused just above his house long enough to feel his surroundings, to amplify his spirit senses. What he perceived was a disruption in the normal energy flow, which had been replaced by turmoil.

This is not good.

Concentrating his own energy field within a tighter ball, he moved upward through the layers to Level Four, where his home away from home was located. Hoping the Circle of Prophets had followed through on their promise, Thunder Child put out an invitation to the spirit of Tecumseh.

As he waited in his clear-domed spiritual Home Among the Stars, he hummed the melody of an old Cherokee song he'd often heard at the Live Oak stomp grounds. That, of course, reminded him of Grandpa Wesley, whom he missed very much.

As he gazed at the stars and thought of Wesley, a strange thing happened. The bright jewels of outer space appeared to transform into millions of tiny, distant campfires.

Beautiful!

As he continued to watch, one of the campfires began burning brighter than the others. A message was coming to Thunder Child from that glowing campfire that said, "I received your invitation, and I accept."

The campfire seemed to begin racing toward the dome, morphing into a burning orb as it approached. As it came closer, the orb evolved further and began looking like a man. Within seconds, this spirit man descended into Thunder Child's space, appearing much like the painting of this very man, Tecumseh, created in the early 1800s, which Thunder Child had seen online.

"My brother told me of your desire to meet," Tecumseh said. "He said you have an unusual request."

"Thank you for visiting me," Thunder Child responded.

The young warrior explained the conditions that were beginning to unfold in the Middleworld, including the probable manifestation of the Underworld beasts and the possible incarnation of Shadow Zone dwellers. He capped it off with his plea for help against the Underworld forces.

"Why would I, or any other Native warrior, help now?" the Shawnee man asked. "American soldiers drove us from our lands and our homes. Missionaries came to rob us of our religion and spirituality. Teachers in boarding schools punished us for speaking our Indigenous languages. They burned our traditional clothing, forcing us to wear their uniforms. Politicians created laws that herded us onto reservations where we starved on rotten food and died of the white man's diseases." He paused for a moment. "Have I left anything out?"

"Everything you said is absolutely true, but please listen to me just for a minute," Thunder Child said.

He, too, paused before proceeding with his counterargument.

"America's population is very different today," he began. "Things have changed a lot since your earthly lifetime. Most people know that the nation's past actions were wrong—against Native Americans, African Americans, Asian Americans. But joining us in the battle against an Underworld takeover isn't just about saving the descendants of colonizers. It's much larger than that. It's about saving the whole world from total chaos, preventing completely negative forces from ruling our lives."

Tecumseh weighed Thunder Child's words carefully.

"You know, I checked you out before this meeting," the Shawnee man said. "You come highly recommended by Morningstar, and you're one of the youngest warriors I've ever met."

"Good to know. Glad he hasn't completely abandoned me."

Thunder Child waited for more.

"I failed at my mission in the early 1800s, so this might be a second chance to do something important for our people," Tecumseh concluded.

He paused before sharing his final decision.

"All right, young warrior. I will join you, and I'll see if I can convince the other Native warriors up here to join you. I've come to know many of them."

"That's a big relief," Thunder Child replied and proceeded to explain the steps he planned to take, activating the Sky Stone with the Fire Crystal and liberating the Sun Chief.

"Sounds like you've still got a lot to do!"

"Someday I hope to tell you all about it."

After shaking spiritual hands, the two parted ways.

Back home, Thunder Child merged with his physical self and considered his next move.

While her boyfriend was traveling out-of-body, Lisa made the call to Raelynn, who answered the call even though it was in the middle of the night.

"What's up, girlfriend?" Little Shield said in a sleepy voice. "Why the after-hours contact?"

Lisa explained what was going on and concluded with "My father and Chigger want to resume the search for the hidden cave. They'll get a boat and go on their own if the FBI won't help."

"Jerry said the Bureau won't approve any more resources or manpower on the search, so I guess we *are* on our own," Raelynn said. "But I think he's about ready to commit to an independent search, and he said his uncle on the police force probably would too."

"Good. I'll keep you posted."

Ethan and the Muskrat drove to the home of Augustus Stevens, a.k.a. Digger, and pounded on the professor's front door. After many loud raps, the front porch light finally came on. A frowning archaeologist peeked out between the drapes to see who could possibly be causing such a racket at that hour.

"What the hell do you guys want at this ungodly hour?" the archaeologist yelled angrily through the door.

Standing on the porch, Chigger and Ethan took turns explaining why they'd come. Stevens yanked open the door and glared at them a moment before blowing out an exasperated lungful of air.

"Come in and tell me more of this tall tale while I make us some coffee," Digger said in a gravelly, but less angry, voice. "Sounds like a job for the Paranormal Patrol!" He paused. "That's not the name we're using anymore, is it?"

"We've got to get you up to speed," the Muskrat said as the three headed into the house.

In the meantime, Cecil had driven his pickup over to the lodge where the shaking tent ceremony had taken place. The rest of the Intertribal Medicine Council had decided to camp out there ever since Thunder Child reactivated the group.

Rather than sound an alarm or make some loud noise to wake up the elders, Cecil began quietly building a fire in the center of the lodge. As the flames cracked and popped to life, people in their sleeping bags, one by one, began to wake up.

Upon rousing, each of them felt the increased presence of negative vibrations and instantly knew why Cecil was there. Having already talked about what to do when this time came, each one found a spot within the lodge and began quietly praying in their native tongue—praying for Thunder Child's strength and guidance.

As the sun began its journey across the sky from the East Coast to the West, everyday Americans awoke in a foul mood and didn't know why. Their lowest traits, their worst tendencies, welled up inside, causing them to begin acting terribly toward those around them. Every form of lower human nature boiled over—criticism, greed, jealousy, anger—you name it.

As the day progressed, the very foundations of civilized society seemed to crumble as the most basic parts of civic duty were abandoned. Many people decided to skip work, play hooky from school, or generally shun their regular responsibilities.

Normal, everyday people began exhibiting these abnormalities on a scale never seen before! Gun violence immediately became the number one means people used to resolve conflicts. The number of injuries and murders across the country skyrocketed to new and alarming heights. Even members of law enforcement became targets for anyone with a firearm.

Chaos ruled the day.

Augustus, Ethan, and the Muskrat headed toward Three Rivers as fast as they could, towing Digger's boat behind them. The chaos all around them extended the road trip to two days. They took turns driving, sleeping, and keeping watch for monsters, both human and supernatural.

During his turn at the steering wheel, Augustus turned on the van radio.

"We've interrupted our regular broadcast to bring you live updates of what must be the beginning of the final Apocalypse!" the radio news reporter proclaimed. "I don't know what else could explain what's happening!"

Back in the Buckhorn's upstairs War Room, James, Rebecca, and Thunder Child watched similar reports online coming from all parts of the country.

"The worst examples of humanity now seem impossibly to be coming back from the dead," a panicked on-camera reporter said. For his own protection, he was reporting from inside an armored police vehicle parked outside the Angola prison. The scene cut to a view of the prison cemetery, where dozens of inmates had been buried after being put to death in recent years.

The reporter's voice continued. "It began in the middle of the night as previously executed inmates started materializing in the field behind the prison, where they had been interred by the state."

Then the camera shot transitioned to the city of New Orleans, where almost two thousand people had died during Hurricane

Katrina in 2005. Hordes of disheveled, wild-eyed people of all races stumbled aimlessly through the streets.

The reporter continued. "But it doesn't seem like *everyone* who died is coming back. The ones showing up are what you might think of as less desirable people released from below! But now they're back here and in the flesh! My advice is to stay inside with your doors locked."

"Didn't see that coming!" Thunder Child told his mom and dad.

One person who was watching the chaos unfold from a remote cabin on the Eastern Cherokee reservation was Amos Yonaguska. Something in the Night Seer's mind had begun shifting weeks ago after he heard the news of the death of Wesley Buckhorn. It was a step too far, as far as the Cherokee sorcerer was concerned. That was why he hadn't responded to the calls from Thomas Two Bears or shown up at Mammoth Cave.

He'd joined the Owl Clan all those years ago only after his own tribe had accused him of being a *skili*. They'd turned their backs on him because of unfounded rumors, so he'd decided to become what they already assumed he was.

But he'd never liked Thomas Two Bears or approved of his leadership methods. Now Yonaguska was horrified as he watched the Owl Clan's long-planned actions come to fruition.

"I can't just sit by and watch this," he told himself. "There's got to be something I can do. But what?"

He knew he'd have to act before it was too late. The seed of an idea began to develop in his mind, a dangerous idea that might wind up getting him killed. But he decided then and there on a course of action. He just had to work out the exact steps he'd take and then follow through.

As Augustus, Ethan, and the Muskrat traveled southward toward Three Rivers to look for Molok's hideout, Lisa made another call to Raelynn Little Shield.

"Raelynn, we can't wait any longer to pull a search team together," she said. "Chigger, my father, and their archaeologist pal are putting their own lives in danger searching for the hidden cave!"

After getting a commitment from Raelynn to "try her best," Lisa had another idea. Driving to the Buckhorn house, she presented the concept to her boyfriend.

"Travis Youngblood from the Cherokee Nation Marshals Service attended the presentation at the amphitheater," she said. "He's now heard the whole unbelievable story of what we're up against. Maybe he'd agree to get the US Marshals involved in the search. Isn't that something they do?"

"Good idea," Thunder Child said. "Worth a shot."

Unexpectedly, the teen pulled his girlfriend closer and kissed her. She wasn't ready for it, so it was rather awkward.

"I'm sorry," she said. "It's been such a long time since we've done this. Please try again."

They kissed again—dramatically, passionately—and then separated. Both of them sighed, releasing pent-up tension they'd been holding for some time.

"I can't wait until this whole thing is over," Thunder Child said.

He smiled, and Lisa smiled back. They both felt emotionally strengthened.

"I'll call Travis Youngblood now," the boy said. "We need all the help we can get."

CHAPTER EIGHTEEN

Beasts Arise

T he conjuring process took longer than Thomas Two Bears expected or would have liked. But the Owl Clan's incantations and conjurations finally began creating the results he was after, plus many other unexpected and undesirable consequences in places none of them wanted.

Off the west coast of Alaska, near the Yupik village of Tununak, a tribal elder who was paddling his kayak and spear fishing in the bay was the first to see it. The Amikuk, known from ancient tribal stories, rose from the icy cold waters holding a fish in its mouth, trying to lure the fisherman to come and get it. The man, who'd heard tales of this legendary beast all his life, knew better than to fall for the ploy.

The elder quickly turned back toward the shore, paddling like he'd never paddled before. He had to warn his tribe of the horrid creature's return. The hairless, leathery-skinned thing was notorious for dragging kayakers under the water for its next meal.

Farther south on an island off the Canadian shore of British Columbia, a Native hunter traipsed through the woods on his tribe's historic lands in search of traditional plants and herbs. A rustling of leaves caught his attention.

He looked up just in time to see what his people called the Wild Man of the Woods coming toward him, offering him food from a seashell. The hunter knew from different tribal stories that the hairy creature was a Bakwas or a Gagit, attempting to lure him to his death.

Outside White Swan, Washington, on the Yakama Indian Reservation, a Native woman was busy harvesting huckleberries as her children played nearby. As the sun was setting beyond the mountains, the woman began hearing the call of a creature she'd never heard before. But, knowing of the warnings of tribal elders, the woman recognized the sound as the call of the hideous mountain dwarves who stole children and carried them off to their caves.

Quickly the woman rounded up her children and ran back toward town, leaving her basket of huckleberries behind. She had to warn the tribe of the little cannibals' return.

Off the shore of Lake Superior in Wisconsin, in the woods near the Red Cliff Reservation's powwow grounds, several Chippewa families were camping out and enjoying the beautiful May weather. As they ate a midday meal, a foul smell wafted over them, coming from a remote part of the forest.

The smell was followed by a sudden drop in air temperature. After grabbing jackets from their tents, members of the family who had camped closest to the woods emerged in time to see what their tribe called a Wendigo. One such creature had mysteriously appeared in a daydream vision Chigger had had weeks ago.

Driven by cravings for human flesh, the two-legged half-deer, half-human creature with piercing red eyes charged directly at the Chippewa campers. Screaming for their lives and running toward their nearby cars, everyone in the camp made it out alive, but just barely.

From the back seat of one car, a twelve-year-old girl had the presence of mind to grab her phone and shoot video of the attacking monster. She immediately posted it to her social media account, and the posting spread like wildfire.

In the lands of the Navajo in Arizona, a half dozen dangerous, cannibalistic creatures began terrorizing people—Native people. In the Zuni territory of western New Mexico, the giant Atasaya, with its bulging eyes, yellow tusks, and wrinkled red face, emerged from a cave in the mountains.

Farther north, the skeletal monster known to the Minnesota Chippewa as Baykok lurked around abandoned rural homesteads, attracted by the smell of humans. On the East Coast, the fanged sea creature known to Natives there as Apotamkin rose out of Passamaquoddy Bay, prowling the shoreline in search of children to eat.

In the Seneca Nation of western New York, tribal legends warned of the Yakwawiak, an enormous man-eating bearlike creature with no fur. Thankfully, none had been seen within recent memory. That was, until this day in the month of May, when one of the beasts climbed out of the Allegheny River in search of food—human-type food.

For several days in early May, this scenario repeated itself in the traditional homelands of Native American tribes across North America. One thing these creatures had in common was their craving for human flesh. The other common denominator was the location of their appearances.

None of them materialized in suburban neighborhoods or areas frequented by the descendants of colonizers. One and all incarnated close to Native communities, pursuing and terrorizing Indigenous people.

Tribal police departments on Indian reservations across America were the first to get phone calls from frightened residents who'd seen or been attacked by these creatures. Initially, these calls weren't taken seriously, labeled prank calls or the hallucinations of drug users. Cops joked among themselves about the sudden burst of wacky-sounding reports.

But when news came in from tribal clinics and reservation hospitals regarding injuries and even deaths from these supposedly false alarms, attitudes changed. Because Indian reservations were protected federal lands, news of these incidents traveled to federal law enforcement bureaus and then to national news agencies.

"Forget Bigfoot," one Native American eyewitness reported on TV news. "These fantastic creatures are beyond anyone's worst and wildest nightmares! I only hope someone figures out what to do about them!"

If the appearance of these legendary creatures, known as cryptids in certain circles, wasn't already baffling enough, they proved to be impervious to bullets and other projectiles. Dwellers of the Middleworld couldn't kill one no matter how hard they tried!

But mythological creatures from Native American legends and dwellers of the Shadow Zone weren't the only life-forms turning up in the Middleworld. Conjuring efforts of the Society of Serpents began to pay off within a few days of the first of May.

The first to respond to the Snake Cult's supernatural call came slithering out of the cave near Natchez, Mississippi, about sixty miles north of Molok's hidden cave. This had been the last cave visited by the UTPT before they arrived at Three Rivers.

As it emerged from the darkness, this Horned Serpent squinted in the bright sunlight. The creature's mind immediately perceived a signal coming from some unknown source, commanding it to avoid human contact while traveling upstream to join its companions.

Six more Horned Serpents slithered forth from six other caves along the Mississippi and Arkansas Rivers, caves visited by the UTPT during their expedition. Each of the beasts, under control of a Serpent Society member, immediately responded to the same message: *Gather in the ancient cave near Solstice City and await the arrival of your ancient master, who will arise very soon!*

Of course, the original Uktena, discovered by Billy and Chigger in the crystal cave, had been living in Molok's hideout for several weeks now. This Horned Serpent was still missing the Fire Crystal from the center of its forehead.

Serpent Society member Norman Redcorn, a Caddo Indian from eastern Oklahoma, was in charge of this particular Uktena. Redcorn was a descendant of the people who built the spiral mounds where the Sun Chief had been buried. This Uktena now waited near the southern entrance to Molok's hidden cave—waited for a Horned Serpent reunion of sorts.

The three searchers—Chigger, Ethan, and Augustus—finally arrived on the morning of the third and launched the motorboat from the Angola Ferry Landing on the west side of the Mississippi River. The launch ramp was just south of the Three Rivers Mounds.

As they transferred food and gear from the van to the boat, the Muskrat checked and double-checked to make sure they had their eye-in-hand medallions on board. Each of them would need to be wearing one before they possibly encountered one of the Horned Serpents.

The danger and absurdity of what they were about to do wasn't lost on the Muskrat.

"I feel like we're adventurers of old, maybe swashbucklers setting sail on the open sea," he told his companions.

"But we're just archaeologists getting into a tiny motorboat we'll launch on the river," Ethan countered.

"No, we're more than that," the Muskrat exclaimed. "We're much more than that. But what?"

Ideas flitted about in his head.

"I know!" he said excitedly. "We're the Three Muskrateers!"

"You mean the Three Musketeers, don't you?" Augustus corrected. "The fictitious French swordsmen from the novels and movies?"

"No, no, no!" the Muskrat protested. He took several bold strides toward the front of the boat, put one foot up on the bow, and brandished his flashlight as if it were a sword. "Time to set sail, ye hardy Muskrateers! Onward to the hideout of the evil, one-eyed Molok!"

After a welcome laugh that released some of the anxiety they were all feeling, Augustus started the boat engine.

"Where to, young Muskrateer?" he said.

Standing near the bow of the boat, the Muskrat closed his eyes and allowed himself to be fully exposed to the purple Underworld energies that swirled around him.

"North of here, near the mounds, I still sense a purple wave coming from across the river. That's the one I felt the first time we came here." He turned his whole body downriver to the south. "But now I feel an even stronger pulse from south of here, also coming from across the river."

Ethan, who was examining a topographical map of the area, said, "That's interesting."

He held out the map so Augustus and the Muskrat could see it, then pointed to a hilly area across the river.

"Behind this ridge of hills on the east bank of the river runs a shallow ravine," he said. "There's an opening between two hills on the north end of the ridge, and a similar one at the south end."

His companions examined the features he described.

"The hidden cave might run under or inside the entire length of that ridge and be accessible from either end," Ethan suggested. "I say we go check it out, starting with the south end, where Chigger, er, the Muskrat, sensed the strongest purple vibe."

Dedicated to their mission, the Three Muskrateers set off on what might have been considered a foolhardy expedition. After traveling downstream for a short twenty-minute ride, the team reached Tunica Bayou, a narrow stream of water that flowed through the ravine they'd seen on the map.

They moved more slowly now, watching for rocks and stumps that could damage their boat in the narrow waterway. When the stream became too shallow for the boat, they parked it and hiked farther up the ridge, each carrying a small backpack filled with items they might need.

The Muskrat was being guided by the purple energy pulse he felt, and the other two Muskrateers followed the teen's lead. After walking about fifteen minutes, the Muskrat stopped abruptly and gave a sharp hand gesture, raising his right fist to a point level with his shoulder.

"What's that supposed to mean?" Ethan asked in a raspy whisper, almost bumping into the boy from behind.

"It means freeze right where you are!" the Muskrat replied in what he thought was a commanding voice. "It's a common army combat signal I saw in a video online."

It was all his older teammates could do to keep from laughing.

The Muskrat turned and squinted sternly at them, doing his best Clint Eastwood impersonation. "Hold it together, guys. This is serious!"

Augustus and Ethan swallowed their giggles and feigned serious expressions.

"Yes, sir, Muskrat, sir!" Ethan replied with a salute.

The Muskrat had turned back toward the mountain ridge and missed seeing the salute. "The purple energy pulse seems to be coming from just on the other side of those boulders," he said.

The Muskrat headed for the boulders, signaling the other two to follow. Ethan looked at the professor with a questioning face, and Augustus whispered, "Best to just play along."

Ethan nodded, and the two proceeded. The Muskrat peeked around a boulder that was twice his size and smiled.

"There's an opening in the rock face," he whispered.

The other two rapidly caught up to their intrepid leader so they could see it. There, in the steep slope of the hillside, was a rift in the rock formation—a hole too small for the men but just the right size for the Muskrat.

"I'm going in," he said. "This is where the Muskrat lives up to his name!"

In real life, muskrats are small, hardy nocturnal rodents that burrow underground near water to build their nests. Chigger realized the muskrat identity wasn't a perfect fit for him, but he'd decided to stick with it anyway.

"I pledge myself to becoming more like the real-life muskrat so that I may be worthy of the name," he'd proclaimed at the time.

Now, just outside the small cave opening, the Muskrat put down his backpack and took out his flashlight and his eye-in-hand medallion. Fitting the medallion's chain around his neck, he placed the serpent-repelling pendant under his shirt.

He looked at the gap in the rocks he was about to enter, turned on the light, took a deep breath, and squeezed into the tight space. Hunched over to keep from hitting his head, he proceeded cautiously through the passageway.

Every instinct in his body told him to turn around and get the heck out of there. The ever-increasing purple energy feeling was the only thing propelling him forward. He knew the whole team was counting on him now. The idea that he was an important part of this team gave him the confidence he needed to continue with what was unquestionably a dangerous path, possibly the most dangerous path of his life.

Get out of your own head, Muskrat, and get on with it!

He pushed on and, to his great relief, the passageway began to expand. He noticed faint light coming from the direction he was headed and, within a few minutes, was surprised to find himself standing at the edge of a very large, dimly lit cavern. Realizing the light was coming from a couple of lights on metal stands, he ducked behind a tall stalagmite so no one would see him.

The scars on his hands were throbbing painfully now, and he realized something.

My hands only throb this much when I'm near the dark purple crystal. That must mean . . . No, that's impossible!

He peeked around the stalagmite to take a quick look at the area. What he saw shocked him. Three cages with metal bars sat on the broad, damp floor of the cavern. Each was about the size of a prison cell, the Muskrat guessed. Inside each cage was a man wearing an orange jumpsuit with *Angola State Pen* stenciled on the back. The three were facing away from the teen.

What the hell? Why are inmates from Angola prison inside this cave?

Suddenly a series of loud bangs came from deeper in the cave, echoing again and again off the hard rock walls. That was followed by the sound of a man yelling, though the teen couldn't understand what was being said.

The Muskrat could tell the caged men were frightened by the noises. They stood at the front edge of their cells, staring in the direction the noises had come from. As the echoes faded and the noise subsided, all became quiet again. The men sat back down on the floor of their cages.

The Muskrat took a deep breath and then tiptoed toward the nearest cage. He quickly reached the caged man and tried to get his attention.

"Hey, buddy, what's going on here?" the Muskrat said in a whispered tone.

The man, frightened by the unexpected noise from behind, jumped and yelled, "Ahhh!"

"Shhhhh!" the Muskrat replied. "Keep quiet. I'm not here to hurt you."

"You gotta get us out of here!" the man whispered after settling down. "They said they're gonna sacrifice us to some sort of serpent god."

The Muskrat didn't know what to say to that, but it triggered the memory of the human skeleton the UTP Team had discovered on a slab in one of the caves they'd explored.

"They keep one of those things in the other part of the cave," the man continued. "It's hypnotized or under a spell or something." He nodded toward the direction the loud noises had come from.

The Muskrat was still processing what he was feeling, witnessing, and hearing, trying to make sense of it. He remembered the Underworld Takeover Prevention Team's visit to the bat cave and the discovery of the missing Uktena with its purple tail crystal.

Could it be? The Uktena is here?

"Stay here," the Muskrat said. "I'll go check it out."

That was when the teen realized what a foolish thing he'd said. Of course the guy wasn't going anywhere. He was in a cage.

"Sorry for the *stay here* thing," he amended.

As the Muskrat tiptoed away, a prisoner whispered, "Be careful!"

Moving as quickly and quietly as he could, the teen reached the bend in the cave in a couple of minutes. Each step brought even stronger painful throbs to his hands. He could also hear several faint voices echoing from somewhere in the cave.

Peeking around another stalagmite, he saw yet another shocking scene. The Horned Serpent, the only one the teen had ever seen in real life, lay on the cave floor. The creature was held down by a crisscross of chains over its long body. A light from a metal stand illuminated the area around the beast. An aluminum ladder stood nearby, and a Native man wearing some sort of weird goggles stood next to the ladder.

The Muskrat did not know this man was Norman Redcorn, the Serpent Society member put in charge of controlling this Uktena. The man held something in one hand that the teen couldn't see. Suddenly the beast raised his head and looked in the teen's direction.

Seeing the boy to whom he'd once been so deeply connected, the Horned Serpent got excited and knocked the man away with one of his horns. As the object catapulted from the man's hand, the Muskrat saw it sparkle with orange, pink, and red highlights as it flew through the air.

The Fire Crystal!

And when the man tumbled to the cave floor, hitting with a crunching sound, the strange goggles fell off his head and onto the ground.

The old Chigger—the one that existed before sneaking into Molok's domain by himself—would have panicked and fled from the cave as quickly as possible. The sight of the beast would have triggered all the teen's fears.

But the Muskrat now inexplicably felt a positive vibration coming from the giant reptile. The scars on his hands stopped throbbing, and the creature's thoughts seemed to reach his mind, emoting an absolute fondness.

"Oh, how I've missed you, my old friend!" the Uktena communicated. "You and I once were so closely connected. The people in this cave want to use me for their own ends. Sure, they're the ones who brought me to life, but only to serve them, to do their bidding."

The Muskrat was frozen in place, shocked by what he saw and heard. Could this be real?

"I'm going to share something with you, and I don't want you to be afraid of it," the serpent said through telepathy. "I've learned to turn the energy level down."

Then the serpent's long tail, which had been hidden from the teen's view, came toward him. The Muskrat saw the purple crystal reattached to the tip of it.

"I thought you might like to hold it once again, for old times' sake," the beast's mind said. "But it won't hurt you this time."

Feeling surprisingly safe, the teen moved toward the tail crystal. The boy didn't sense any pulsating negative energy coming from it now. Instead, there was a welcoming, inviting vibration. He slowly extended one hand toward it.

Instantly, on contact, a whole energy ball of information was downloaded into the teen's mind from the serpent's mind. It was as if he'd been plugged into a computer mainframe filled with the Uktena's knowledge, secrets, and plans. The transfer only lasted a few seconds, but what was revealed needed to be shared immediately with Thunder Child and the UTP Team!

Part of the revealed information included what had been going on here in the cave just before the Muskrat arrived on the scene. Molok and the rest of the Nine were busy in another part, in an area closer to the larger, northern cave entrance. A concealment spell was in place to hide that entrance, like the one Carmelita Tuckaleechee had used to make it hard to find the kidnapped Lisa.

Also, after being separated for so many years, the Fire Crystal was about to be reattached to the place it belonged in the middle of the Uktena's forehead, which would restore full power to the beast!

But in the moment before it was attached, the Horned Serpent had sensed the Muskrat's nearness, and for some odd reason it had decided the boy should be the one to reinsert the dazzling crystal between the serpent's eyes. So the beast had knocked over Redcorn, causing him to fall to the ground. The Muskrat now knew he was expected to retrieve the crystal from where it had fallen and place it back in the empty spot on the creature's forehead.

With a big fake smile plastered across his face, the teen turned on his flashlight and searched on the cave floor for the precious gem. His eyes swept across a wider view of the cavernous room, and he could see passageways that led to other underground chambers.

Then, out of the corner of his eye, flashes of orange, red, and pink from within the crystal attracted his attention. He spotted it a few feet from Redcorn's body. Also lying on the cave floor near the crystal was the tube used to store the Sun Chief's staff and feathered cape.

No time for the tube, staff, or cape, he thought.

The Muskrat knew he had to act quickly if he was going to snatch the crystal and make his escape. The boy dashed past the man, who was beginning to wake up, and grabbed the gem. Seeing the curious goggles nearby, he grabbed those too.

Quickly turning back to the Uktena and using the eye-in-hand medallion as a shield, he shone the flashlight's beam into one of the creature's eyes. The angle of the reflected light hit Redcorn squarely in the face just as he opened his eyes, temporarily blinding the man just as the light from the night watchman's own flashlight had done at Spiral Mounds on a night last winter.

Being careful not to look into the Uktena's eyes, the Muskrat made a dash around the corner and back toward the cave's tiny back entrance. Realizing it had been betrayed, the beast released a fiendish, deafening roar as it strained against the chains that bound it.

"I'll send someone to rescue you!" the teen shouted as he raced by the caged men.

He stopped momentarily to get a better grip on the flashlight, crystal, and goggles and to make sure nothing was dropped. He then vanished into the tight little passageway he'd come through and scrambled out the other end as fast as humanly possible. He squinted in the sunlight as he tried to catch his breath. He looked down at what he held.

Under his arm was tucked the pair of dark goggles, which really seemed like something a World War II aviator might wear. His right hand held the flashlight. His left hand held the long-sought Fire Crystal, which sparkled and seemed to dance in the sunlight. He was mesmerized by the gem, but approaching foot-steps broke his concentration.

Locating the backpack he'd stashed beside the cave opening, the Muskrat quickly stuffed the gem, goggles, and flashlight inside.

"Well, what was in there?" Ethan asked as he rounded a nearby boulder. "Did you find Molok or Greenstone or whatever his name is?"

The Muskrat couldn't answer because he was still huffing and puffing—and still thinking about what he'd tell them. "I've got important stuff to tell you, but give me a minute while I catch my breath!" he asserted.

In truth, his mind was still coming to grips with the fact that he now possessed the Fire Crystal but wasn't sure what he was going to do about it. The gem seemed like it wanted him to keep it. A couple of extra deep breaths allowed the teen to delay his response while still trying to figure out what he'd say.

"I've got to call Thunder Child on the sat phone!" the teen finally said. Looking at Augustus, he added, "Our Uktena, the one from the bat cave, is in there, and he's got his purple tail crystal back."

"Oh dear, that's not good" was all the man could say, re-membering when he had been attacked by the creature in his basement office.

"He let me read his mind, though, and now I've got more in-formation in my head than I know what to do with," the teen continued. "I'd better spill it to Billy before I forget some of it."

Inside the cave, when the teen first held the Fire Crystal in his closed fist, the pinkish-orange crystal had reminded him a lit-tle of how the purple crystal had first felt in his hands, all warm, enchanting, and beguiling. But this crystal—even though as-sociated with fire—felt cool, purifying, and rejuvenating. He'd decided at that moment to keep his possession of the gem a secret for a while.

Now I know why the Sun Chief placed this crystal on top of his staff!

"Well, what are we waiting for?" Ethan said, interrupting the Muskrat's thoughts. "Let's get to the sat phone!"

That jolted the teen into action. As the three scurried down the slope to the boat, the Muskrat began sharing some of what he'd learned with his two compatriots.

"You know those caves we explored during the spring break expedition?" he said.

"Of course," Ethan answered.

"There's an Uktena for each one of them, and they're all headed to a cave up the Mississippi River near St. Louis for a big snake reunion."

"That doesn't sound good," Augustus replied.

"And they're all excited because the head snake, the one with wings, is gonna be here too!"

"So, the Winged Serpent is real!" Ethan said.

"And that's not all!" Chigger said as they reached the boat. "The Sun Chief's twin brother is planning on showing up for some big rematch, a final showdown, at Cahokia!"

The two archaeologists were dumbfounded by everything the teen was telling them. When they reached the boat, the Muskrat oddly continued to clutch the backpack tightly to his chest. To him, the gem in the bag continued to feel like a living being that wanted to share its powers with him. So the boy's mind was fractured into two competing divisions.

One part knew he needed to hand over the crystal and help the UTPT stop the Underworld takeover. The other part wanted to lock himself in his room and caress the priceless crystal. Struggling with the internal conflict, he tried to focus on the job at hand.

"I have to call Marshal Youngblood so he can organize a rescue of the three men trapped in cages in that cave who are waiting to be sacrificed," the teen said.

"Now you're just making stuff up," Augustus said dismissively. "That can't be true."

Chigger gave the older man a look.

"Holy crap," the man replied after realizing the teen wasn't embellishing his story.

Chigger punched in the marshal's sat phone number, and as he waited, it felt like something inside him shifted. A stronger sense of confidence settled in, and, among other things, he suddenly realized how silly his identity as the Muskrat had been.

"What a weirdo!" he said under his breath. And then, to his fellow searchers, he said, "I've come to an important conclusion, guys. I'm no longer the Muskrat. I'm just Chigger again."

The marshal came on the line, and Chigger talked nonstop to the man, explaining more about how to find the north cave entrance and the need to rescue the trapped men. After the call, the teen oddly felt he was ready to take charge of things.

"Let's get to the boat launch and back to Oklahoma," he said. "We have a lot to do and a very short time to do it in."

The men agreed, and the boat ride gave Chigger time to think things through a little more. He knew Billy desperately needed the Fire Crystal to overcome Underworld forces, but he wasn't exactly sure why, since he hadn't heard all the details about the prophecy and the Sky Stone.

But he did remember something Wesley had said about the crystal during the days of the Paranormal Patrol: "The Fire Crystal is said to impart great powers to anyone who possesses it, but all those that have tried died in the attempt."

Chigger reasoned that if he held on to the crystal, he would be better able to help his best friend Billy when it came time to fight the Underworld. And if he himself took the gem to Cahokia—a place Chigger had never been to—he'd be able to use his powers during the showdown, whatever that meant.

"I thought you were in a hurry to call Thunder Child," Ethan said after they'd been riding in the boat for a while.

"Oh, right," Chigger replied and punched a new set of numbers into the sat phone.

Having just settled into a chair in the upstairs War Room of the Buckhorn home, Thunder Child immediately picked up his sat phone, which he always kept with him.

Again, in a rush of words, Chigger delivered *most* of the incredible news he'd learned from the Uktena, and then he followed that up with a report on his conversation with Marshal Youngblood.

"This is incredible news! Good work!" Thunder Child said.

"Just so you know," Chigger said near the end of the call, "I was right about the cave's location when we first arrived at Three Rivers."

"Oh, yeah, how's that?" Thunder Child asked.

"The cave's north entrance is directly across the river from the Three Rivers spiral mound. No one could find it because of the snake man's concealment spell."

"You felt that negative purple energy coming from there, didn't you?" Thunder Child said. "Good for you, Chig—er, I mean the Muskrat."

"Oh, don't bother. I realized how silly that all was. Chigger is back."

"That's a relief!" Thunder Child said, blowing out a breath. "None of us knew how much longer we could keep calling you that."

After the call ended, Chigger felt the need to hug his backpack close to him. He realized the Fire Crystal was calling to him, and he was ready to respond to that call. Playing it very low key, he quietly unzipped the backpack, slipped one hand inside, and grasped the Fire Crystal.

The cool, refreshing feeling washed over him again, but this time the gem also provided the teen with another image.

Superimposed over Chigger's regular vision was a different view, much like seeing the output of a surveillance camera. Defocusing his physical sight allowed him to concentrate on the overlaying view, which seemed to be coming from inside the cave.

I'm seeing what the Uktena sees!

Chigger was so thoroughly shocked that he withdrew his hand from the backpack, zipped it up, and put it down beside him in the boat. His decision about what to do had just gotten even harder!

During the phone call from Chigger, Thunder Child sensed that something was off with his friend. He wasn't sure what it was, so he put it out of his mind. He had more important things to worry about, like whether he was really ready for what was to come.

He decided it was time to take stock of all the assets, skills, and resources that were available to him to fight whatever the Underworld was about to throw at him.

He had the thirteen magical spells he'd learned from the members of the Intertribal Medicine Council. He also had the council members themselves. He could do spirit travel, and he could read people's energy fields. He had his physical bow and quiver of arrows, but more importantly, he had his Lightning Lance, a gift from Morningstar and the Thunders.

There were new Nahuatl spells that he'd discovered in the back of Blacksnake's medicine book, as well as newly discovered ways to undo the spells someone else had cast. Finally, there were the Native American warriors of the past who, he hoped, would break through from the spirit world to fight alongside him.

What am I forgetting?

An image of Grandpa Wesley appeared in his mind, prompting him to remember the deerskin medicine pouch the elder had given him during the initiation ceremony. The pouch contained the most powerful warrior medicine available to a Cherokee: a scale from the skin of an Uktena. Thunder Child had put it away in a drawer in his room so he wouldn't lose it, but now he took the pouch out of the drawer and hung it around his neck so he'd have it if the going got tough.

One additional important thought popped into his mind, this one from the Circle of Prophets: *When in doubt, rely on yourself. That means all the multiple dimensions of yourself that exist in multiple time frames.*

The idea was just as puzzling as when he'd first heard it. Unexpectedly, the house phone sitting on his father's desk rang, interrupting his deliberations.

Now, who could that be? No one uses landlines anymore.

He picked up the receiver, half expecting it to be a salesperson, scammer, or wrong number. "*Osiyo,*" he said into the mouthpiece.

"*Osiyo,*" came the unexpected reply from an elderly man's voice. "Is this the Buckhorn house?"

"Yes. Yes, it is," Thunder Child said. "Who's this?"

"Amos Yonaguska," the man replied. "Calling from—"

"The Eastern Cherokee reservation," Thunder Child said, instantly recognizing the name. "Some people thought you were dead."

The last time the teen heard that name, it came from the mind of the Tlanuwa bird with metallic wings as the creature looked down at him from a cave above the Oconaluftee River.

"As a lifetime member of the Night Seers of the Owl Clan, I did some despicable things to people," the old man said. "But when I heard that two Night Seers, with the blessing of our leader, had murdered your grandfather—well, that was a step too far."

This confirmed what the Buckhorns and Lookouts had already suspected, but Thunder Child had no response to this confession.

Yonaguska continued. "I knew I had to do something about it, but I wasn't sure what."

The old Cherokee paused. The young Cherokee waited.

"I'm calling to make you an offer that I hope you accept," Yonaguska said. "It may help you prevent the Owls and Snakes from completing their mission."

"I'm listening," Thunder Child replied.

And the young Cherokee was glad he did, because by the end of the call, he had one more weapon in his arsenal to use against his devious and deceitful foes. It was as if Thunder Child's thoughts had reached the old man eight hundred miles away.

Thunder Child's thoughts must've reached someone else as well. Or that someone decided now would be a good time to reach out to him.

"Rely on yourself," a voice told him. "All the multiple dimensions of yourself that exist in multiple time frames."

The teen looked around but saw no one else in the War Room. "Who are you? Who is talking to me?"

"I am you, Billy 'Thunder Child' Buckhorn—the future you," the voice replied. "I'm here to help you put the pieces of the puzzle together."

"Okay, now I've really lost it," Thunder Child said.

"You are *not* imagining this," the voice said. "I'm very real and chose this exact time to appear to you."

"All right, let's say I believe you. What have you got for me?"

"There's one item you forgot to mention in your list of skills, assets, and resources," the voice said.

"What's that?"

"Out-of-body time travel."

"You're absolutely right. I had totally forgotten about it," Thunder Child replied.

"As your future self, I am using that skill right now," the future self said. "And after we've finished talking, you'll use the same ability to go back in time to take care of some extremely important business."

The future Thunder Child proceeded to provide the current Thunder Child with knowledge that could only have come from direct experience, and the current Thunder Child listened intently.

CHAPTER NINETEEN

Enemies and Allies

A thousand years is a meaningless length of time when you reside in a realm where time doesn't exist. The Afterworld, Underworld, and Upperworld are all such realms. Or, more accurately, the further away you are from physical life on planet earth, the less relevant are concepts such as time and space.

Monkata, the Snake Priest, had learned this lesson very well during his thousand-year stay in the Underworld, but he'd known what to expect before he got there and had planned ahead. A well-known supernatural truth stated that "like attracts like" in nonphysical realms. Therefore, his twisted mind and ambitious soul attracted him to like-minded residents.

Upon his physical death during his army's attack on Solstice City, his soul immediately plummeted to the fourth Underworld level, the Valley of the Stalking Skeletons, location of the House of Bones. As part of the Negative Afterworld Belief Zone, it was a natural stopping place for the soul of a man who'd spent his earthly life on the dark side.

Monkata knew very well that the idea of a "final judgment of the soul" was a religious myth first invented by the ancient Egyptians. Rising to one of the seven heavens or descending to one of the nine hells was part of that belief. Where would your soul end up?

He believed he knew the destination of a soul after death was, instead, purely a function of natural, or rather supernatural, laws, not the result of a mighty higher power weighing life's deeds on some cosmic scale.

Nothing much scared the Snake Priest while on earth, and nothing much frightened him in the lower world either. That trait served him well, for it freed him from fears that troubled other souls down there. And he had a goal in mind that also helped him survive. That was to reach the lowest level of the Underworld, abode of the Winged Serpent, and win the beast's confidence.

After much methodical, concentrated effort, he eventually reached that goal.

Upon arrival in Level Nine, Monkata set about the task of eliminating all the competition for the title of Servant to the Serpent. The lowest region was filled with the dark souls of all the Snake Priests who'd ever lived from whatever nation they'd lived in, because the Serpent God had been worshipped by people all over the ancient world for thousands of years.

How do the dead wage war on those who are also dead? There were deals to be made. "You help me and I'll help you" kinds of arrangements. Manipulation and betrayal played large parts in the game, because lower-world deal makers weren't necessarily trustworthy, were they?

The punishment for losing? Expulsion from the Winged One's realm. Like a season of the TV show *Survivor*, you'd get voted off the island, except the word *voted* isn't a strong enough term. Expulsion landed you in one of the other levels, the Shadow Zone, the Valley of Stalking Skeletons, or the Territories of Torment.

CHAPTER NINETEEN

Those regions were filled with common, ordinary outlaws, offenders, delinquents, and addicts.

But Underworld dwellers came from cultures all over the world and from times long forgotten by most earthlings. Native American beliefs about the Afterworld made up only a very small percentage of the actual realms and conditions in the lower zones.

Native American magical practices made up a tiny fraction of all the possible rituals and spells used in the dark magical arts worldwide. For every positive, selfless higher use of magic and medicine for healing in the Middleworld, there were contrasting harmful, selfish, and destructive versions.

For Monkata, the physical deformity that plagued him during his life on earth at first tormented him in the Afterworld. But he quickly acquired the skills of a Soul Eater from a fellow Indigenous sorcerer and began preying on the unsuspecting newly dead. The vitality of his own soul increased with every meal.

The Solstice City outcast then absorbed every form of magic he could find, strengthening his abilities to a point that no one could challenge his right to abide with and serve the Winged One. The powers and reputation of this Indigenous sorcerer grew until he became the dark master that other souls wanted to learn from.

However, the disadvantage of being so far removed from the physical plane of existence was the difficulty in keeping up with news from the Middleworld. And Monkata needed to hear the latest in a specific kind of news—news about preparations for the Thinning of the Veil, news about the reunion of the Owls and Snakes, news about the status of the bones and soul of his twin brother, Shakuru.

The long and the short of it was this: he needed an ally who could regularly provide these kinds of updates. That was when he met Shadow Zone dweller and former Owl Clan leader Benjamin Blacksnake. The two quickly recognized each other as kindred spirits, having similar goals and parallel ambitions. They readily forged an alliance—a secret alliance.

For Blacksnake, it was a sorcerer's dream come true, the best of both the Middleworld and the Underworld. It was easy for the Cherokee Raven Stalker to pretend to be helping Thomas Two Bears and Nahash Molok while simultaneously and secretly aiding Monkata with his plans for ultimate domination of the physical world. Being on the Winged Serpent's winning team would put Blacksnake where he always knew he belonged: among the immortals!

"I hope you bring good news this time, comrade," Monkata told Blacksnake when they met in the Shadow Zone just before the Grand Thinning began. "Are our secret arrangements still unknown to the Owls and Snakes? Do they suspect anything?"

"All seems to be unfolding as we planned," Blacksnake confirmed. "Coyotl took care of positioning Shakuru's remains in the cave south of Cahokia, uh, Solstice City, just as you asked. The Aztec and I will be ready to assist you with the spell to destroy your twin forever."

"Good, good," the Snake Priest said. "I can't even think of executing the rest of our takeover plans until I've vanquished that usurper of the Sun Chief's throne once and for all! Then, as the Winged Serpent and I ride across the sky, I'll destroy that puny Thunder Child character and put an end to the dreams he and his followers have of ruling the Middleworld!"

"Well, don't forget the part me and my Shadow Zone army will play in ridding the world of Shakuru's physical descendants," Blacksnake said, "and the quick work we'll make of any Upperworld forces that materialize. They won't stand a chance!"

Unaware of the secret alliance formed between Blacksnake, Monkata, and Coyotl, Brother Molok pushed his Serpent Society members to work long hours in the hidden cave to conjure the Winged Serpent from below. By Molok's calculations, the

Grand Thinning would be at its most potent point at the thirteenth hour of the third day of May.

"Almost time," Snake-Eye told his fellow Serpent Society members as that time and date approached.

Everything seemed to be progressing well until midmorning, when unexpected noises came from the southern chamber of the cave. Molok knew that Norman Redcorn was back there working to reattach the Fire Crystal to his Uktena's forehead in readiness for the reunion of the Uktenas with their leader, the Winged One.

Molok's secret hideout had long ago been fitted with the best in communications technology, lighting, furnishings for up to fifty people to live comfortably, and all the luxuries his collection of sorcerers would ever need. It also still contained features and relics left over from the glory days of the Mound Builder era more than a thousand years ago.

"Is everything all right back there, Redcorn?" Molok asked, speaking into an intercom system. "Do you need assistance?"

No response came back. Rather than disrupt the work of the rest of the Serpent Society, Molok sent one of his assistants to go find out what happened. Ruthann, who did double duty as manager of the Serpent World tourist destination, volunteered to go check it out.

Although she always pretended to outsiders that she didn't know what Greyson Greenstone, a.k.a. Nahash Molok, a.k.a. Snake-Eye, was up to, that was just a ruse. The older teen was very familiar with all of Greenstone's properties, including the hidden cave's many chambers.

What she loved most about the cave was the incredibly beautiful outcroppings of purple and green crystals. Patches of these formations were visible all through the subterranean space.

The cave's central passageway, from the main north entrance all the way to the back room, featured a tall, vaulted ceiling and a shallow channel of water that came in from the river. Just above and beside the channel ran a hard stone surface wide enough to drive an electric cart on.

Ruthann hopped on the battery-powered all-terrain vehicle they kept charged for the purpose and was about to head for the cave's back chamber when her boss stopped her.

"Remember to put on your protective goggles," he said.

"Oh, right. Thanks."

From a storage cabinet, she pulled out one of the pairs of special protective eyewear that Coyotl had created. Without them, the beast could blind you, paralyze you, or kill you with one wrong look, especially after the Fire Crystal had been reinserted.

Placing the goggles beside her in the cart, she sped away. At the midpoint of the cave, she knew to slow down considerably as she passed by the large, round opening in the cave floor known as the Gateway to the Underworld. The ruins of ancient stone structures lay scattered about around the Gateway.

Almost any cave in the world with deep passageways was a possible supernatural portal to the nether world, but the massive hole in the middle of this particular cave was *the* main one, used by ancient Native American Snake Priests to conjure the Winged One centuries ago.

In the past, the Gateway was also the source of mind-altering gasses that had been used by Snake Priests to help them receive and interpret messages from the Underworld. But, wherever the hallucinogenic fumes had come from before, they no longer poured out of the Gateway.

Just as she passed that opening, Ruthann heard a loud roar coming from the back of the cave. The sound echoed and reverberated off the walls around her. She knew it to be the angry call of Redcorn's Uktena, so she revved up her speed as much as the little electric motor could handle. Before reaching the back room of the cave, the girl stopped the cart and put on the safety goggles, making sure the eye coverings fit snuggly.

"Pedal to the metal," she said and sped onward.

She found the Uktena right where it was supposed to be and a dazed Norman Redcorn sitting on a rock with his back toward the beast. He was rubbing his head.

"Where are your goggles?" Ruthann asked. "What happened?"

"I'm not exactly sure," Redcorn replied. "My Uktena knocked me down, and I hit my head. When I came to, the Fire Crystal was gone and so were my goggles. There might have been somebody else in here."

The girl scanned the ground around them to confirm the man's statement. Seeing neither the gem nor the eyewear, she walked toward the back of the cave and peeked around the corner.

"The guys are still in their cages, so they couldn't have done it," she said.

At that moment, an explosive ripping noise came from the direction of the Gateway, followed by a hot blast of foul-smelling air that hit Redcorn and Ruthann in the face hard.

"What the hell was that?" the girl asked.

"The Gateway has been breached," Redcorn said, standing up. "I think Monkata and the Winged One just crossed the dimension barrier."

The man took off running, and Ruthann climbed into her cart.

At the far end of the cave, Molok and the rest of his Serpent Society had heard the ripping sound, felt the blast, and smelled the odor.

"The energies of the Grand Thinning have peaked," Molok remarked. "Well done, Serpents! Your efforts—our efforts— have succeeded!"

Brother Molok and his followers stood in awe, watching the giant purple-and-green Winged Serpent step into their meeting chambers. The reptile looked like some kind of composite creature from a twisted fairy tale. Its leathery wings resembled those of a bat, but unlike a regular snake, its body was supported by back legs with clawed feet. A pair of antler-type horns—much like those sported by the Uktenas—adorned its head, and its mouth was rimmed with sharp teeth.

Monkata sat astride the back of the beast's ridged neck, tightly holding on to one of its textured spikes. His entire body emitted a purplish glow, especially the eyes. The jagged lines on his bronze-colored face looked as though they'd been carved in ancient, cracked stone.

The clothing worn by this resurrected Snake Priest was something a Mound Builder warrior might have worn in the past. An obsidian dagger was visible on his reptilian belt, and a round war shield was strapped across his chest, easily accessible in time for battle.

"I bring you greetings from Level Nine," Monkata said as he slipped down off the beast's back. "The reign of a new era, a new kingdom, is about to begin, and you are the first witnesses of this history."

Seeing the one-eyed Molok, the ancient Snake Priest approached the man. "Is everything in readiness for our return?"

"Yes, yes, very much so," the man answered. "As the Snake Priest of this modern era, I greet and welcome you, the Snake Priest of the golden age of our past."

Molok bowed slightly to display respect for his guest, then extended his hand in friendship.

"Ah, you've pinpointed a prime issue right from the start. How appropriate!" Monkata said, ignoring the extended hand. He took a couple of steps to the side and turned back toward the Winged One. "You see, there can be only one Snake Priest in each era, and therefore I must sadly bid you farewell."

Monkata pointed at Molok. "*Yehcoah!*" he commanded. "Finish it!"

The giant reptile lowered its head and stretched out its neck toward the shocked Molok, who had begun to retreat.

"You can't do this," Snake-Eye protested. "I'm your own flesh and blood, and I've worked my whole life toward—"

The beast expelled a single breath of hot, foul-smelling air at Molok. There was no fire and no visible evidence of anything deadly, but the man immediately grimaced in pain, gasped for air, and fell to the ground. For a moment, his body writhed and convulsed, and then it eventually stopped moving altogether.

"Now, unless any of you care to join him, we'll proceed with the takeover using my own set of plans," the Snake Priest asserted.

"We're with you one hundred percent," Coyotl, who had been prepared for this sequence of events, said on behalf of the group.

Nervous nodding heads confirmed the statement.

"And my Aztec friend here will be my second-in-command," the Underworld dweller said, surprising everyone else. Monkata looked at Coyotl. "Time to meet Blacksnake at Solstice City."

The Winged Serpent lowered his head, allowing the Snake Priest to climb onto the beast's neck.

At the same time as these events were unfolding, up on Ohio Street in the city of St. Louis, Cody Lookout stood on the man-made mound next to his home on the western shore of the Mississippi River. His grandfather Cecil had been away for weeks, down in Cherokee territory, taking care of the most important spiritual matters ever faced by Indigenous people.

But Cody had stayed behind, promising that he'd continue to carry out regular prayer ceremonies at Cahokia across the river, the city his tribe built more than a thousand years ago. Cecil explained that someone in the Lookout family had to maintain those rituals on behalf of the Intertribal Medicine Council.

After donning his tribal regalia, the fifteen-year-old drove eastward across the 150-year-old Eads Bridge, the first structure in St. Louis to ever span the mighty Mississippi. For much of his life, the young man had regularly traveled the same thirteen-mile route to Cahokia for the same purpose: to perform one ancient tribal ceremony or another to help keep alive his tribe's connection to the site that was once the jewel of the Mississippian Mound Builder culture.

He parked, as usual, in the visitor parking lot at Cahokia Mounds state park and climbed the steps that took tourists to the top of Monk's Mound, so named by the archaeologists who excavated it. The mound had once been the largest flat-top earthen mound ever built in North America. After centuries of disuse and erosion, it only hinted at the grandeur of its former self.

The mound, the site of the Sun Chief's palatial home, was still tall enough to rise above the morning mist that often clung to the low-lying grounds that surrounded it.

Following a pattern similar to the Cherokee ritual Billy Buckhorn followed, Cody began his prayers to the Four Winds by facing east and asking for blessings from the spirit of that direction. Then, rotating clockwise, he prayed to the south and then to the west. Finally, after making his last turn, he was ready to pray for a blessing from the spirit of the north, when he thought he saw movement within the mist.

North of Cahokia sat flat fields of low-lying farmlands, and just north of those sat the large but shallow Horseshoe Lake. The lake, originally formed as a sharp curve in the Mississippi River, was as old or older than the mounds. Cahokia, the lake, and the farmlands were surrounded by the urban sprawl of East St. Louis.

At first, Cody couldn't believe what he was seeing. There were multiple dark gray figures moving about in the mist not far from Monk's Mound. North of that, the boy noticed more of the figures coming up from the shallow lake. They seemed to almost emerge from the liquid and awkwardly march onto the shore.

The figures stumbled around on two legs, but their bodies seemed like they weren't fully developed yet. Once they arrived onshore, they just milled around aimlessly and looked like they were waiting to be told where to go and what to do. Cody's mind searched for an explanation for what he was witnessing.

What is this? The zombie apocalypse?

That was when the boy remembered something his grandfather had told him.

"When the Underworld comes," Cecil had said. "It will rise from the waters and step from the caves."

That was when he knew!

It's here! The prophecy of the Underworld takeover is coming to pass! I have to call Grandpa Cecil!

One more quick look to the north confirmed it. These were human souls from somewhere in the Afterworld in the process of becoming flesh-and-blood physical beings again.

In a panic, the Osage teen called his grandfather at about the same time Chigger called Thunder Child to report on his discoveries in Molok's hidden cave.

CHAPTER TWENTY

Breath of Death

By the time Chigger reached Travis Youngblood on the sat phone, the marshal had already heard from Raelynn and agreed to head up the unofficial search team, so he was ready to act.

And act he did.

His first action was to deputize the four new members of the unofficial search-and-rescue team made up of himself, Raelynn Little Shield, Police Chief Swimmer, his nephew Jerry, and Lisa Lookout, the group's only civilian.

His second action was to alert the US Marshals' Tactical Division of the immediate need for manpower and equipment to raid Molok's hidden cave. Fortunately, the Tactical Division's headquarters were in Pineville, Louisiana, only 120 miles west of the intended search site.

His third action was to commit his own office's resources to the team, which included the use of a helicopter large enough to transport the five of them to the Three Rivers area. At a flight speed of one hundred miles an hour, the trip took about five hours.

Youngblood put the copter down on a flat piece of land just north of the Three Rivers Mounds site, which was right across the river from the cave's north entrance. Or so Chigger claimed, based on his "sensitivity to negativity," as the teen described it.

Another team of US marshals was already on site with two boats, one for Youngblood's group and one for a second, more official search team. After introductions all around, Travis's group boarded the second boat, and off they went.

The two boats quickly and easily reached the canyon-like inlet across the river Chigger had described. The teen had also alerted them to the fact that they might not see the cave entrance due to some sort of camouflage magical spell set up by Molok's Snake Cult.

Much to their surprise, the mouth of the cave was readily visible as they approached. All was quiet and still.

"Why would this have been so hard to find?" Youngblood asked no one in particular.

Lisa, the only one with any experience in these matters, offered a possibility. "Something has changed since the last search was carried out," she said. "The spell that concealed the entrance has been broken or canceled."

"If you say so," the marshal replied. "But what could cause that to happen?"

"One of three things," the teen said. "The sorcerer who originally cast the spell canceled it. Or another sorcerer used a more powerful spell to override the original spell. Or . . ."

"Or what other story are you going to tell us?" Jerry Swimmer interrupted as he jumped out of his seat. "I think this whole magic-medicine, evil-spell thing is a crock of crap! I can't believe all of you fall for this stuff."

"You were at the amphitheater and heard the whole story, and still you're questioning it?" Raelynn responded. "Why are you even here?"

"Enough, you two!" Youngblood shouted. "We've got more important things to do than listen to you argue! We're here to conduct a search for men in cages and to see if we can discover anything else about this evil group's activities."

The pair grew quiet and simultaneously said, "Sorry."

"We're going in," Youngblood said and gently nudged the boat's throttle.

The other vessel moved alongside the marshals' boat, and both crafts beached on the narrow sandy shore at the cave's mouth. Guns drawn, the five marshals from the other boat jumped onto the shore and quietly made their way inland. They were followed first by Youngblood and the two Swimmers, who also had their weapons at the ready.

Finally, the two unarmed members of the team disembarked. Lisa thought to grab her phone and began making a video recording of their search to show Thunder Child and Chigger later. The first team quickly determined there was no one in the front part of the cave, but the men were amazed at what they did find.

"You've got to see this setup," one of the marshals told Youngblood over the walkie-talkie.

Youngblood's crew quickly caught up to see what all the fuss was about. The well-lit main room contained luxurious seating for nine people around a large oval table. Each station included the strangest black viewing screen any of them, except Lisa, had ever seen. Along the outer walls of the room were cabinets and shelves filled with bottles and baskets full of dried herbs and funny-looking liquids.

"Everything a proper Native American witch or wizard would ever need," Lisa said when she saw the surroundings and the furnishings, "including spirit viewers for each of them."

One of the nine chairs was larger and more ornate than the others, and the Aztec mirror in front of it was larger as well. Lisa moved toward the larger chair.

"This was probably the snake man's station at the head of the table," she observed.

Then she noticed something crumpled and flattened near the back wall of the main room and became curious. Raelynn followed Lisa's line of sight and became curious as well.

Lisa was the first to reach the object and gasped loudly when she realized what it was. "Oh my god!" she said, more as a raspy whisper.

Seconds later, Raelynn reacted with a quiet "What the hell?"

The rest of the team rushed over to see what the two were reacting to. Lying there on the ground was the body of a man that looked more like a mummy whose liquids had long ago been drained away. The leathery ashen skin clung to the skeletal structure as if the mummy were hundreds of years old. The figure's most distinguishing feature was the eye patch that covered one of its eye sockets.

"Chigger said the leader of the Snake Cult was a one-eyed man," Lisa remarked. "This must be what's left of Brother Nahash Molok, also known as Greyson Greenstone."

"Incredible!" Marshal Youngblood said. "This just gets weirder and weirder."

Jerry Swimmer took out his cell phone and began taking pictures and videos of the corpse. "This dehydrated corpse is supposedly the number one suspect in the murders of the warden and the guard," he said in disbelief. "I personally think testing will prove these remains to be at least two hundred years old and not our suspect."

One of the marshal's men had picked up a bottle of dried herbs. When he accidentally dropped it, the sound of breaking glass echoed off the cave walls and traveled deeper into the underground chamber. That brought echoing shouts back from the deeper region.

"The men in cages!" Youngblood shouted.

The team of marshals scrambled toward the shouts, responding with shouting of their own. More slowly, Lisa's group moved cautiously through the cavernous space. When they reached the deep dark hole in the middle, Lisa paused and gazed intently downward.

She couldn't see a bottom to it, but uncomfortable shivers ran up and down her spine. She rushed to catch up with the others, thinking she'd revisit the hole on her way out of the cave. The marshals freed the orange-suited men, handcuffed them, and escorted them toward the mouth of the cave.

"Out of the cage and back to prison," one of the inmates said as he passed. "I'll take being in a cell over waiting to be sacrificed to a serpent demon any day."

Lisa and her team followed after them, but the girl paused again at the bottomless pit.

"You guys go on," she said. "I'll catch up."

As Raelynn and the Swimmers moved on, the Osage girl closed her eyes and tried to feel with her Spider Woman senses what that opening was all about. The word *gateway* came to her, along with the quick flash of an image. The sight of that image jolted her back to normal consciousness.

Her whole body jerked, and she quickly turned, intending to catch up to the others. She didn't expect to see Raelynn standing there beside her.

"You saw something, didn't you?" the investigator said. "What did you see?"

"The Winged Serpent," Lisa said matter-of-factly. "It came out of this hole earlier today."

"*The* Winged Serpent?" Raelynn asked. "The lord of the Underworld Winged Serpent that Thunder Child spoke about?"

"That's the one," Lisa confirmed. "We gotta go. It's good we found the trapped men, but now we gotta go. We gotta tell Thunder Child and the others about this."

The two women did not know that hours before their discovery, under the command of Monkata, the Winged One and the Society of Serpents had vacated the hidden cave, leaving behind the mummified remains of the mastermind who had orchestrated the entire Underworld takeover campaign. He would not witness the final fruits of his dedicated efforts, and he would not be among those who expected to rule the Middleworld.

After a lifetime of disservice to humanity, the soul of Snake-Eye was destined to fall, as naturally as an apple falls from a tree, into the deeper levels of the lower regions, where he would remain.

At the Grand Thinning's most potent point, the Winged Serpent had risen from the hidden cave's Gateway. Immediately afterward, the dimensional rift closed again. No one else would be admitted to the Middleworld from the Underworld, and the doorway would remain closed for at least another Long Count of 5,125 years.

Having witnessed the brutal demise of her boss from a corner of the cave room, Ruthann, the assistant, had elected to quietly slip away on her own after all the serpents had vacated the premises. She was never seen or heard from again.

Riding through the sky on the back of the Winged Serpent, Monkata and Coyotl presented an unbelievable sight to people on the ground. Reports of UFOs, dragons, and various other flying monsters flooded into police stations all along the route, which followed the Mississippi River. Traveling about six hundred miles, the three made good time and reached a cave south of Cahokia in less than five hours.

This underground cavern, known locally as the Cliffside Cave, sat at the bottom of a sheer rock face at the water's edge.

It was significant to Monkata because he'd launched his attack on Solstice City a thousand years ago from this very cave. And after the Uktenas finally arrived in a few hours, it would be from this same cave he would launch his conquest of Cahokia and the rest of the Middleworld!

The last person to gain access to this underground chamber was the Aztec, who'd put a combination lock on the gate protecting the entrance. Coyotl had been in and out of this cave several times, making sure all was in readiness for the Snake Priest's glorious return.

One of the *most* important preparations concerned the physical skeletal remains of Monkata's twin brother, Shakuru. These bones had either been in Coyotl's possession or inside this cave ever since the Aztec picked them up from the Reverend Dr. Miller in Texas.

And the whereabouts of the skeleton had been kept under wraps thanks to the Nahuatl concealment spell Coyotl had applied to them. On top of that, he'd also strengthened the imprisonment formula that kept Shakuru's spirit bound to the bones.

"You just can't imagine how I've looked forward to this very hour," Monkata told Coyotl as they headed for the cave's gated entrance. "The thought of destroying Shakuru once and for all is really the only thing that's kept me going."

"Tonight's the night you'll be able to end your brother's existence forever," Coyotl said. "Once I've enacted the destruction spell, his old, brittle bones will be easy to grind into powder. Then, after Blacksnake's Shadow Zone army overcomes whatever meager resistance the Mundanes try to muster, you can spread that dust over the fields of Solstice City, and his soul will cease to exist."

A broad smile spread across Monkata's face as the Aztec unlocked the gate. Coyotl found the bones right where he'd left them, but something seemed amiss. The skeleton, though intact, was no longer enclosed in the protective energy field he'd put around it. And Coyotl's concealment spell had been undone, along with the formula he'd used to contain Shakuru's spirit within the cave!

"I don't understand it," he said in a state of bewilderment. "You've got to believe me! I used the most powerful and effective Aztec spells possible, and yet your brother's spirit is just plain gone! I have no explanation for it."

Monkata's shock quickly transformed into anger that became visible on his face. He shouted, "What fools am I surrounded by?"

Stomping out of the cave, the Snake Priest returned to the Winged One and issued the same Nahuatl death command he'd used earlier that day.

"*Yehcoah!*" he said, pointing toward the Aztec sorcerer.

Coyotl had all of two seconds to experience the feeling of sheer terror before the warm breath of death washed over him and he fell to the cave floor.

"I was already tired of you anyway," the Snake Priest said as he watched the man writhe on the ground. "I'll take it from here."

Coyotl's blunder wasn't the only disappointment Monkata would experience within his first twenty-four hours back in the Middleworld.

That afternoon in Oklahoma, Cecil and Thunder Child made an important decision. Because the Fire Crystal hadn't been found, they were going to plan B, a plan they just made up on the spot.

All thirteen members of the Intertribal Medicine Council would join Thunder Child at Cahokia. Together, they would all attempt to manifest Tecumseh and the spirit warriors using Cecil's medicine skill of materializing spirit beings in the physical plane, his own version of a reembodiment formula.

Although Cecil had only used the spell a few times in his life to help the souls of the deceased temporarily appear to their living loved ones, Thunder Child felt it could actually be used to make spirits become flesh if it was amplified. The way to amplify it, he thought, was to have a circle of all thirteen medicine makers perform the ritual at the same time.

There was no guarantee this backup plan would work, but it was all they had at the time.

So a caravan of cars and vans, filled with thirteen elders, two parents, and one sixteen-year-old, headed up Interstate 44 toward St. Louis. Cecil carried the Sky Stone with him, and Thunder Child, of course, brought the Lightning Lance, along with his most prized warrior medicine: the Uktena scale.

Earlier, down in Louisiana, when the boat carrying the Three Muskrateers returned to the ramp they'd launched from, Chigger made a request of his fellow expeditioners.

"If the information I got from the Uktena is right, we should head for Cahokia immediately," the teen advised. "Everybody who's anybody will be there."

Ethan and Augustus looked at each other questioningly.

"What do you think?" Augustus asked.

"The boy's been right about things so far," Ethan replied. "He's on a roll, and I think we should keep rolling with him."

Augustus nodded. "Okay, Cahokia, here we come!"

Towing the boat behind them, the Three Muskrateers headed north, taking turns behind the wheel during the long trip.

After leaving the hidden cave hours later, Lisa called her boyfriend. She told him about her vision of the Winged Serpent coming through the Gateway. He shared his news that a caravan of cars was headed to Cahokia. After the call, the girl spoke to Travis Youngblood as the rest of the search team listened in.

"I need to get to Cahokia, east of St. Louis," she said. "Have you heard of it?"

"The site of some old eroded Native mounds?"

"Can you give me a ride in the copter?" Lisa asked.

"What's going on there?" the marshal responded.

"Well, for one thing, the people who kept those men in cages will probably be there."

"Say no more," he replied. "That's enough reason to go."

"I need to go too," Jerry said. "I want to be on hand when nothing actually happens, and this group realizes it's all a big supernatural hoax!"

"Count me in too," Raelynn said. "I want to be there when this dimwit FBI agent finally sees the truth! I want to hear him say he was wrong, and I was right!"

"This should be loads of fun!" Youngblood replied sarcastically as his team disembarked from the boat on the west side of the river.

The five of them scrambled for the Marshals Service helicopter as its pilot fired up the engine.

"Okay, all aboard the crazy copter!" the marshal shouted over the sound of the rotors. "First stop is Tactical headquarters so we can refuel."

After they reached their cruising altitude, Youngblood asked Lisa, "How are we supposed to recognize the Snake Cult members?"

"Chigger told us they all usually wear Winged Serpent medallions," she said as another thought struck her. "I bet the Night Seers will all be there too."

"Great—this is shaping up to be an old-fashioned Wild West gunfight at the O.K. Corral," the marshal said, referring to the famous Tombstone shootout of the 1880s.

"Chigger called it the Showdown at Cahokia," Lisa replied.

"Sounds about right," the marshal concluded.

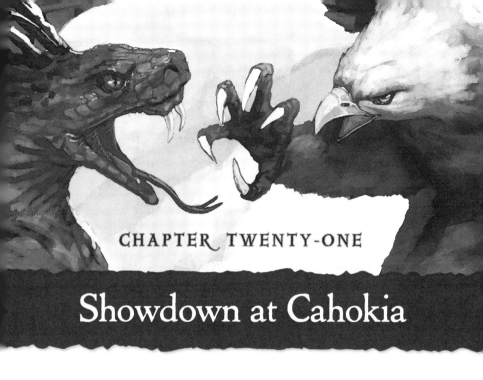

Showdown at Cahokia

As he and the Medicine Council elders made their way to Cahokia, Thunder Child realized all the far-flung members of the Underworld Takeover Prevention Team might arrive at about the same time.

Ready or not, this is it, the War of Worlds, he thought. *I've done all I can do. The team has done all it can do. All that's left now is to pray and hope and fight.*

Another thought nagged at him though. Why didn't anyone find the Fire Crystal? The Sun Chief's staff and feather cape were there in the hidden cave. But the gem was missing. Did the Society of Serpents put it back on the creature's forehead? Billy realized he may never know.

As Chigger rode toward Cahokia with the two archaeologists, he told them he needed to take a nap. Hugging his backpack close to his chest, he lay down out of sight in the back of the van. The Fire Crystal had been calling to him since they'd departed for Cahokia, and now he could respond.

Quietly unzipping the bag, he stuck his hand inside and grasped the gem. Holding the precious stone gave him an enjoyable and empowering feeling he couldn't describe. But, at the same time, it also opened his connection to the Uktena. This gave him a front-row seat not only to what the Horned Serpents were *doing* but also to what they might be *experiencing*.

How's that possible? the teen thought.

The first thing he sensed was confusion among the beasts. An outside source, probably Serpent Society members who'd conjured them, were controlling the creatures, pushing them to rapidly swim northward. But Chigger's Uktena, the one he was connected to now, resisted that command.

That Horned Serpent suddenly broke from the others who were swimming in formation up the river. It now seemed to move toward Chigger's position. That realization made the boy release his hold on the gem. The visual connection ceased.

This can't really be happening. I must be imagining it.

To test his theory, he waited a couple of minutes and then wrapped his fingers around the stone again. He immediately saw what the Uktena saw. It appeared that Chigger's Uktena had actually been leading the others upriver when the creature turned to look in Chigger's direction.

Chigger knew the van was traveling on a freeway east of the Mississippi River. Not only did the Uktena look in that direction, but it also turned toward the eastern shore, and the other Uktenas followed.

My Uktena is the leader of the pack!

Chigger's mind began churning with ideas about what this discovery might mean and what he should do about it. He fantasized about climbing onto the Uktena's back and riding it up the river. He imagined all the Uktenas following him to Cahokia and then bowing down to him as their leader.

His final fantasy was that of him riding on the back of the Winged Serpent as they flew above thousands of adoring subjects in a restored Cahokia. It felt so glorious!

The ringing of the boy's cell phone burst Chigger's imagination bubble. Without looking at the caller ID, Chigger answered.

"I feel like you're holding something back," Thunder Child said. "What are you not telling me?"

In total shock, the once mighty Muskrat remained silent for a moment. His secret had somehow been discovered, and he felt ashamed.

"I wanted to tell you, but holding it felt so good, so . . . I don't know," Chigger said in an almost whiny voice. "I thought I might be able to somehow help you defeat the Underworld if I kept it and used it myself."

"But you've already done so many brave and surprising things and helped so much," Thunder Child said in an understanding tone. "It's time to let me do my job."

His friend didn't scold him or get angry, and that was disarming to Chigger.

"You're right," he replied. "I'm on my way to Cahokia now with Ethan and Digger. We should be there in a couple hours. I'll give it to you as soon as we get there."

"Good," Thunder Child replied. "I'm looking forward to it. Then I want you and Lisa to go to Cecil's house in St. Louis to be safe. She knows where it is."

"Okay, buddy. See you soon."

After ending the call, Chigger realized he still had some time to possibly put the Fire Crystal to good use. An idea was forming in his mind that might prove to be a significant contribution to the Underworld Takeover Prevention Team. But would it work? He wouldn't know for sure until events unfolded later at Cahokia.

Thunder Child and the elders of the Medicine Council arrived at the two-thousand-acre Cahokia state park first. At about two hours before sunrise, their caravan headed straight for the site's interpretive center on the east side of the park. Everyone on the Chosen One's support team would be meeting there.

During the past few days, while Lisa, Chigger, and various law enforcement agencies had been focused on the hidden cave near Three Rivers, Thunder Child had been very busy with other matters.

One such matter was the adoption of the Tlanuwa. On May 1, Amos Yonaguska had driven his prized, but slightly rusted, 1955 Ford pickup from the Eastern Cherokee reservation to the Cherokee Nation of Oklahoma while telepathically guiding the metallic-winged bird as it flew in the sky above him.

The elder and the teen had agreed to meet on the remote and abandoned property at Buzzard Bend once belonging to Carmelita Tuckaleechee.

"I was so sorry to hear about the death of your grandfather," the medicine man said when they met and shook hands. "I should've reached out to you sooner."

"No matter—you're here now," Thunder Child replied. "I need all the help I can get."

The retired Night Seer transferred control of the strange, giant bird to Thunder Child and demonstrated how to command the creature's every move with his mind. Yonaguska also agreed to remain on site while the teen bonded with the bird and practiced riding on its back.

When it came time for the Medicine Council's caravan to head for Cahokia, Thunder Child commanded the Tlanuwa to fly to the perfect place to hide. It was another large cave in the cliffs just north of St. Louis right on the Mississippi River. Long ago, the cave had been home to another legendary flying creature, called by the local tribe the Piasa Bird.

Now, with a brilliant star field overhead, the Medicine Council elders parked their cars, trucks, and vans in the interpretive center's main parking lot. Over Thunder Child's protests, his parents, James and Rebecca, had driven their son to the site in the family Jeep. It was definitely a dangerous place for them to be.

Many sets of eyes scanned the skies, searching for any sign of the feared Winged Serpent. Many other sets of eyes focused on the ground to the north, searching for signs of the shadowy figures Cody had reported seeing. Everyone wondered why there hadn't already been an attack of some kind.

Thunder Child was the first to hear the whirring of blades as Lisa's search team approached the historical site. What first appeared as merely a glowing dot against the dark western sky eventually became recognizable as a helicopter with running lights.

After setting the whirlybird down on flat turf, the pilot killed the engine, and his passengers disembarked. Lisa sprinted across the grass to hug both her boyfriend and her cousin, Cody, who'd driven out from St. Louis to participate in the gathering.

"When we're done activating the Sky Stone, I want you to get everyone over to Cecil's house and wait till you hear from me," Thunder Child told Lisa. "It should be safe there."

"But I need to stay to—"

"That includes you," her boyfriend said sternly. "And Chigger, if he gets here in the next few minutes."

The girl reluctantly nodded.

"If this is going to be such a big damn deal, why haven't you called for military support or law enforcement backup?" Marshal Youngblood asked angrily. "You're sitting ducks out here in this field."

Thunder Child stepped toward the marshal and spoke softly. "Because, as I understand it, bullets and bayonets, wielded by those with physical bodies, will have no effect on our enemies from the Underworld," the Chosen One said.

"That doesn't make any sense," Youngblood insisted. "How do you even know that?"

"We know that because reservation police from all across the country have reported it," James Buckhorn said as he stepped in closer to the conversation. "Cryptid creatures, once thought to be figments of the imagination, have been appearing in rural communities for some time now, but, so far, physical weapons don't seem to harm them and can't stop them."

Cecil interrupted the two men. "No time for chitchat," he said. "Time to chant."

The men moved away as Cecil stepped into the center of the gathered group. Then, carrying the assembled Sky Stone, he led the elders and the Chosen One to a central area of the park that had once been part of Solstice City's main plaza. It was near the very spot the meteorite, the original Sky Stone, had plowed into the earth on that fateful day in AD 1054.

Not knowing when all hell might break loose around them, the group immediately formed a circle in the flat area with the Chosen One in the center.

"Chigger will be here with the Fire Crystal any minute now," Thunder Child told them. "I know he will."

"I hope that's true," Cecil said. "But in case he's delayed, we'll still follow through with our plan B."

The teen nodded, and Cecil signaled to the group. The elders joined hands and began an Osage incantation they'd learned from the Keeper of the Center just for this occasion. As arranged earlier, Lisa and Cody smudged everyone in the circle with sage as the incantation continued.

Standing in the circle's center, Thunder Child could feel a wave of positive energy radiating toward him from every direction. One way or another, he knew this burst of added power would benefit him in the coming clash.

The incantation ended, but the swell of added energy remained with Thunder Child. He was about to make an announcement to the crowd when the sound of a honking horn broke the silence, and in the faint predawn light, a pair of headlights approached from the main road.

It wasn't long before a van towing a boat pulled into the parking lot, where the overhead parking lights were still on. Before the vehicle came to a complete stop, a back door swung open, and out popped Chigger carrying the Fire Crystal.

It was the first time most of the people there had seen the legendary gem, and they saw firsthand why the word *fire* had been used to describe it. Caught in the glow of the parking lot lights, the pinkish-orange facets inside the crystal seemed to dance like firelight.

"Stand back!" Chigger commanded dramatically as he trotted from the van. "Special delivery for Thunder Child! Fire Crystal coming through!"

At first, Lisa was shocked when she learned Chigger was the one who'd found the crystal, and yet part of her wasn't surprised at all.

Typical Chigger, she thought.

"I guess you're running on Indian time," Thunder Child told Chigger as he approached with the gem. "Not a minute too soon, not a minute too late."

Ever the showman, Chigger presented the Fire Crystal with a dramatic flair. "Your Spiritual Highness, I present the legendary Fire Crystal, recently retrieved from the Society of Serpents' hidden cave."

That brought unexpected supportive shouts of "Aho!" from Native men in the crowd and a series of "lulus" from Native women, which were meant to honor Chigger, the young warrior, for having bravely *counted coup* on an enemy.

"Enough with the drama," Thunder Child said sharply. "Give me the crystal."

Chigger handed over the gem and then retreated back into the crowd.

"I want to thank all of you for your support, but now it's time for all civilians to evacuate," Thunder Child announced. "And by civilians, I mean anyone who is not a member of the Intertribal Medicine Council."

Both Lisa and Chigger stepped toward the circle of elders.

"After all we've been through together, I'm not about to miss this!" Lisa said.

"Yeah, and I'm your best friend forever!" Chigger protested. "Doesn't that count for something?"

Irritated that these two wouldn't listen to him, Thunder Child exclaimed, "Go, don't go, do whatever you want to do! I have to focus now!"

"Everyone to the interpretive center!" Youngblood shouted, taking charge of the situation. "Let's get going so he can get on with it."

Raelynn, the Buckhorns, the two archaeologists, the two Swimmers, the marshal and his helicopter pilot, Lisa, Cody, and Chigger all headed for the building that sat about a hundred yards away.

Turning his attention back to his primary mission, the Chosen One signaled Cecil. The elders of the Medicine Council encircled the teen, and, when they were all in place, the Keeper of the Center presented the Sky Stone to Thunder Child. With one hand still on the stone, Cecil recited a short prayer he'd been practicing for a long time.

"We welcome our crystal brother back to his home in the Sky Stone," the elder said in the Osage language. "We humbly ask Upperworld spirits to come forth to join the Chosen One in returning balance to us here in the Middleworld."

When the prayer ended, Thunder Child inserted the Fire Crystal into the keyhole slot in the middle of the five-piece Sky

Stone. Even after hundreds of years, it fit perfectly. He twisted the crystal to the right one-quarter turn, as Cecil had previously instructed.

A sudden blast of energy radiated out from the stone in every direction, accompanied by a sonic boom usually heard when a jet plane breaks the sound barrier. Every elder standing in that circle felt the shock wave, which struck them like a blast of wind in a hurricane.

In the next instant, the stone and crystal flew out of the teen's hand and shot straight up into the night sky. Within a few seconds, there came an explosive burst high overhead, like miniature fireworks on the Fourth of July. Particles of light lingered in the air, illuminating the ground below. Shortly afterward, the brightness of the stars and constellations high above the earth intensified noticeably.

Thunder Child had never witnessed anything like it before. Light coming from the particles created a glow on the ground that enhanced the faint light of early dawn. But this light was more than just physical illumination. It seemed to emanate from a supernatural source, breaking through the dimensional barrier separating the physical and the celestial.

"You never told me exactly what would happen when we activated the Sky Stone!" Thunder Child whispered to Cecil.

"I never knew exactly," Cecil replied, wide eyed.

On the fringes of Cahokia's fields, the soft muted light revealed much that had been lurking in the dark of night.

To the north, Benjamin Blacksnake and his Shadow Zone army became visible. Appearing as a mobile mass of blackness, they'd been lurking in the darkness, waiting for a signal to attack. To the south, the remaining seven members of the Serpent Society were also in standby mode, their silver-and-black medallions visible in the overhead light. They anxiously anticipated the arrival of the eight Uktenas, which were overdue.

To the east, Thomas Two Bears and the Night Seers stood poised and ready to strike, using various forms of their black magic medicine. Behind them, a dozen or so nervous cryptids, conjured and barely controlled by the Owl Clan, were gnashing their teeth and losing patience.

Finally, to the west, Monkata became visible, seemingly ready for hand-to-hand combat. He was sitting atop the massive Winged Serpent, and what a formidable sight the pair presented! The purple-and-green being snapped and snarled as its rider strained to maintain mastery over the beast. The Snake Priest, who also expected the imminent arrival of the eight Horned Serpents, looked to the west toward the Mississippi River.

"The Underworld is literally all around us now," Thunder Child told Cecil. "I've got to create the protection bubble we talked about!"

"Elders, gather round me," Cecil said. "Make a tight circle."

Moving in closer, all thirteen medicine makers squeezed together. Then Thunder Child took hold of the warrior medicine pouch he wore and repeated the protection formula he'd learned from Blackfoot medicine man Ryder Heavy Runner. A defensive dome of protective energy began forming over the huddled group.

Just in time too, because that was when Monkata made his first move. With a loud, growling hiss, the Winged Serpent leaped into action. The creature spread its massive batlike wings and propelled the pair upward.

"You puny, pathetic collection of raggedy old relics," the Snake Priest shouted from his hovering position. "One fatal breath from the Winged One will end you forever!"

He and the serpent glided toward the cluster of medicine elders, who stood their ground, hoping their supercharged protection spell could repel the attack. The flying reptile passed above them, expelling its deadly, foul-smelling breath toward them.

When absolutely no harm came to the medicine makers, the Snake Priest turned his anger toward Thunder Child.

"I suppose you're responsible for the spell that protects them," Monkata said. "Pretty good trick if I do say so myself. Let's see how you handle this!"

Quickly, Thunder Child grabbed his warrior medicine bag with one hand and thrust the Lightning Lance out before him with the other. He uttered the magic words to activate his own protective shield.

"*Yehcoah! Yehcoah! Yehcoah!*" Monkata commanded, repeating the destructive Nahuatl phrase.

With an extra burst of strength, the serpent blew out its breath toward Thunder Child for an extended length of time. But the result was the same. Nothing happened. His anger turning to rage, the Snake Priest remembered another group he needed to deal with.

"I'll be back to finish you off in a minute," the Underworld dweller said. Then he refocused his attention to the south. Flying directly toward the gathered remnant of the Serpent Society, he demanded, "Where are my Horned Serpents? They were due here long ago!"

No one in the group spoke.

Hovering above and in front of the group, he focused on one. "Redcorn, you're in charge of the Uktena that's leading the others here. Where are they? What happened to them?"

"Something got them off course," the nervous man replied. "Try as I might, I can't get the creature to respond to me or even acknowledge my control."

"Anyone else got an explanation for this?" Monkata asked as his anger grew. "How about you, Jonna Boudreaux? You're one of Molok's most trusted followers. What do you have to say?"

"My Horned Serpent followed the others as expected," she replied weakly. "But they all seem to be waiting at the Cliffside Cave for a signal from someone outside the society."

"You worthless excuses for medicine makers!" the serpent rider yelled. "What good are you? I never want to see your miserable faces again. *Yehcoah!*" he commanded one more time, and the beast responded as before.

The conjurers turned to flee, but their last-minute attempt at escape was futile. The seven unprotected mortals, once part of a dark and powerful force, perished where they stood. Their bodies were immediately dehydrated of all fluids, leaving behind nothing but desiccated carcasses.

The sound of people gasping in horror reached Monkata's ears. The presence of Lisa, Chigger, and the others had escaped the Snake Priest's notice until that very moment. He set his gaze to the west, looking for the source of the sound.

That was when Cecil realized the terrible thing that might happen next.

"Quickly, to the interpretive center," he told the elders, "We must provide a shield for them."

Moving more quickly than a group of aging elders could expect to, the thirteen ran for the interpretive center.

"Stand in a circle around them and link arms," Cecil instructed as the out-of-breath group arrived.

Facing outward, the elders encircled the group of civilians, as Thunder Child had called them. They braced for the next deadly breath, which came quickly. Thankfully, again it produced no results. Failing once more, the Snake Priest screamed at the top of his lungs in frustration.

Then he thought of Blacksnake and his army waiting to the north. He started to prompt his flying ally to move in that direction when some sort of motion in the west caught his eye.

Only Thunder Child expected what happened next.

A tall, muscular male figure emerged from the western edge of the field and stepped into view, carrying a short copper sword in one hand and a shield in the other. His gold-fringed regalia glistened in the faint light as he looked up at the Winged One and Monkata.

"My brother," the man shouted, "you asked for a rematch here on the land where you were defeated long ago. So here I am. Come and get me."

"It's the Sun Chief!" Thunder Child exclaimed loud enough for Cecil and the others to hear. "I thought he'd never show up!"

Cecil had long ago given up on the possibility of ever finding the Sun Chief's spirit, so his appearance was surprising and confusing. "How?" the elder shouted back.

"I'll explain later," Thunder Child said.

Monkata nudged the serpent, and the beast quickly covered the distance from the interpretive center to his brother's position.

"At long last," Monkata said. "I'll relish this moment the rest of my life."

Swooping down, the Winged One expelled a breath from his lungs that was aimed right for Shakuru. Again, it had no effect.

A troubled and perplexed Monkata hovered above his twin.

"Your Underworld weapons and wizardry can't harm me," Shakuru announced. "They only work on mortals made of flesh and bone. My physical bones still lie in that cave where your Aztec coyote friend put them. This body I'm in now formed when Thunder Child activated the Sky Stone. Nothing within your power can harm it."

"I don't know how you escaped the Aztec magician's spells in the cave," the Snake Priest said, "but this isn't over."

"Get off that hideous beast, come down here, and face me man to man," Shakuru shouted.

Ignoring his brother's taunt and turning northward, Monkata signaled Blacksnake to release the Shadow Zone army that he commanded. The Cherokee sorcerer uttered a string of unintelligible words to the horde, and the Underworld brutes rallied, running toward the center of the field.

That was when Thunder Child noticed a low-lying cluster of twinkling stars, which seemed to linger while others had faded as the light of dawn grew brighter. They appeared to be burning brighter and becoming larger. But he soon realized they weren't getting brighter or larger. They were getting closer.

In the next instant, the stars were racing toward earth with fiery trails behind them. But instead of crashing into the ground like meteors, they transformed into warriors carrying weapons, who landed feetfirst on Cahokia's soil.

Thunder Child recognized Tecumseh as the leader of this celestial war party. The man acknowledged the teen's presence as dozens of other Star People began to arrive. Many of those Thunder Child knew from historical photos or paintings. There was Sitting Bull, the Lakota chief; Red Cloud, Oglala Sioux; Chief Joseph, Nez Percé; Dragging Canoe, Cherokee; Osceola, Seminole; and Geronimo, Apache. Many, many more dropped from the sky and stood ready to fight.

Immediately jumping into action, they fired arrows, threw spears, and pitched tomahawks toward the shadow fighters. Blacksnake, originally displaying vicious intentions, watched helplessly as his untrained, inexperienced squad suffered serious losses.

"I thought you said weapons couldn't stop them," the sorcerer yelled to Monkata.

"Physical weapons used by mortal humans from the Middleworld absolutely cannot harm them," the Snake Priest responded. "I didn't expect there to be Upperworld weapons wielded by Afterworld warriors on this battlefield. This changes everything."

As the hand-to-hand battle raged between the residents of opposite worlds, Thunder Child called out telepathically to his own secret weapon, the giant metallic-winged bird waiting in the Piasa Cave near the river.

The Tlanuwa, roughly the size of the Winged Serpent, responded immediately and came to the teen as easily as a pet dog answers the call of its master. Monkata, absorbed in watching the battle between the warriors and the shadows, didn't notice the arrival of Thunder Child's raptor.

After mounting the bird, Thunder Child prompted the magnificent creature to lift off. As it rose, it screeched loudly, sounding much like a red-tailed hawk. The sound immediately caught the Snake Priest's attention, and he prodded his serpent to confront the new adversary. With Yonaguska's help, Thunder Child had practiced many aerial combat maneuvers and was prepared for this very encounter.

The flying serpent's built-in defenses included a mouth full of sharp teeth, a set of antlered horns, clawed back feet, and a talon tip on the top of each wing. The Tlanuwa's defensive equipment included impenetrable metal feathers, strong grasping claws, an indestructible beak, and a remarkable agility in the air.

Add to that Thunder Child's Lightning Lance, and the combination was awe inspiring.

"Let's do this!" Thunder Child uttered to no one in particular, and the action began.

He quickly had the giant fowl rising higher into the sky, which gave him the upper hand over Monkata and the serpent. Diving down toward the Underworld duo, the Tlanuwa targeted the serpent while Thunder Child targeted its rider.

Midflight, the teen activated the Lightning Lance, and a bolt of lightning passed from the sky through the tip. Redirecting the electricity, Thunder Child propelled the amplified charge toward the Snake Priest.

Monkata was woefully unprepared for any of the counterattacks mounted by Thunder Child, the medicine elders, and the Upperworld. He'd planned to first destroy Shakuru at

Cahokia with the help of Coyotl's Aztec sorcery and then unleash the eight Horned Serpents on anyone and everyone who got in the way of his master Underworld takeover strategy.

The possibility of this aerial battle had never entered his mind, nor had the thought of practicing for a classic midair dogfight.

Lightning from Thunder Child's lance hit the Snake Priest squarely in the chest, knocking him from the beast's back and onto the ground several feet below. As he lay on the turf trying to catch his breath and regain strength, the confrontation continued above him.

Free of the Snake Priest's weight and control, the Winged Serpent fully engaged in the aerial conflict. Thunder Child realized he also needed to give the Tlanuwa free rein to act and react as needed in the struggle. A quick mental message gave the bird the freedom to maneuver as needed as Thunder Child clung to the creature's back with one hand and his lance with the other.

The two winged beasts circled one another as they rose higher in the atmosphere, each seeking an advantage. When none was found, the metal-winged bird charged for the snake beast, which responded by flipping backward to repel the attack claws-first. The Tlanuwa mirrored the move, also coming in with claws extended.

Locking talons, the two began a midair tug-of-war as they twisted and twirled in a dangerous ballet. Flapping, flailing wings failed to keep the pair afloat, and they tumbled toward the ground. At the last possible minute, the Tlanuwa released its grip and momentarily glided parallel to the earth to regain aerial speed.

The greater density of the Underworld serpent caused it to crash into the ground. From a source deep within, the grounded beast emitted a loud growling hiss expressing its pain and anger. Then, scrambling to quickly recover, it once again launched itself skyward.

Suddenly, the purple crystal in the creature's tail began to glow as the tail seemed to take on a life of its own. The added power from the tail propelled the serpent toward its opponents with incredible speed. Just as the winged beasts prepared to engage again, the tip of the reptile's tail hit Thunder Child from behind. He was knocked off the Tlanuwa, and his Lightning Lance flew from his hand.

As the teen hurtled toward the ground, the metallic-feathered bird disengaged from its foe and sped to the rescue. An extended wing buffered the fall, allowing Thunder Child to safely step onto the grassy field.

Now's my chance, Monkata thought to himself.

Standing up on the spot where he'd fallen, he drew his dagger, readied his shield, and called to Thunder Child with a sneer, "Over here, boy! Let's see what you can do without your little lightning stick!"

"Not so fast," a voice called from behind Monkata. He turned to find his brother standing a few yards away.

As the twins faced off, Thunder Child retrieved the Lightning Lance and signaled his metal-feathered friend.

Above him, the two winged ones had continued to fight. Using the edge of one of its metal wings, the Tlanuwa slashed a gash in the Winged Serpent's neck before responding to its master's call.

Purple blood gurgled from the monster's wound, and it withdrew from the fight momentarily. This gave the Tlanuwa time to pick up Thunder Child and return to the sky.

On the ground, Monkata quickly executed magical formulas to enhance the powers of his own dagger and shield. Both objects began to emit a purplish glow, and the Snake Priest was ready to do battle. Warily, he approached his brother.

In the sky above, Thunder Child recognized an opportunity and took it. He spurred his bird to action, and the pair quickly climbed above their wounded winged opponent. Having gained a superior position, the Tlanuwa dive-bombed the purple-and-green monster, allowing Thunder Child time to trigger his Lightning Lance.

In response, the Winged One surged upward toward his descending foes—too late!

A bolt of electricity struck the serpent right in its open teeth-rimmed mouth, blasting through the back of its throat. Purple blood and tissue exploded from the gaping hole.

Choking, gurgling sounds erupted from its windpipe, but its wings somehow continued to operate. It was as if the beast was in autopilot mode for a few beats before the wings got the message there was serious trouble in another part of the body.

A few seconds later, the wings quit functioning, and the heavy reptilian body plummeted to earth only a few feet from the Snake Priest.

The impact shook the ground beneath Monkata's feet, distracting him from his face-off with his brother. Backing away from Shakuru, the Snake Priest remembered he had one more weapon in his arsenal: the Owl Clan and their collection of dangerous, hungry creatures.

"Release the banished beasts!" he called to Thomas Two Bears and the Night Seers.

But no response came from that direction. Only silence. The Snake Priest looked for any signs of activity or movement there but couldn't see or hear anything.

Still hovering above the scene, Thunder Child heard sudden war cries from Tecumseh's warriors. Shouts of "Hoka hey!" came repeatedly as the fighters broke through a final line of shadow soldiers who'd been protecting Benjamin Blacksnake. The teen's searching eye found Tecumseh in the melee just as the warrior thrust his spirit spear into the sorcerer's black heart.

That thrust not only ended Blacksnake's short-lived reincarnation; it also ended the very existence of his Shadow Zone army. The horde of dark denizens of the Underworld all felt that thrust at the same time. One minute they were engaged in battle, and the next they disintegrated, ceasing to exist at all.

In utter shock and disbelief, Monkata also witnessed that moment. How could things have gone so seriously wrong? What happened to his mighty conquest of the Middleworld?

"Now it's my turn," Shakuru declared. "A chance to face off, just like you wanted."

Monkata turned back to his twin just in time to see a glint of morning light reflecting off Shakuru's copper blade right before it struck him in the side of the neck. Dark purple blood spurted from the cut, and the Snake Priest struggled to remain upright.

Wide eyed, disillusioned, and defeated, he weakly spoke one last time. "A curse I cast upon all our living descendants, brother," he whispered. "I will, at least, be remembered for that for all eternity."

"You will be remembered for nothing!" Shakuru replied, adding, "As you die, so do your conjured accomplishments."

The Sun Chief struck a second blow to the same spot as the first, decapitating the Snake Priest. Monkata's head fell to the ground in one direction as his torso and legs toppled in the other.

It was over.

As Thunder Child and Shakuru watched, the bodies of Monkata and the Winged Serpent disintegrated into piles of ash. Puddles of their purple blood that had pooled on the grass seemed to just drain into the ground.

All was silent for a moment before joyous cheers erupted from the interpretive center. Everyone who'd gathered there rushed onto the grassy field in celebration. Thunder Child, Shakuru, and the spirit warriors congregated at Cahokia's center field in a silent moment of mutual appreciation.

"We shall meet again," Shakuru told his victorious fighting companions. "You can be sure of it." And to Thunder Child, he added, "Thanks to you I can finally join my relatives on the Path of Souls. Call on me anytime. I am forever at your service."

With that, the incarnated spirits dematerialized, breaking into thousands of tiny glimmering particles that drifted upward before disappearing.

Feeling elated and exhausted, Thunder Child mounted the Tlanuwa, and together they flew a victory lap above Cahokia as members of the Underworld Takeover Prevention Team celebrated on the ground.

CHAPTER TWENTY-TWO

A New Normal

For two weeks, Thunder Child wanted no interaction with anyone, and no one understood why. Everyone in the teen's support circle wanted to celebrate the incredible outcome of the frightful and tumultuous time.

The teen spent most of those two weeks visiting familiar places in the backcountry of the Cherokee Nation. Favorite fishing spots. Well-worn trails he'd walked with his grandfather. The woods where he'd hunted with his bow. The places he'd gathered medicinal herbs. The areas he'd perfected his blow-gun techniques.

He realized he was looking for normal, the feeling of normal—what life was like before the lightning strike, before his death and rebirth.

He'd been putting it off, but finally on Memorial Day, the last Monday in May, he visited the cemetery where his grandmother and grandfather were buried. Their bodies lay side by side in the Live Oak cemetery located on the old stomp grounds.

But, of course, he knew they weren't anywhere near that plot of land.

"Well, as you probably know, it's all over," the teen said, looking at their tombstones. "Thunder Child did his job, and Billy has returned—and I'm glad."

"We know every detail of every event," Awinita said as her spirit came into view.

"We were there every step of the way," Wesley said as he, too, appeared.

"Grandma! Grandpa!" Billy yelled. "It's so good to see you again. Where have you been? I needed you so much!"

"We realize that," Awinita replied. "But Creator let us know we needed to step back and allow you to carry on with only a few little assists every now and then."

"We always believed in you," Wesley added. "And you didn't disappoint."

"We are with you always," Awinita added.

After their brief spirited conversation, Billy did feel like things were getting back to normal. In fact, he was ready to end his life as a hermit and join the whole UTP Team at the barbecue they'd planned for later that day.

As he drove toward the cookout, several ideas began forming in his mind, including a project he wanted to launch. It felt like the concept came directly from his Buckhorn elders.

As he pulled up in front of Grandpa Wesley's house, he heard laughter coming from the backyard and smelled the aroma of meat cooking on a grill. With new energy, he bounded up onto the porch and stepped into the living room.

There he found Lisa chatting with Raelynn on the sofa. Seeing her boyfriend and sensing his newly found upbeat attitude, she jumped up and sprang into his embrace.

"Well, well, well," she said jokingly. "Look who decided to grace us with his royal presence. If it isn't the celebrated Thunder Child himself!"

The broad smile on her face told Billy she was only kidding, and they kissed. And to Billy it felt very normal, so they kept kissing.

"Yoo-hoo," Raelynn said finally. "There are other people present, and they're feeling rather ignored."

The couple finally broke it off with one last lingering look into each other's eyes.

"By the way, I'm no longer Thunder Child. I'm just Billy."

"Hello, just Billy," Lisa said. "I'm just Lisa, your long-lost girlfriend."

"Okay, you two," Raelynn interjected. "Enough! Why don't we go out back where everyone's enjoying themselves?"

As the couple followed the investigator toward the back, Billy said, "I'm sorry I've been distant the past two weeks. I had to sort out a few things in my mind."

"No problem. I figured you needed time to process everything that happened."

Raelynn announced Billy's arrival to everyone gathered around card tables and folding chairs in the backyard. Chigger was the first to welcome his friend with some news he couldn't wait to share.

"Billy, I've been dying to tell you about the comic book I've started writing!" he said, not waiting for anyone else to speak.

"Oh, yeah, what's it called?" Billy asked.

"*Nathan Nighthawk and the Tale of the Banished Beasts*," he said. "It's filled with all those nightmarish creatures I dreamed about."

"Sounds fantastic, my friend," Billy said. "Too bad no one will believe it."

"I believe it," Jerry Swimmer said. "Every word. In fact, I'll tell everyone I know to buy a copy. I had a front-row seat to the most unbelievable series of events anyone on earth has ever witnessed. So I tried to tell everyone I encountered all about it."

"And what was their response?" Raelynn asked.

"They all think I'm crazy."

She gave him a little peck on the cheek. "I told you he'd come around," she said and grabbed her FBI boyfriend's arm.

After everyone had their chance to greet Billy, Cecil announced, "Time to eat the roast beast," playing off Chigger's comic book theme.

The gathering provided Billy with the perfect occasion to share his new idea and answer the questions the UTP Team had been asking. After devouring a classic summertime plate of sliced barbecue beef, baked beans, potato salad, and cole-slaw—followed by a slice of ripe watermelon—Billy was ready to converse.

"The first question I'll answer came from Cecil back at Cahokia when the Sun Chief appeared."

"That's right," the elder said. "After all our failed attempts to find his bones so we could free him from the Snake Cult's curse, how did you make that happen?"

"I simply followed the advice of someone who was a little older and wiser than I was at the time," Billy answered.

That reply puzzled everyone there.

"One of the things I learned from Morningstar was how to do out-of-body time travel," he said.

"Wow!" Chigger interrupted. "I think I just found the storyline for my next comic book!"

"Anyway," Billy continued, "before the Showdown at Cahokia, my future self paid me a very timely visit."

He paused to let that sink in.

Using his hand, Chigger made the gesture of something flying over his head. "You're blowing my mind here, buddy," he said.

"You're blowing all our minds," Lisa echoed.

"After telling me to rely on myself, he briefed me on a few important upcoming events," Billy continued. "Then he suggested I use the time travel trick to go back and follow Coyotl's timeline, starting the day he got Shakuru's bones, to see where the Aztec took them."

Billy paused again to make sure his listeners were keeping up.

"That allowed me to see the code to the combination lock on the Cliffside Cave's gate and then listen to the Nahuatl words Coyotl used to reestablish the concealment and imprisonment spells. The day before the Showdown, I physically visited the cave and used a Nahuatl spell I found in the back of Blacksnake's book to undo Coyotl's spells."

"Sounds like basic procedures from the spy's international handbook," Chigger commented.

"But what about the Uktenas?" Cecil asked. "What happened to them?"

"Your granddaughter can fill us in on those details," Billy replied.

"By the time we got the US Marshals' helicopter refueled, it was already dark," Lisa's account began. "We flew north over the Mississippi River, but it was too dark to see much of anything below. That is until I saw a very curious sight about the time we passed by Memphis."

"What, what, what?" Chigger effused.

"There were seven small, odd glowing objects moving northward in the river," Lisa continued. "I asked our pilot to get us closer so I could take a better look. When we were directly above the objects, he aimed a spotlight down on them, and I was shocked to see seven Horned Serpents merrily swimming along. The spotlight also revealed a trail of dead fish floating in the water behind the serpents, and withered and dying plants along the shoreline."

"Why only seven serpents?" Lisa's grandfather asked. "I thought there were eight."

"There *were* eight, but only seven of them still had their glowing Fire Crystals in the middle of their foreheads," Lisa answered.

"The eighth one, the one without the crystal, was out in front, apparently leading the pack."

"Oh, that explains a lot," Chigger said. "I wondered when and how you started putting things together."

"You're right. That's when I began wondering about what happened to that missing Fire Crystal. And I remembered the story Billy told me about how Chigger kept the purple tail crystal belonging to the Uktena in the bat cave."

"Smart girl," Billy said.

"I called Billy and told him my suspicions about where that crystal might be," Lisa concluded.

The crowd at this backyard cookout waited quietly and patiently for more details to unfold. You could hear a pin drop in the silence.

"Then I called my oldest, bestest friend, who was riding in the van toward Cahokia at the time, and asked a very vague question," Billy said. "Is there something you're not telling me?"

"Man, you got me good," Chigger replied with a chuckle. "I thought you already knew for sure I had the crystal. I spilled my guts immediately, didn't I?"

"I'm glad you did," Billy said. "Think about what might've happened if you didn't."

Chigger picked up the story from there. "I realized the lead Uktena was paying attention to me and seemed to want to follow me because I had his Fire Crystal," he explained. "I still wanted to do something to help the Underworld Takeover Prevention Team, so I came up with the idea of trying to slow them down."

"I have to say that was good thinking," Lisa responded.

"I appreciate that, Lisa. I tried communicating this idea through the crystal, and my Uktena—I called him my Uktena because he seemed to like me—understood me."

"I think your superpower was still at work," Billy commented.

"No doubt. I checked in on them as we kept driving toward Cahokia. They stopped at that Cliffside Cave south of St. Louis, waiting for further instructions. I'm pretty sure they'd already been programmed by the Serpent Society to do that. But now they were waiting for me to tell them what to do next."

"Good deductive reasoning, Sherlock," Billy said. "When the Snake Priest killed the remaining Serpent Society members at Cahokia, the Uktenas they controlled bit the dust at the same time."

"This is all incredible, but I have one more question," Cecil said.

"What happened to the Night Seers and their collection of cryptid creatures?" Billy said. "That's what you want to know, right?"

Cecil nodded.

"We have Amos Yonaguska to thank for helping us with that problem," Billy said.

The Eastern Cherokee medicine man, sitting quietly in the back, had joined them for the barbecue at Billy's invitation.

"Amos, where are you?" Billy called out.

A tall, thin man with a craggy face rose from his folding chair. "Hello, everyone," he said. "I feel blessed because Billy chose to forgive me for my past transgressions and welcome me into this community. I hope you all can do the same."

"Not only did he transfer control of the Tlanuwa to me," Billy explained. "As a former member of the Owl Clan, he was also able to block the attack of their beasts at Cahokia. Once that happened, the Night Seers scattered and escaped as quick as they could, because they'd already witnessed the execution of the serpent sorcerers who failed Monkata."

"I only wish I'd acted sooner, before any of the banished beasts had been released from the Underworld," Yonaguska said. "Now, every last one of them has been sent back where they belong."

"Except for one," Billy corrected. "Our Tlanuwa still remains, living in a remote mountain area far away from humans. Amos and I will keep an eye on him."

"We've become quite attached," Amos added.

"To you, Amos, I say *Wado*—thank you—for what you did," Billy replied. "And to everyone here, please welcome Amos as our new ally and friend."

Cecil was the first of many to approach Amos and shake his hand.

"But will the Night Seers just get away without being punished for what they did?" Billy's dad asked.

"Not if we can help it," Jerry Swimmer replied. "Amos gave us the names and addresses of all the Night Seers, and we expect to arrest every last one of them for the murders of your parents, Wesley and Awinita Buckhorn. They'll also be charged with acts of domestic terrorism for their role in releasing dangerous, life-threatening beasts onto several Indian reservations."

Spontaneous shouts of "Aho" and "Amen" and "Hoka hey" and "Hallelujah" came from various members of the assembled partyers as the celebration kicked into high gear.

Billy decided announcements about his own future plans could wait until another time. In fact, the delay allowed him the opportunity to huddle up with his parents and the Lookout family to make those plans more concrete.

Then, on the night of June 21, the summer solstice and his seventeenth birthday, Billy made the announcement to the hundred or so invitees who'd gathered at the Cherokee Nation Cultural Grounds. The medicine lodge, site of the shaking tent ceremony earlier in the year, still stood on those grounds, thanks to permission given by the tribe's principal chief.

"Thanks to a very generous donation from an anonymous donor," Billy said as he stood before the assembled crowd, "I'm proud to announce the creation of the Awinita and Wesley Buckhorn Center for Healing and Cultural Education, which will be located in the renovated house that once belonged to my grandparents."

Vigorous applause flowed from the audience, which included everyone who'd recently attended the gathering at the abandoned amphitheater.

"I've consulted with my parents, my grandparents—who send their regards from the Afterworld—and the Lookout family, and we've decided to make it a place where traditional Cherokee medicine merges with modern medical treatments in a holistic approach. And now my partner in this project will give you some more details. Lisa?"

Billy gave his girlfriend a quick peck on the cheek as she stepped forward, immensely embarrassing the girl. It showed on her face. Smiling, she gave him a little swat on the shoulder as he stepped aside.

"My partner, the sometimes-annoying Billy Buckhorn, will serve as the primary provider of traditional healing services, carrying on the practice of his grandparents," Lisa said. "But he's inviting other members of the Cherokee Nation Medicine Keepers to also treat patients here, if they want to."

"I really like the sound of that," Wilma Wohali replied from where she stood in the crowd. "Spoken in the true spirit of Awinita and Wesley."

"Billy plans on continuing the even older tradition of connecting Native people with the spirits of their deceased loved ones," Lisa continued. "A scene etched into the wall of the crystal cave provided a glimpse of this ancient practice."

That announcement was received with mixed reactions. Not everyone at the event approved of such activities.

"Excuse me," a woman standing in the back of the audience said. "I'd like to say something, if I may."

Billy recognized Mattie Acorn, a Cherokee woman who'd come to him seeking consolation after her son's death. She came forward and stood beside Lisa.

"First, I need to apologize to you, young man," she said, looking at Billy. "When my son died, I came to you seeking a comforting message, but what you gave me was the truth. When you saw a vision of him dying by suicide, I pretended it wasn't true and called you a liar."

There were gasps from a few in the audience.

"You weren't lying," she went on, "and I'm sorry for accusing you of that. When you open your new healing center, I want to be the first in line, and maybe we can connect with my son."

Billy stepped closer to the woman, and he reached out to her, grasping her hand. "I'd be honored to help you, but why wait?" he said. "Let's find a quiet, private place and see if we can talk to him now."

As they retreated to an out-of-the-way corner of the cultural grounds, Lisa invited guests to enjoy refreshments available inside the lodge, and everyone mixed and mingled in a subdued mood.

A few evenings later, Lisa and Chigger joined Billy for a little night fishing on Lake Tenkiller. The skiff, which had been neglected the past few weeks, drifted on the water as the three dropped their fishing lines overboard. A dark velvet sky filled with a brilliant field of stars floated overhead.

"I had hoped for a little alone time with my boyfriend," Lisa complained as she sat in the soft glow of the camping lantern.

"Ah, but Lisa," Chigger replied, "this is the new reality. You, me, and Billy are truly the Three Muskrateers!"

"My dad said you, he, and Augustus were the Three Muskrateers back when you were searching for the hidden cave."

"I was just trying out the name then, but I now realize that name was meant for us," Chigger said. "One for all, and all for one."

"And I was hoping for a quiet night of fishing with *no talking*!" Billy said a little too loudly.

"Shhhh!" Chigger admonished. "You'll scare the fish or wake those Underworld shadow spirits."

That gave all three of them the shivers.

"I for one don't want to get any of that started again," Billy said, and no one said anything after that.

Looking up, Billy thought he saw the campfires of the ancestors burn more brightly for a few seconds and then fade back to their usual appearance. The muggy June air clung to his skin like a familiar wet blanket, and he felt that things were almost normal once again.

BIBLIOGRAPHY OF SOURCES

Conley, Robert J. *Cherokee Medicine Man: The Life and Work of a Modern-Day Healer*. Norman, OK: University of Oklahoma Press, 2005.

Diaz-Granados, Carol, James R. Duncan, and F. Kent Reilly III, eds. *Picture Cave: Unraveling the Mysteries of the Mississippian Cosmos*. Austin, TX: University of Texas Press, 2015.

Garrett, J. T. and Michael Garrett. *Medicine of the Cherokee: The Way of Right Relationship*. Rochester, VT: Bear & Company, 1996.

Jefferson, Warren. *Reincarnation Beliefs of North American Indians: Soul Journeys, Metamorphoses, and Near-Death Experiences*. Summertown, TN: Native Voices, 2009.

Kilpatrick, Alan. *The Night Has a Naked Soul: Witchcraft and Sorcery Among the Western Cherokee*. Syracuse, NY: Syracuse University Press, 1997.

Kilpatrick, Jack F. and Anna G. Kilpatrick. *Friends of Thunder: Folktales of the Oklahoma Cherokees*. Norman, OK: University of Oklahoma Press, 1995.

Little, Gregory L. *The Illustrated Encyclopedia of Native American Indian Mounds and Earthworks*. Memphis, TN: Eagle Wing Books, 2016.

Little, Gregory. *Path of Souls: The Native American Death Journey*. Memphis, TN: ATA Archetype Books, 2014.

Mooney, James. "The Sacred Formulas of the Cherokees." *Seventh Annual Report of the Bureau of Ethnology*, 1886, 301-397, Bureau of American Ethnology.

Monroe, Robert A. *Ultimate Journey*. New York: Doubleday, 1994.

Pauketat, Timothy R. *Cahokia: Ancient America's Great City on the Mississippi*. New York: Penguin Books, 2009.

Zimmerman, Fritz. *The Native American Book of the Dead*. Self-published, 2020.

ABOUT THE AUTHOR

G ary Robinson, a writer and filmmaker of Cherokee and Choctaw Indian descent, has spent more than thirty years collaborating with American Indian communities to tell the historical and contemporary stories of Native people in all forms of media.

His most recent books include *Native Actors and Filmmakers: Visual Storytellers* and *Be Your Own Best Friend Forever*, both published by 7th Generation in 2021.

His historical novel series, *Lands of Our Ancestors*, portrays California history from a Native American perspective. It is used in many classrooms in the state, and has been praised by teachers and students alike.

He has also written several other teen novels, including *Billy Buckhorn and the Book of Spells*, *Billy Buckhorn and the Rise of the Night Seers*, *Standing Strong*, *Thunder on the Plains*, *Tribal Journey*, *Little Brother of War*, and *Son Who Returns*. His two children's books share aspects of Native American culture through popular holiday themes: *Native American Night Before Christmas* and *Native American Twelve Days of Christmas*.

He lives in rural central California.

Billy Buckhorn and the Thunder Child Prophecy Trilogy

BOOK ONE

BILLY BUCKHORN
and the Book of Spells

"Strange changes are afoot,"
Awinita said. "An ancient evil has
returned to the Cherokee Nation."

This ominous message, conveyed to sixteen-year-old Billy Buckhorn by the spirit of his deceased grandmother, opens the door to astounding supernatural events. Struck by lightning and brought back from the brink of death, Billy must contend with extraordinary visions and psychic insights. Little does Billy know that this is just the beginning of a prophesied quest to vanquish mythical evil forces that have materialized and now threaten to overtake the Cherokee Nation.

BOOK TWO

BILLY BUCKHORN
and the Rise of the Night Seers

"The Night Seers' attempt to trap Billy's spirit
means he's already on their radar and seen
as a serious threat," Cecil Lookout said.
"More proof that he is indeed the One chosen
by the Thunders in the prophecy."

Cherokee teen Billy Buckhorn has come to terms that he is the long-awaited Chosen One, and is destined to battle dark ancient forces that are planning to retake control of the Middleworld. As he comes to accept his prophesied new role, he must also learn to accept that he and his loved ones are now targets of the most powerful shape-shifting Native American witches and sorcerers on Turtle Island, the Night Seers of the Owl Clan.

7th
GENERATION

For more information, visit: **nativevoicesbooks.com**

Book Publishing Company • PO Box 99 • Summertown, TN 38483 • 888-260-8458

Free shipping and handling on all orders.